Mistress by Marriage

D1031520

Mistress by Marriage

MAGGIE ROBINSON

WITHDRAWN

BRAVA

KENSINGTON PUBLISHING CORP.

www.kensingtonbooks.com

BRAVA BOOKS are published by

Kensington Publishing Corp.
119 West 40th Street
New York, NY 10018

Copyright © 2011 Maggie Robinson

All rights reserved. No part of this book may be reproduced in any form or by any means without the prior written consent of the Publisher, excepting brief quotes used in reviews.

All Kensington titles, imprints, and distributed lines are available at special quantity discounts for bulk purchases for sales promotion, premiums, fund-raising, educational, or institutional use.

Special book excerpts or customized printings can also be created to fit specific needs. For details, write or phone the office of the Kensington Special Sales Manager: Kensington Publishing Corp., 119 West 40th Street, New York, NY 10018. Attn. Special Sales Department. Phone: 1-800-221-2647.

Brava and the B logo are Reg. U.S. Pat. & TM Off.

ISBN-13: 978-0-7582-5103-9
ISBN-10: 0-7582-5103-3

First Kensington Trade Paperback Printing: September 2011

10 9 8 7 6 5 4 3 2 1

Printed in the United States of America

Prologue

London, 1820

Edward Christie had been an utter fool six years ago. True, he'd had plenty of company. Every man in the room gaped when Caroline Parker entered Lady Huntington's ballroom. Conversation stilled. Hearts hammered. Shoulders straightened. Chests and areas lower swelled.

There were many reasons for those changes. Her hair, masses of it, red as lava, was swirled up with diamonds. Diamond earrings, a diamond necklace, and diamond bracelets were festooned all over her creamy skin—skin so delicious every man whose tongue was hanging out longed to lap it. Her eyes were liquid silver, bright as stars and fringed with midnight black lashes, so at odds with her hair. And her dress, a shocking scarlet for an unmarried woman—for *any* woman—had a diamond brooch hovering over the most spectacular assets he'd ever seen. The jewels were all paste, as he was later to find out, but her breasts were very real.

There were known drawbacks, which quickly circulated about the room, prodded along by spiteful cats who were quite eclipsed by Caroline's magnificence. She was old, at least twenty-five, and her family—what there was of it—was dirt poor and touched by scandal. Some said her brother died in a duel; others said he was killed by one of his many mistresses. She had a sister in Canada, living in some godforsaken outpost in the snow with her lieutenant husband and howling wolves. Her parents were long dead and she was clinging to the ton by the weakest of threads. The distant cousin who had inherited her brother's title was anxious to get her off his hands before he put his hands all over her and irritated his irritable wife.

Edward had obliged in a courtship of less than five days. Baron Christie had spent his first thirty-four years never, ever being impulsive, and his sudden marriage by special license to a woman who looked like an expensive courtesan was the *on dit* of the season. He had buried one wife, the perfectly staid and proper Alice, whose brown hair would never be compared to living fire and whose brown eyes could only be compared to mud. Alice, who'd quickly and quietly done her duty had provided him with an heir, a spare, and a little girl who looked just as angular and forbidding as her father. Alice, who'd caught a chill one week and died the next was no doubt rolling over in her grave to be supplanted by Caroline Parker.

Edward had no one to blame but himself. He didn't need more children, and Caroline hadn't any money. But what she did have—what she *was*—had upended Edward's life for one hellish year before he came to his senses and put her away.

Caroline had no one to blame but herself. It was her pride, her dreadful Parker pride that had prevented her from saying one simple word—no. If only her rosy lips had opened and she had managed to get her tongue to the roof of her mouth and expelled sufficient air, she would not find herself living on Jane Street, home to the most notorious courtesans in London.

When Edward asked her to marry him after less than a week's acquaintance, she should have said no. When he'd asked her that horrible, vile, *impertinent* question five years ago, she should have said no. But instead she'd said yes to the first question, rather gratefully if truth be told, and hadn't said a word to the second, just cast her husband the most scornful look she could conjure up and showed him her back.

Caroline was no man's mistress, despite her exclusive Jane Street address and rumors to the contrary. In the five years since she and her husband separated, he had come to her door but once a year, the anniversary of the night she was unable to utter that one syllable word. They took ruthless pleasure in each other, and then Edward disappeared again. She, however, remained, ostracized from polite society, completely celibate, and despite her ardent hopes, a mother only to the curious contingent of young women who shared her street. The children changed, but the game remained the same. From experienced opera dancers to fresh-faced country girls who had been led astray by rich gentlemen, Caroline watched the parade of mistresses come and go. She passed teacups and handkerchiefs and advice, feeling much older than her almost thirty-one years.

But when she looked in her pier glass, she was still relatively youthful, her red curls shiny, her gray eyes bright. She might have been stouter than she wished, but the prideful Parkers were known to run to fat in middle age. For some reason Edward had let her keep some of the lesser Christie jewels, so there was always a sparkle on her person even if there was no spark to her life. She made the best of it, however, and had some surprising success writing wicked novels that she couldn't seem to write fast enough. Her avocation would have stunned her old governess, as Caroline had showed no aptitude whatsoever for grammar lessons or spelling as a girl. Fortunately, her publisher was grammatical and spelled accurately enough for both of them. Her *Courtesan Court* series was highly popular with society members and their servants alike. There were happy endings galore for the innocent girls led astray, and the wicked always got what was coming to them. She modeled nearly every villain on Edward. It was most satisfactory to shoot him or toss him off a cliff in the final pages. Once she crushed him in a mining mishap, his elegant sinewy body and dark head entombed for all eternity with coal that was as black as his heart.

Of course, sometimes her heroes were modeled on him, too—men with pride nearly as perverse as the Parkers, facile fingers that knew *just* where to touch a girl, and particularly long, thick, entirely perfect penises. Caroline missed Edward's penis, although she didn't miss his conversation much. He was so damned proper and critical, and had been beyond boring to live with. Controlled. Controlling. Humorless. Once he'd installed her as his baroness, it was as if he woke up horrified at what he'd actually done, and whom he'd actually married. It was no wonder that she—

No, she couldn't blame him. She had no one to blame but herself.

Chapter 1

He had been the coldest man in England. They
called him Frozen Frazier. How fitting it was for him
to be encased in ice at the bottom of the alp.
—The Count's Courtesan

"If you don't do something about your wife, we will."
Edward looked at the two gentlemen, viscounts both,
who had already helped themselves to his best conciliatory
brandy. He knew as soon as he'd received Lord Pope's note he
was in for it. Caroline had gone too far. But when hadn't she?

"It's libel. Or slander. I cannot remember which. But we'll
sue you for every groat you've got, Christie, and the publisher too, unless you control that woman. We've got friends
in high places."

Edward wore his impassive Christie face. His grandfather
had been known for it. His father had been known for it.
Now it was his turn. The house could be engulfed in flames,
the ship sinking, the heart breaking, but a Christie was always cool and collected. He'd heard the sobriquet "Cold
Christie" a time or two and wasn't offended. It suited him
perfectly most of the time. "I have very little influence over
Caroline. We've lived apart for years."

"But you keep a roof over her head and the clothes on her
back!" Lord Douglass objected. It was rumored he was to
appear in the much-anticipated *The Senorita's Senor,* and he
wasn't clacking his castanets about it. His ex-mistress Victorina Castellano had apparently described Douglass's masculine equipment in an entirely unflattering but anatomically
correct way.

Edward shook his head. "That's not precisely true. She

earns enough to dispense with her allowance. My man of business tells me she hasn't touched much at all since she's been writing her books."

"Books! As if the trash she writes deserves such elevation. She's worse than the worst scandal sheet," Pope blustered. "Because of her my wife left me!"

"Surely the fact that you caned your mistress nearly to death had something to do with that," Edward murmured. He watched as Pope's fist clutched his brandy glass, expecting it to shatter at any moment. The fist or the glass, he wasn't sure which.

Each of the so-called gentlemen in Edward's library was the thinly-disguised villain in one of Caroline's wildly successful novels. He didn't read them himself, of course, could only reluctantly permit himself to imagine their lurid content, but his sister Beth gave him regular book reports on their irregular content. The slender books came out monthly, and Beth was amongst the first who lined up eagerly to buy them. Edward was quite sure Beth lived to torture him with every salacious revelation. But he couldn't throw his widowed sister out, as she was helping him raise his children. Not that either one of them was doing a particularly creditable job. The boys, and especially little Alice, were nearly as bad as when Caroline was their stepmother. Perhaps in some ways worse.

He'd made a dreadful mistake—just the one—and was paying for it every day. A dutiful son, when he was one and twenty he'd married the sweet seventeen-year-old girl his parents picked for him from her cradle. They were neighbors, grew up together. He'd liked her well enough. Alice had been raised to be his perfect wife. Her behavior was faultless, her conversation unexceptional, their lives organized. They'd been lucky with his heir Neddie, a honeymoon baby, and then two years later Jack came along. Little Alice didn't even remember her mother, and all three had needed a new one.

If he was honest, Edward had been lonely, too. Alice had been good company, soothing and steady. Then he laid eyes on Caroline Parker, glittering, glossy, and entirely unmotherly. Steady as a fault line. Soothing as a razor blade at one's throat.

It had been a disaster. Nearly every day of it, if not the nights. He and Caroline disagreed on the most fundamental things. She babbled incessantly at breakfast; he wanted nothing more than to be left alone with his toast and the *Times*. She encouraged the children to mischief—they'd gone through five governesses in the year she lived with them. And even though Caroline had indulged their every whim, the children hadn't really known what to make of her. She was nothing at all like his wife. She was nothing at all like anyone he'd ever known.

Now she was writing about lords and their ladybirds, books that were so—so—*graphic* they'd put a blush to a whore's cheek. Or at least that's what Beth said.

Edward put his glass down. It was June 14. He'd see Caroline tonight; it wasn't as if he had to make a special trip. It was their night to remember their last. "I'll speak to her. That's the best I can do. I hear most Jane Street gentlemen are flattered by her work."

Pope was crimson. "Well, *we* are not. She can't be allowed to destroy lives and champion those whores. Why, she's just a whore herself."

Edward's long fingers were suddenly wrapped around Pope's cravat, whose knot he inconveniently tightened. "I suggest you leave now, both of you. If I hear from my wife you have threatened her in any way, I shall do more than this." He shoved Pope down on his arse. He'd have to get the carpet cleaned tomorrow.

Hell and damnation. It wasn't as if Caroline needed the money to write such rubbish. He'd piled an enormous amount in her account the past five years. Guilt money. Guilt for asking such an unsuitable woman—a *stranger*—to marry him. Guilt for letting her down, because he couldn't, wouldn't, *shouldn't have to* change. Guilt for still wanting her as much as he ever had. Guilt, because unless one of them died, their lives were absolutely ruined by his single, mad, impulsive mistake.

He shouldn't go to her tonight. He could send a note, or simply not turn up at all. Perhaps she didn't even mark the date. Maybe she was still in the country with her sister. But no, he knew she'd been back for days, probably came back just to see him . . .

Or have one of her damn tea parties, where the courtesans confessed. He really should warn Conover now that he had set up his mistress. But maybe Con wouldn't care if his tattoo turned up on some poor chump's shoulder in the next installment of the *Courtesan Court* series.

Edward picked up his glass, then set it down again. He needed to be clearheaded, though one minute with Caroline turned him into a prize idiot. In her company, the only head he thought with fought to get free of his breeches at the earliest opportunity.

It was time to discuss a bill of divorce. It would be criminally expensive, embarrassing, endless, and, if successful, a scandal even worse than the one they were living. But he had the letters, and right was on his side.

Or he could step in front of a fast-moving carriage.

Or go on as he was.

What he could not do was live with Caroline. That had been tried, and found wanting.

When she woke up, Caroline knew perfectly well what day it was and wished she'd never come back from her sister's home in the country. Not only had her garden completely gone to seed and weeds, but she'd pulled a muscle in her back trying to fix it which had made solid sleep the past few nights nearly impossible.

But Mary had been much too happy with her decorated major, who had been knighted for his frostbitten Canadian service to the Crown. Their twin boys and two daughters were the most adorable children on earth, their puppy well behaved, their small manor house charming. And Mary was pregnant again, swollen and beautiful. It had been three weeks of absolute, unadulterated, harmonious hell. Caroline thought she'd turn green with envy, and toward the end she could barely lift the corners of her lips to smile. Even her cat Harold had enough and coughed up an enormous hairball on Mary's new brocade settee.

She hated feeling this way, so base, so jealous. Her sister had endured dreadful hardships—blizzards, wild Indians, wars—and deserved every idyllic minute of her new life. Mary's husband Sir Jared was missing two toes and three fingers, for heaven's sake. How dare Caroline begrudge her sister the happiness that would never be hers?

So she'd plunged right into her Jane Street life when she came home, met her new neighbors, hosted her tea, and felt an enormous pit of emptiness, which would only get deeper when Edward came tonight. And he must come. If he didn't—

Well, she'd simply go on. Alone, alone, alone.

My, but she was being maudlin. Positively lachrymose. Lugubrious. Sepulchral. She spent much of her time with a dictionary handy trying to broaden her vocabulary for her novels. After all, one had a duty to educate one's readers.

How ironic that she, Queen of the Happy Ending, was stuck somewhere in the mucky middle of a never-ending tragedy. No, that wasn't right—it was a farce.

She would ask Edward to divorce her. He had the evidence; it was only his prickly, nearly-Parkerian pride that was holding them back from any sort of resolution. Then she might leave the Jane Street house and move where no one had ever heard of her or her novels.

Or she might become exactly what everyone thought her to be.

She doubted she could find a worthy man to sleep with her. Edward only seemed to do it for some sort of punishment. Whether he intended to punish himself or her, it had the same result. Caroline pulled the sheet over her face to block out the infernal sunshine, not at all ready to face the day or the night.

Her maid tapped timidly on the door, as she did every morning. Poor Lizzie had once been mistress of her own Jane Street house, until Lord Pope had scarred her body and scared her witless. Caroline had offered her protection, and done what she could to ensure that no other girl would fall victim to the appetites of Randolph Pope. Although she'd called him Randy Poop (quite juvenile of her, really), everyone in the ton and beyond now knew of the viscount's unnatural proclivities after they read *The Vicious Viscount*. He'd once had the audacity to come round to Number Seven, but Caroline had kneed him in his withered balls just as her brother Nicky had taught her to do, then poked him out the front door with her best parasol from the umbrella stand. It had not been nearly enough, but it had been a satisfying start.

"Good morning, Lizzie. How are you?"

"Just fine, Lady Christie. Will you be wanting your breakfast in bed?"

Caroline didn't want to step out of bed for a week, but she supposed she could laze away the day tomorrow, doing a postmortem on Edward's performance, reliving each glorious inch of his penile perfection. It simply wasn't fair that at forty, he was more handsome than he'd ever been, the dusting of silver at his temples so distinguished, the planes of his cheeks so sharp, his chin completely resistant to doubling. She had seen him standing ramrod straight on the street quite by accident four months ago, his head bare against the winter wind, his hazel eyes keenly fastened upon a very attractive fur-clad woman with whom he was conversing. Caroline had crossed the street and hidden in a tobacco shop until he kissed the woman on the cheek and walked away. She'd had to buy a box of Spanish cigars for her publisher to kill the time.

But what if there was no penile perfection to savor? Caroline had gained at least a stone this year, worrying over Lizzie, writing six books, untangling her girls from unwise entanglements, stewing in Surrey with her sister and her family. It was probable that Edward would not find her at all attractive, or even kiss her on the cheek.

Hell and damnation. She was crying over milk that hadn't even had a chance to spill yet. And anyway, she wanted a divorce. It wouldn't do to keep sleeping with a man who despised her and broke her heart every June 14.

"I'm up, I'm up," Caroline muttered. "Tell Mrs. Hazlett I'll be downstairs in an hour. Poached eggs, please. Toast, but no butter or jam."

Lizzie lifted a blond eyebrow. Her face was as fair as ever; Pope had at least spared her that.

"Oh, very well. Jam. *And* butter. But no bacon. And kippers are out of the question. I mean it."

Lizzie curtsied, grinning just a bit at her victory. "Very well, my lady. I'll bring up your washing water in a trice."

"Don't hurry. You know I'm working on my special project." Caroline stretched and reached for an old but exquisite Chinese robe embroidered with giant red poppies. Edward had hated it. It did not match her plain white muslin night rail, but she considered it her writing uniform. For the next forty-five minutes she sat at her desk and poured ink on the pages of the notebook she currently called *Pride and Artifice*. No doubt her publisher would want to change the title, but she thought it very clever, if a bit derivative. The hero, a widower with three children and an enormous sense of self-consequence, was soon to meet a shallow red-headed vixen who would change his life forever in one turn around a ballroom.

When she was done, she washed the ink off her fingers and face and went downstairs to eat. The rest of the morning was spent revising *The Harlot's Husband*, as her publisher wanted her to be more explicit. Caroline wasn't sure she could use all the naughty words he suggested, but she'd try.

After a light luncheon that she was too nervous to eat, she spent approximately four hours in a bathtub, scrubbing every nook and cranny, calling on Lizzie for more hot water and lotions to turn her into temptation incarnate. Her husband, that vexing man with an enormous sense of self-consequence, was coming for dinner.

Chapter 2

Camilla gazed up at the rigging, where the terrifyingly
tall pirate blocked the scorching sun. "Drop to your
death," she whispered. "May the winds blow and your
brains be battered across the deck."
                                    —*The Captain's Concubine*

At first it had been for the sex and the anger, but for the
last two years, Edward had arrived early enough for dinner. Caroline, for all her hoydenish ways, was a creature of
habit. She always dined at eight if she was at home. Judging
from the blaze of lights at Seven Jane Street as daylight was
hours from waning, she was home. Candles were costly, but
since Caroline had become a writing sensation, she spent her
money without economization. Her money, not his. As he
had told Douglass and Pope, she was nearly self-sufficient.
Edward imagined it suited her pride to be as independent
from him as possible, not having to beg for pin money. As far
as he knew, she didn't gamble or entertain lavishly, unless
one counted her weekly teas with the other residents on the
street.

He had meant to punish her by setting her up on Jane
Street—but how like Caroline to turn the punishment into
pleasure, consorting with courtesans like some sort of fairy
godmother. He should have known she would find a way to
thwart him. She always did.

He passed muster with the two night security guards at the
mouth of the little cul-de-sac, hired by the eleven men and
one woman who owned the dozen houses to keep out gawk-
ers and undesirables. Not that Caroline owned her house
outright, but it was she who tended to the particulars of Jane

Street residency. She was the queen of her little lane, and her female subjects adored her. Some of the gentlemen, as evinced by Pope and Douglass, were probably less enthusiastic.

There had been some trouble recently, and the guard duty had been doubled at the elaborate iron gate. Edward had stood in irritation as the two men poured over a list, finally satisfying themselves that Edward Christie was an approved, if rare, visitor.

Before his fist hit the door, Caroline's butler Hazlett opened it. Her staff was small, suitable for the little jewel box of a house: Hazlett, his wife who was the cook/housekeeper, an orphaned kitchen boy, and the poor maid whom Pope had beaten so savagely. Edward knew it only because he bribed Hazlett an enormous amount to keep him informed of Caroline's activities. His dustup with Pope that afternoon worried him, and he would be sure to warn Hazlett when he took his leave.

"Good evening, Lord Christie. You're expected." Hazlett took Edward's gloves and placed them carefully on the waxed credenza in the tiled hall. Edward hadn't worn a hat in years, no matter the weather, and the butler looked at his bare head with some disapproval. For a man who was employed on the most sinful street in London, Hazlett was an amusingly high stickler.

Edward glanced into the empty drawing room and dining room beyond. The table was as bare as his head.

"Lady Christie asked that dinner be served in the upstairs parlor. She is waiting for you there."

Good. Closer to her bedroom. Edward had been hard as marble since he left his town house and walked the few long blocks to Jane Street. He hadn't had a woman since his last visit to Caroline. Ridiculous, but true. He had to set an example for his boys, so he'd not broken his marriage vows. Yet. He'd been tempted once or twice, but something had always come up. Or gone down. His hand and his imagination had served him adequately for the past five years, but he did feel he was wasting what few good years he had left to him. Perhaps that issue would be settled tonight.

He might not ever marry again, but at least if he was free he could find some comfort in the arms of a willing widow if he could ever not see Caroline behind his eyelids, her riot of red hair teasing his nipples as she moved over him, her lush hips rising up on his cock as she cried out—

He lost his balance on the stairs and nearly took a tumble. Aye, he could break his neck fantasizing about that little witch. If only he'd stayed home with his account books and not gone to Lady Huntington's ball six years ago, he wouldn't have a year-long case of blue balls. How he was to sit through dinner he had no idea.

Caroline sat on a plum velvet sofa. She'd redecorated the room since he was last there, and seemed to be dressed to match it. She wore the amethyst set he had given her, and a pale filmy lilac-gray gown that barely covered her nipples. Her hair was half up and half down, as though she couldn't quite decide whether to look like a queen or a school girl. His mouth dried and his cock betrayed him with a ferocious twitch. She was exquisite. She was perfect. She was Caroline.

"You're looking well," he said blandly.

"As are you, Edward. Do sit. May I get you some champagne?"

Her voice was low, all honey and sex. One could come to crisis simply listening to her read newspaper advertisements in *The London List*: Wanted, one man to muck out stalls. Serious inquiries only. Semen would be everywhere.

"Yes, thank you. That would be pleasant."

He watched her float off the sofa; there was no other word for it. She moved to a table topped with a silver ice bucket and flutes, expertly popped the cork, and poured two fizzy glasses. Leaning over him, her breasts nearly spilling out of the gauzy bodice, she pressed a glass into his sweaty hand. "To us."

He wanted to bury his face between the fragrant crease of

pearl-white bosom. Instead, he raised his glass, and looked at her. "To us. Tonight."

Caroline smiled without showing her teeth. "Ever a caveat. How have you been keeping, Edward? How are the children?"

"Ned's at university, drinking and wenching and presumably learning something, although I can't see what. Since he's been home, he's shown no aptitude for anything but courting trouble. Jack's off to join him at Cambridge in the fall and is bound to be just as bad. Little Alice is—well, she's not little. She's thirteen and nearly as tall as Jack. I confess I don't know what's to be done with her." *Hell and damnation.* What had come over him? He had not planned on blurting out his problems, one after the other with barely a pause for breath, and was appalled at himself for doing so. Caroline's lips were pursed in concern, and he knew he was about to get a lecture on child rearing from the most inexpert expert imaginable.

"Poor thing! I hope you don't criticize—Allie can't help it that she takes after you. I'm sure she'll grow into her looks and be a stunner. She's at such an awkward age, and to be singled out—"

Edward set his glass down in annoyance, mostly at himself for opening up this can of worms. It wasn't as if his wife could be of any practical help to him. "Give me some credit, Caro. Beth and I praise her at every turn. She has dancing lessons. Riding lessons. Music. Art. She's execrable at everything but we'd never say."

"But she knows anyway. Do—do you think she'd be happier away at school?"

"She won't go." Why on earth were they having this conversation? It was not at all to the point. "I'm not here to discuss my children with you, Caroline."

"I know," she said quietly, the spark of sympathy gone out of her silver eyes. "You're here to fuck me. Shall we have dinner first or get right to it?"

"Don't be so vulgar. Those filthy books you write have

gone to your head." *Hell and damnation.* She put his back up and made him sound like a perfect prig—which, at the heart of it, he was.

"Yes, that must be it. I'll ring for dinner then. It's your favorite, roast beef with Yorkshire pudding. You'll have to endure some oysters and a lobster soufflé first. Mrs. Hazlett insisted."

She glided over to the bellpull and Edward yearned to yank it off the wall. He wanted nothing to feast upon save her firm white flesh, spilling over her wispy dress and into his mouth. He would unpin all her hair and wrap it tight around his hands, the better to control her. He shut his eyes for a moment to savor the fantasy.

When he opened them, she was back on the sofa, playing with the catch of the amethyst bracelet. Her wedding rings twinkled in the candlelight. He'd stopped wearing his ring five years ago. He didn't even know where it was.

"How is Beth, or are we not to discuss her either?"

"She's well. Busy."

"And your work in Parliament?"

"Dead boring. Thank God we're nearly ready to recess."

"Will you spend the summer in town?"

"Good Lord, no. I'll be at Christie Park with the children. London will be hot as hell." The superficial conversation was quite easy. Short sentences. Subject, verb. No confessional complaints over his family. No need to imagine Caroline beneath him, writhing in ecstasy. Soon she would be. He put his champagne glass down. *Clearheaded.* He had to be clearheaded. "I understand your brother-in-law has settled into his new holding in Surrey."

"Yes. I visited them recently, but you know that. Hazlett gave his report, did he not? By the way, you pay him far too much to do so. He tells *me* everything, too." She cast him a sly smile.

Hell and damnation. He was not a spy. But he had a right to know what she was up to. She was still his wife.

Caroline took another sip of champagne, licking a wayward drop from her lips. To his disappointment, her tongue disappeared from view so she could continue to speak. "Jared and Mary seem quite content. She's increasing again."

She had said it lightly, but it must hurt. Caroline was barren, but that had been a blessing after all.

The perfidious Hazlett interrupted the scintillating conversation, inquiring if they were ready for dinner. Edward, who wanted to "get on with it" more than life itself, nodded. Both Hazletts were back within moments, carrying silver trays and chafing dishes to the sideboard. Edward and Caroline were silent until the servants left, shutting the door behind them.

"Shall we?"

Caroline didn't wait for him to lead her to the small dining table at the end of the room. It was set with a dazzling array of silver and crystal, all new. "Very nice," he said. First quality, and expensive, too. Her writing business must indeed be lucrative.

"Yes. Please help yourself."

"After you."

Edward was fairly sure the food was delicious, but he tasted nothing but regret. His wife picked at her plate, occasionally asking an innocuous question. He watched her tilt her head and slip an oyster down her throat, and had a vision of her on her knees. A vision he was determined to bring to reality shortly. After an appropriate amount of time, they rose in mutual understanding, leaving dessert for later.

"I want you, Caroline," he said, his voice rough. "Damn my soul."

"Damn it to Hell," she agreed, throwing open the door to her bedroom.

For such a cold man, Edward was a marvel in bed. Of course, she had very little to compare him to, but it seemed from the observations of her neighbors, not all men were as equipped or as efficient as Edward. And by efficient, Caroline did not mean speedy. Edward was agonizingly, teasingly, thoroughly slow, but guaranteed to bring her to orgasm every single time. Not just one puny little frisson, but wave upon wave of cliff climbing, precipitous descent, and shrieking.

Caroline knew her responsiveness frightened him; no doubt his first wife, the paragon Alice, had just lain there and said, "Thank you," if she said anything at all. Caroline's language was substantially more colorful and less constrained. She lay in the wreck of her bed, dripping everywhere from delicious depravity.

Edward stared up at the ceiling, his mouth puckered. "There's a mirror up there."

"Yes, it came with the house. Have you never noticed it before?"

"I have not. We never made it to the bed last year as I recall."

"But it *was* there the two years previous. I assure you I did not install it."

"What do you do with it?"

"I? Why nothing. Scare myself silly when I wake up in the morning." She grinned, meeting his eyes in the mirror. His dark hair was a bit mussed, but she looked like she'd been caught in a tempest at sea, washed overboard, and with her last gasping breath barely crawled to shore in time.

"It's indecent."

She shrugged. "So am I. If you don't care for it, I can have it removed."

Edward sat up. "Don't bother. My preferences will not count in the future. There will be no need for Yorkshire pudding. I—we—cannot do this thing, whatever it is, anymore."

Despite the flattering candlelight, he had seen she was heavier. Older. She fought to keep the fear out of her voice. "I didn't please you?"

"This has nothing to do with pleasing. If you must know, you make me burn, Caroline. I cannot find myself around you. I disappear in some puff of sulfur and become the Devil himself. It must stop."

She put a reassuring hand on his forearm. "You're just a mortal man, Edward, with carnal needs like any other. If you indulged yourself more frequently—"

"Indulge! This is more than indulgence. This is disease! Sickness!"

Caroline forced a laugh. "How melodramatic! What a Puritan you are. It's just sexual congress, Edward. Everyone does it."

But she knew it was more, too. For a buttoned-up man like Edward, the loss of self-control was like a loss of honor. He hated her for striking his flinty heart and igniting flames of passion that he couldn't control. Just as she hated him . . . when she wasn't loving him.

"I'm going to talk to Will. He can advise me on how best I can bring suit for divorce. Neither of us can continue this charade. If you hadn't—" He paused. Caroline wanted him to say it. Needed him to say it so she could finally say her own piece. But he didn't. "No, I'll not blame you. We simply don't suit and never have."

He had turned away from her, his face in profile, his voice wooden. In the mirror above she saw the muscle in his chiseled cheek flick. It was costing him to be so dispassionate. Caroline wished he'd explode, be anyone but this calm, reasonable stranger, but she knew better. Edward was always calm and reasonable, even when his world was imploding.

He should yell at her. Shake her. Call her names for her incredible indiscretions.

Caroline untwisted the sheet to cover her suddenly embarrassing nudity. "Your family name will be—will be ruined." Why did she care? She'd planned to discuss divorce herself this evening, but Edward had preempted her and hurt her before she had the chance to hurt him.

He bent to reach for his pants. Caroline could see each bump of his spine on his long narrow back and wanted to touch them.

"I'm a laughingstock already. It will be up to Ned to retrieve my dignity if he can, but I'm not counting on it." He shook out the length of his trousers but didn't put them on.

"The children—"

"It's a bit too late for you to think about them now, Caroline. I don't know how my daughter will ever find a decent husband after what we've put the family through."

Oh, he was cruel. "I can stop writing the books." At first they'd been a lark, a shot over Edward's bow to wake him up, to make him as unhappy as he had made her. The money had been incidental. The Christie name was not on the covers, but somehow word had leaked out that she was the authoress. She had been almost glad.

"This is not about the books. Although you should watch out for Pope and Douglass. Mention that to Hazlett. They both came to see me today and are threatening legal action."

"Pope! He's nothing but a disgusting pervert. He's lucky he's not in prison. Garrett won't back down. We're completely within our rights."

Edward shifted on the bed, his hazel eyes the color of a stormy sea. "Ah, yes. Garrett. How is your lover?"

Caroline felt a mounting fury. She knew it was pointless to argue as Edward's mind was made up, but she couldn't help herself. "He is not my lover! Ask your spy Hazlett if you don't believe me!"

"There are some things I dare not ask anymore. And even you can be discreet if you wish to be."

Yes, she was discreet. She lived like a veritable nun. And Garrett *would* be her lover, if she let him. Perhaps it was time to do so.

Just like that, she gave up the hope of Edward in her life, even for the one day a year. It was past time.

She sat up against the pillows, chin lifted, spirit sunk. There were three steps to divorce—she had researched it herself. Expected it eventually. First, Edward would have to sue her lover for alienation of affection. Then he would sue her in an ecclesiastical court. Because he was a peer, they would still not be done with each other. Parliament would have to pass a bill of divorcement. No wonder estranged couples stayed yoked in marriage for what was surely hell on earth. "Fine. Do whatever you wish, Edward. You have the letters. I'll confess if it will make things go faster. I'm sure you could easily persuade Andrew to say whatever is necessary. He always needs money, and truth is just a meaningless five letter word to him. Be done with me once and for all and put me out of my misery."

"You've not been more miserable than I."

"The misery contest is not one you will win, Edward. You at least still move about in society. People speak to you. You have the company of your family. I, on the other hand, have the company of courtesans thanks to the 'gift' you made me of this house. Come to think of it, buying it for me was probably the most emotional thing you've ever done. You must have been so very angry."

"I'm angry still. You make me angry."

One would never know it from his tone. He might as well have said, "Please pass the butter." He was motionless beside her, his breeches in his lap, looking down at them as though he wasn't sure which part of the body they were intended for.

"It's not a sin to feel things, you know."

He barked out a laugh, rusty from disuse. "You feel enough for both of us, Caroline. You are—too much for me."

"But yet not enough. I'm not Alice, good and pure."

"Don't drag my wife into this!" There was satisfactory heat to his voice; her barb hit home.

It had been tedious—no, torture—to be compared with the incomparable Alice, even when he never said a word out loud. "*I* am your wife, at least until Parliament says otherwise, in case you've forgotten. I can't help who I am. God knows, I tried, but it was never enough." Even as she made the claim, she knew she lied. There had been many days when she had gone out of her way to provoke him.

He snorted. "One would never know it. Our life was a circus. To what purpose is this analysis of our marriage? We never shall see eye-to-eye."

"You're quite correct. As always. I shall miss you, though. Miss the idea of you. So solemn and judgmental. I shall simply have to take up with a Calvinist next."

"I wish the poor fellow luck. I'll even pray for him."

"Why, Edward. Are you making a joke?"

"I suppose I am. This is the end then." He made no attempt to get off the bed.

"As you wish." Caroline tried to stop the betraying tears by closing her eyes. She could not bear to see the back of him as he walked out of her bedroom, his posture straight and unyielding, making him look even taller than he was.

But she didn't have to watch him leave. He took her in his arms and laid her back on the bed. His lips were gentle as butterfly wings, his warm hand tugging the sheet away to press her against his chest. He held her as if she were porcelain, his fingertips skimming her skin, teasing the tiny copper hairs on her arms, circling her pale pink nipples, dipping lower to stroke her drenched bud. His mouth never left hers, their tongues tangling, tasting, promising something more than a farewell kiss. His tenderness tumbled into something else altogether as her hand locked around his rigid cock. Just as he knew every peak and valley of her body, every strength and weakness, she knew his. If only they could just stay abed and never speak.

He broke the kiss and entered her again in one wonderfully hard thrust, his arms corded on either side of her and his hands bunched on the rumpled sheets, gliding in and sliding out as her hips rose frantically to meet him—to catch him and never let him go. He made her work for it, taunting her each time he withdrew, rocking back into her so completely she thought she would die of pleasure. He stopped for a moment, buried deep within her, forcing her to respond to his power as she spasmed around him. They watched each other, gray eyes to green, until her tears blurred the angles of his face. He bent to lick them away, his tongue cool on her flushed cheeks. He whispered something—she could feel his lips thrum against her temple as the next climax hit, spinning his words away.

She couldn't hear. She couldn't see. She could only feel—when he took a peaked nipple between his teeth, when his fingernail scraped an invisible line down her throat, when the heat of his skin set fire to her own at each point of contact, when he angled himself just so to create exquisite friction.

He flooded her, collapsed and held her to his beating heart, imprinting himself onto her slick body, every inch of separation between them gone.

They lay like that until she thought he had fallen asleep. His breathing was even, yet his arms did not relax their hold. She dared not sleep herself and miss a minute of that perfect closeness, his long, lanky body cradling hers. But at the clock's midnight chime, he rolled away.

"Where are you going?"

"Home, Caro. I must. I *must*," he repeated, as if he had to convince one of them. He didn't glance her way as he rounded up the clothing that had been tossed aside in such haste. The candles still guttered on the mantel, but she couldn't take one last look as he removed himself from her life. She stared up at the mirror instead, where she was a shadowy forlorn form, indistinguishable from the white mound of bedding.

"Good-bye." He said it from the doorway, his voice travelling the miles between them. There was no last kiss, no last caress. The door shut with a soft click, and her heart broke once again.

Chapter 3

"Poison?" The duke clutched at his throat, his long, elegant hand turning into the claw of death.
—*The Dark Duke's Dilemma*

It was impossible to sleep. Caroline changed the sheets and pillowcases herself, rolling up the traces of Edward's scent and semen into an unwieldy ball. Lizzie could deal with the laundry pile tomorrow. Wringing out her sponge in the basin of cold water, she scrubbed her body with vicious indifference, barely noting the pink and purple marks Edward's hands and lips had left. She ran a comb through her tangles and put on a plain navy dressing gown, a far cry from her exotic writing robe. Feeling an urge to banish every shadow, she lit branches of candles in her upstairs parlor until the room was lit like Christmas. The remains of dinner had been taken away at some point—she hoped the Hazletts had not been too horrified by the commotion beyond the bedroom door. They had left dessert behind, two sad puddles of caramel and cream. Caroline ate the entire contents of both parfait glasses without a thought to her hips or her chin, then pulled a book from the shelves and curled up on her purple sofa.

Unfortunately the words swam about the pages like little black fish. She snapped the book shut and stared into the empty fireplace. Tomorrow she'd cut some pink hydrangeas and place them in the hearth in one of the Chinese pots. She could ask some of the girls on the street in for tea. It wasn't her usual Thursday reception day, but perhaps someone would be at loose ends. The two newest Jane Street mistresses, Laurette and Charlotte, had already moved out before they ever really settled in. Laurette had gone to the country with her marquess, while Charlotte had simply disappeared, which was probably just as well. Charlotte was simply not cut out to be any man's plaything.

Nor was Caroline. She was no longer at the mercy of Edward's single night a year.

She might never see him again, unless it was by chance. She expected that his advocate would contact her over what needed to be done. She'd prefer legal counsel of her own, although she knew perfectly well she had no rights under English law. Only a man could bring charges of infidelity in a petition for divorce, and most men were not quite furious enough to do so. Her reputation, tarnished now, would be irretrievably black once the act of Parliament became fact.

She didn't have a solicitor. She'd best ask Garrett for a recommendation—which would mean Garrett would know her circumstances were about to change and it would be even more difficult to keep him at arms' length.

A trial would be public and mortifying. Every bit of her dirty laundry—far worse than her soiled sheets—would be published for all the world to know. The truth would come out about Andrew, and possibly even her brother. Mary's Surrey serenity might be affected as well. Maybe she would decide at last that Caroline was not a fit sister to consort with.

It had finally come to this. All Caroline's past machinations to salvage her Parker pride had been worse than useless.

But a divorce could take years. Perhaps Guy Fawkes could return from the dead and blow up Parliament successfully this time and she wouldn't have to worry.

The brisk rapping of her door knocker shocked her out of her musings. Edward! He'd come back! She flew downstairs barefoot before Hazlett woke. It was well past two, but the gas lamps of the street were bright enough for her to see one of the Jane Street guards on her steps through the sidelight. Puzzled, she pulled the door open.

"Beggin' your pardon, Lady Christie, but I saw your lights,

else I wouldn't bother you. There's a young gentlemen here to see you. Says his name is Edward Christie, but the other man claimin' to be Edward Christie just left a while ago, so that's a lie. We've got our list, you know. Nobody gets in or out at night without us knowin'. Thought I'd double-check before we send the boy on his way."

Security on Jane Street was strictly enforced. The men who kept their mistresses there protected their investments from dusk to dawn. They might be unfaithful to their wives, but their mistresses would stay true whether they wanted to or not. Of course there was plenty of daylight for dalliance, a foolishly overlooked fact.

"There must be some mistake."

"That's what we thought. These young bucks get in their cups and want to see the Janes for themselves, poor devils. Their time will come. I'll get rid of him." He tipped his cap and turned.

"Wait! What does this boy look like?"

"A nice-lookin' lad. Quality. Dark hair. Real tall and skinny, all arms and legs, although his legs won't be holdin' him up much longer. Dead drunk, he is."

Ned. Dear Lord. He'd been almost as tall and just as handsome as his father five years ago. She should let the guards send him home. Edward would be furious with them both. "It's all right. I believe it must be my stepson. Please bring him to my door."

"Aye, if you're sure." The man looked at her, doubt written all over his face.

"It's quite all right. I'll wake my butler."

"That's a good idea, my lady. You never know what a fellow might do when he's jug-bitten."

Caroline stepped back into the dark hallway. Hazlett was already coming down the stairs with a candle, a robe thrown over his striped butler's pants.

"Lady Christie, I do hope everything is all right. I heard the disturbance and came as fast as I could."

Poor Hazlett. His wiry white hair stood on end. If it was

how he woke up every morning, he must give Mrs. Hazlett quite a chuckle. Caroline had never seen him at such a disadvantage, but then she rarely had callers in the middle of the night. "We have an unexpected visitor. Ned Christie, my husband's oldest son. Or at least I believe it's he who is at the gate. The guard says he's not well."

"Oh, dear. Shall I fetch a doctor?"

"I don't think that will be necessary, but you could prepare a pot of coffee. Perhaps a sandwich. You needn't wake Mrs. Hazlett."

"No indeed. That is all within the realm of my capability. Would you like me to wait with you to assist the young gentleman into the drawing room?"

Caroline had dealt with her father's, and then brother's drinking for years. They had been easy to maneuver. Parkers were was not nearly as tall as Christies, however. She would hate to have Ned topple to the tile and ruin his pretty face. "Thank you, Hazlett. Your assistance will be most welcome."

There was a fair amount of commotion in the street—some cursing by both parties, a snatch of song, and the unmistakable sound of retching—but at last a chastened Ned stumbled up the steps in the arms of the guard. Caroline would have to tip the poor man for his efforts tomorrow. For tonight, at least, she'd send Hazlett out with coffee and extra sandwiches.

"Caro!" Ned said with a loopy grin. He seemed to think that explained everything.

"Come sit down, Neddie. Ned." Between the guard and Hazlett, they deposited Ned on a sofa in the downstairs drawing room. Caroline had redecorated recently with the proceeds from *The Maid's Master*, her most popular volume yet, and hoped the boy had cast up his accounts sufficiently to keep her new green brocade safe. Somewhere along the way of his evening Ned had lost his neckcloth and one glove. His pants were torn, and his dark hair rivaled Hazlett's in its

defiance of gravity. She gave Hazlett instructions and the butler disappeared to the kitchen.

"I have not set eyes on you in five years. What brings you
to my doorstep? And in this condition! Your father will not
approve. He's forbidden me from seeing any of you, you
know." Caroline tried her best to summon sternness, but was
checking his forehead for fever and brushing his coat of
crumbs.

"F-father never approves of anything he didn't think of
first. Pay no attention to him. Don't m-myself." He hiccupped.

"Easy for you to say. Oh, Neddie! Why are you here? I
should send you home now that I know you're not at death's
door."

"Might be. Don't feel at all the thing, Caro." He looked
up at her pleadingly with his father's hazel eyes.

Caroline repressed a desire to slap some sense into him,
and sniffed in disdain. "I should think not. You've fallen into
an ale barrel."

"Brandy, too. Inferior stuff. N-nasty."

"I'm going to fill you with some coffee and send you home
in a hack. And you must not tell your father you were here.
Why *are* you here?"

" 'Twas a m-mission of mercy. Wouldn't come if it weren't
'portant. Know I'm s'posed to cut you. L-like you never
ex-existed. The old man will flay me alive for finding you,
but I don't c-care. The fellows tonight got to talkin' about
parents. Parents are the v-very devil, you know. Cut off one's
'lowance for no good reason. Rules and r-regulations. One
l-long and boring lecture after 'nother for the m-merest in-
fraction. A Christie never does this. A Christie never does
that. And then *they* do just as they please. Do y'know Father
wants me to m-marry my cousin when I come of age? S-safe,
he says, as if a fellow wants safe. She's got a squint, and no
chest to speak of. I won't do it. But that's not—no, I'm here

for m'friend Rory. His father is the worst. He keeps a fancy whore here on J-jane Street while p-poor Rory doesn't have a shilling to his name and his mama is home crying all the time." He turned a mottled shade of red which clashed with his green hue. "Sorry. No doubt the wh-whore is a friend of yours. And I was going to tell you—" he trailed off, as if he really had no idea what he was supposed to say on poor Rory's behalf.

So her location and reputation had trickled down to Ned. She felt instantly stricken for that which must be a considerable source of embarrassment for him. To know that his stepmother was installed on Jane Street—Edward could not possibly have told him. Even though Edward had been cruel, he had been the soul of discretion. It was she who had let her whereabouts slip a time or two.

Caroline had an idea which Jane was involved in this love triangle—square, if one counted the destitute Rory. Sophie Rydell at Number Two complained long and loud about Lord Carmichael, who brought his domestic troubles with his wife and son into her bed more often than an erection, and was somewhat stingy with his gifts besides. "Does Rory's father beat him or his mother?"

Ned gaped at her as if she'd grown two heads. In his inebriated state, she probably had. "I should say not! Rory would knock him flat. Good with his f-fists, he is."

"Then I suggest you explain to your friend that gentlemen often seek dalliance outside the bonds of marriage. It's the way of the ton. He'll probably do the same to his wife when he marries."

Ned's dark brows drew together. "That's it? You w-won't talk to the girl?"

"And what am I to say to her?" Caroline asked in impatience. "Leave your comfortable house and go back on the street to sell oranges because some spoiled drunken boy is unhappy that his allowance is cut? Lord Carmichael will only find another mistress, I assure you."

Ned hiccupped. "You r-really are a wonder. You *do* know everything. I n-never even said his name."

The rattle of cups heralded Hazlett's return. Ned declined a sandwich but gulped the hot coffee gratefully.

"Hazlett, if you don't mind, wrap up the sandwiches and take them and a flask of coffee out to the guards. They've earned them tonight."

"Very good, Lady Christie. Shall I procure a hackney cab for the young master as well?"

Ned was slumped over the table, all sharp elbows and knees. He had yet to fill out, but gave the promise of being as lean and elegant as his father. Caroline sighed. Ned could not become her reclamation project. She had been quite out of her league as a stepmother, as Edward had pointed out to her again and again.

"Yes. Although it's awfully late. I wonder if you'll have any luck."

" 'Snot that far," Ned mumbled. "I can walk."

"I should like to see you try." Jane Street was ideally located in the heart of Mayfair, so handy for gentlemen to slip away from their homes and slip into their mistresses. But she could picture Ned sprawled facedown on the sidewalk. He wouldn't freeze to death as it was nearly summer, but he'd be a target for pickpockets and gossip.

She plied Ned with more coffee, and he did indeed seem to come somewhat to his senses. She was treated to rambling tales of his siblings Allie and Jack. Caroline had missed Allie most of all, that sullen, gangly, impossible child who had made her married life a living nightmare. Well, to be fair, Edward did that, but Allie had helped him with a concerted, conscientious effort. The boys had been easier to deal with, being mostly away at school. When they came home, she was reminded of her scapegrace brother Nicky, and Andrew, God rot his soul.

Hazlett came back after more than a quarter of an hour, unsuccessful in procuring a means of transportation to remove Edward Allerton Christie the Younger from her sofa. It was just as well. Despite the coffee, Ned was snoring. Grunting. And farting. There was a noxious aroma in Caroline's parlor from which she was anxious to escape. Leaving poor Hazlett to find a pillow, a blanket, and a bucket, she climbed the stairs to her lonely bed, wondering what the morning would bring.

The morning brought disaster. Ned had been sick in the night. Although his aim had been more or less on target, Caroline's parlor smelled even worse than it had earlier. A ghost-white Ned lay on his back on the divan clutching his belly, his long legs dangling off to the carpet. At regular intervals he'd spasm and gasp, "Knew it. The oysters were off." At first she thought he'd helped himself to her dinner's leftovers, but he explained—between vomiting and a manly form of crying—that he and his friends had ordered two platters of oysters in an alehouse as they discussed the vicissitudes of their wicked yet dull fathers. Between bad seafood and worse drink, Ned was suffering, and Caroline was suffering right along with him. Food poisoning could be deadly, although she hoped the worst of it had wound up in the bucket. Hazlett had already summoned the doctor, and she had most reluctantly written a note to Edward, trying to explain in the very vaguest of terms why his son spent the night on her sofa.

Dr. Turner arrived first. He shooed her out of the room, so she gratefully went to her little garden for fresh air. It was an oasis of peace to her, although at the moment she needed to deadhead the spent flowers. Sometimes she held her weekly teas there when the weather was fine, or sat by herself even when the weather was not. The sky was sufficiently cloudy, promising a storm. When Edward marched outside, she knew the storm had arrived a few hours early. She tossed her gardening gloves on the bench and sat down in resignation. She'd barely slept, and knew she did not look her best. A glance in the mirror had her wanting to put a sack over her head to spare the public.

But Edward looked worse. Apart from his fury, his hazel eyes were sunken in between gray smudges and his full lips were bloodless. She hoped he'd lain awake all night in torment realizing he'd never have her body again.

"What is the meaning of this?" he thundered.

Caroline stared up at him, nearly cracking her neck—he was so awfully tall. He would make a perfect fire and brimstone preacher, she decided. One look at him and all the commandments would be obeyed instantly without question. But she'd never been much of a rules-follower.

"I wrote to you. Neddie turned up late last night, and he was ill. Surely you've spoken to the doctor."

"He'll be fine," Edward snapped. "The young fool. Why didn't you send him directly home?"

"I tried to, but there were no cabs to be had at that hour."

He pointed a long finger at her. "If this is some sort of trick to get me back here, Caroline, you've misjudged badly. I won't have you in collusion with my children again."

"A trick? Do you think I planned to get Neddie drunk and throw up and defecate all over my house? I suppose I paid off all his stupid friends to make him eat bad oysters to make my grand plan even more diabolical. Go round to Lord Carmichael's house and see how his son Rory is faring. I have no reason to lure Carmichael here—I don't even know him."

"What the devil are you talking about?"

"I don't even know." Caroline decapitated the head of a bright pink pelargonium, crushing the petals between her fingers. "Go home, Edward, and take Neddie with you. And stop lecturing him so. He doesn't like it. And furthermore," she said, tossing the flower to the ground, "let him pick out his own wife."

Edward looked at her, his pale face glacial. "Don't you dare tell me how to raise my children."

"And don't you come to my home and tell me what to do!

I've kept my end of the bargain—I never once tried to see *your* children these past five years. *Your* children, not ours, never ours. It was crystal clear from our wedding day that you didn't want my help with them."

Edward snorted. "Help! As if you had one inkling in that rackety brain of yours how to be a mother. And this is *my* house. Don't forget it."

She had quite enough. Recalling the satisfaction her next-door neighbor had after smashing statuary in her garden, Caroline snatched up the heavy pot of pelargonium and dropped it very close to Edward's foot. "Get out! You gave me a life interest in this house, and my sole interest is to keep you out of it! If you are to lord your ownership over me, I'll leave London. I have enough money now. I'm no longer dependent upon your scraps of generosity."

Edward opened his mouth, then shut it. The muscle in his cheek danced the tarantella. She had never seen him in such a towering rage, and was nearly giddy from it. It was time he felt as frustrated as she was.

His next words were barely audible, yet deadly just the same. "I've already sent Ned home. You and I are going upstairs. Now."

"Are you mad? What will you do? Beat me to confess? I told you, I did not invite Ned here!"

"You are still my wife, and you will obey me."

Caroline laughed a little wildly. The lack of sleep had softened his brain. "Now wait a minute. Last night you said you were going to divorce me. Don't tell me you've changed your mind."

"I have not. But until the matter comes before the House of Lords, I expect to resume my marital rights. Not just for one night a year, but whenever I choose. I choose now. You will serve as my mistress."

"You *are* mad."

"If I am, you have driven me to it. I will get you out of my system one way or another."

Caroline clutched her gloves, feeling dizzy. "By—by forcing me? You are not that kind of man, Edward."

"I don't believe much force will be necessary." He smiled a perfectly dreadful smile.

Caroline swallowed. Her cold, controlled husband had obviously lost his mind. "I will not cooperate."

"We'll see about that." Scooping her up, he carried her into the house.

Chapter 4

"I've got you now, my fine filly, and soon you'll be
ridden hard and put away wet," Lord Carrolton
exclaimed, a leer upon his long, lecherous countenance.
    Catriona careened down the staircase of Carrolton
Manor, praying for someone to save her.

—*The Maid's Master*

The little hellcat had bitten him. And she was not as easy
to carry as she used to be. He'd noticed last night she
was rounder and deliciously soft. But he adored every inch of
her alabaster skin, skin so fine he could watch blue veins
pulse, skin so pearlescent she nearly glowed in the dark. It
was not dark now, of course, not even noon on a rainy spring
day. She had lied to him, betrayed him, tricked him, yet still
he couldn't wait to sink himself deep within her pink folds.

But he needed to catch her first. She had locked herself in
her dressing room as soon as he tossed her onto the bed,
scrambling like a cat and twisting about the room, flinging
the odd object at him. He avoided the shattered vase and
brushed the rice powder from his jacket, then hung it neatly
on the chair beside her desk. A notebook lay open, her careless loopy writing covering one-third of the page. He didn't
have his spectacles with him, and wouldn't read her nonsense
even if he did. Beth had told him, with a triumphant big-
sister smirk, that Caroline seemed fond of killing off rangy,
pompous, dark-haired aristocrats in her books. It would be
unlucky to read about his premature demise.

Hell and damnation. What had come over him in the garden? There she sat, a red lily in the midst of pastel blooms,
taunting him. She had been so haughty about Ned and the
house he'd simply snapped. He had wanted somehow to

teach her something. He wasn't sure what—his mastery, his domination, his perfect *rightness*. What he had proposed to her had shocked him as much as it shocked her. *His estranged wife as his mistress*. It was patently absurd. Their one night a year already took him forever to marshal his thoughts again, and he was planning to multiply that night by many. A hundred if he could. She would drive him to Bedlam, but first he'd fuck her until he stopped wanting to. Surely she'd bore him eventually.

She'd made him suffer enough. If she'd begun their marriage by telling him the truth, he believed he could have born it, and forgiven her. He realized her other faults had been merely a diversion from the core of their difficulty, rather like the icing over a rotten cake.

Perhaps he was being unfair. If she'd had more time, she might have revealed her past during a normal courtship. But he didn't give her time, couldn't give her time—he'd had to have her. A *coup de foudre*. He'd never believed in love at first sight, but it was certainly lust at first sight. Edward had known someone else would propose if he didn't.

He should have made her his mistress instead. Well, it wasn't too late.

He poked his head out the bedroom door. Hazlett was hovering in the hallway, looking conflicted as well he should. Technically, Caroline might be his employer, but it was Edward who paid his exorbitant salary and padded his pockets besides.

"I'm not going to kill her," Edward said dryly. "I don't suppose you have the key to her dressing room on that chain, do you?"

Hazlett shuffled his feet and sighed. "I had a hard night, my lord, and I'm not as young as I used to be."

"I'll give you a pony if you give me the goddamn key."

The butler lifted two fuzzy white eyebrows in surprise. Perhaps the key could have come cheaper than twenty-five pounds. "I want your word that you won't harm her. Mrs. Hazlett and I are very fond of Lady Christie, and that's a fact.

She may appear reckless and gay, and a bit—well, *naughty*— but she's a good girl. Warmhearted."

"I'm sure she appreciates your loyalty. The key, please."

Hazlett stared meaningfully at Edward.

"I'm good for it. I haven't any money on me. I left the house in haste," Edward said, annoyed. When Caroline's note came, he'd nearly choked on his solitary breakfast and flown out of the house. It was a wonder he was not still in his dressing gown.

"I'll take your word as a gentleman about the pony *and* your promise to treat Lady Christie with care." Hazlett's keys jangled as he searched for the right one. "Here it is."

Edward grabbed it before the man changed his mind. "Hazlett, why don't you and Mrs. Hazlett take the rest of the day off? Go for a walk. Take in the sights. The maid Lizzie, too."

"It's raining, my lord. And I'm not sure as we should. Lady Christie might need us."

"She won't. Stay upstairs in your rooms, then. Take a nap. We'll try not to make too much noise. But under no circumstances are you to interrupt us, no matter if Lady Christie is screaming bloody murder. *Especially* if Lady Christie is screaming murder. Understood?"

Two bright red patches stood out on the old butler's cheeks, but he nodded his head.

Edward shut the bedroom door with a satisfying click and stalked over to the dressing room. Before he could fit the key to the lock, Caroline flung it open. She had changed into that horrible robe, the one with ugly flowers that looked like splotches of blood. No doubt she thought it might put him off, but he was not so easily deterred. It swirled behind her like a trail of fire as she paced the carpet, her cheeks nearly as crimson as the poppies. Or Hazlett's.

"That traitor! I heard every word. Once you finish with me, I'm firing him."

"You can't. He comes with the house. Please lie down. You're making me addled with your traipsing about."

Caroline shot him a withering look, then tore the ribbon at

her throat. The robe puddled at her feet and she was singularly, gloriously naked. "To love, honor and obey, isn't that what I said? Well, I lied."

Edward found his voice. "You'll obey me, at least."

"Oh, indeed, it seems I must in order to get rid of you. I'll be watching the clock, however." She lay flat on the bed, hands clasped like a virgin martyr in prayer and closed her eyes.

Edward went to the mantel. A pretty little china clock covered in rosebuds told him he'd been awake almost thirty straight hours. He pitched it against the wall, where it joined the vase shards in porcelain death.

"Add destruction of property to your other sins," Caroline said, her eyes still closed.

Edward examined his hand, wondering what had come over it. "I can see why you do it. It does feel—rather *good.*"

"If you enjoy it so much, may I recommend you go downstairs to the kitchen? There's plenty of crockery there."

"Do you remember the night at Christie Park when we went downstairs for the leftover trifle? I took you on the kitchen table as I recall. You got a splinter."

Caroline bit her lip, but he watched the flush spread to her chest and the tips of her shell-like ears. Yes, she remembered. He began to systematically remove his clothes, carefully folding them because he had to walk through Mayfair later in daylight . . . unless he stayed until evening . . . which he just might do.

He wondered why he'd never hit upon this scheme before. Certainly he was furious with her, certainly he wanted to divorce her, but she was right—he was a mortal man, with manly needs, and he still had a wife to assuage them. Thanks to that blackguard Andrew Rossiter she was as skilled as any courtesan. She lived amongst them and there were any number of things she might have added to her repertoire. Why should he deny himself like some tonsured monk? The evil genius of it all stunned him.

He could visit Jane Street every day if he had a mind to. It was he who'd decreed that silly June 14 agenda, he who'd limited their contact by virtue of his nettlesome pride. She had begged him for another chance. Well, here it was.

Caroline had removed her nether curls for him, as he preferred once he realized it could be done. Edward took advantage of her smooth white skin by firmly pushing her legs apart and dipping his tongue to part her more yielding flesh. Her bud was ripe, rigid and pink, and he set patiently to taste her. Consume her. He had never done this with Alice, couldn't imagine his sheltered first wife ever permitting him such liberties. He shoved the thoughts of innocent Alice out of his mind and concentrated on his wicked Caro, who was writhing and mewling with pleasure. Her fingertips skittered through his hair and danced across his shoulders with increasing urgency, and he knew it was time to insert his fingertip. She splintered—like the vase, like the clock—one more broken possession that could not be made whole but could be mended for a little while.

He quickly sheathed himself within her, reaping the instant benefit of her orgasm. Each wave milked him, drove him deeper. For a woman who was not particularly tall, she stretched and melted like magic around his long body. He felt her everywhere, inside and out. Her eyes were shut, as though she was pretending he was just a dream. Or perhaps another lover, but it didn't matter at the moment. He would leave no doubt that she was still his. He kissed her hard so she could taste herself, nearly bruising her mouth with his insistence, and she bruised him right back, her lips and teeth and tongue frantic, her nails raking the length of his back.

His heart stuttered as his cock erupted, the breath left his lungs, his throat constricted. He could easily die where he was, and wouldn't that teach him a lesson? One he couldn't unlearn. Caroline could kill him without even trying. He gasped and withdrew, rolling off her sweat-satined body, sucking in air in the suddenly close room.

"Are you done?"

Edward had to give her credit—now that she'd had her

pleasure she sounded bored, as if she had another appointment. He wasn't fooled for a minute.

"For now."

"I'm hungry, and you've sent the servants away," she said peevishly, struggling to sit up. He hid his smile; it was as if her arms and legs were made of blancmange. He knew just how she felt, weak as a kitten after a tiger's attack. He couldn't decide which one of them had been the tiger. Perhaps they'd taken turns.

"I didn't have a decent breakfast, you know. The Hazletts and I had our hands full with Neddie. There wasn't time for the smallest muffin crumb."

"I was called away from my breakfast as well, if you recall. I thought my son was dying."

Caroline sniffed, tucking a long red curl behind an ear. "Nonsense! I'm sure my letter was not meant to give that impression."

"And you claim to be a writer. I assure you your words— what I could read of them—were most alarming, worthy of a Gothic novel. It's no wonder you're so popular with the masses."

It was clear Caroline didn't know whether to be flattered or insulted. She looked on the verge of speech but covered herself with a sheet instead.

"Why don't you get dressed and fetch us some provisions, Caro? It's going to be a long afternoon."

"I b-beg your pardon?"

"You're hungry. I'm hungry," he said, all reason. "There must be something in the pantry. Last night's dessert, perchance? I know we never touched it."

"I—you—why don't *you* go downstairs? It's all your fault anyway!"

"Our mutual hunger? Well, I suppose Ned *is* my son, although I didn't ask him to land on your doorstep foxed to the gills. And I had nothing do with the oysters."

"Oh!" She stood up, clamping the sheet to her breasts. "Go home. Please. You've caused me enough grief. Just when

I thought you were done playing games with me, you've started up another round."

He felt the muscle in his cheek jump. "You of all people know I don't play games, Caroline. But I do set the rules, and you'd be wise to follow them." He ducked the pillow she threw at his head. "Be careful what you throw next. You wouldn't want to make me angry."

"Yes, I would! I should love to see you angry—furious— livid, wild, and ungovernable!" She looked wild and un- governable herself, her eyes flashing, her tangled hair worthy of Medusa.

"I do so hate to disappoint you." He folded his hands over his cock, the act both self-preserving and calming. He was not going to rise to the occasion by temperament or tempta- tion. "Something simple will do. A heel of bread. Some cheese. Wine. And that dessert, if you didn't already eat it."

The bedroom door slammed with a vengeance. Edward smiled at himself in the mirror above him. He'd forgotten all about the mirror, but would make good use of it later.

Caroline tripped down the stairs, her feet tangling in the sheet. Would Edward even notice if she fell to her death? She supposed if he got hungry enough he might come looking for her, find her broken body, step over it and continue on to the kitchen.

This new Edward—this stolid yet different, *demonic* Ed- ward—was a puzzle. What was she to do with him? Did he really expect to resume his conjugal rights while they lived apart and he sought a divorce? It was cruel in the extreme. She'd tried so hard to forget him, to make a life for herself, and he was ordering her about, doing all manner of things to her that she simply could not forget. She wrapped the sheet tighter for the next set of stairs. How the Romans had man- aged was a mystery.

She shouldered her way through the kitchen door, wonder- ing how she'd keep the sheet up as she foraged for food. Four sets of eyes looked up in surprise. The traitorous Hazlett was not napping, but having a substantial lunch with his wife, Lizzie, and Ben the kitchen lad. They rose in unison, talking over each other.

"Lady Christie, I hope you understand—"

"Good Lord, you'll catch your death, dear—"

"Oh! This is so romantic!"

"Gor!"

"Be quiet, all of you," Caroline grumbled. "I cannot fire you, Hazlett, but I want to. You have aligned yourself with *him* one too many times."

"My lady," the butler blustered, "he assured me he wouldn't harm one red hair on your head! What has the villain done to you?"

"Oh, be quiet. And fetch a ham out of the larder. Make us some sandwiches. You're good at that. Find me a bottle of the most inferior wine we have. For *him*. Mrs. Hazlett, if I could trouble you for a cup of tea, I'd be very grateful. I need my wits about me. Ben, you are to go out to the garden immediately and forget you ever saw me in such disarray. Oh, hell and damnation, it's raining. Sit in the shed, then, until Mr. Hazlett tells you to come back in. And Lizzie, please do something with my hair. I cannot go on like this."

Tea and hairpins and sandwiches miraculously appeared as a goggle-eyed Ben disappeared. Caroline sat silent as the three servants went out of their way to soothe her. A tray was laden and poor old Hazlett mounted the steps with it. She stood like a doll while Lizzie and Mrs. Hazlett draped and knotted the sheet so she was nearly presentable. No doubt Edward would strip her of it at the first opportunity, but at least she could walk upstairs without incident.

Steeling herself, she returned to the scene of the crime. Edward was sitting in bed propped against pillows like an eastern potentate, a sandwich in one hand, a goblet of inferior wine in the other. She supposed she was designated to be the dancing girl.

"You look very fetching in that sheet, Caro. You might even start a new fashion craze. Come join me."

She raised her haughty chin. "I'm not hungry."

"Come, come. This was all your idea. Have a bite." He extended his sandwich toward her.

The bread was fresh and studded with fragrant seeds, the mustard sharp in her nostrils. She could bite his pink thumb off and pretend she mistook it for ham. "No, thank you."

"Suit yourself. Old Hazlett made enough for an army. I'm sure we'll work up an appetite and get to it later. He tells me that caramel dessert was nowhere to be found, but there's pie. I know how you like your pie."

Oh, he was wicked. Andrew had told him about the Cherry Pie Incident and she had not denied it because she couldn't. Andrew had told him so much that day, but not the whole truth, thank God. She'd been rooted to the floor, mute, disheveled. It had been the worst day of her life . . .

Except for around midnight last night, when she thought Edward was gone forever. Now it seemed she couldn't get rid of him. And she wanted to. She did.

She collapsed on her dressing table chair. Lizzie had done wonders braiding her hair and pinning it into a rather regal coronet. She could pass for some Roman goddess, one of the obscure ones. Clementia, goddess of forgiveness, although just at present Caroline was full of righteous outrage. Sentia, who helped children develop. She'd helped Edward's, hadn't she, as best she could? And Ben, too. But never Disciplina. Caroline had been unable to control her passions all her life.

Edward was not supposed to become her passion, just her husband. She'd seen his sangfroid as a benefit, not a detraction, when they'd first met. True, he was precipitous in his proposal, but she'd taken the ton by storm and was very much in demand. It was only sensible that a sensible man move quickly if he wanted to secure her hand in marriage. And it was only sensible of her to move quickly and accept, before her unpleasant past caught up with her. Edward was steady, reliable, boring, living in a world very different than the one she was trying so desperately to escape. But it had taken Andrew so little effort to insinuate himself into Edward's world and back into her life. Her year of marriage had been fraught with peril far beyond the management of three obstreperous children.

"Penny for your thoughts, Caroline."

Her hand shook as she wiped away a tear. "I am tired, Edward. I didn't sleep a wink."

"Tsk, tsk. Didn't sleep. Didn't eat." He patted the bed. "We'll rest a while. Come here, Caro. Now."

Because she had no righteous outrage left, she went.

Chapter 5

"This contract is illegal," she sputtered. Her mama had taught her to read before she was forced onto the streets to lead her life of sorry sin.

"So, sue me," Lord Grant grinned. "I'll have you, and have you now."

—*The Viscount's Willing Victim*

She lay curled up like a child beside him, her hairpins scattered on the pillow. Idly he toyed with her braid, losing his fingers in the red silk as he unraveled it. It was a sin to confine hair like that, and words were inadequate to describe its color—not Titian nor auburn nor russet nor ginger. His own Boudicca, although not precisely tall or terrifying.

They'd slept several hours, and slept only. She had been truthful admitting she was tired, as was he. Perhaps because he'd gone so long without sleep he'd made an irrevocable mistake taking her to bed again, but he wasn't sorry. Yet.

Tomorrow he would go to his old friend Sir William Maclean's chambers to hammer out what needed to be done to end the marriage. Will would know what to do, and do it quietly until it was necessary to unleash his rapier-like tongue. A bill of divorcement before Parliament was not a light undertaking; it truly might be years before the thing was settled. Edward had the letters, but the damn things were undated, so getting Rossiter on board was imperative. Ironic that his entire future was in the hands of such a man. Rossiter would have to be sued, but Edward was well aware it would be he who would wind up paying the damages to himself. He had a severe dislike for the man, whom he kept tripping over in the most unlikely social situations. Rossiter was no better than a male courtesan, stylish and sleek, always looking to advance himself. Caroline had been foolish in the extreme when she gave her virginity to him without sufficient payment.

Edward looked at his sleeping wife, her face smoothed of artifice. He had hoped her to be an innocent when he married her, but was not too terribly disappointed to find she was not. She did her damnedest to cry out and feign ignorance on their wedding night, but Edward was not a complete innocent himself. There had been his virginal, hesitant Alice, and a few other women besides. It had seemed important to Caroline to continue the fiction that he was her first, so he let it go. She had been five and twenty after all, living a shockingly unsupervised life with her ramshackle brother in the wilds of Cumbria, never coming to town.

Town went to them. Certain elements of it, at any rate. Nicholas had been a viscount with a tumbledown estate and a penchant for sin; his parties had been legendary, reaching even Edward's staid ears. But her brother was dead and Caroline had seemed eager for a new life. If Edward had not been thinking with his cock for the first time in his life, he would have seen how wrong she was for him and his children. But he couldn't think then, and now he was thinking too much.

She sighed and stirred, and he drew her closer. Her eyes flew open, black lashes bent and tangled from their encounter with the pillow. "Oh, it *is* true."

"What?"

"You're here. I thought it was a dream."

Edward chuckled. "Yes, I am every maiden's fantasy."

"I'm hardly a maiden."

Edward thought it safer not to comment. Her sexual experience had proved to be one of her few virtues.

She squirmed in his arms. "When are you going home? I need to write. I have a deadline."

"I'm sure you'll find some way or other to placate Garrett."

She pushed at him harder, but he didn't release her. "You

will never think the best of me, will you? Garrett is a friend, a business partner, no more."

"But he would like to be something more, wouldn't he? He's rich. I suppose you could call him handsome. I wonder why it is you've suddenly become so proper." He watched her flush and felt her nails dig into his chest.

She sent him an equally piercing look. "I never mix business with pleasure."

"Ah, so you'd sleep with a stranger. Or perhaps an old acquaintance."

"Or an old husband," she said tartly.

"Touché." He let her go. The shadows had deepened; it was nearing dusk. They had slept much longer than he thought. Any acrobatics in front of the mirror would have to be postponed. She left the bed in an instant and wrapped herself back in the garish robe.

"Really, Edward, since we are to be lovers, you'll need to give me some sort of schedule. I do have a life, you know."

"I'll have to consult my calendar and get back to you. I should think four or five times a week should do the trick."

"Four or five times!" she screeched.

"Oh, all right, more often if I must."

She simply stared at him openmouthed as if he'd grown an additional penis.

He was gratified that he'd robbed the famous author of words. "We'll settle for six. Thursdays off, since that's your entertaining day. You might be too fatigued from all the gossip with your neighbors, and I prefer you to be fully responsive."

"You—you—I will not, I can *not* give six nights a week to you!"

"No one said anything about nights. There are tedious social events I must attend before I leave for the country. As I said, I'll consult my schedule and write down the dates and hours. You'll still have plenty of time to write your books. And it won't be for very long, not even a month. We'll see how I feel in the fall when I return from Christie Park." He waited for her to say something, do something, throw something, but she stood absolutely still. "That's that, then. As it happens, I have an engagement this evening. And I suppose I should check up on Ned and give him a piece of my mind." He rose and began to dress, keeping an eye on Caroline in case he had to parry an attack. But she was curiously, disconcertingly passive. Her silence unsettled him more than he liked to admit. He was used to her tirades of temper. He'd seen more than enough of them in the year they were married.

Once he had tied his cravat to his satisfaction, he kissed her quickly on a pale cheek. "Good-bye. I'll be in touch." He had nearly reached the bottom stairstep when he heard a remarkably vile curse and a satisfying crash. Something wooden this time, he thought. No doubt he'd find out what it was the next time he came to call.

"Hell and damnation!" She heaved the carved jewel box against the wall. There was an explosion of topaz and pearls, amethysts and aquamarines, a diamond or two. Caroline was disgusted. Her room looked like a battle zone. The sheets were still balled in a corner and she'd already cut her foot on a Meissen fragment from the earlier vase mishap. She'd been fond of the jewel box, too, a long-ago Christmas gift from her brother. He'd teased her that she'd have a proper place for her paste jewelry, and that one day their fortune would improve and he'd buy her something real. Her gemstones were real now, if mostly inexpensive, but her fortune was as lamentable as ever.

She limped back to the bed, not having the energy to strip it again. Edward's spoor was everywhere. She'd better get used to it. Apparently he would be tormenting her on a daily basis. Except for Thursdays. She let out a howl and threw herself facedown on the pillow.

There came the tentative tap on the door. Poor Lizzie. Caroline had made a dreadful mess, and it wasn't fair to make her maid pick up after her. "I'm all right. Go away, Lizzie."

"Are you sure, Lady Christie? It sounds—it sounds as if something broke again."

"You mean *I* broke something again. You might as well enter, but don't say I didn't warn you."

The blonde maid opened the door a crack. "I've seen worse. I think."

"Oh, God. What am I going to do?"

"Well, first, you should put your slippers on. Your foot is bleeding on the bedding," Lizzie said sensibly. "Then you should gather up your jewelry, because I'm not to be trusted. I might abscond with that sapphire choker. I've always been fond of it."

Caroline grinned in spite of everything. She loved it when Lizzie showed some of her old spark. She had been a delightful, mischievous girl before Pope had beaten the daylights out of her.

Caroline climbed off the bed, scooped up the necklace and handed it to Lizzie. It was not from Edward—she had bought it herself to celebrate her first year as an author, and the stones were not so very large or valuable. "It's yours."

"Oh, Caroline—Lady Christie, no! I couldn't take it from you! And where would I wear it anyway?"

Caroline tucked the necklace in the pocket of Lizzie's apron. "You won't always be my maid, Lizzie. Someday you'll have jewels again, and furs, and a fine gentleman to see to your comfort."

"Now you're writing me into one of your stories. Not everyone gets their happy ending."

"Don't I know it." Caroline bent over and winced. Whatever she had done to her back while gardening would not go away. Rutting like a wild beast with Edward hadn't helped much either. She straightened up with difficulty. "I'm sorry, Lizzie. You'll have to pick up the rest and steal me blind. My back is killing me. I didn't think of the consequences of my anger. I never do."

"Sit down while I change the sheets. We'll put you to bed with a hot brick after a nice hot bath."

That sounded like heaven. Caroline hobbled to a wing chair by the window. The street was empty of Edward and every other living thing. Most of her neighbors slept their days away since their nights were quite busy. "I'm an awful lot of work for you."

"Nonsense. I'd do anything for you, Lady Christie."

Caroline leaned back in the chair. Her cat Childe Harold, Harold for short, had made himself scarce while Edward was visiting. He jumped onto her lap now and purred. When she named the cat for the hero of Lord Byron's epic poem, it had seemed fitting that as a writer she should give a nod to literature, although truthfully she found Byron rather hard going. Being a girl, she'd not been educated in the classics; being a woman, she found Byron's antics even more scandalous than her brother's. Her tastes were simpler, her life distilled into manageable bites.

Edward was going to gobble her up and ruin everything.

Lizzie moved to and fro, sweeping, straightening, lugging water for Caroline's bath up to the dressing room with an embarrassed Ben. Despite her nap in Edward's arms, she was still exhausted, and watching poor Lizzie and Ben tired her out even more. But her room was aired and fresh, her bath and clean sheets awaited. She was promised wine and soup and vanilla pudding for supper, things she wouldn't even have to chew. She sat in the tub like a child, permitting Lizzie to wash her hair and sponge her off, then retired to her bed with a tray, the brick on one side, Harold on the other. She fell asleep before the last ray of sunshine hit the spire of the local church she was too ashamed to attend.

And dreamed. She and Nicky were in the haymeadow at sunset, lying on the ground holding hands. Above, a flock of birds wheeled and swooped, their delicate shadows dappling the earth. Although his lips were moving, she couldn't hear what he said over the chatter of the birds. He pushed her braid away and pressed his lips to her ear, and suddenly she was waltzing with Edward, his long legs gliding effortlessly on the polished floor. He spun her in circles until she was dizzy, her dress a red blur—as red as the blood that seeped from Nicky's wound.

She woke with a start and sat up. Harold objected, kneading the coverlet until he was comfortable again. The room was black, the house quiet. Wiping the tears from her face, she punched down the pillow and started her night all over again.

But sleep wouldn't come. She hated nights like that, when her old demons took root and wouldn't leave. She supposed she deserved every minute of their haunting—she'd courted sin with naïve fervor, caught it, embraced it.

She'd loved Nicky with all her heart. He was nearly her twin, born just fifteen months before she was. They'd been inseparable until he was sent off to school. Caroline was nearly joyful when her father couldn't afford to send him to university. But by then he had a new friend, a better friend, Andrew Rossiter. When Caroline's father died suddenly over a hand of bad cards, Nicky invited Andrew to live with them. An orphan himself with no particular place to go, Andrew had happily assented. Their guardian, a man as improvident as their father, didn't trouble himself to supervise them, preferring to spend their tiny inheritance in far-off London. When then sensible Mary eloped with her soldier, the three of them had the house to themselves.

There was no one to tell them what to do. There was no one to tell them what not to do. So they did everything, until the money ran out.

It was Andrew who got the bright idea to turn their home into a kind of hotel for vice. Gentlemen who wanted to escape the strictures of town were happy to comply with their exorbitant tariffs. Every month of the year they came for one week of unlimited food, unlimited wine, unlimited sex, gambling, drugs—everything and anything was available for the right price chez Parker. There was no limit to Andrew's connections or imagination. Caroline was sheltered from most of the debauchery, actually locked safe in her room, because Nicky foolishly hoped she'd make a good marriage someday.

He was far more anxious than she was for her to find a rich man to improve the family coffers.

Caroline had already found the man she wanted. He wasn't rich, but he had the key to her room, and *he* had found *her*.

She'd been too stupid to see *why* he wanted her, imagining it was her beauty—which was undeniable and not at all vain for her to acknowledge—her carefree spirit, her loving heart. She was a most willing pupil in each and every one of Andrew Rossiter's lessons, odd as they had sometimes seemed. She grew used to everything, and then he made her crave it.

It wasn't until her brother shot himself that she found out the truth. And by then, it was too late for all of them.

Caroline's entire life was filled with "too lates." It was certainly too late to be awake, reliving a nightmare. It was too late to find happiness with Edward, too late to be a mother. Even her manuscript would arrive too late, unless she could find a way to churn the words out faster between servicing her husband on his schedule and regretting she had ever met him.

But it was just for a few weeks. She could endure anything. She already had.

Chapter 6

His appetites were insatiable, keeping her a slave from morning until night, until the hours turned into days and Mariette heard no cock crow but his.
—*Dreams at Dawn*

There was the faintest tickling on her nose. The damn cat and its tail. Caroline blew out a stream of air to shoo him away, but didn't open her eyes, unwilling to see Harold's equipment so close and so early in the morning. But the sensation increased, dancing across her eyelids like little fairy feet. Caroline scrunched up her face and rolled to the side. A feather-light stroke from her jaw to her clavicle made her reconsider. Either Harold had developed opposable thumbs, or she was being touched by a human. She waited, wondering if she should cry out for help or lie back and enjoy the gentle assault. A quick glance up to the mirror on the ceiling gave her the answer.

She had finally slept like the dead, never hearing Edward's footsteps, never seeing him undress, never smelling his lime-scented skin. But she felt him now, and soon she would taste him—as he was tasting her. A gossamer kiss on her bare shoulder. A nip at the base of her throat. His warm tongue edging into her ear, which always drove her mad.

"Don't pretend you are still asleep. You cannot be."

But she would pretend. Just to see how far he'd go.

She didn't have long to wait to find out. He pulled her nightgown up, fitting himself behind her, hard and hot. One hand cupped a breast, thumbing her nipple to a tight peak. That task accomplished, he traced a line from her belly to her hip, coming to rest, palm flat. She felt each warm finger splayed in ownership.

Surely he wasn't going to stop *there*. She wiggled up against him to urge him on.

She felt his lips curve on her back. She'd seen his smug smile before; he had every right to it. "I knew you were awake. Ask me nicely, and I'll wish you a very good morning."

"Nicely," she whispered, and he complied. A long finger teased her arse, then swept forward to her slit, dipped into its moisture, then rubbed against the top of her sex. He circled diligently until the room spun, Caroline clenching her nightgown to keep from touching herself. She wanted his skin covering hers, his weight overpowering her. She wanted to see him in the mirror splitting her apart. Understanding her unspoken need, he pushed her back and tore the nightgown over her head.

His mouth blanketed her cry as he penetrated her, his tongue mimicking each thrust. They were joined from head to toe, layered so close the only parts of her the mirror reflected were her wide eyes, the red of her hair on the pillow and her hands scoring his back. Her legs locked beneath him, then he twisted, lifting her from the bed as she rose to become even closer. He had never been so deep; she had never been so deep in trouble. For what was she to do when he left her again?

He mistook her sob for pleasure, then made it true, driving into her with reckless abandon, freeing them both. Stroke upon stroke, thrust upon thrust they tumbled together, heedless of anything but the electric unity of his skin to hers. She curled into him, transported, her mouth soft with love. But she swallowed the words—he would hear only desperation. Manipulation. They had never claimed to love each other, and he wouldn't trust her.

Her orgasm took her hopeless speech away anyway. She felt nothing but the pure sin of his cock spilling inside her, his hand wedged between them pressing and circling her clitoris, his teeth at her throat. She bit him back. Let the House of Lords weigh *that* evidence.

When she spoke, it was with careful disinterest. "I expect you've brought the timetable with you."

Edward flopped onto his back and looked chagrinned. "I'm afraid I didn't have time to draw one up. I'll work it out later and send it 'round."

She kept her tone severe, schoolmistressy. "I can't have any more unscheduled incidents like this. I want sufficient notice in the future."

"You didn't throw me out of bed." He looked far too proud of himself. His facial expression implied a woman would have to be an idiot to throw Edward Christie out of bed.

Well, she was an idiot. "I was asleep! And then it was too late. Get up, Edward. I have a busy day ahead and want some privacy."

He hesitated only a moment. "All right, Caro. I got what I came for. More than I expected, actually. It was very pleasant."

She knew he was baiting her. She thought the top of her head was exploding when she orgasmed. Surely he felt the same. "Yes. I suppose it was adequate. Have a nice day." She slipped into her dressing room to use the commode, hoping he'd have the good taste to leave.

When she came out, he was gone. Baron Christie was indeed the epitome of good taste. And an exceptionally fast dresser. Remembering poor Lizzie, she squelched the desire to throw something, and rang for breakfast instead. She would write today. And write and write and write.

Her *Pride and Artifice* notebook lay where anyone could find it. Now that Edward was a fixture in her bedroom, that would have to change. Perhaps it was still safe—Edward had always complained about her handwriting, claiming he couldn't read it. Perhaps that was why he'd been in such a tizzy when he read her letter and learned that Ned had been there. Fortunately Garrett had no such difficulty editing her novels. *His* handwriting was even worse than hers.

She had been the bane of her governess's existence, but the schoolroom had held no interest for her when there were fells to walk and her brother to chase after. Nicky had no luck with his tutors either, and was sent off to school quite young—more to rid her father of one more distraction than his desire to see his heir educated properly. School was where Nicky changed and forged his deadly friendship with Andrew Rossiter. The poet (not the viscount) Pope's words were never truer—

A little learning is a dangerous thing;
Drink deep, or taste not the Pierian spring:
There shallow draughts intoxicate the brain,
And drinking largely sobers us again.

Well, apparently something had sunk in, Caroline thought wryly. Wasn't she just a font of poetry and philosophy this morning? She dipped her pen in the little crystal pot of ink and let it hover over the page. A tiny drop spread onto the page just as she felt Edward's semen gush forth. She needed a bath desperately, but working on the book each morning was like drilling before going into battle. It made her limber so she could maneuver over the hills and valleys of her pages for Garrett. He would not be pleased to know she spent an hour each day wasting her words. She shut her eyes, picturing Edward at his most insufferable. It was not a difficult image to summon, and she began to write.

"You shall do as I say. You will obey me in every-
thing. And I mean everything." The baron flexed
his long fingers, as though he couldn't wait to have
her at his mercy.
"Not while I have breath!" Constance's eyes flashed,
her heart beating wildly. Desperately, she dashed to
the door.
"It is locked, and only I have the key."

> *He advanced toward her, his green eyes glittering like evil glass.*

Hell and damnation. Glass could not be evil, could it? Caroline drew a black line through *evil glass*, then struck through the entire passage. Her muse had departed rather suddenly and locked her in the room with the baron and Constance. At that moment Caroline didn't care if the baron used his long fingers to strangle Constance. Her private book was not going at all well. The baron, despite his evil glassy eyes, was really a gentleman at heart. She was very much afraid he was turning into a hopeless hero, not that Constance deserved him. She was simply too stupid to live.

As for Caroline's next heroine, the harlot, she was locked up firmly in a dark drawer, along with her future husband. Her story had degenerated so badly, Garrett would never publish it as is, if she ever finished it. Her deadline was just days away and for the life of her, she couldn't care about the next installment of *Courtesan Court.* It was as if Edward's shadow fell over her shoulder, blotting out her writing sun.

Caroline closed the notebook, wishing she could close her thoughts away with such ease. Edward's wretched little schedule was to arrive later. For the next three weeks, he would detail to the hour and the minute when he expected her to be available to him. Probably no two days would be alike—Edward was a busy man with numerous obligations. She was prepared to be perpetually off balance. For a woman who had fought a lengthy battle to wrestle her haphazard life into some order, it was like offering opium to an addict. She'd be in a haze for the foreseeable future.

But perhaps Edward would be similarly afflicted. She could only hope he'd be so befuddled from lust and lack of sleep he'd walk in front of a dray cart and be crushed. That had happened to the hero in *Love Lane.* The heroine had nursed him back to health, but Caroline would do no such thing. It would be preferable to be a widow rather than a divorcee, not that she really wished Edward dead or ever expected to join the ranks of society again. He had seen to that when he moved her to Jane Street, and she'd compounded the problem when she began to write her books.

It was ludicrous that people read them to escape their everyday problems, when her own life was so complicated. She was hardly a relationship expert, and it was by far easier to reform a rake or bring a villain to justice on the page than it was to live with a flesh-and-blood man. Not that Edward had ever been a rake or a villain. It might have gone easier for her if he had.

She put the pen down on its tray and capped the ink. It was pointless to think she'd be able to write anything. Thoughts of Edward and the life she'd lost were swamping her, drowning her, making her feel uncharacteristically sorry for herself. Most days she shrugged off her blues, pinned a jewel to her breast, poured a cup of tea, pulled up a weed, or lent an ear to someone even less fortunate.

Would he understand if she told him everything? She couldn't imagine telling him all her secrets. If he held her in contempt knowing just a fraction of them, she couldn't fathom what he'd feel if he knew the whole. His own green eyes would glitter like evil glass. She would wind up in court, not for a divorce but for murder.

She glanced at the new clock on the mantel. He might be back tonight. She had the whole day before her to have a long bath and do something, if she could only think what. She'd already planned the menus for the week, filled her un-broken vases with flowers, inspected Harold for fleas. She had no friends to write to, children's clothes to mend, piano to play. Caroline tried to remember what she did to fill her days before Edward stepped back into them, but she was as blank as the page of her manuscript.

She could go shopping. She *would* go shopping—to buy red dresses that Edward would hate. She'd pledged to her friend Charlotte she would do so. If Caroline had to endure Edward underfoot, she would make him suffer, at least visu-ally.

She had been wearing a red dress when she met him, a dress the color of ripe cherries designed to make a lasting impression. Its audacity had scandalized her cousin's wife and every other woman in Lady Huntington's ballroom. It had shocked the gentlemen too, but in precisely the way Caroline hoped. There wasn't time or money to flutter about in pasty pastels. Caroline had needed a husband fast.

Once they were married, Edward expected her to hang that red dress in the closet. There were a great many things she'd had to give up to please Edward and his impeccable Christie standards, and the closet got crowded. But she had been eager for change, for structure, for respectability. Perhaps if she'd had a few more months, she could have pounded herself into submission.

Oh, who was she kidding? She was a red dress girl at heart.

"Lizzie! Fetch my bonnet and gloves, and yours too. We're going shopping to find the reddest dress in all of London!"

Edward wore his Christie face. His son had not perfected his own. Ned was a veritable barometer of emotion, his mercury rising and falling, shame-faced one moment, defiant the next. It was all Edward could do to keep himself from reaching across his mahogany desk to throttle the boy.

One was mistaken to assume Edward had no feelings, but they were kept carefully in check. It was better that way. Slow and steady won the race, although he wondered if the rules might have changed lately while he wasn't looking. He'd always obeyed his parents, firmly convinced they knew what was best for him. They'd not gone wrong with Alice, as comfortable a wife as a man could have. Why, if he hadn't married her, his handsome sullen son and heir would not be sitting in front of him, prattling nonsense about his cousin Amelia, of all things.

Edward interrupted. "You have explained the reason you sought out my estranged wife, Ned, despite my express, explicit orders forbidding you to contact her. A barely satisfactory explanation, fueled by foolishness and an excess of drink. One must choose one's friends carefully, Ned. A Christie examines the character of an acquaintance, not just the convenience. I am aware Rory Carmichael is a school chum, but I wouldn't choose him as a friend for you."

"Rory has plenty of character! It's his father who's at fault with a whore on Jane Street. I thought Caro—" Ned flushed, apparently realizing he hadn't thought at all.

"You do realize you put her in an awkward situation, and breached her hospitality most egregiously. I expect you will write her a letter to apologize."

Ned shifted in his straight-back chair. Edward had purposely told the boy to bring it over to sit on. He wasn't worthy yet of the comfortable leather chair just a few feet away. "Why can't I apologize in person? Take flowers or something."

"She already has a garden, Ned. Quite a fine one. Your flowers would be superfluous. You're not to have further contact with her. I forbid it. Again, and *this* time you will listen."

Ned looked mulish. "I don't see why. She's very nice, even if you don't like her."

"I like her well enough." Edward looked down at his desk blotter, remembering the morning. How very inadequate the word *like* was. "But we don't suit as man and wife. I haven't told anyone yet, but I've resolved to divorce her. You can see why a visit from you would be unwelcome."

Ned's complexion reverted to yesterday's hangover pallor. "Divorce! But you can't! A Christie cannot get divorced!"

Edward sat back in his leather chair, surprised at the vehemence of his son. "I am fully aware of the scandal that will result, which is why I am taking you into my confidence to prepare for it. It will not be easy—for any of us."

"But Caro—she'll be a complete outcast!"

"Divorce is a mere formality. She is already proscribed from polite society."

"By you! Because you bought her that damn house!"

Edward's hand curled around a glass paperweight. "Edward Allerton Christie, do not use that tone with me."

Ned stood up, shaking. "Well, it's true! If she was unfaithful, it's because you're the coldest man in creation! And I'll not be saddled with Amelia in two years, because I am *not* cold. You can tell Uncle Roger that I'd rather marry a Jane Street courtesan than his flat-chested lackwit! Have you ever *talked* to Cousin Amelia? She's positively insipid!"

Edward stared at his son with icy hauteur. "I fail to see why you keep inserting Amelia into this conversation. Her father and I have a long-standing arrangement. You will do your duty to the family."

"Just as you're doing yours by dragging the Christie name through the mud?" Suddenly, Ned grinned. "Wait a minute! Uncle Roger will be so scandalized he'll break the betrothal contract. He's even higher in the instep than you are! Yes. Get your divorce. You have my blessing. You'll have your freedom, and I'll have mine!" He let out a childish whoop and practically ran out of the study.

"Neddie! Ned! Come back here! We are not finished!" Edward heard the reverberating slam of the front door. *Hell and damnation.* He pinched the headache back from between his brows. How had he sired such an impetuous imbecile? If Alice had lived, her children would be circumspect. Respectful. He'd never caned Ned in his life, and was regretting it. His fingers twitched to do so.

It was Alice's fondest wish that Ned marry her brother's girl. They had talked about it when the children were the merest babes. Amelia was perfectly acceptable. Perhaps not a raving beauty, but she was neat in her appearance and habits and had a handsome dowry, not that the Christies needed an infusion of cash. Edward's investments were conservative. Sound. Lucrative. Amelia expected Ned to marry her when he came of age, just as Alice had expected to marry Edward twenty years ago. The poor girl would be heartbroken.

What kind of husband Ned would make was now in question. Drinking, carousing, showing execrable judgment. Edward flushed. He was *not* the coldest man in creation, but as warm-blooded as the next man. But he was prudent. Practical. His son had two years to get his education, pull himself together and rise to the occasion. Two years was a long time. Anything could happen, even the reformation of Edward the Younger.

Thinking of time, Edward consulted his appointment book and penned a brief but detailed letter to Caroline, feeling somewhat more in control afterward. Then he negated that by opening his desk drawer and removing the hinged gilt case that held Alice's miniature. It had been some years since he'd talked aloud to his dead wife, but sometimes just looking at her painted pink face eased his heart. Not today. Prying the case open, he didn't see the usual sympathy from her large brown eyes, but an accusatory glare.

"You're right. Everything is all bollixed up. I—I've lost my way, ever since Caroline. Sometimes I wonder if you're in heaven punishing me for marrying again, but that doesn't seem very heavenly. I couldn't seem to help myself, you know. Caro is—well, I don't think you'd understand her. God knows, I don't. I'm going to try to set it all to rights—if only I can figure out how."

Feeling foolish, he snapped the case shut. Next he'd be talking to plants or imaginary friends. Whom he should be talking to was Will Maclean about the divorce. He returned the portrait to the dark of the drawer and headed out to do just that, being careful not to slam the door behind him.

Edward had had a full and frustrating day—his early interlude with Caroline, his aborted interview with Ned, the somewhat alarming appointment with Will Maclean, his appearance for appearance's sake in Parliament late in the afternoon to vote on a bill he hadn't even read. But he knew which way his party expected him to vote, and he did his duty as he always did. He was Baron Christie.

Finally, he was off to be just Edward, to find a few hours of easy, mindless pleasure again in the arms of his soon-to-be ex-wife. Well, not soon. Certainly not soon if Will was to be believed, and Will was as honest and upright as any man in Britain. There had been discussion of formal separation versus divorce, but Edward's mind was made up. Will had thrown every conceivable spanner in the works to test him, raised every possible objection as devil's advocate, but Edward stood firm.

Firm was his watchword. Firm he was. The thought of Caroline's fiery hair across the white linen of her pillow made him as randy as a schoolboy. Perhaps that was Ned's problem—Amelia's mousy blond hair held no similar attraction. Maybe Edward had been too demanding, expecting his son to deny his baser instincts. He would try to talk to him again, when their tempers cooled.

Edward startled the two Jane Street guards by appearing three times in three nights. He startled himself that he had the stamina, considering he'd been there that morning too. But the street was not patrolled in the daytime, as though one's sexuality only came alive at night. That certainly was not true in his case.

Though he might be forty, he was still fit. The Christies were fortunate with their physiognomy—each generation was taller and leaner than the last. Ned topped him by an inch, and Jack was catching up. Little Alice was a worry, however. Even her Aunt Beth, a tall woman herself, seemed unable to untangle his daughter's coltish awkwardness. Allie was all sharp angles in body and in tongue.

Enough. No more fatherly thoughts and worries. He was on Caroline's steps to sin, and sin well—if one could sin with one's wife. He rather thought one could.

Once again, Hazlett was prompt opening the door. "Good evening, Lord Christie. Lady Christie is in the downstairs drawing room."

Well, damn. She was going to make him work to get her upstairs. It wouldn't harm him to brush up on his flirting skills—if one could flirt with one's wife. He rather thought one should.

His breath hitched when he spotted Caroline, a brilliant ruby in an emerald sea. She reclined on her green couch reading a book, wearing the most . . . the most incendiary . . . something. His mental words deserted him. One could hardly call it a dress. Perhaps a peignoir. Whatever it was, the pearl white of her bosom spilled over the flimsiest of bodices. Her skirt had been raised so one unstockinged ivory leg lay most visible on the sofa cushions. Her eyes finally lifted, bright as polished silver. Her hair streamed over her shoulders like rose-gold and molten copper in the candlelight.

Good Lord, he was thinking like a jeweler in a trance.

He woke up abruptly as Caroline made a show of yawning and stretching. "Let's get this over with, Edward. I'm quite fatigued."

Rubbish. She looked well rested, her skin glowing, her eyes gleaming like silver. She looked like a woman who had been shopping, had spent a fortune on a dress and knew its worth and her own.

"Is that a new gown? If you recall, I don't favor red." Critical Baron Christie had slipped into Easy Edward's shadow. That did not sound a bit flirtatious. Certainly if Caroline appeared in public is such dishabille, there would be cause for criticism. But there was no one to see her—nearly all of her that was worth seeing—except for him. He began again. "Although you look very—vibrant."

Caroline's silver eyes shot silver bullets at him. "Your good opinion matters little to me. I received a note from your friend Will Maclean a little while ago, no doubt designed to rob me of my sleep. You wasted no time after this morning, did you?"

Edward was mistaken; her eyes were not like silver, but ice. While he had urged Will to spare no speed or expense, he had not expected him to contact Caroline that very day. "You knew my intentions," he said, his back stiffening.

"Indeed. Forgive me if I cannot reconcile the chill of your heart to the heat of your manhood. The dichotomy must cause you some confusion as well."

He would not acknowledge he'd had his own faint mis-givings over the current path he'd chosen to tread. "I'm not confused. I am exercising my marital rights. You yourself en-couraged me to appease my carnal nature."

"When have you ever listened to a thing I said? You think I'm cork-brained—you've said it often enough." She snapped her book shut, no doubt wishing Edward's head was between the covers.

He removed the simple gold stickpin from his cravat and tucked it in his pocket. "I did not come here to argue."

"Or discuss your children! And there's no roast, either, so let's get on with it." Much to Edward's regret, Caroline tossed her ruched skirt back over her exposed leg. He contin-ued removing his tie.

"About the other night, I've talked to Ned, and he recog-nizes how inappropriate his visit was. You can expect to re-ceive an apology." He wound the length of linen around one hand, dropping it on a pie crust table. It appeared once again they would not make it all the way upstairs to the bed.

"I don't need an apology. He was befuddled—he's just a boy."

"He's nearly twenty. At his age, I was not vomiting in the streets."

Caroline's eyes narrowed. "No. You were probably at home, reading your Bible."

"There's no need to be blasphemous, Caroline. I've never made any pretense of being a saint. Or even particularly reli-gious."

"But you have made a habit of being *good*." She pro-nounced the word with contempt, as if good was bad. Per-haps in Caroline's world, it was.

"Look," Edward said quietly, getting a grip on himself. "You obviously want to provoke me. You are dressed as a harlot, in a color I abhor. You've arranged yourself like temp-tation on a platter to make me sorry for wanting you. I can't be. I want you, Caro—just not as my wife. Just as you don't want me for a husband. I don't mean to hurt you—or myself—anymore. You know divorce is the most sensible solution."

"Yes. You are perfectly right as usual." With one violent tug, she ripped the diaphanous fabric of her bodice straight down, freeing her breasts. There was nothing between the dress and the snowy velvet of her body. Edward stared for a moment, slow to find words.

"That was unnecessary. You won't be able to mend it."

She shrugged. "It doesn't matter. I bought more dresses. And you had better get used to the color. Close the door, would you? We wouldn't want Hazlett to have an apoplexy."

He didn't quibble at the order, but slid the pocket door shut and turned the lock with a click. Somewhat disappointed that the bedroom ceiling mirror would not be an accessory to their activities, he reminded himself there were still twenty-two more days before he left for Christie Park—if he didn't have an apoplexy of his own.

Caroline slipped from the sofa to her knees, rising like a white light from a pool of crimson fire. There was no hesitation for either of them. She made quick work of his falls without resorting to the destruction she'd exhibited a moment ago, cupped his balls and took him in the warm wet heaven of her mouth. He tried to stem his orgasm by counting each long black eyelash as they fluttered against her cheek, but never made it much past one hundred before he lost himself. She smiled, satisfied with her explicit power over him.

"There." She stood, fishing her torn gown from the floor and draping it about her as best she could. "You can go home now."

Edward collapsed on the couch, his pants still down. He reached into a pocket, handed her a handkerchief and watched her delicately blot her lips. He tried to smile, but his facial muscles were as slack as his brain. "I think I had better reciprocate, don't you?"

She wrinkled her nose. "Completely unnecessary. I am fully capable of attending to my own needs, thank you."

"Is that how you spend your nights, Caro? With your fingers—or an object? I confess, I think I'd like to watch."

She blushed. "You presume too much."

He caught her hand and brought it to his mouth. The dress dropped to the floor again. She was still as he kissed each knuckle, then inserted her longest finger into his mouth, imitating her earlier act. He suckled until her blush deepened, circling her palm lazily with his hand. She soon buckled and fell into his lap.

"Maybe I have a lover," she rasped.

He released her finger and pressed it against her slit. "Show me, Caro. Show me what you do." He helped her get started, stroking over her hand until she was boneless, her head back against his shoulder. Her jasmine-scented hair tickled his throat. He wished he'd removed his clothing, but at least his cock was free, hardening and nestled in the cleft of her arse. His left hand was busy with her full breasts, teasing each nipple to pink marble.

He knew she was close. Her honey dripped, and he took his hand away. She went still instantly.

"Finish it, Caro. Come for me."

She groaned in frustration. He chose that moment to nip her ear, then sweep his tongue inside. Clumsy at first, her fingers circled again as he'd taught her. He watched, riveted, heard her shallow breaths, felt her tremble straight through his skin to his bones. A wicked rose flush crept over her chest to her belly. He held her to him as she crested, crying out. It was too soon for him, but he needed to feel closer. Lifting her hips, he sank into her and concentrated on the way she contracted around him. He pushed her hand aside, touching her himself, pinching and stroking until she spasmed endlessly around him. Somewhat of a miracle, his own tension mounted and he experienced another orgasm nearly as strong as the first.

They sat in a mutual stupor, consciousness clouded, their hearts erratic. Edward glanced at the case clock. He'd not been there quite half an hour and he was wrecked. He should go home. But he had no inclination to displace Caroline from his lap, her scent of jasmine and sex drugging him to complacency. The couch was too narrow for them to sleep on; at some point he would have to let her go.

He had an early day tomorrow as well. Some last-minute minutiae before Parliament recessed for the season—if it would. Edward had heard rumblings that did not sit well with him. He longed for the sweeping green of Christie Park, Alice's garden in riotous bloom, riding with his sons and daughter. He and Ned would visit the barony's tenants, perhaps go so far as lending a hand in the mowing and haying, getting their backs brown from honest labor. Ned would have an opportunity to reacquaint himself with his neighboring cousin Amelia, and perhaps discover she was not so insipid after all.

Edward took his responsibilities seriously, as a member of the government and as landlord and manager of a considerable estate. But right now, all he wanted to do was drowse in Caro's arms.

"Edward."

"Mmpf." His lips brushed her temple and she twitched.

"I really am very tired."

"As am I. I find you quite exhausting." He traced a pattern on her rounded stomach as she swatted him away.

"Be serious. I have an appointment with my publisher tomorrow, where I must plead for an extension for next month's book. He won't be happy with me."

Privately, Edward wished Garrett Marburn to the deepest hole of unhappiness possible. The natural son of an earl, he had all the posturing but none of the paternity of his class. Marburn had been well educated, and chose to skewer his father and his friends with scandalous accounts of society mischief. Caroline's *Courtesan Court* books were only a portion of his publishing empire, and the least salacious of the lot, which was saying something. Rumor had it that Marburn was desperate to acquire a Jane Street house for himself, but the closest he'd come was to inveigle Caroline into writing about it for him. Deeds to Jane Street passed only in the most special of circumstances, and so far Marburn had not qualified despite his personal wealth.

"Are you suggesting that I leave?"

"I am *insisting* that you leave. If you stay the night, we won't get a bit of rest. A woman my age needs her beauty sleep."

"Don't flatter me, and don't fish for compliments. You're holding up very well."

"I've gained more than a stone. Perhaps even two."

"I hadn't noticed," Edward lied. That explained the subtle difference—Caroline was softer, although her tongue was sharp as ever. He believed the extra weight suited her, made her slightly more mortal. She had lived like a goddess on a pedestal in his mind for too long.

"I need to get up. Please release me."

"In a moment." Edward shifted to retrieve Caroline's dress. "Well, I'll be damned. It's—it's *engineered* to come apart like that. You didn't tear it at all."

"Clever, isn't it? And most effective."

Edward laughed and set Caroline next to him on the sofa. "My God, you're a witch. If you were a man, I bet you could have exiled Napoleon to Elba far sooner."

"Poor man. I hear his treatment at St. Helena is a scandal." Caroline took the garment from him and fastened it so she could go upstairs without undue curiosity. He supposed he'd better hike up his breeches as well—his long shanks made him a figure of fun.

"One reaps what one sows," Edward said. He couldn't squeeze out much sympathy for the man who'd upended the world for all of his adult life. "I shall see you tomorrow evening. For dinner, if I remember correctly."

Caroline frowned. "Yes. You know you're a bit of a tyrant. What if your dates don't suit mine?"

"One must eat, Caro, even a skinny fellow like me, and so must you. I shan't take up too much of your time."

"Promises, promises," Caroline muttered. She whirled away in a scarlet flash, leaving him to see himself out.

Tomorrow night, he'd get her upstairs, or enjoy trying. Whistling most unlike a Christie, he buttoned up his trousers and walked into the balmy London evening.

Chapter 7

*There was nothing she liked so much as matchmaking,
but Lady Laura lived alone, doomed to press her
lightly-freckled nose against the glass and watch the
world in love without her.*

— *Lady Laura's Lesson*

The occasion called for diamonds, not as celebration but distraction. Caroline had only her engagement and wedding rings, and a simple spray of smallish stones set into a pin that had belonged to Edward's mother. The major Christie jewels were locked up as they should be, waiting for the boys to marry and Allie to grow up. Caroline set the pin aside as not battle-worthy and picked up the topaz drop. Since her bronzy gown was cut conveniently low, it would do. She'd just need to be careful not to entice Garrett too thoroughly. He was getting more dogged by the day for her to break her vow of celibacy. Little did he know she had done so already with her husband.

She would ask Garrett's opinion on the divorce, and show him the annoying communication from Sir William Maclean. Will had always been worse than Edward when it came to propriety. The barrister had been opposed to Edward's second marriage, and made no bones about it. Caroline hoped if *he* ever married, justice would finally be served. His wife could bring him before Cupid's court without mercy. Rob him of all his dry legal language until he blithered like a bedlamite. Imprison him in a cage of lust so he knew for once what it felt like. Caroline would love to sit on the sidelines and watch the great Maclean unmanned.

Lizzie knocked quietly at the bedroom door. "Mr. Marburn is downstairs, Lady Christie. Shall I show him up?"

Caroline and Garrett often used her upstairs sitting room to discuss business, but she wanted the formality of the downstairs drawing room today. Then she remembered last night and its extreme informality and felt the heat on her cheeks. Soon there would be no room in her house that would be safe from Edward's aura.

She couldn't very well meet with Garrett in the kitchen, so she might as well stay put. "Yes, Lizzie, please. And bring up the lunch tray in half an hour or so—with whiskey for Mr. Marburn."

Lizzie bobbed and did as she was bid. Caroline tucked herself in a corner of her plum sofa and fanned some papers to cool herself off. Her notebooks were stacked neatly on the table, not that Garrett would give her credit for order. He was likely to be very irritated with her indeed.

He strode into the room, looking every inch the gentleman. His light brown hair was perfectly arranged, the cut of his clothes exquisite. Evidently he felt she looked her best, too. Placing a hand over his heart, he grinned. "Caroline the Divine. How I've missed you."

She had planned to wait for the topaz or the whiskey to take effect, but decided to get it over with. "I hope I stay in your good graces, Garrett. I'm afraid I have some bad news for you."

Garrett lifted a groomed eyebrow. "Should I sit or stand ready to flee?"

She patted the sofa. A mistake. He sat too close and she felt it was not only the topaz which absorbed his attention. "I've had a bit of a setback with *The Harlot's Husband*. I don't believe it will be quite ready to publish on the usual schedule."

Garrett waved a careless hand. "Let your public wait then. A delay will only serve to make them more eager. Are we talking days or weeks?"

"You—you're not upset?"

"Caroline, darling, the only thing that would upset me

would be if you told me you'd found your conscience and refused to write what we both know to be utter drivel."

Caroline gave him a little shove, not half so hard as she
wanted. "It is not drivel! I'll have you know I work very hard
assuring the quality of my stories!"

"Yes, yes," he said dismissively. "Art and all that. It's sex
your public wants, and secrets. Let's not put pearls on the
pig."

Caroline was vexed and sat up straight. While she knew
she was not writing the great English novel, Garrett's words
stung. He reminded her quite forcibly of Edward at the moment.

She poked a finger into his chest, which was still too near.
"*You* try churning out a novel a month!"

He inched backward a fraction. "Caroline, you aren't trying to increase your advance, are you? Not that you're not
worth every penny. But summer's upon us. The ton are leaving the city for their boring country estates and sales always
drop. You have that husband of yours to support you. Hit
the dullard up for extra cash if you're short."

"Oh!" Caroline stamped her foot, managing to clip the tip
of Garrett's boot. "Sorry. No, I'm not short of money. What
I am short of is time. Something"—*someone*—"has come
up."

"Caroline, I'm a businessman first. I'm not making a fuss
that you're failing your contractual obligation to me. Finish
the damn book whenever. But I'll not give you another penny
unless you stop playing games with me and finally let me into
your bed."

"Oh!" Her foot came down harder. Garrett just laughed.

"Why are you paying any attention to me at this late date?
You know I just like to tease you. A man like me can hope."
He cupped her chin.

Caroline blinked, but not soon enough. A tear splashed on
her powdered cheek.

"Something's riled you, and it's not me."

"Yes. No. Oh, Garrett." She swallowed, feeling very like one of her stupid heroines. "Edward is divorcing me."

Garrett's steady brown eyes met hers. "Good."

"Is it? I'll still have this house, and I suppose he'll settle some money on me, but—but—" She looked down at the diamonds twinkling on her finger. She would keep wearing them, even after.

"Good Christ. You still love him." He stood up, angry. "I've never understood why a warm-blooded woman like you fell for such a dry stick. By God, he even looks like a stick, like some sort of mutant tree."

"You're just jealous because he's taller than you. Edward is a very attractive man."

Garrett shot her an incredulous look. "Don't expect me to notice. I'm not Andrew Rossiter."

Caroline shivered. "Unfair," she whispered. "I'm sorry I ever told you."

"Well, I'm not. I could kill them both with my bare hands for hurting you."

Despite the seriousness of her situation, Caroline smiled. "You cannot kill a peer of the realm. But I would have no objection to you going a few rounds with Andrew."

"A few rounds? Don't be absurd. I'd flatten him in seconds, bastard to bastard. Caroline, what can I do to help? Do you want me to talk to Christie?"

"Good Lord, no. He wouldn't see you at any rate."

"I've got my ways," Garrett said darkly. "He needs to be told."

"No!" Caroline said, alarmed. "You promised."

"That was when you were just an estranged wife. But if he means to divorce you—why, he can't, can he? He'll have to prove you were unfaithful."

"Andrew will lie if the price is right. There are the letters, too. No one need know they predate my marriage."

Garrett sat back down, gripping her hands in his. "Do you want this divorce, Caroline? If you do, you needn't have anything to do with Rossiter. I can give evidence."

The idea had some appeal. She would prefer she never had her name linked to Andrew Rossiter in any way. But Garrett Marburn was too good a friend, and the scandal could affect his business adversely. "Your reputation would be ruined, Garrett."

He barked out a laugh. "Aye, illegitimate son that I am. And *in trade*, even worse. I'm already persona non grata. But people will still buy my newspapers and books, Caroline. They cannot help themselves." He gave her hands a quick squeeze. "You know as well as I do some people think we're lovers as it is."

She shook her head. "I know you mean well, but I cannot bring you into this any more than you are already. I wanted to warn you Sir William Maclean will probably contact you. Don't lie for me, Garrett. We've done nothing to be ashamed of."

"Not that I haven't tried, Caroline. I wonder, does Christie even know what he's giving up? You've never let me touch you, but I know it would be good between us. More than good. You're light and fire, Caroline, meant for love. For life. For laughter."

She did love Garrett, but not in the right way. Caroline pulled her hands free and wiped her face. "You are supposed to cheer me up, not make me blubber."

"Well, I thought that was a very pretty speech if I do say so myself, and I expect to read it verbatim, if not in *The Harlot's Husband* then in some other volume. What's the name of the next one? *The Duke's Doxy?*" He winked at her.

"You didn't mean one word! Oh, you are incorrigible."

"Every minute of the day." He moved his foot before she could stomp it again.

"There's something else, too," said Caroline, remembering. "Edward told me that Lords Pope and Douglass visited him the other day, threatening legal action over my books."

Garrett laughed. "Cold Christie must have had a spasm entertaining those two. How I wish I had been there. I'd have set them straight."

"I know you have legal representation, and you say we are safe, but—"

"We are, Caroline. Don't add that to your list of worries. If it will make you feel any better, I can have one of my men move in to guard you."

"Guard me! Surely it won't come to that. We're all perfectly safe here on Jane Street."

Garrett frowned. "I hope so. You know there was some sort of incident involving Sir Michael Bayard. The watchman was knocked on the head."

"There are two watchmen now, and Charlotte's gone. The house is empty." Caroline smiled. There was nothing left of her friend but some cupid dust in the garden. There was plenty of essence of angel to protect all the women who lived there.

A clatter at the door signaled Lizzie was up with lunch. Garrett went to the door and let her in. "Lizzie, my love, you get more beautiful every time I see you. That mobcap is rather criminal, though, covering all that golden hair." In an instant, he plucked it off her head. Lizzie was openmouthed, the heavy tray preventing her from retaliation.

"I'll take the whiskey back downstairs if you don't give it back this instant."

Garrett swept the tray out of her hands. "Indeed you will not. Caroline, you don't insist your maid wear that ridiculous headgear, do you? Bad enough the poor girl's all in black with an apron concealing her luscious curves."

"Garrett!"

"Mr. Marburn!"

"Ah, the outrage. I'm a man. I have eyes." He set the tray down on the small dining table. "And I've a powerful thirst." He poured two fingers from the decanter into the glass. "To the ladies of Jane Street. May the future be bright for you both." He tossed back the liquor as Lizzie fled the room.

Caroline came to the table and distributed the plates and cutlery. "It's one thing to tease me, Garrett, but don't be so cavalier with Lizzie. She's had a hard year."

Garrett popped an olive into his mouth. "Who says I'm being cavalier? I find her very fetching. She's wasted as your maid."

"She can't go back to being a whore. Pope made sure of that."

"Who said anything about her being a whore?"

Caroline put her fork down. "Garrett," she said carefully, "what are your intentions toward my maid?"

Garrett speared a chunk of chicken and waved it across the table. "My intentions? Are you the girl's mother?"

"She was brutally beaten. Her back is a mess and her spirits worse. Don't toy with her."

"Caroline, I don't know if I ever told you. My mother was a Jane. Lived in Number Ten under my father's protection. I have no objection to her former profession. I'm that rare thing—a true son of a whore. And I remember when your Lizzie was Eliza Reynolds, one of the most beautiful girls on the stage. Couldn't dance well, but didn't need to."

"That was years ago. There were men before Pope, you know."

Garrett shook his head. "You must decide whether you're championing Lizzie or championing me. Leave it, Caroline."

Caroline took a sip of wine. Could it be she was jealous? No, not at all. She didn't want Garrett for herself, like some sort of trained lapdog who danced for his treat. He was her best friend at present, not a potential lover. But Garrett and Lizzie? She took another sip and choked. My word, it all sounded like a possible plot for a book—*The Bastard's Battered Beauty*. It was too perfect for words. She might be able to get her digs in again against the wretched Randolph Pope. But no. Garrett wouldn't publish such a thing, although perhaps he could live it.

"What do you think of Queen Caroline coming home?" she asked, changing the subject as requested. If anyone knew the latest *on dit*, it would be the man at her luncheon table. As Garrett ate and gestured, Caroline drifted off, plotting the next romance, one she had every intention of orchestrating from the ground up.

"Hell and damnation!" Edward tossed the missive into the farthest corner of his study and set his eyeglasses on their tray. According to a friend in high places who knew the secret machinations of their monarch, it seemed he would be condemned to stay in town all summer to haggle over the marital situation of his king and his unlucky wife. A Bill of Pain and Penalties was being prepared, a completely apt name as far as Edward was concerned. There would be untold pain and penalties for him. He could, of course, send the children to the country for their planned holiday with his sister, but he was doomed to sit in the heat and misery to discuss the cold and miserable state of George IV's marriage. Queen Caroline was already parading all over London, and every peer, bishop, and judge would be required to attend the trial, which could go on indefinitely. Interminably.

Odd that two Carolines were the key to his discomfort. In the few days he'd returned to Caro's bed, he had been unable to wean himself from wanting her with an intensity that was somewhat frightening. He'd looked forward to escaping to Christie Park to contemplate his newly single state. Now his days would be tied up in the stuffy confines of an annex to the House of Lords, and his nights—

Caro would know his plans had changed. The whole of England was privy to the Queen Consort's and George's difficulty, and this latest step of the king's to remove the boil that was his wife from his backside was sure to attract the interest of all his subjects. Everyone knew they had been mismatched and unfaithful to each other for years, yet even after the 'Delicate Investigation' fourteen years ago, George had been unsuccessful in untethering himself from his German cousin.

A new movement was afoot to be rid of Caroline of Brunswick once and for all. When she returned from abroad, the fragile deal that had been forged splintered apart. Edward supposed he should consider himself lucky. His Caroline had never been quite as indiscreet—nor as demanding—as George's unwanted wife.

Would Caro still expect him to provide her with a new schedule once she learned he wasn't going to leave for the country after all? Could he even stick to a schedule, when every conscious minute of the day included thoughts of her? Resuming his marital rights had only reminded him how empty and dull his life had been without Caro in it. He had been well and truly hoisted on his own petard.

How ironic that all his future days were to be tied up in the dissolution of a marriage not his own. What it would do to advance his own plight he had no idea. If the government was to rehash the scandal about Queen Caroline and her Italian secretary for the foreseeable future—shades of Mary Queen of Scots!—there might not be opportunity to shoehorn in his own petition.

Edward let out an uncharacteristic growl. It was followed some seconds later by a gentle knock on his study door.

He was not in the mood to deal with anything but his own self-pity. "Go away!"

"It's only me, Papa. I promise I won't bother you long."

Damn. Only Little Alice, as if there were anything *only* about her. Edward pinched the space between his brows. At the rate all this was going, he'd wear his skin away. "Come in, then."

His daughter peeked around the door. Two dark braids framed her long face, the childish hairstyle at odds with her great height. "Are you angry about something, Papa?"

"Nothing you've done." He'd never liked either of the damn Georges, not that he'd utter such treason. A Christie would never be such a cretin. "Come in, sit. Li—Allie, what may I do for you this fine day?"

"It's raining again, Papa."

"I meant—it's just a turn of phrase, Allie. It's not necessary for the sun to be shining to be considered a fine day."

His daughter looked on solemnly, no doubt thinking he certainly *was* a cretin. "I should like to make an appointment with you to discuss a very serious matter."

"Good heavens. If it's so serious, we must deal with it now." He ignored the shooting pain that pierced his skull. His daughter needed him, and he could not fail her.

"I know you've said eavesdroppers get just what they deserve." She twisted her slender fingers, embarrassed.

"I eavesdropped—quite by accident—and overheard Neddie and Jack talk about something disgusting."

Oh, God. Surely she wasn't going to ask about the birds and the bees. Beth or her governess should have that subject in hand, should they not? He kept his mouth firmly closed, but nodded.

"I just can't believe it," she continued. "A Christie wouldn't do such a thing, bring such shame upon the family."

Ah. Ned must have bragged about his drunken, debauched night, rubbing Jack's nose in the fact that he breached Jane Street's defenses. "Young men are often very foolish, Allie, most especially your elder brother. You must pay no mind to what they do or say."

"You're not young, Papa, you're old!"

The pain cleaved his head in two. "I beg your pardon?"

"Neddie said you're going to divorce Caroline. We'll be in all the newspapers. And I'll never get married, not that anyone will ever want me anyway."

There were simply too many ideas to respond to, but he seized upon the one that gave him the most concern. "Allie! You're not to say such things. You are a lovely girl and will grow into a lovely woman."

"Pooh. You have to say that. You're my father. But don't change the subject. What about Caroline?"

"You are too young to understand. You never liked her anyway. I should think you'd be delighted that I'm seeking to formally end my ties with her."

" 'What therefore God hath joined together, let not man

put asunder.' It's in the Bible, you know." Her lips pursed primly.

"A great many things are in the Bible. There is, as I recall, an entire passage dedicated as to how a father can sell his daughter into slavery," he teased.

"That has to do with a betrothal contract, I believe."

Maybe Allie could become an Anglican nun. He cleared his throat. "I am aware this is indeed a serious matter. It is not a decision I've come to lightly. Caroline and I have been separated for five years. She—I—we made a mistake after too brief an acquaintance, which is why it is so important to not jump into things. When it comes time, I will not expect you to marry at the end of your first season. You should be courted long enough so you are comfortable with your intended. Know his character, his tastes and opinions."

"Just as he should know mine."

"Why, yes. Of course. I knew your mother very well before we were married. We were ideally suited."

"Do you still love her? Is that why you and Caroline couldn't stay married? I know I should hate to live in another woman's shadow with another woman's children."

Edward was amazed at his daughter's conclusion, but oddly enough, Caroline had never once complained about her role as stepmother. "Of course I still love your mother, and always shall. But you children were not in any way to blame for what went wrong with my marriage to Caroline," he said firmly.

"I was horrid to her." There was some regret in her voice.

"You were just a little girl. You weren't used to having a mother at all. You had run quite wild. My fault. I had hoped my second marriage would settle the family. It proved to do just the opposite."

Allie's dark brows scrunched. "I do not see why we cannot just go on as we are. You are too old to marry again, and you already have an heir. Although"—she sniffed in disdain—"he is a grave disappointment at present. But there is always Jack, should something, God forbid, befall your firstborn.

Jack's much less of a loose screw. If you go through with this divorce, you will ruin our lives. We'll be shunned. Snubbed. Cut by everyone who counts."

Edward bit back his irritation. His daughter was out-Christie-ing him, reminding him of all his earlier reservations, and sanctimonious as only a child could be. Life was complicated. And he most certainly was *not* too old for anything and longed to tell her so. But that was hardly a fit subject to discuss with one's precocious thirteen-year-old daughter.

"My mind is made up, Allie. Caroline is in agreement as well. Imagine for a moment how this state of limbo has affected her. She might prefer to live quietly in the country, perhaps even get married again. She is not nearly so old as I, you know," he added, slightly sarcastic.

"Then buy her a house in the country! Let her live at Christie Park, for that matter. The house is so huge you never need see her."

Caroline under the same roof—disastrous. As if he could confine her to a wing like some mad aunt. "You do have an answer for everything. I expect Miss Linnet is very pleased with your schoolwork."

"She thinks I am a dunce. Don't try to change the subject, Papa." She looked at him earnestly with her mother's large brown eyes, her lower lip quivering. "If you proceed along this course, I shall not be responsible for what I do."

He nearly smiled. "Alice Elizabeth Christie, are you threatening me? Since we're tossing the Bible about, what about this? 'Honor thy father and thy mother, as the Lord thy God hath commanded thee; that thy days may be prolonged, and that it may go well with thee, in the land which the Lord thy God giveth thee.'"

"I won't want my days prolonged if you divorce Caroline! I shall run away!"

All traces of his good humor disappeared. Edward rose like an Old Testament figure, towering over his daughter in somewhat righteous wrath. "Go to your room. You're too young to have sufficient understanding of this matter, and I refuse to discuss it with you any further. I believe I know what's best for this family, and you will abide by my judgment."

"Very well, Papa. 'All go unto one place; all are of the dust, and all turn to dust again.' Some of us are dustier than others," she said cryptically. "Don't say I didn't give you warning." She flounced out of the room, pigtails flying.

Really! The impudence! Perhaps it was time to put his foot down and send her to some girls' school in Bath where she could bedevil complete strangers.

Well, he'd heard from two of his children. Neddie was all for the divorce, assuming he could weasel out of his betrothal. Allie seemed very much opposed, more on social than Biblical grounds. Jack might understand, but somehow Edward was not eager to ask him at the moment.

He sat back down and put on his spectacles. Opening up his appointment book, he noted there were six hours until he found relief in Caroline's arms. That simply wouldn't do. Caroline might view his early arrival more favorably if he arrived early with some token—some jewelry, for example. Caroline had a weakness for jewelry. Like a redheaded magpie, she was very fond of shiny things. He would stop at Garrard's on the way.

Maybe he should get Allie something there too, for the crime of banishing her to her room. It was clear she was growing up, whether he liked it or not.

Chapter 8

Violet would tell the truth at last, though no one, least of all Sir Rupert, would believe her.

—*Ravishing Revenge*

Edward was snoring gently beside her. Caroline supposed she should wake him so he could go home to his family in time to have breakfast with them, but she didn't. She rather jealously put a protective hand on his muscled chest, the better to examine the pearl and diamond ring he'd placed upon her finger when he arrived yesterday afternoon. She had not been at all ready for him. Caroline had been ink-smudged, wearing her oldest daygown—it was not one of her naughty new red dresses—her hair a veritable nest, but he had swept her into his arms and covered her with hungry kisses. Kisses that flashed across her skin like lightning. Kisses that made her knees buckle and her womb ache. Kisses that made her forget everything, including why she hated him.

The ring was very pretty, the kind of gift a man gave his wife, not his mistress. A pearl was a symbol of purity, but Caroline was most assuredly not pure. However, the halo of diamonds surrounding it glittered in the early morning sunlight, adding a touch of refreshing wickedness set in gold. The pearl was Caroline's June birthstone, although Edward certainly never wished her a happy birthday on June 14, if he even remembered. Celebration was to be avoided entirely. Caroline's birthday was irretrievably bound with the date she lost Edward's trust for good.

In sleep he appeared trusting, as innocent as his son Neddie—now called Ned, all grown up. Caroline wondered what Jack and Allie looked like. Five years was an eternity in a child's life. She might not recognize either of them, although they were destined to be tall and loose-limbed, the Christie countenance. But judging from Ned, the Christie composure might not have taken root quite yet.

She had tried her best with the children. The boys mainly ignored her but Allie viewed her as an interloper, although the girl had no memory of her mother. Caroline sympathized. Her own mother had died when she was born, and her father had never been up to the task of raising three children alone. Her childhood was so free of restrictions and restraint it had been hard to find her footing. In the end, she slipped and tumbled onto Jane Street.

Edward had not given her a reason for his sudden appearance yesterday, but if Garrett was right with the latest gossip, Parliament would not be recessing after all—which meant that Edward was not retiring to Christie Park. Perhaps the pearl ring was a good-bye gift. He could not expect to conduct their affair indefinitely. Caroline's lips curved. Could one have an affair with one's husband? Apparently so.

She eased out of bed to go to her dressing room, careful not to disturb him. Once she relieved herself and cleaned her teeth, she came back wearing a sheer peach peignoir and a cloud of perfume. Her hair seemed hopeless, but she sat at the dressing table and attacked it anyway, the brush crackling through its coppery mass. If Edward was to take his leave of her, she wished to appear so perfect it would pain him to do so.

If he left, she could write to her heart's content, never worry about interruptions. It would not be as much fun to wear her red dresses without his glare of approbation, but that was a small sacrifice. She looked her best in Madame Dulac's creations and could impress some other man.

As if she wanted to.

"Good morning. What are you doing so far away?"

Caroline glanced over her shoulder. Edward was stretching his long arms, a boyish smile on his face. He looked too relaxed to be giving her a farewell speech.

"Brushing my hair, and from the looks of things, I should brush yours, too."

One hand went to his head, sweeping his dark hair back over his forehead. "There. Am I presentable?"

"Very nearly." Caroline got up, taking the brush with her. She raised it over Edward's head, but his hand encircled her wrist.

"I have a better idea."

Caroline noted the tenting sheet. "I can see that." She dropped the hairbrush on the bed and the peignoir to the floor.

He tugged her down gently to kiss her. His lips were soft and warm, his tongue dallying first at the corner of her mouth, then slipping within. To her disappointment, he broke the kiss before it had a chance to claim her.

"Umm. Toothpowder. Should I follow your example?"

Edward tasted delicious as usual. She shook her head. She couldn't put off her need of him. He made a thorough assault on her senses, probing deeper until she thought he might swallow her up for breakfast. While his tongue was busy, she felt the bristles of the hairbrush graze her back, stroking slowly on her sensitive skin. Each soft boar hair tickled its way down to the cleft of her bottom, then trailed up like a thousand feathers. Sinuous, then straight, then serpentine lines, designed to lull her like a pampered pet. Torn between total collapse and giggling flight, Caroline's decision was made for her as Edward flipped her to her back. She watched as he gazed down, fisting himself to spear into her. She was sure he had no thought of divorce, but of dominance. He was all stark male beauty, and she pretended she would belong to him forever.

There was no gradual entrance, but a pure instant, instinctive thrust. Edward's face was triumphant, not that she had put up any resistance whatsoever. She closed her eyes, afraid to fall deeper in love with her husband.

She didn't even know *why* she loved him. She hadn't meant to. He wasn't her type at all—not a teasing, playful bone in his long, upright body. Everything about Edward was upright. Tight. She'd chosen him for that very reason. They were supposed to have a marriage of convenience, but somehow passion had overtaken good sense. Not that she had any. Edward was supposed to have enough good sense for both of them. He was a Christie, legendary for his control. You couldn't build a marriage on sexual pleasure alone.

But how effortless it was to rise to meet him, to feel each stroke, to mold herself against him. She had not forgotten how good it was between them, even when she was full of inarticulate rage and he with chilly contempt. It was probably too late to have the conversation they should have had in the few days before their whirlwind wedding. Edward would never understand anyway. If anything, disclosure would only cement his determination to rid himself of her.

Even with those grim thoughts, her heart beat faster, her breath hitched, her skin heated. She had that peculiar sensation of her nose tingling into numbness, which always heralded her orgasm. How Andrew had laughed and mocked her when she told him. She had never repeated the same mistake with Edward.

Her legs stiffened, toes curling in obligatory fashion, teeth clenched in pained ecstasy. Sensation ripped through her, wave after humbling wave, reminding her she was at Edward's mercy for the exquisite relief. He followed her soon after, flooding her. Her barrenness was a fact. There was no need for him to act the gentleman.

They lay entwined in exhaustion. He brushed the tear from her cheek. "Did I hurt you? I am not myself these days."

Caroline shook her head. He hurt her in ways she couldn't explain. "You will remember I urged you to indulge your carnal side. You are simply making up for lost time."

He rolled away, staring at the ceiling. Caroline could see the thoughts moving across his angular face; he had something of import to tell her. She braced herself for the unpleasant truth, pulling up the crumpled sheet to cover herself. To be miserable and naked in the bargain was nothing to aspire to.

"About this." He gestured at the space between them. "I will be required to stay in town for the duration of the case against Queen Caroline. I know I had promised you a short—fling, if you will—before we parted ways for the summer."

"Before we parted ways forever," she reminded him.

"Yes. I do not wish to be unfair, to press you to accept a further association. I know I've been high-handed in this arrangement. You have obligations."

Ah, yes. Her busy life. Taking tea once a week with courtesans. Digging in her little patch of dirt in the back garden. Struggling over each and every word lately. Was there any point to telling him she was blocked in her writing? She found her characters needlessly frivolous and her villains far too predictable. The harlot would never find her husband at the rate she was going. And worse, the story she was writing for herself was turning into a tragedy with no happy ending in sight. The only thing she lived for were his visits. Lord, but she was a fool.

"Are we done then?" Her voice was surprisingly light.

Edward said nothing. She could not meet his eyes in the mirror above. The new clock ticked on the mantelpiece as the sunlight filtered through the blinds. Discreet movement was audible downstairs signaling the household had risen. Edward should go home to his children and his own obligations before she fell apart.

He cleared his throat. "Do you want us to be? I confess, I don't. But don't misunderstand. I have every intention of pursuing the dissolution of our marriage." His laugh was hollow. "I'm as despicable as those men you write about. I'm using you, Caro. There's absolutely no justification for what we've—for what I've—been doing. I'm betraying my principles. It's as though I've been bewitched again. I should know better."

Perfect, cruelly honest Edward. He'd never been able to dissemble. That was her forte.

"How you flatter me. Do you suppose I put something in your wine? Chanted a spell? Red hair was once associated with witchcraft, you know."

"I'm serious, Caro. I despise myself for my weakness."

"Well, as long as you're not despising me." She sat up, hoping he would not admit that he did.

Her inner witch spun from vapor to solid form, compelling her to speak her mind for once. For one final time, because she was determined that they be done. It was far too late to change anything, to reassemble the shattered trust of their marriage, but she needed to spare her heart. Each time she saw his face, she lost more than her ability with the written word. "Look, Edward, neither of us is dead yet. We are healthy, consenting adults. You need not feel any guilt for wanting to sleep with your legal wife. Once we're divorced, you'll probably take up a mistress, perhaps even turn up here now and then for old times' sake. I might not turn you away."

"Caro!"

"Oh, don't sound so shocked. I've no intention of spending the rest of my life denying my nature and living like a nun. I like sex, Edward. No, I love it. I need it. I was corrupted at an early age. These past five years have been agony. Whether you believe me or not, there has been no other man since I spoke our wedding vows, but I mean to change that."

There. She'd said it. It couldn't be plainer. She had finally answered his question. She had never ever meant to revisit that long-ago afternoon, but at least she wasn't begging him to forgive her. She watched him pale in the mirror. "That's right. Although I have no doubt Andrew will happily cooperate with you for the criminal conversation portion of the divorce for the right price, he will be perjuring himself. What's one more lie to him if you pay him well?"

Edward's brows were lifted in disbelief. "I saw you with my own eyes."

"I know what you thought you saw. I don't blame you for leaping to conclusions. If you hadn't come in when you did—" She stopped. She *would* have slept with Andrew again. She might as well have. The results had turned out the same. She'd seen no other way out of her predicament then. If she hadn't actually sinned, she'd had lust in her heart and the requisite guilt over it. "But you certainly have grounds for fraud. I was not a virgin when we married. Either way, you are right to seek an end to this farce."

"But—"

In just that one wavering word, Caroline heard the doubt in his voice. Fine, let him doubt. Let him think she was lying to him again. What did it matter? She retrieved the peach robe from the floor, wishing it were something boringly flannel which would cover her from head to toe instead of an insubstantial scrap of wisp. Wrapping it as tightly as she could, she settled herself at her desk and picked up a pen.

"Go home, Edward. I'm tired already and the day has just begun. I think your little experiment has run its course, has it not? We are surely done with each other, whether you are ready or not. I'll expect to hear how the legalities are progressing. And thank you for the ring. It's lovely." Deliberately turning her back to him, she scratched out a few phrases in her notebook. She pretended indifference as he moved silently about the room. Only when she heard the door click shut did she give in to the tears that swam in her eyes, blurring the words before her.

Edward felt shell-shocked. While he had never served in the military, he'd heard enough from friends who, deep in their cups, finally revealed the grim reality of war's glory. He could barely put one foot in front of the other on his short walk home. To a passerby, he must resemble a man awakened too soon from a drunken evening. Instead, he was waking from five years of self-imposed delusion.

If what Caroline said was true, he could not possibly go through with the divorce. He'd been ready to lessen Rossiter's pain with an infusion of cash—the man couldn't afford the damages likely to be assigned by a court. Edward had not thought of it as tampering, just ensuring the necessary first step of the entire procedure. Rossiter had an affair with his wife; he was guilty of alienating her affection, if she in fact had ever looked upon Edward with anything other than a naked desire for financial security. He had seen them in the most compromising of positions with his own eyes. He'd heard Rossiter's taunts with his own ears. He'd read every word of those damning letters, so many times whole passages were forever emblazoned in his brain.

But if Caroline was innocent—oh, not innocent, she could never be that—but had not committed adultery then, he had no basis to divorce her. Their marriage had been consummated and he was certainly not impotent. He could have a hundred mistresses and Lady Justice would remove her blindfold to simply wink at him. It mattered only if a wife was unfaithful.

Edward couldn't go home. He stumbled past his street and hailed a passing cab. It was much too early for Will to be at his chambers, so he gave the driver Will's home address and settled back into the dingy squabs. All his cautiously constructed plans for his future had just been razed. He was doomed to live in limbo until death claimed him. Feeling distinctly un-Christielike, he punched a fist into the seat, releasing a cloud of dust. What had Allie said just yesterday? *All go unto one place; all are of the dust, and all turn to dust again.* It was just happening for him sooner than he expected.

He paid the driver and climbed the stairs to Will's bachelor apartments. Sir William Maclean could have afforded a house anywhere in the city, but he was snug with his books and antiquities and comfortably looked after by a valet and a daily housekeeper. It was the immaculately turned-out valet, Arbuthnot, who opened the door to Edward's noisy pounding.

"Good morning, Lord Christie."

There was the faintest reproof in Arbuthnot's voice. Edward knew he looked unkempt and felt worse. "Good morning to you, Arbuthnot. I apologize for this early call. Is your master up yet?"

"He is taking his breakfast in the study. If you wait here, I shall see if Sir William will receive you."

Edward suppressed his frustration and cooled his heels in the foyer. A bust of Pericles sat on a round table, the statesman's marble eyes fixed on a painting of ancient Athens hanging on the wall opposite. Will had been to Greece recently, and had brought back as much of the country as he could pack in crates with him.

Arbuthnot returned. "If you will follow me, Lord Christie."

Edward needed no guide to navigate Will's rooms. Everything was located off a dark narrow hallway. He had spent enough evenings there in the past five years, and plenty before that. Will had been a friend for ages, a pillar of strength when Alice died, a sympathetic ear when Edward thought Caroline had betrayed him. The barrister had been begging him for a while to end his marriage legally, as distasteful as divorce was to both of them.

Arbuthnot paused before the open study door. "Shall I ask Mrs. Wallace to prepare you breakfast, Lord Christie? You look as though you might need some sustenance."

Eggs were insufficient for his current needs, but he nodded and went into the room. Large windows bathed the space in light, causing the gilt letters on hundreds of books to twinkle and the coffee service to blind Edward with its gleam. He blinked owlishly at his friend, who was still in his striped satin dressing gown crunching a muffin.

"Bad night?" Will asked, once he had swallowed.

Edward poured himself coffee in a spare cup. "The night was in fact excellent. It is the morning which is proving to be a challenge. How far along are you with the divorce proceedings?"

Will wrinkled his substantial nose. "I met with that blackguard Rossiter yesterday. An hour with him and I was forced to leave my chambers early to come home to take a bath. He was peculiarly gentlemanly on the subject of your estranged wife, but I'm sure he'll come round."

Edward took a sip of bitter coffee. It was only what he deserved. "What did he say?"

"Not a great deal. That he had known her since she was a child. And when he said 'known,' Edward, there was no mistaking he meant in the Biblical sense. But that was all. He sat silent throughout the rest of my proposal. Played with his *hair*, for God's sake. The man has more curls than all of Carracci's cherubs. If I didn't know better, I'd think he was flirting with me."

"There have been those rumors," Edward said, amused at the thought of his oldest friend's discomfort. If Will had not chosen the law, he would have made a perfectly terrifying fire-and-brimstone clergyman. Life was largely black and white to Sir William Maclean. Either something was good or it was evil. Rossiter clearly fell into the latter category.

Will shuddered. "I may be a confirmed bachelor, but not for *that* reason. Women are impossible to please in the long run—or perhaps I am. What's all this about, Edward? You look like the dog's dinner. Never say you've changed your mind about untangling yourself from that unsuitable woman. We've discussed it for five years."

"Yes, I know. But there's been a hitch. I've come to believe Caroline may not have had an affair after all."

Will dropped his fork with an alarming clink. "Are you mad? You saw them yourself. Oh my God. You've been seeing her again, haven't you? And not just on June fourteenth." He rose and began to pace the study, his eggs and ham abandoned on his plate, his finger pointing as if Edward sat on a jury. "I have told you from the first to cease from celebrating that foolish anniversary—it does no one any good. Now she's wormed her way back in. Don't you see, Edward? You've allowed yourself to be manipulated! She's an adventuress. Lord only knows what she was up to all that time in Cumbria. You know about her brother's life. Those house parties. No, no, man, I can't have you change your mind now! And there's Garrett Marburn as well. Wake up! "

Edward felt a prickle of anger at Will's bluntness. His friend spoke with absolute conviction, but he didn't know Caroline. He had never liked her. Hadn't wiped regret from her cheek. Hadn't seen the slant of her shoulders and her defiant chin when she sent him away this morning.

"You know as well as I do, she had nothing whatever to do with her brother's business. That, at least, was one thing I investigated before I asked her to marry me. No one had ever laid eyes on her until the Huntingtons' ball. All I'm saying is that we may have been mistaken about Rossiter, not that I'm going to resume my marriage. You've nothing to fear there. It's quite hopeless."

Will stopped marching around and examined his embroidered slippers, the gift of some poor woman who had once hoped to become Lady Maclean by demonstrating her skill with a needle. Dragons done in the Chinese style looked particularly menacing on a foot Will's size. "Forgive me, Edward. I've overstepped my bounds. It's just that you are my oldest friend. I hate to see you the victim of deception. Is she denying they were ever intimate?"

Edward's jaw felt like a block of wood. It was more than difficult for him to have this conversation. "No. She did not go into detail, but it's clear they had a relationship prior to our marriage. One of long standing, not just a quick fling. *Something* went on after to be sure—Rossiter was in my house for a reason. He might have been using the letters to exert influence over her. I knew—well, never mind. It's to my shame I put up with her as long as I did. Things were wrong from the start."

After a discreet tap, Arbuthnot entered with a plate for Edward, then left, closing the door behind him. Edward wondered just how much the valet had overheard, but it was far too late to salvage his dignity. Will settled back down in the chair and fixed an eye on the steam rising from the heap of scrambled eggs and fresh gammon steak. "I say, my food's gone quite cold. You don't mind sharing, do you? Mrs. Wallace must think you're still a growing boy."

Edward passed the plate across the table. "I haven't any appetite anyway. Sorry to have disrupted your morning routine."

"Nonsense. I'll bill you for it." He grinned and sliced into the meat. "Rossiter can still be useful to us, I'm sure, if we want him to be. What about Marburn?"

Edward shook his head. "She says not."

"Edward, why are you suddenly so convinced of her virtue?"

"I don't know." By mutual agreement, he and Caroline had never discussed the details of the day he found her with Rossiter. She had too much pride to dignify his question with an answer, and he had too much pride to ask it again.

As Will ate his second breakfast, Edward got up and examined the volumes on the shelves, reflecting on the denouement of his marriage. He had come home to Kent unexpectedly, as Parliament was still in session. It was her birthday and he'd had an unaccountable itch for his wife—or perhaps a suspicion that something was afoot. Whatever had brought him home, his peace was most thoroughly shattered. Rossiter had been in her bedroom, for Christ's sake, and Caroline in his arms. She had been wearing that horrible poppy-covered robe, its belt loose. Her hair had tumbled down over her shoulders, barely covering her breasts. Her lips were swollen from kisses, her eyes bright with tears. Guilt was written on every inch of her face when Edward walked in. Rossiter had smirked and began to recount the ways he knew Caroline far better than Edward did, than Edward ever would. To Edward's everlasting shame, he had stood still for all of it, kept his fists at his sides, his tongue between his teeth. When it was finally loosened, he had looked at Caroline with utter indifference and asked, "Have you whored yourself out to anyone else?"

Caroline had turned away and gone to the window, her fingertips pressed white against the pane of glass. Alice's gardens were in bloom below. He had forbidden Caroline from making any alterations, planting anything new, cutting so much as a blade of grass. Perhaps he had not been wise there, setting her in the long shadow of his late wife. Even Allie had something to say about that the other day.

If Caroline had been ice until Rossiter slunk away, Edward was a glacier, immovable. Quite treacherous beneath the surface as well, planning how to make her suffer for her betrayal. She expressed no emotion as he divested himself of her until the very end of his chilly speech, and then it was an insincere and frankly unbelievable suggestion that they begin anew. As if forced tears and a half-swallowed sob would have any effect. Edward had her packed and thrown out of the house by sunset, banished to the dower house and away from the children until he could make other arrangements.

When he returned to London, he made a lucky purchase of the Jane Street house. Deeds passed rarely and through exceptional circumstances. His luck was another's misfortune. Guy de Winter had been shot dead by his wife right in the bedroom of Number Seven, his mistress, too. Guy's young son was anxious to rid himself quickly of the reminder of his parents' foolishness, and Edward was at hand, seated opposite with a bottle of port and a sympathetic ear, trying to drown his own sorrows. If the new Lord de Winter had thought it odd the paragon of rectitude and reason, Edward Christie, had need of a love nest, he did nothing but affix his name to a sales agreement.

De Winter's murder had resulted in the security detail that was to be found at the end of the street every evening, lest other wives become emboldened like poor, mad Eloise de Winter. Edward had thought Caroline safe and properly identified as the whore she was. He knew she had no choice but to live there—her cousin and his wife would never take her back, and she was absolutely penniless save for the few trinkets he'd purchased for her during their year of marriage. Jane Street had seemed heaven-sent, but now Edward wondered if he had not condemned his wife to her own little corner of Hell.

He realized after a moment that all sounds of chewing and chomping were over. Will was staring at him, avid speculation in his dark eyes. "So, sit back down, Edward. Another cup of coffee?"

Edward looked into what was left in his cup, half filled and cold like the current state of his heart. He shook his head.

"What do you want me to do? You know as well as I we can still proceed. With those letters and Rossiter's need for filthy lucre, we can cobble together enough of a case."

"It would be built on a lie."

"Damn it, man! Your marriage was built on a lie."

Caroline had never verbally claimed to be a virgin. Hell, they'd barely said any significant words between them before he snatched her off the Marriage Mart and wed her by special license. He had felt rather heroic, rescuing her from the drudgery of the Cumbrian cousins. And smug, as his suit prospered over the salivating young bucks.

"I think it best to put everything on hold."

Will's saturnine face displayed his displeasure, but he voiced no objection.

"I'm sorry you had to endure that interview with Rossiter. Where did you find him?"

"At the Albany, if you can believe it. In one of their lesser sets, however. It's said very quietly that the Everdeens foot the bill. They claim him as a cousin of some sort." It was clear Will didn't believe any of that.

Edward tamped down his revulsion. George and Laura Everdeen were simply names to him, but if Rossiter was in their orbit, he wouldn't want their friendship. People who would tolerate his sexual amorality—

A cold chill descended upon him. Rossiter had lived with Nicky and Caroline Parker for years. Caroline had been seduced by him when she was barely out of the schoolroom. But what if she were not the only Parker under his spell? He tipped his coffee cup over in his haste to rise.

"What the devil's come over you?"

"Sorry, Will. I've got to go."

He found himself on the street again, the June sunlight filtering through a haze of coal smoke and clouds. London was a filthy place, and he was stuck there for the foreseeable future. But it would give him time to sort out what had really ruined his marriage. And if he couldn't talk to Caroline, he had an idea of who to ask.

Chapter 9

The tabbies of the ton called him The Thief of Hearts,
but in truth, he had not one of his own to steal.
—*The Thief of Hearts*

Andrew Rossiter was stealth itself. He slipped from the
bed in the darkened room, glancing back at Sir George
and Lady Everdeen, both sated, both snoring. There would
be a cuckoo in the Everdeens' nest if he'd been successful
tonight, not that he cared. They paid him enough just for his
pleasure. To be a sort of conduit, a job he'd had much experience with, the only job he'd really ever had. When he took
up with Caroline and Nicky Parker, they'd put him on his
crooked path, although that had not been their intention. He
had discovered his dual nature in pleasing them both and decided why limit oneself to only half the population? Andrew
looked like an angel with gold curls and October sky eyes,
but knew he was the devil himself.

Except—yesterday he'd had a most discomfiting interview
with a stiff-necked barrister informing him he was about to
be sued by stiffer-necked Edward Christie. A substantial sum
had been offered for his cooperation, but he'd suddenly discovered he had some scruples. Caro was unaccountably dear
to him, rather like a first or second love if one were to be so
maudlin, and he wasn't sure it was in her best interests to
perjure himself. Certainly he'd fucked her, and certainly he'd
tried to fuck her after her marriage to that dead bore
Christie, but it wasn't the same thing. As far as Andrew
knew, despite his concerted efforts, she'd never broken her

marriage vows. The poor girl was simply desperate to become like everybody else, saddling herself with a cold fish, three brats, and a house in the country. Poor Caro. It was like snuffing out a bright-burning candle.

He'd made her life worse—out of pique. If he were the sort to feel shame about anything, it would be the day Edward Christie caught them in their negotiations. Andrew had not cared for the man's attitude or assumptions. He had said some things that were better left unsaid. The packet of letters he tossed Christie out of spite was the final nail in their dead marriage's coffin.

The letters were conveniently undated. Not so convenient for Caro. She'd been plunked down on Jane Street almost immediately but refused to see him. His name would never be on the famous list the guards kept to ward off undesirables, and Andrew was as undesirable as they came. He'd spent the past five years insuring that.

Now it seemed Caroline Christie's happiness rested in his dirty hands.

Andrew got dressed in the dark, let himself out of the Everdeens' townhouse and walked to his bachelor lodgings. He preferred accommodations in his clients' houses, but the Everdeens paid his rent, so he was going home to *think*, not a commonplace occurrence. Best not to, when thoughts would turn to Nicky Parker and that last night.

Poor Nicky, he hadn't even gotten killing himself right. He'd lived a week, sightless, deaf to his sister's cries, a permanent look of childlike wonder on his face until the end. Andrew had done the right thing, the humane thing. Caroline didn't blame him for it. She knew he did it for her.

It meant he'd lost both of them that night, something he thought he could live with. Most of the time he managed, and managed well. He had the morals of an alley cat and, like a cat, the ability to land on his feet. He wasn't so sure about the nine lives—he fancied he'd exceeded that limit already.

He ambled down the street in the gray dawn, perfectly at home as the nightwalkers disappeared from corners and sought their beds. The decent city was just waking as the indecent craved sleep. The echo of his footsteps joined with the jostling of carts on the cobbled streets and the raising of windows to let what passed for fresh air in. He caught sight of a pretty red-haired maid through the glass of a second story window and tipped his hat. He still had a weakness for redheads.

Andrew let himself into his rooms and stripped off his neckcloth. Fucking for a living was surprisingly arduous work, and he treated himself to a brandy for breakfast. The Everdeens' generosity had not included the services of a valet, but Andrew didn't mind much. He could be himself in his comfortable rooms, no need of posturing or propriety. His library, what there was of it, had recently been enhanced with a purchase of part of an amazing collection from a notoriously wicked baron. The illustrations provided Andrew with enough fodder to get him through the mechanics of coupling—make that tripling—with George and Laura Everdeen.

He took down a heretofore unexplored volume but lost interest after the first few pages. He was proficient enough to have penned the manual himself. There were only so many ways humans could interlock in that age-old puzzle. Perhaps he should rustle up a bit of cheese and bread, go to the communal bathing chamber and have a good soak. He had nothing much to do until tonight, when the Everdeens would expect him to service them again.

His bed, still unmade from the previous day, called to him instead. Within seconds he was naked beneath the sheets, within minutes fast asleep as only the truly wicked could be. He'd squelched whatever was left of his conscience for later examination and was deep in slumber when rapid knocking roused him. With a curse, he turned, pulling the covers up over his ears. The steady tattoo at the door was impossible to ignore.

It couldn't be bill collectors. Old George had been most dependable, settling Andrew's few accounts per their agreement. Andrew was careful nowadays anyhow. One never knew how long one would go between engagements. His services were not universally recognized or appreciated, but he had quite a little nest egg saved. He planned to spend the winter in Italy, where the weather was milder and the morals somewhat wilder.

Andrew smiled despite his irritation. If it was that plaguey lawyer of Christie's again, he deserved everything that was about to come to him. It would teach him to disturb a man two days running before the sun hit its apex. Andrew strutted to the door naked, his most superior expression firmly in place. Let Maclean be so startled he'd lose the gift of speech.

It was Andrew who was surprised. Edward Christie was on his doorstep, looking much like a wind-blown scarecrow, his clothing wrinkled, his usually slick-backed dark hair disordered, a day's growth of beard softening his long jaw. For the first time Andrew could understand what Caroline saw in him—untidy, he was altogether delicious. But boring as hell, Andrew reminded himself, as he swept a well-muscled arm toward his chamber.

"This is an unexpected pleasure, Lord Christie," he said smoothly. "Come in. As you see, you've caught me at a disadvantage. Please make yourself comfortable while I find my dressing gown."

Christie blanched, looking everywhere about the room save at Andrew's gloriously naked self, and Andrew couldn't resist deepening his discomfort. "Tell me. Do you think my exercise regimen has been beneficial?"

Christie made a choking sound, and Andrew winked one of his bright blue eyes. He was being outrageous, he knew, but the temptation was irresistible. Edward did not look one bit amused, however, so he quickly stepped into his small bedroom and retrieved his robe from where he'd tossed it days ago. He'd have to clean up a bit before his charwoman came, but on the whole he was relatively satisfied with his abode. It wasn't as if he entertained there, although the interview with Edward Christie might prove entertaining.

Andrew found him standing like a marble statue over the abandoned book. If the baron had picked it up out of curiosity, he'd put it down in a hurry. Andrew chose the most comfortable chair and sat. "Now then. Do sit down. How may I help you?"

Christie remained upright, his countenance rather fearsome if one were to pay close attention. "Sir William Maclean came to see you at my behest yesterday."

"Yes, he did. I'm afraid I did not answer his questions in precisely the manner he hoped for. Have you come to try your hand at the inquisition?" He reached for the brandy bottle and splashed some into his used glass. "I don't expect you'd like to join me in a drink."

"Certainly not."

"Oh, save the curling lip for someone who cares. You can't shame me, Christie. I'm beyond all that nonsense." He took a swallow, hoping the warm golden liquid would steady him. Despite his bold words, having Christie stand in his modest parlor was disconcerting. "Make your case and then get out. I'll listen for a while."

He leaned back, watching as Edward twisted his long fingers nervously. The room was dim and still, the heavy curtains shutting out the light and London noise. After an age, Edward lowered himself to the sofa.

"Five years ago, I found you with my wife. You said some things—" His face looked pained.

Andrew couldn't quite remember everything he'd said, but was sure he'd said too much. Or not enough, depending on one's viewpoint.

"You want to know if I fucked her. Yes, I did." Andrew felt triumphant as Christie's pale face paled further. "But not that day. Not, in fact, any day since she married you. And not the year or three before that, when she was under the thumb of that wretched cousin of hers and his wife. Terrible people.

I believe we can agree on that at least. It was no wonder she jumped at your offer to marry her. You saved her, Christie, even if you didn't set her world on fire. She was going mad, you know. Imagine a girl like Caroline, buried alive with those horrible people in the middle of nowhere. At least when Nicky was still with us we tried to make it amusing for her." He swallowed more brandy. Christie's face might have been carved of stone, impervious to insult. Despite his robe, Andrew shivered at the palpable cold leaching across the room.

"So you see, if you are to abide by strict legalities—cross all those Ts and dot all those Is your barrister friend Maclean seems so fond of—you haven't really got a case for adultery. It looked bad, I admit. If I'd had a few more minutes to persuade her, I have no doubt I would have been successful. She was incredibly unhappy, you know."

"I know."

Andrew could barely hear the admission or see Christie's chiseled lips move. The man had a fine mouth, but seemed entirely passionless. Poor Caro. "So you understand my reluctance to lie and assist you with your divorce petition."

"You want more money."

Andrew waved a dismissive hand. "Don't insult me, sir. Even men like me have their standards. I'm very fond of Caro, for old times' sake if nothing else. If it's in her best interests to unshackle herself from you, then I'll cooperate. But I'd need to hear it from her."

"You're not to go near her." There was no mistaking the passion in his voice. Christie looked like a mad prophet rising from the sofa, his fists bunched.

"Sit down, man. The time to hit me is five years past. I have no interest in you breaking my nose. My face is my fortune, you know." Andrew hoped he sounded nonchalant, but the reality of it was that he was extremely sorry he ever opened his door. Christie stood over him, radiating fury. "Let's discuss this as gentlemen. Surely you have talked to your wife about all this. I fail to see why you're here."

"There is more to it than what she has said—or what you have said. I want to hear the whole of it."

Andrew picked at a loose thread on his cuff. "I don't believe you do. Let it rest, Christie. Your wife and I were lovers when we were very young. She didn't deserve my ill-treatment of her then, nor yours now. But if you mean to divorce her, you'll have to do it without me." He raised his eyes to Christie's green glare. "I still have the slightest shred of honor left. Tell Caro hello, and that she has nothing to fear from me."

Christie looked on the verge of saying something, but turned on his heel and left.

Andrew exhaled the breath he didn't even know he was holding. Perhaps it was time to leave for Italy a bit sooner than he planned. Another week or two with the Everdeens and he could free himself from obligation. They were relentlessly insipid anyway, believing themselves to be naughty when all the while they were just mired in a ridiculous quest for the succession of a baronetcy. It wasn't as if poor George was a duke, after all. If the child was a girl, they'd have to find another stud. Andrew was done.

He poured another few fingers of brandy into his glass and drank it down. Yes, it was time to leave for hillsides covered with flowers and balmy ocean breezes. Alessandro and his wife would be happy to receive him ahead of schedule. Andrew would see how much his golden-haired son had grown. Giulietta was anxious for a daughter, and Alessandro's letters were ever more urgent, both for his wife's needs and his own. The portly Alessandro was, quite simply, hopelessly in love with Andrew's lean perfection and no one else would do.

He would write to them this very day, removing himself from any danger that Christie could conjure. Andrew was never anything less than practical when it came to his affairs, save that one time when he lost his soul.

Edward had visited friends in the Albany for years, it being the premier place for gentlemen who didn't want the bother of a house in town, yet wanted amenities galore. There was a dining room, luxurious communal baths; even Angelo had his fabled fencing studio there. On the whole, the place was far too grand for scum like Andrew Rossiter, who had sprung up from who knows where. But today's visit with the man had surprised him, so at odds with what Edward thought he once knew.

Edward had succumbed to the investigation Will had urged upon him five years ago. Rossiter and Caroline's brother had been school chums, partners in the sex hotel scheme they ran when they were little more than schoolboys. His origins were completely obscured; his tuition was paid for by some Scottish industrialist, likely his natural father. The man had died and the source of Rossiter's funds dried up. When Nicky Parker offered him a home, he'd been quick to agree, and their house parties became legendary. But once Parker died, Rossiter had moved with remarkable ease across England and the Continent as if he belonged in the finest drawing rooms, leaving Caroline to fend for herself with the new viscount.

It was not really surprising to see Rossiter come to the door bare naked, a Grecian statue come to golden life. It was absurd. Obscene. But entirely expected from a man like Rossiter, leering and winking at him from the doorway. If what he said was true after he'd donned his paisley robe, Edward had done Caroline a grave injustice. Five years of banishment for nothing.

No, not nothing. She'd admitted she'd sinned, then and now, and her choice to write all those wretched books had only confirmed she was a dissolute woman.

He should never have married her. Caroline had never fit easily into his routine. He had felt smothered by her affectionate attention, appalled by her artless conversation, her endless schemes, her temper. She had no place in his carefully constructed Christie world.

Except in bed.

The sooner he went home to the calm and comfort of his own house, the sooner he could work out what he'd heard.

Caroline. Will. Rossiter. Each of them one side of the triangle whose sharp corners pierced his consciousness.

Stumbling into the street, he hailed his third cab of the day, grateful he still had some pocket change. But it would take more than money to solve his problem, if it was even possible to solve.

Chapter 10

*The flames licked each corner of the letter until nothing
was left but the lingering loss in Lucinda's heart.*
                                        —*The Orphan Princess*

Caroline had a serious case of the blue devils. She had
made her unwanted confession and sent Edward away.
She couldn't write—couldn't eat.

But she could read, and was in the mood to torture herself
even further. Shoving some papers aside, she felt for the tiny
indentation on the back panel of her desk drawer and popped
it. A plain brass key lay alone in the hidden compartment.
She weighed it her hand a few minutes before going into her
dressing room. A small black trunk awaited, filled with the
remnants of her girlhood—her diaries. And Nicky's.

It had been a revelation after his death to find her brother
had been just as scrupulous as she recording their madcap
existence, only he was the superior speller. She often read
both sets, comparing their observations. Learning her false-
hoods. Learning his truths. Some of the passages brought a
smile to her face. Most broke her heart, as she had broken
Nicky's without ever trying.

She knew which volume to pick up—1806. Fourteen years
ago. The spring Andrew came to them. Prior to that, her life
had been unexceptional, although she supposed she had been
granted far more freedom than most girls her age. In fact, her
father ignored her most assiduously. But it wasn't until Andrew's arrival that she felt truly alive.

Even in her own hand, she had tried to fool herself about
what he was to her.

Nicky's friend Andrew Rossiter has come to stay. He is, I suppose, what one might call handsome—lots of yellow curls like a slipped halo. So now Mary and I have two people to cook for and clean up after. They do nothing but amuse each other at our expense.

Caroline smiled. She had been in the throes of calf-love. Andrew was the most beautiful creature she had ever seen. How careful she'd been to limit her praise and not gush even to herself on the pages of the diary. She thought of the night when she prepared yet another dreadful meal. The night Andrew changed their lives.

"Jesus God, Caro." Nicky spat a mouthful right onto the scrubbed pine kitchen table. Caroline had taken pains, going so far as to polish the candelabra which halfheartedly shone beneath the candle stubs. The flickering light from the fire in the hearth did nothing to make the gray mess on the plates appealing, and now it had been proven that its looks were definitely not deceiving. She burst into tears.

"Nick, have a heart. She slaved away the whole day." Andrew passed his crumpled linen napkin to Caroline, who abandoned all pretense at ladylike demeanor and blew her nose into it soundly.

"I can't h-help it," Caroline hiccupped. "Mrs. Revere took her cookery books with her. Mary's r-run away. I don't kn-know how to do anything!"

Andrew gifted her with one of his beatific smiles. "Rubbish. It's not your fault you don't know how to cook. A viscount's sister is not expected to be proficient at the stove."

"All the years I was at school, Caro—did you never hang about here? Watch the water boil? Mrs. Revere wasn't such a bad old trout."

Caroline sniffed. She had hung about. There was nothing better to do with Nicky away. It had always looked so simple when Mrs. Revere set the stewpot over the fire. "She said I was ham-handed. A hoyden. A h-hell-cat."

"Alliterative, was she?" Andrew murmured. "Don't cry, Caro. You'll turn your eyes as red as your hair."

Caroline pushed the long braids behind her ears. She was far too old for such a hairstyle, but with Mary gone, no maid to help her dress and all the housework to do, there was no choice. Nicky and Andrew spent their days jogging about the countryside on the last two horses trying to cadge a free meal with the distant neighbors. Goodness, the horses ate better than they did.

Nicky got up to warm himself near the fire. Although it was June, the house was damp and cold. Caroline had hoped dinner cooked in the fireplace would accomplish two things— feed them and take the chill off the gloomy kitchen. She was wrong, as usual. Her brother's ginger hair glowed brighter than her candlestick, but she saw where she'd missed a spot when she barbered him last week. He kicked back a loose coal. "I've shut up most of the house. I don't see what else I can do. No one will work here. The wretched state of the Parker finances is known by every unlettered urchin in the vicinity. It's not as if we can offer free room and board. The roof caved in on the servant's wing."

"Where is our beloved guardian? Why cannot he be found to help us?" Caroline asked bitterly.

Nicky snorted. "As if a friend of Father's could be at all useful." He paused, rubbing his hands. "Caro, Andrew and I have made inquiries. I didn't want to worry you—I know how hard you've tried. According to a reputable source, Gossler took everything we had and was bound for the West Indies. I hope the boat sinks."

That was the first Caroline had heard of it. What else had her brother and his friend withheld from her in their efforts to protect her? Despondent, she pushed her plate away.

"I'll make some tea," Andrew offered in his soft Scottish burr.

"There isn't any."

"None at all? Not even a few flakes? You'd be surprised what I can do with the bare minimum." Andrew smiled

again. He was always so kind to her. He'd been orphaned too, at a much earlier age. If it hadn't been for his Uncle Donal, he never would have had the advantages he did. But when his uncle died, there had been a mix-up in his will. Andrew was even poorer than they were, happy to accept Nicky's invitation to throw his lot in with them. He and Nicky were so close they sometimes knew what the other was thinking without ever uttering a word. Caroline had been jealous of their friendship at first, but Andrew was too nice—and too beautiful—to dislike.

She knew she was beautiful too, even in her patched dress and her unraveling braids, like a Cumberland Cinderella. But unlike Cinderella, there was no ball to attend to attract a prince. She was seventeen years old and doomed to a life of spinsterhood with her impoverished brother and his friend in a decaying country house. She cried a bit harder.

"Oh, give way, Caro. It's only supper," Nicky said impatiently. "Andrew can try his hand at it tomorrow night."

"The-there's plenty of vegetables in the garden." Caroline had one domestic talent at least—her garden was thriving. She would have preferred to grow flowers instead of vegetables, but was at least practical enough to plant carrots and turnips and potatoes. Onions and beets and four kinds of lettuce, too. They'd eaten every asparagus stalk this spring along with the strawberries in the raised beds Andrew built for her. The beans were running up the poles Andrew had helped her set, and she hadn't ruined the bright green peas that sat in a cracked white bowl on the table. She reached for them and put some on her plate, being careful to edge them away from the goo that was meant to be mutton stew.

"Peas," grumbled Nicky, returning to the table. "You know I don't like them." He spooned a large amount on his plate, made a face and dug in.

"At least there's wine, Nick old man," Andrew said heartily, tipping the bottle. He gave Caroline a wink. "You deserve some, too, after your kitchen drudgery, Caro. Pass me your glass."

Her papa had kept a good cellar at least. What was left of the Parker family fortune was stored below in the cool dark vault. She rose to add some water from the jug at the sink but Andrew stopped her.

"Water this wine? Heresy! You're old enough to drink it straight with us, Caro."

"Old enough to marry," said Nicky through a mouthful of peas. "Why can't you snag a rich husband who can set this place to rights?"

Caroline felt her face grow hot. "And where am I to meet this man? Why don't you find a rich girl? I thought that's what you and Andrew did all day, riding all over to take tea with the ladies. What about Bessie Abernathy?"

Andrew made a choking sound. Caroline knew why. Bessie Abernathy was twenty-five if she was a day and plain as a scuffed boot, but her father owned half of Cumberland.

"Her father would think me a fortune hunter."

"Well, you are." Caroline swallowed more wine, enjoying the warm rush to her tongue. No wonder gentlemen were constantly in their cups. It was delicious.

"I'm too young to marry. Isn't that right, Andrew?"

"Much." A look passed between them that Caroline didn't understand. Young men were a mystery, and at the rate she was going she'd never solve it.

"What we need is an industry," Nicky said, putting his fork down. "Perhaps there's a coal seam on the property. Or tin."

Caroline laughed, although the thought of ripping up their beautiful acreage was not amusing at all. "Don't you think Papa investigated all that? I was forever tripping over some engineer lured up here by one of his crazed schemes. We've nothing but rocks and grass."

"Sheep then."

"And what money will you use to buy them? Don't you remember, Papa tried sheep when we were little. They all caught some disease and died, poor things. I can hardly see

you and Andrew with your sleeves rolled up shearing and lambing."

Glum, Nicky poured himself more wine. Andrew cleared his throat. "Let's be logical. List assets and debits."

"Ha. Don't bring up the estates' debts—I'll never live long enough to pay them all."

"What about the house?" Andrew asked.

"You know it's entailed. I can't sell it. It will all go to some fifth cousin twice removed."

"You'll marry, Nicky. Someday. Your son will live here and I'll be the dotty aunt in the attic."

"No, no. I mean the house is an asset," interrupted Andrew.

"May I remind you it's missing part of a roof?"

"Yes, but it's a lovely old place. Plenty big, and the grounds are beautiful. You're doing wonders with the gardens, Caro."

"Th-thank you, Andrew." Caroline was pleased he noticed. Her brother didn't seem to give her credit for anything except not burning the kitchen down. She examined her work-roughened hands, wondering if they'd ever be soft again.

"What if we cleaned it up as best we could, and held house parties here?"

Nicky put the wine bottle down with a clunk. "Are you insane? Invite a bunch of people to eat and drink us to death? Who would cook? Caroline? I say, Andrew, you've had too much wine."

"You misunderstand. They would pay their way for a week or two. Pay a lot."

"You mean turn this dump into some sort of a hotel? Only Bedlamites would pay to stay here."

Andrew pushed the curls from his forehead. "We could attract the right people if we offered the right amusements. Privacy. Privilege."

Nicky knit his bronze brows. "You mean a club of some sort. I don't think that's at all wise, Andrew."

*"A man needs to escape from the strictures of society now
and then. A woman, too," he nodded at Caroline. "We could
sell subscriptions, use the money to do some fixing up and
have plenty left over. Offer unlimited—everything. For a very
hefty price. You know as well as I do, we could succeed in
this."*

"I don't quite understand," said Caroline.

*"You're not meant to," Nicky replied, rising from the
table. "Let's take a walk, Andrew. I want you to tell me
more."*

*Caroline watched in disgust as they went out the kitchen
door, leaving her with the cleaning up. Again. If they thought
to turn her into some drudge catering for silly society people,
they could think again.*

*But perhaps some young buck would arrive on the
doorstep and sweep her away from the ashes. Caroline closed
her eyes and let her imagination run wild. He would be tall.
Golden-haired. And bear a very suspicious resemblance to
Andrew Rossiter.*

That had been the beginning of the downfall. The three of
them spent the next few months scrounging for cash and
connections, fixing up the house as best they could. Andrew
had gone to London to have the subscription offers printed,
coming back with half of them sold. Caroline didn't know
how he'd done it then, but now she had a fair idea of just exactly *what* he'd offered. Their Christmas debut was a wild
success. No one thought to go to the midnight service, although for their souls' sake, they should have considered it.

Caroline lived a nearly normal life the other three weeks of
the month. As normal as can be when one is falling headlong
in love with a young man who had been bent to sin at an
early age. Her diary entries became shorter—she didn't dare
put into words what was happening, in fear that Nicky might
find her journal and despise her.

If only he had.

She flipped ahead. There was a date, and just two words. *Cherry pie.*

Caroline heard the lock tumble. Andrew slipped into the room balancing a plate on his palm.

"*It's very late,*" *Caroline scolded.* "*I thought you weren't coming.*" *She pushed the covers off, revealing every inch of her marble-white skin.*

"*It's a madhouse out there. Here, I saved you some dessert. Tarte aux cerises.*"

Yum. Her favorite. There was someone else to cook now, a wizened French chef who treated them like dirt but was masterful in the kitchen. He gloried in the week of debauchery, preparing the most elegant, expensive dishes. The rest of the time, Andrew and the Parkers were as likely to get a bowl of cold oatmeal and a burnt muffin—which was economical. They didn't profit so much from the scheme as they hoped. Their guests were ever more demanding. Apparently one could never be bad enough, and badness was costly.

Caroline opened her mouth, waiting for Andrew to spear a chunk of sweet dough and tart cherries and feed her.

"*Ah. No. You're going to have to work for this, Caro.*"

"*What do you mean?*"

"*You'll see.*" *He put the plate on the dresser and stripped himself of his evening clothes. Caroline was well acquainted with his body, but he never ceased to awe her with his perfection. They had not discussed marriage, but she was hopeful Nicky could be persuaded to agree to let her marry a man with no background and no money. After all, Andrew was his best friend and business partner. She and Andrew could continue to live and work at Parker Hall.*

Raising a family there would be tricky, however. They took every precaution and position to prevent her getting with child. But if by some miracle she became pregnant, her brother would have no choice but to give his blessing.

Andrew padded across the bare wood floor with the pie.

Caroline's mouth dropped open when she saw where he put it. He lifted a golden eyebrow. "Hungry?"

Yes, she was, She would always be hungry for him.

Even after all the years, Caroline flushed in embarrassment remembering. Andrew had used that night to taunt Edward, to prove he had more sway over Caroline than her husband ever would. Andrew was wrong. As much as Caroline the girl had loved Andrew, Caroline the woman loved Edward more. She'd learned a bit about honor and betrayal, discovered that character mattered. Whatever one said about Edward Christie, his character was beyond reproach—which was all the more reason for her to give him up for good. She was damaged, and seemed to damage everyone she loved.

She dropped the red leather journal back into the chest and looked for Nicky's last volume. She needed to remind herself just why her marriage had been doomed from the start despite her nearly manic effort to be continuously gay during the first months of it.

Pushing the darkness away had been a temporary solution. In the end, all she'd done was annoy Edward and ruin her life.

She weighed Nicky's book in her hand. She'd read it one last time, then burn the lot. It was time to put an end to it all.

Despite her misery, she smiled. She sounded like a gothic heroine. She wouldn't do away with herself quite yet—she'd bought those gorgeous new red dresses and hadn't even worn them all. People like Lizzie depended on her. If she was to put the past behind her—her guilt, her marriage, all of it—getting rid of the diaries would ensure she not be tempted to dwell on what could never be changed. The future would consist of clean white pages yet to be written.

The diary fell open to Nicky's last entry. She began to read.

March 11, 1810

It's agony. I watch my sister and my lover entwined, knowing that every second I spend at the peephole I come closer to losing my resolve. The devil of it is that Andrew knows I sit here and goes to her anyway, daring me to come in and put a stop to it. Or join in. God help me but I have considered it.

Somehow the power between us has shifted over the past few years. All those midnight confessions have caught up with me and are taking a toll. He's no longer the grateful cub who'd been corrupted and maltreated, but a sleek young entrepreneur responsible for recovery of my birthright—not that we've a fortune. But life is better now. The house parties are a wild success, with an ever-increasing number of people who seek membership in our little secret society. Most of the debts have been repaid and the curtains rehung and the furniture recovered. The whole house looks perfectly reputable and our disreputable clientele never leaves unsatisfied. Caro has surprised me with an unerring eye for cheap comfort and beauty. How could she not notice Andrew?

I haven't even bothered with a glass tonight. No one is here to see me drink my brandy directly from the bottle. I'm exhausted but can't sleep despite ever-increasing doses of laudanum and whatever else I can get my hands on. No drug-induced hallucinations could be worse than the nightmare vision before me.

I am losing Andrew; we both know it. Oh, he knows what to do to make me happy, but serves me more out of duty than desire. It is Caro who captures him now, beautiful Caro who is every bit as wicked as Andrew and I are combined.

I've been blind to it for too long, preoccupied with the business, too proud to imagine Andrew would ever seek comfort elsewhere. Andrew flirts with everything that walks, but it never meant anything before. It is I who am naturally unnatural. Andrew simply bent out of necessity.

*I can't go on this way much longer. I should cut
Andrew loose—throw him out. Throw Caro out, too.
The pair of them can find somebody else to torment.*

*I see that I have dropped my bottle. It has slipped
from my fingers, rolling harmlessly on the carpet. Not
a drop wasted. It was empty. Time to head to the cellar
for more to blot out the ivory and gold lovers' knot
beyond the wall.*

*I don't blame Caro. Andrew is irresistible, growing
more angelic by the day while I bloat from drink and
pale from drugs. If I'm not careful, I might fall to my
death on the cellar stairs and I'm much too young to
die.*

*But truly, would that be so bad a fate? My life is
purposeless without Andrew in it. Even if he comes to
me later tonight, I will smell Caro's jasmine perfume
on his skin.*

*There is a young footman in the hall. It still isn't
easy retaining servants, despite the fact there is money
now to pay them. The demands of the house parties are
more than most will agree to. This boy—Harry, is it?—
was hired off the streets because he will do most
anything without a blush. Much like Andrew when
we first met.*

*If I ask him, will he come? Will there be a flicker
of disgust on Harry's face? No matter. I am lord and
master here, and if the boy wants to eat, he'll do as
he's told.*

Caroline closed the book gently. Her brother had been a
tortured soul, hanging by a frayed thread. When she'd confronted him, he cut that thread, spreading his misery to the
two people he loved the most. There was no pretending that
everything would be all right. That they could go on together.
So Caroline had become a drudge for her cousins and Andrew debased himself whenever and wherever he could.

Lizzie would think it odd to make a roaring fire in summer. Caroline started it in her bedroom hearth herself. The heat of it scorched her cheeks and dampened her hairline. One by one, she fed the books into the flames, inhaling the noxious aroma of burning glue and leather and ink. She opened the windows, but the scent of despair lingered.

Chapter 11

*Twas nothing but midnight madness. Mischief. Yet
somehow the words hung in the air like tattered sheets
on a clothesline.*

—Whispers in the Dark

Hard as it was, Andrew sat half asleep on the secluded
stone bench. He'd come out to the garden to escape the
Everdeens' soiree, the stench of human sweat, and the vain
attempts to conceal it with heavy French perfume. The air
outside was little better—London in the summer was a mi-
asma of evil, and those left in town equally repugnant. Except, of course, for the peers deciding Queen Caroline's fate,
and they were certainly not to be found within the infamous
walls of Sir George Everdeen's town house. The party was a
dead bore because of its too-conscious attempt at wickedness, but then everything bored him lately.

Thank God in a few days he would leave the city for the
sunny climes of Italy. Some wine and pasta and palm trees
would perk him up, not to mention seeing his little son. Andrew knew perfectly well that the child was being raised with
all the advantages he'd never had and would inherit Alessandro's title besides, but a part of him felt proprietary. Territorial. Marco was *his* son, his image. Thank heavens that
Giulietta was blond as well, or else the crème of Savona society would question his parentage. Andrew knew what it was
like to be a bastard, and wished that fate upon no one.

He took his pocket watch out, calculating how much
longer before he'd be celebrating the Everdeens' social triumph in their bed. Hours yet. Disgusted, he leaned back
again and closed his eyes but opened them quickly when he

heard footsteps on the brick path beyond the hedge. If George was coming out for an appetizer, he had better be prepared to wait until the last guest left. Andrew had no intention of getting caught in the bushes with his pants down.

"It's a brilliant plan, I tell you," came the slurred words.

Not George. Not anyone he recognized. But someone nearly as drunk.

There was a silence, then a grudging "Perhaps."

"We'll hold her for ransom until Christie pays and puts a stop to it. Or better yet—the bitch disappears for good."

Andrew was instantly alert, craning his neck to catch each incriminating word. Unfortunately, the two plotters decided to lower their voices, and raucous laughter from the ballroom's open windows above drowned out any subsequent sounds. By the time he rose from the bench and rounded the hedge, he saw only two shadowy forms heading up the garden stairs through the French doors in the wavering torchlight.

Blast. He sprinted up the steps, once inside nearly sliding on the polished parquet floor. The room was filled with a motley assortment of lower-tier ton. If the stratification of society were a house, those people would be relegated to a subterranean vault beneath the cellars with the rats. There were actually a few peers among them, tarnished though by a scandal—or several. For a minute Andrew questioned why he had chosen to accede to the Everdeens' wishes, but it was too late for regrets. What he needed to do instead of feeling sorry for himself was find those men. He only knew that one of them was conspicuously drunk, and that would describe at least three-quarters of the people in the room. Cheeks and noses were raddled with red patches, laughter was too loud, not-quite-ladies' bosoms were virtually bared to the leering glances of not-quite-gentlemen. The scene resembled one of those hellish paintings by that fellow Bosch.

Andrew circulated, holding on to a glass but not drinking, attentive to the sounds around him. But he never heard the voices again. When he could stand it no longer, he whispered into Laura Everdeen's ear that he was feeling unwell and had to leave. She was so tipsy he thought she might not remember, but would surely notice his absence when she fell into her bed alone.

He walked home quickly, formulating his plan. He could write a letter, but it was better by far to appear in person and warn Christie of what he'd heard, unpleasant as that prospect was. Baron Christie had left no doubt he considered Andrew no better than a bug beneath his shoe. Well, the bug was about to fly up and buzz in his ear. What Christie would do with the information was up to him.

Edward put his napkin down carefully. It was all he could do to keep his composure. His butler would be shocked if Lord Christie ever behaved in an untoward manner, but Andrew Rossiter's presence in his foyer was circumstance enough to throw the breakfast dishes. Edward was convinced he'd seen the last of the man a few weeks ago. Perhaps he'd changed his mind about the money and would cooperate with the divorce proceedings. Even though Edward had shelved the whole process for the time being, he had cut himself off from Caroline anyway. He didn't dare contact her in his unsettled state, and she had indicated she had no further interest in him. For all he knew she had become some man's mistress as she'd threatened.

He really didn't know. He'd not pumped old Hazlett for information, not wanting to torture himself. *Something* needed to be done, but Edward had no idea what at present. He hadn't had a decent night's sleep since he'd left Caroline's bed and quite simply couldn't think straight.

"Put Mr. Rossiter in my study. I'll join him there shortly." Edward picked up his coffee cup, but his roiling stomach objected to its bitterness too much to bring it to his lips. There was no point in delaying. The sooner he concluded the interview with Rossiter the better.

Edward found the man perusing an atlas, seeming as tired as Edward felt. Even Rossiter's famous curls were limp. He looked up and met Edward's eyes.

"Good morning. Thank you for seeing me."

"I take it you've changed your mind."

"No! Not at all," Rossiter said, surprised. "Whatever your plans are for Caro, they cannot in good conscience include me. I have a somewhat mysterious matter I need to discuss with you before I leave for the Continent. I overheard something that may affect you."

Edward sat down behind his desk. "I suppose you want money for this information."

Rossiter laughed. "You do hold me in utter contempt, don't you? No, Lord Christie, this information is free and without strings of any kind. What you choose to do with it is your business. But I cannot sit back and do nothing when Caro's safety may be compromised."

"What the devil do you mean?"

Rossiter eased his long form onto a chair. "There was a party last night at the Everdeens'. Not at all the sort of thing that would interest you, or even me, for that matter. I was half asleep when I heard two men talking in the garden." He leaned back in the chair and closed his eyes as if replicating his pose. "Let me see. I haven't got the exact words, but it went something like this. One man, very drunk he was, said 'I've got a good plan.' The other said, 'Perhaps.' I woke up for the next sentence. 'We'll hold her for ransom until Christie pays and puts a stop to it. Or maybe the bitch should disappear forever.'"

Edward's stomach roiled again. "Who were they?"

"I haven't the foggiest idea. I followed them, but they vanished into the crowd."

Edward gritted his teeth.

"I *did* try to find them, so stop growling at me. I wandered about as long as I could stand to, listening for a familiar voice. Nothing. I went home, didn't sleep, and am, as you see, here at the crack of dawn to warn you."

"They didn't mention Caroline by name."

Rossiter shook his head. "I suppose not. What other females are under your protection?"

"My daughter. My sister."

"Not precisely bitches, I take it."

Edward rose and began pacing. "A while back I had a visit from Lord Pope and Lord Douglass. Were they present at this party?"

Rossiter's forehead wrinkled. "I'm not sure. It was a dreadful crush. Pope is known to me and I usually avoid him at all costs. I don't remember seeing him there, but it's possible that he was. I'm not acquainted with the other."

"Caroline has written about both of them. And not in a flattering way."

"Ah." Rossiter had the audacity to smile. "Did she kill them off as gruesomely as she's killed you off? If I recall correctly, you've been swept off an alp by a frozen mountain goat and drowned in a serpent-infested moat."

"I don't read such rubbish," Edward snapped.

"Well, you should. Caro's writing is singularly edifying. *Everyone* reads her books, from chambermaids to duchesses."

"I don't! I suppose I should thank you for the warning, Rossiter." Edward expected the man to get up and leave, but watched as Rossiter steepled his fingers in thought.

"I'm quite hurt that I haven't ever recognized myself as the hero *or* the villain in any of the dozen books I've read."

Edward couldn't resist the taunt. "Maybe you were never that important to her."

Rather than take offense, Rossiter grinned again like a naughty angel. "I believe you must be right. Thank you for that insight—my conscience is much relieved. I do have one, you know, rusty and feeble as it is. I never meant to harm Caro. I loved her as much as I was able. I imagine I love her still. Please watch out for her."

Speechless, Edward watched Rossiter saunter out the door, his notion of the man forever altered. If what Rossiter overheard was true, what should he do? There wasn't much to go on; he might not even be the Christie in question, although he couldn't see Ned at the center of some nefarious plot. He'd already spoken to Caroline about Pope and Douglass, and she'd dismissed the matter out of hand. But if they, or someone like them, intended violence to either her, his sister, or Allie, he couldn't sit idly by in his study and curse Andrew Rossiter.

Beth and the children were already in Kent. A quick word to his bailiff to beef up protection around the house was a simple matter. Ned and Jack could feel useful and manly protecting their aunt and little sister.

Expecting Hazlett to act as a security guard on Jane Street was not logical, however. Loyal as the butler was to Caroline, he was nearing seventy if not actually past it. Edward had a brief image of Hazlett clocking Pope with his bunch of keys and smiled despite the seriousness of the situation.

There was only one thing to be done. Convincing Caroline to agree to it would be a challenge.

Caroline pinched at the sleeve of a new red dress. Either Madame Dulac was stingy with the fabric, or Caroline was continuing to gain weight. Her upper arms were turning wobblier by the day. Of course it didn't help that she'd just indulged herself at one of her Thursday teas in the shade of her fragrant garden. Mrs. Hazlett had outdone herself with honey buns studded with candied violets, lemon curd tarts, ginger curls, and a cherry cake, not to mention the tiny savory sandwiches stacked upon a silver platter. Caroline's courtesan neighbors had rolled home to work off their excesses by vigorous bedsport. However, Caroline did not face that energetic prospect. She would have only her cat Harold's company, and he was even more sedentary than she.

Edward had taken her at her word a few weeks ago and made no effort to return to her or her bed. She supposed he must still be in town, engaged in the government's business of trying poor Queen Caroline. Citizen Caroline knew there were demonstrations in the street in support of the woman, but on the whole she was indifferent to the whole subject. Let the entire world seek divorce, starting with her. Everyone could start their life fresh, like the crisp white pages of her notebook that were yet to absorb any ink.

She had finished *The Harlot's Husband*, after several sleepless nights and days and quite a bit of Mrs. Hazlett's plum brandy, and it was dreadful. Not the brandy, which had an enormously powerful kick, but the book. Garrett had frowned a bit as he skimmed it in her parlor yesterday but assured her it would do. After all, she had inserted every naughty phrase he had suggested, and a few more besides. She had killed off the Edward character by an attack of ravening wolves in the forest. There wasn't a scrap left save for his cravat and walking stick. Eating Edward would not make for much of a meal for wolves though—he really was too thin. Whereas she was beginning to resemble an over-stuffed pillow minus the tassels and cording.

Jack Sprat could eat no fat. His wife could eat no lean. Had Caroline and Edward stayed married, they would have become figures of fun in the ton. As it was, she felt the disapproval every time she stepped into a shopping arcade or theater box. It was much easier to send Lizzie out with a list, or entertain herself at home by writing ridiculous fantasies that had no basis in reality.

Bother. She was feeling incomparably sorry for herself. Where was the Caroline of old, who was bold and spirited, a reckless hoyden, the girl who climbed the fells and swam naked in lakes and danced in Andrew's arms as her brother hummed off-key? That Caroline had disappeared inch by inch after her brother died and it became clear Andrew was not going to save her from her cousin James and his wife Maria. Andrew had stayed with her out of duty until they came to claim the house, then vanished without a word.

Caroline had thought she knew why. Andrew hadn't any money; she was still a viscount's sister, no matter how disgraced. A part of her heart hoped he was off to seek his fortune so he could return for her. It wasn't until she found Nicky's diary that she discovered what a fool she'd been.

Nicky and Andrew had done their best to shield her from the salacious house parties, but she had half an idea of what was transpiring in the guest wing. She wasn't deaf or blind. Sometimes she had felt like Rapunzel trapped in the tower, gazing down into the gardens as all manner of pleasure was taken publicly. Their guests came each month for a week of seasonal frivolity. It was up to her to appoint the house with every luxury, but once the carriages began to arrive, she was tucked behind her bedroom door. If they were not busy directing the diversions of their company, Nicky and Andrew delivered her meals to her, but most often trays were brought by one of the temporary maids who had been hired for the week. She could bear the loneliness for seven days, knowing Andrew would come to her after.

Caroline had found her youthful experiences useful for her novels, though the bulk of her knowledge came from her neighbors. They were perfectly willing to tell their secrets for biscuits, tea, and a sympathetic ear. Caroline had spent the past five years listening to various tales of woe and solving as many problems as she could. Lizzie was not the only girl she had helped.

But no one was available to help her, now or then. It had been a killing blow to realize, as she read Nicky's diaries that she was not the only Parker Andrew had pledged his love to. Nicky's darker fantasies about her had shocked her to her core. She'd put the books away, nearly burning them many times over before finally consigning them to the fire, but could not erase the words from her heart. When she felt especially pitiful, as she had the other day, she tortured herself with Nicky's careful entries. She felt as responsible for his death as if she had pulled the trigger herself. But his words and hers were now ash, swept away by Ben the kitchen boy. Too bad her memories were not so easily disposed of.

The brass mermaid knocker startled her from her thoughts.

It was probably one of the girls, arriving much too late for tea, but Caroline could use the company. Mr. Hazlett was outside helping clear up the garden party, so she opened the door herself.

"Edward!" She stared at him, quite stupid in her surprise. Realizing she must look like a booby, she dropped her eyes to the step and saw the large portmanteau at his feet. She had given it to him the only Christmas they celebrated together, his initials EAC inscribed in gilt on the leather. Raising her eyes in confusion, they landed on two carters removing trunks and boxes from a wagon on the street.

"Good afternoon, Caroline. Forgive me for not contacting you earlier. May I come in?"

"Wh-what's the meaning of this? Did I forget something when you threw me out five years ago?"

"Just let me come in and I'll explain everything."

Caroline crossed her arms over her chest and heard an ominous rip. Bother Madame Dulac and her careless stitches. "I fail to see how you can explain why it appears you are moving into my house lock, stock, and barrel."

"I have an excellent explanation, I promise you."

"You *are* moving in?" Caroline squeaked. "You cannot! I won't allow it."

The men stopped shoving the boxes around and were looking very engaged in the spectacle before them. Caroline could almost hear what was going on in their heads—the great and proper Baron Christie begging admittance to a Jane Street joyhouse while the fat little doxy denied him. Edward's lips were quite white. No doubt he was anguished by the public display on her steps before workmen and could imagine their thoughts, too. The scene would make an excellent chapter in a book, but only if she pushed Edward backward to fall flat on his arse on the pavement below.

"Caroline, we will continue this conversation indoors."

"Indeed we will not! I told you the last time I saw you that we were through. Finished. Spent. Terminated."

"Stop sounding like a dictionary." He softened his voice. "*Please*, Caro. This is important."

Caroline pointed to the men on the sidewalk. "Tell them to wait while you make your case. *Not* that I will change my mind. You must be absolutely mad to think you can come in here and order me about. Just because I'm your wife does not mean I'll obey your every whim."

The carters stood in open-mouthed awe. "Coo, this is better than a play," one of them muttered quite audibly.

"Tragedy or farce?" Caroline snapped. "Don't you two dare move an inch." Uncertain, the men seemed to freeze where they were. "Oh, do sit down on a box or something. We won't be long." Caroline turned on her heel, leaving Edward in the open doorway. He followed her into her green downstairs parlor.

She threw herself onto the sofa, spreading her crimson skirts so there was no room for him to join her. "You have five minutes."

Edward went to her drinks cupboard and poured them both a finger of brandy. She refused hers, but Edward swallowed his in one gulp.

"Dutch courage?" she asked contemptuously.

Edward set the glass down. "Andrew Rossiter came to see me."

Caroline felt her stomach knot. "You've come to terms with him about the divorce then?"

"No. He is not assisting me in any way. In fact, he's leaving the country. But he overheard something that troubled him enough for him to come to me, and I am troubled as well."

She didn't know what to make of the way Edward dismissed the divorce so casually. It was as if he didn't care about pursuing it any longer. He must have something else planned with that wretched Will Maclean. "Well, what has got you in such a tizzy?"

"We believe your life is at risk, Caroline."

"I beg your pardon?" Caroline watched his face for any sign of a joke. There was nothing but firm resolve.

"I think it may be Pope and Douglass who are moving against you, but really, it could be anyone whom you've libeled in your books. There is a plot afoot to kidnap you. And worse."

"W-worse?" Caroline stammered.

"A death threat, my dear. Apparently you've made enemies. It may have all been drunken talk, but I'm not willing to be so cavalier when it comes to your safety."

The only man she had truly maligned in her books was pacing magnificently before the empty grate in her parlor. "Jane Street is guarded. I am perfectly safe."

"The watchmen are only here at night. I got past the gates this afternoon, didn't I? Those carters outside could be hired ruffians come to box you up in one of the trunks. Drop you right into the Thames."

"*Earrings from the Earl*," Caroline said absently. She had used that very plot device once as the Edward character bobbed out to sea only to become fish food.

"I met with an investigator earlier today, a Mr. Mulgrew. He comes highly recommended. You've heard of the Egremont case, I expect. He and his agents will discover who is behind these threats. In the mean time, I will move in here. When I'm in Parliament, my valet Cameron will see that the house is secure. He served with honor on the Peninsula and knows his way around a pistol."

Caroline was reeling. She supposed she had no objection to taking in Edward's man—with a gun!—as a precaution but she couldn't possibly allow Edward to move in. Even if it were little more than a closet, this Cameron fellow could share young Ben's room on the third floor, but where would Edward sleep?

"This is ridiculous. There must be some mistake."

"Don't be stubborn. Even Marburn agrees with me that something needs to be done."

"You've spoken to Garrett?" Caroline was incredulous. To her knowledge, they had never spoken before. Edward would never give Garrett the time of day unless the situation was serious. Or at least he thought it was. How she would have liked to be a fly on that wall.

Edward nodded. "He was present at my meeting with Mulgrew. If you are a target, then he may be as well."

"I don't understand this at all. Perhaps you should start from the beginning."

Edward sighed. "I am paying those men by the hour, Caroline. At least let them unload the cart."

"This is not the time to think of your pocketbook! If you must be so cheeseparing, *I'll* see to it they get their wages and send them back where they belong."

Edward ran a hand through his perfect, brushed-back hair, then gave a little smile. "Very well. I was at the breakfast table this morning. Kippers. Eggs. Stewed fruit. Toast and *The Times*. Just the usual. Do you want to know what I was wearing?"

Good Lord. He was making a joke. "Stop it!"

"Full of orders today, I see. Rossiter came to see me. He'd been up all night worrying about you. I have no doubt that what he heard disturbed him greatly—he was genuinely upset. Last evening he was at a party and overheard two men talking. My name was mentioned in conjunction with the term ransom. From the words used, it is unlikely that any other female attached to me was the object of this crime except for you, but I've taken steps to protect Allie and Beth. Mulgrew will get the guest list to help us narrow down the conspirators. You can figure out which of the gentlemen you've pilloried and we'll take it from there."

Caroline felt the blood drain from her body. If anything she'd ever written in her silly books resulted in harm to Allie, she'd never forgive herself. "Edward—" Her voice broke.

"Here. I know this is a shock. Drink your brandy."

Caroline obediently swallowed from the glass Edward

held to her lips. Her hands shook too badly to take it from him.

"I never meant to cause any harm."

"I know. From what Marburn said, you've been scrupulously careful, flattering most of the men you've based your characters on. Really, the only aggrieved parties he could think of were Pope and Douglass. And me, of course," he added wryly.

"But Pope's book came out months ago! Why would he be so desperate to hurt me now?"

"They say revenge is a dish best served cold. Things have not been easy for him of late. His position in society is tenuous at best. Most decent people cut him."

"As they should! He's a horrible, horrible man." Caroline shuddered, remembering the night Lizzie came to her.

"Until we know the precise nature of the threat against you, it's best if you limit your activities. I can escort you when necessary."

The thought of Edward looming over her everywhere she went sent a little thrill through her, not that she went out much anymore. "But your valet can do that."

"So he can if he must. But I would prefer to see to your safety myself. You are my wife, Caroline."

"Just for the time being."

Edward looked away. "About the divorce—"

"Just one disaster at a time if you please! I'll allow you to move in until we get all this nonsense settled. It shouldn't take more than a few days for your Mr. Mulgrew to do his detecting. But I will not share a bed with you again, not ever. I want that to be very clear." Caroline hoped she sounded resolute. All she really wanted was to be enveloped in Edward's arms. Feel his wiry strength. Smell the lime of his aftershave.

And not simply because she was afraid of this amorphous threat. Perhaps she should be, but she wasn't. She feared herself. She wanted Edward as she always had, and he would break her heart as he always had. He needed to be kept at arms' length if she were to move forward with her life—if she had a life to live.

Oh, she was being melodramatic, worthy of one of her featherbrained heroines. Surely her life wasn't really in danger. Andrew might have gone to Edward as some sort of deranged joke. He'd always had a very odd sense of humor, although Nicky's death had changed him irrevocably.

She could put up with Edward for a day or two. Perhaps even as long as a week. And then—

"I'll let Mrs. Hazlett know you're staying for dinner."

Edward smiled. "And breakfast, too."

Chapter 12

Henrietta hung shackled to the walls of the dungeon,
each hopeless cry echoing on the damp walls like the
laugh of The Devil.

—The Grenadier's Ghost

He was an idiot. He could have hired a hundred men to
protect Caroline. But no. Instead he was sleeping on the
floor beside her bed.

Of course, he wasn't *sleeping*. How could he when every
sigh, every stretch, every shake of the covers reverberated in
the bedroom like a shotgun. And her scent—jasmine and
clean skin and Caroline—was driving him absolutely mad.
He was as hard as the floor.

After a relatively civilized supper, he had every hope of
joining her in bed under that intriguing mirror. There were
times during dinner when Edward thought Caroline was actually flirting with him over the filet of Dover sole and baked
figs. She had changed into another low-cut red dress, and
damn if the color was not growing on him. The contrast between its ruby brilliance and the pearl of her body was entirely entrancing. She had swept her coppery curls up with
garnet clips and needed no rouge or lip salve on the warm
August night to lend her color. Edward had lost his train of
thought several times while he basked in her beauty.

When the time came to retire, Caroline had handed him a
pillow and a sheet and invited him to sleep on the little couch
in her upstairs purple parlor. Unless he wished to triple-up
with Cameron and the kitchen boy in the attic, she had suggested sweetly. Edward had tried to oblige, but he was a long
man and the couch was short. It didn't take any time at all

before he was tapping on her bedroom door, reminding her he could better protect her if they were in the same room. Caroline had pointedly pointed to the floor.

So he was wakeful and woebegone. She had the audacity to be asleep, gently snoring. He didn't remember her snoring during their marriage, but then he'd rarely spent the entire night in the same bed with her. He had taken his pleasure—an unseemly amount of pleasure—then retreated to the propriety of his own rooms, just as all men of his station did. If he had ever noticed Caroline's disappointment as he untangled himself from her arms, he had shut it out of his ordered existence and gone about the business of being Baron Christie. No Christie had ever allowed himself to become the victim of his animal nature, and apart from Edward's precipitous proposal, he had managed to confine Caroline's power over him to the hours bracketing midnight. The last weeks of their reacquaintance on Jane Street, he'd been so sated he'd actually slept right through to morning. But he was definitely dissatisfied tonight, in need, in agony. The thought of Caroline, fragrant and warm, so very close above him, was enough to keep every inch of him alert—his cock in particular.

Punching down the pillow, he rolled away on the carpet, snagging his nightshirt under him in a bulky lump. After a few seconds of frantic tugs, all was smooth again, but certainly not comfortable. The French windows were open to the night air of Caroline's garden, and its perfume joined with hers to permeate his senses and make sleep impossible. Edward pulled himself up and stepped onto the little balcony overlooking the walled yard, wishing he had a cheroot or brandy to soothe his nerves. His nightshirt tented comically in front of him.

All seemed quiet on Jane Street and in the houses beyond. Here and there a flicker of candlelight indicated someone else was as wide awake as he was. Night jasmine, planted not for its beauty but its fragrance, lay below, its pale yellow blooms faint in the bright moonlight. The only sound came from the Marquess of Conover's garden fountain two doors down. It splashed like a regular rainfall, possibly soothing someone, but not Edward.

He had heard in his club that Conover was getting married again, to some childhood friend. The man had wandered across the world for a decade. Perhaps this new wife would keep him home, steady him as Alice had done to Edward, providing him with a well-ordered household and dependable affection.

Not like Caroline. While her dinners were served on time, one never knew what mad dish would be under the covers. She collected cookery books much as some women collected porcelain figurines, nearly forcing his cooks to quit with her interfering ways, both in town and in the country. Edward had finally forbidden her from the kitchens to protect his staff and the assault to his stomach.

Caroline was all spice—ginger and hot pepper, curry and cardamom. She kept an herb patch in the city—leaves of something exotic had seasoned his soup tonight. Taking a deep breath, he inhaled the tiny Eden she had created below to blanket out the rest of London. He tensed as a rustle came from bushes, but it was only Caroline's cat. Harold had taken one look at Edward earlier and decided to spend the night outdoors. The cat's green eyes glowed up at him in disdain, then disappeared into the shrubbery.

Shunned by the cat. Shunned by Caroline. He supposed he deserved it. Edward felt rather useless. The safety of Jane Street's inhabitants was assured by the hired watchmen who stood armed at the gates with their list. Leaving his man Cameron there by day was more than likely enough to protect Caroline, but Edward had not been content with that solution. He wanted to see Caroline again after the abysmal weeks of staying away.

Devil take him. He was damned no matter what happened. Had been damned from the moment Caroline Parker stepped beneath the chandelier in all her crimson glory at Lady Huntington's ball.

"Edward? What's the matter? Is someone out there?"

She whispered, but he heard her anxiety. He had frightened her by simply standing at the window thinking too much. "No, Caro. Everything is fine. I just couldn't sleep."

"Well, you *would* choose to sleep on the floor instead of the couch."

"I'd much rather be in your bed," he mumbled.

"What's that?"

"Nothing. Go back to sleep." He heard her strike the flint and the bedside candle flared along with her laughter.

"Good heavens. I don't believe I've ever seen your hair so disordered."

Edward ran his hand through his straight dark hair. He was in desperate need of a haircut. "Cameron can give me a trim tomorrow before I leave for Parliament."

"I could do it. I used to cut my brother Nicky's hair."

"Well, you won't cut mine. I wouldn't trust you near me with a pair of scissors."

Caroline chuckled. "I'm no Delilah. And I wouldn't harm a hair on your head. Or hurt you anywhere else."

By God, he wished she would hurt him. What he wouldn't give for her hands to be all over him, nails raking, fingers probing. Her sleep-honeyed voice alone was making him crazy. "I'm going below stairs for something to drink. May I bring anything back to you?" He watched her stretch into the pillows, her full round breasts straining against the filmy material of her nightdress, the dusky pink of her nipples visible. He suppressed a groan.

"I'll come with you. I know I shouldn't be hungry, but I am."

He'd always been amused by Caroline's appetite. She was not one of those pale, dainty things that minced their food into bird-like portions. During their marriage, he sometimes thought she'd gone without food during her youth and was making up for it. She could make a banquet of apples from his orchard, hitching up her skirts and climbing the tree herself. Her choice of outlandish dishes, her love of vibrant color, her childlike enthusiasm to try new things—they should have warned him from the first. She was entirely unsuitable. Cheerfully unsteady. He'd made them both suffer for his thoughtless lust.

For that was all he felt, wasn't it? Pure lust—with a dash of territorial protectiveness to keep what was his safe. For she *was* still his, at least in the eyes of the law.

"Suit yourself," he said gruffly. "I can't stop you."

"No, you can't." She bounced out of bed, the candleholder wavering in her hand and casting gobliny shadows in the room. "It is still my home, for as long as I live, at least according to those papers Will Maclean drew up for you. Tenancy for life. Very generous terms for a fallen woman like me, according to him. He was quite put out about it as I recall. But," she said, a mischievous smile on her face, "perhaps you want this mysterious duo to kill me off. I imagine you'd get a pretty penny for the house if you sold it."

"Don't be absurd. I'd not give up the comfort of Christie House and find myself on your dusty floor if I wanted you dead."

She reached up and stroked his cheek. Her fingertips were warm and gentle. Edward felt as if five butterflies had landed, causing his skin to tingle. "Poor thing. I'm sure the floor is not dusty. Mrs. Hazlett would permit no such thing."

"Hmpf." He wished she'd drop her hand. He wished she'd drop it lower. He stepped backward. "What do you suppose she has in the larder?"

"I'm sure I don't know. She's quite immune to my suggestions."

"A wise woman."

Caroline swatted at him. "How can you say that? I'm quite a good cook, you know. I taught myself after a bit of trial and error. Just because you never eat anything but dull and bland and boring fare—"

"Are you calling me dull and bland *and* boring?"

She shrugged. "Dull and boring—I'm repeating myself,

aren't I? Not very accomplished for a wordsmith, but it is very late and I'm very tired. You must admit you are not one bit adventurous when it comes to your palate."

For an instant, Edward remembered how she tasted when he kissed her smooth pink inner folds. Sweet. Tangy. Undeniably Caroline. He wondered if she had allowed her nether hair to grow back in the time they had parted, and wondered too if she would ever permit him to taste her there again. His mind in a fog, he bumped into a table in the hallway.

"Watch your step. If you fall, you'll wake the whole household."

Edward concentrated on navigating down the stairs. He'd concentrate on another deadly sin, gluttony. He'd torture himself watching Caroline eat, licking her lips and fingers, biting into some juicy morsel with relish. He shivered as they reached the landing.

"You aren't cold, are you? I vow, I've never experienced a hotter summer." Tempting tendrils had escaped from her strict braid, and she pushed them behind her ears. She had not donned a robe for their late night snack, so her ripe body was on display under the sheer nightdress. Edward was certain she must be aware of the image she presented, saucy and sweetly disheveled. Caroline was deliberately setting out to make him the sorriest man in England.

She flitted around the kitchen, lighting lamps which only illuminated her near-nakedness. He'd had the sense to put on his dressing gown, which at least disguised his rampant manhood from her too-knowing silver eyes. It was hotter than hell, but he belted the robe tighter.

"Now, let's see. You said you were thirsty. Ale or wine? Or perhaps tea? I could put the kettle on."

The thought of hot liquid vying with his hot blood was too much for the summer night. "Just water, if you please."

She set a tumbler and a jug before him. "See? Just as I said. Dull. I keep a very good cellar. Some wine might help you sleep."

Some wine would loosen his tongue. Loosen his resolve.

There was something to be said for the watchful tension he felt in Caroline's presence. He shook his head and poured a splash of water into the glass. As he drank, he examined her pert backside as she assembled a plate at the sideboard. It resembled the peach she balanced on the scalloped edge. "You will join me, I hope. I've fixed enough for two." She placed the little feast beside him and dragged a chair closer.

It was simple fare—two thick slices of bread, a wedge of cheese, a cluster of grapes, two figs, and the golden peach. Caroline popped a deep purple grape in her mouth and sighed. "Almost as good as wine. I forgot it. There's a half bottle left from our dinner in the pantry. Would you get it please? And a glass, too." She ripped a corner off her bread with determination and held it under her nose. "There's nothing I love so much as the smell of fresh bread." She smiled up at him and extended the chunk to his mouth, brushing it against his lips. "Isn't it divine?"

Edward had no choice but to eat it. It was damn good bread. Caroline nibbled on another piece topped with a sliver of cheese and offered him the same, the ribbon tie of her nightdress slipping down her shoulder. She leaned forward seemingly oblivious to the fact that she was losing what little clothing she had on. From his height advantage, her breasts were impossible to conceal from his starved gaze. No amount of food would quell that particular desire. Once he finished chewing, he reared up quickly from his chair to fetch the wine. He was glad to escape, glad to get away from the sinful bread and cheese and his entirely enticing wife. If bread and cheese had that effect on him, what would happen if she served him oysters? He knocked his forehead into the cabinet in an attempt to draw his blood upward.

"Edward? What was that noise?"

"Nothing, nothing. I'm just clumsy tonight." Grasping the bottle of wine and a goblet, he returned to the kitchen and poured them a healthy tot. Caroline was in the midst of a fig, its jewel-like center glistening in the lamplight. Her tongue darted across her lower lip to catch a sticky wayward seed. He downed his wine in one swallow.

"Here. Let me cut up the peach. They seem to be especially delicious this year. I meant to make some peach chutney, but they are too good to spoil with vinegar and onion." She picked up the silver fruit knife and sliced through to the stone, carefully pulling the peach in half. Edward stared at the golden circle in her palm, its juicy center tinged deep pink. *Dear God.*

"I'm not hungry," he rasped.

"You don't know what you are missing." Her teeth sank into the flesh of the fruit and her eyes closed in bliss. "So very sweet, Edward. You must taste it." She held out the peach half. He would choke on it, but she was not to be resisted. He took a bite and the consummate flavor of summer burst in his mouth. He'd never tasted anything so incredible in all his forty years.

Except for Caroline. She would taste of peaches and herself tonight, a combination he could no longer fight. She was busy with her own half of heaven, clear nectar edging from the corner of her mouth. Edward longed to lick her clean and make her dirty again on the spotless kitchen table. He imagined her arching up against him, her flimsy nightrail tattered—no, torn off and thrown in the banked fire. She would be as golden as the peach, beneath him in the amber lamplight, as pink within and hot as the summer night. He could feel her hands sweep his back, hear her fevered cries, bury himself so deep—

Her cool hand on his cheek broke the spell. There was nothing but concern in her huge gray eyes. "Edward, are you ill? You look very odd."

He mopped his brow with a linen napkin. "You're right. It's excessively warm this evening. I think I'll just step out into the garden. Try to catch a breeze."

"Mind Harold. He's out there somewhere. I don't know why he dislikes you so."

Edward knew why. Anyone who usurped his pillow in his

mistress's bed was the enemy. Well, Harold had nothing to worry about. Edward was relegated to the floor forever.

Caroline stifled her giggle just long enough to hear the tradesmen's door close. Oh, but she was wicked. When she had woken up to find Edward on the balcony, his body lit by moonlight, she had seen how very, very uncomfortable he was, and not from lying on her carpet. The man was stiff as a poker and nearly as long. She had done nothing that past half hour but prolong his agony.

She straightened the strap of her nightrail. Usually she wore something prim and practical to bed, but tonight she had sent Lizzie to Victorina's to borrow the indecent bit of tissued silk. Even if Edward was moving in because of some sudden urge to become her knight in shining armor, she did not want him to get complacent—to take her for granted as he had. Oh, she knew it would not be long before he was elevated from the floor to the mattress, but he would have to suffer a bit first.

She sipped her wine and plucked a few more grapes from the stem. She really was famished. Food had become much too comforting to her since Edward disappeared again. It was a good thing Mrs. Hazlett didn't permit her in the kitchen, else she'd be up to her eyelashes sampling new recipes that she surely didn't need. All her new crimson clothes would soon be useless to her.

Too bad Victorina was not in possession of a red nightgown, but the whispery cream silk was temptingly transparent. It had served its purpose, but something new would be necessary for tomorrow. Caroline would send Lizzie forth to borrow more courtesanal nightwear for the duration of Edward's stay. It would be frivolous to order such things to hang permanently in her dressing room cupboard, and she knew the Jane Street girls would not mind contributing to the downfall of Baron Edward Christie. When Caroline was through with him, he would be contrition itself.

If she was still alive, of course.

Chapter 13

There was nothing like a little good company to light her lonely life. A pity there were nothing but bats and spiders skittering about in the dark.

—*Saving Cecilia*

Caroline waited in the kitchen for Edward until every last crumb was gone from the plate. He must have found the garden absolutely fascinating, for she grew weary waiting for him. Maybe he was making friends with the cat. More likely, he was using his hand to relieve his masculine need that she had set out to inflame. If so, she would be safe from him in the bedroom, if not from herself. Putting their dishes in the scullery first, she climbed the stairs with her candle stub and crawled back into bed. She was nearly asleep when the door opened and Edward quietly returned to his spot on the carpet.

After a decent interval, she rolled to the edge of the bed and peered down. Edward had removed his nightshirt but was half covered with a sheet, his broad shoulders gleaming in the slanting shaft of moonlight. His lips were parted, warm breaths rising to Caroline's face, his lashes dark crescents above his chiseled cheekbones. She could throw one leg over the bed and step on him if she chose. But his breathing was even, and it would be a shame to rob him of sleep, no matter how irritating he was. She didn't believe she was truly in danger, but it was gratifying to know Edward's concern.

The air was still. The room felt close, cloistered, especially with Edward's long form radiating scorching heat. He must be quite naked beneath the sheet. Caroline settled back in the middle of her lonely bed and gazed up at the mirrored ceiling. Although the room was bathed in moonlight, there was nothing to be seen in the silvered glass save shifting shadows.

When Caroline and Nicky were children, they'd done much of their exploring by moonlight, wandering far afield to catch glimpses of nature by night. In the winter when the blanket of snow reflected the January moon so brilliantly, they had even deigned to take their schoolbooks outside to see if they could read them. When Caroline recounted that tale to Andrew, he had been disbelieving. So they'd stepped out into the snow to test its dazzlement and read love poems to each other, then he had taken her atop and beneath fur blankets in the frost-covered garden. She had thought then it was the most remarkable, romantic night of her life. She'd felt nothing but his heat as she opened to him, tasting brandy on his tongue, shivering not from cold but desire.

It was so long ago. She never let herself think of Andrew. That chapter of her life was not to be reread.

She had forgiven herself for her stupidity, and nearly forgiven Andrew for his duplicity. Nicky's journal had been most explicit. Andrew had suffered unimaginable torment from the time he was a child. It was no wonder he couldn't comprehend right from wrong, why he used whatever was convenient to advance himself.

When he came to her with the letters, he'd been almost apologetic as he attempted extortion. She had the feeling he would have preferred her body over the pounds he had requested, and she had been so miserable she would have given it. Almost had—until Edward walked in and saved her even as he condemned her.

Caroline pushed the covers off. It was far too hot, and her brain was broiling with unpleasant thoughts. In a fit of pique she pulled Victorina's nightgown off and tossed it to the floor. Not on Edward's side, of course. She wouldn't want him to smother in silk, although his light snoring was annoying. It had awakened her earlier and abandoned her to night devils.

She was perfectly naked. No, not perfect. Her *poitrine* was *opulente* if she remembered her French correctly, but the rest of her was growing as well. With a rueful sigh, she stroked her belly, then allowed her fingers to dip lower. She was still as smooth as Edward required. For some odd reason she had remained so throughout their five-year separation. It would be so easy to wake Edward, but she was not ready to cede control to him just yet. Slipping her fingers within to stroke the plump fleshy bud, she held back her groan of satisfaction, pressing and circling above it as she had so very many nights alone. She knew what she needed, and knew who held the favored spot in her fantasy.

It didn't take her long. It never did. She waited for God to smite her or Edward to wake—either one would be disastrous, but the waves of blessed relief juddering through her body were almost worth it. Still greedy, she continued to touch herself until she was exhausted from her pleasure. Surely now she could fall asleep, boneless and sated. With a sigh, she pulled the sheet up and curved into the mattress.

On the floor, Edward lay rigid. It seemed Caroline had just done the very thing he did for himself in the garden, in much less than half the time. Of course he'd had the blasted cat to contend with. He'd practically seen Harold sneering in the flower bed.

Lord, but they were a pair of fools. Edward hoped Caroline would not ignore the crackling heat between them forever. He'd have to pressure Mulgrew for fast results. Sleeping on Caroline's floor was torture of every kind—like the state of their marriage. Punching his pillow, Edward cursed and willed himself back to sleep. He had a busy day ahead and couldn't afford to be a lovesick lad at his age.

Things had improved for Edward, at least in terms of his physical comfort. The ubiquitous Cameron had found a camp bed for him, and it was set up near the threshold of Caroline's bedroom door. No longer could she feel his warm breath or feel the waves of desire emanating from him throughout the night. He was at a safe, if dissatisfying, distance. They were scrupulously polite to each other as their days intersected and circled. Caroline had even stopped flirting, as it didn't seem to be effective. Edward was determined to be valiant and chivalrous and too damned *good*.

After several days stuck indoors, Caroline was going mad. Cameron was hovering as usual. He took his duties far too seriously, steadfast in Edward's absence. She had tried without success to sic Lizzie on him as a distraction, but her maid was far too besotted with Garrett Marburn to bother flirting with Edward's valet, no matter how handsome he was.

Even Caroline, who was resistant to the allure of most men thanks to her unfortunate past, thought Cameron was a prime specimen, if a bit humorless. Nearly as tall as Edward, she could imagine him in a scarlet coat tramping through Europe with his musket shooting at the French without a blink. At present, he had a wicked little pistol strapped to his chest and a frown on his face. She had been arguing with him the past quarter hour trying to leave the house. There was a game of loo that afternoon at Victorina's. There was always delicious Spanish wine, Caroline nearly always won, plus she needed to return her borrowed nightgowns and obtain more. Despite the fact that Edward didn't seem to notice her dishabille, she had her Parker pride to contend with. Each night she looked ready to be ravished, not that Edward had laid a finger on her. Yet.

"You can stand guard right outside the house," Caroline suggested for the fourth time. "Or wait inside. I'm sure the girls won't mind a bit."

Cameron colored. " 'Tain't proper. Baron Christie would have my hide if he thought I was hanging about with a house full of loose ladies. Beggin' your pardon, Lady Christie. I know they're your friends and all—the baron did explain— but he wants you to stay inside for now. His instructions were very clear."

"So I'm to be kept a prisoner in my own home?" Caroline flared. Really, this was going too far. Whatever amorphous threat had been uttered at a drunken party, surely she was safe on her own street. It wasn't as if she could be snatched away without incident. After Pope's assault on Lizzie, she had helped train the girls in rudimentary self-defense skills, and each of them would be armed with hatpins, fingernails, and a judiciously placed knee at the very least.

Cameron folded his arms, looking stalwart. "Sorry. My mind's made up. You're to stay put, my lady."

Caroline subdued her desire to fly into a frenzy and attack the man. He was a war hero, after all, and her hands would only wind up bruising against his broad chest. Edward and Cameron were well matched—both calm, controlled, and utterly pigheaded.

"I need fresh air. I assume you'll let me go into the garden?"

"Only if I accompany you. I know about the doors in the garden walls, you see. You'll lift the latch and be down the street in no time."

Hell and damnation. Cameron was no fool. He'd made a thorough reconnaissance of the situation. Each back garden was walled, but there were indeed doors on either side so the Janes could visit each other without stepping out their front doors. Caroline had first made the acquaintance of her old neighbor Charlotte Fallon after hearing her sobbing next door and had hurried through the wall to soothe her. *Blast.*

"Oh, very well." *Insufferable man.* Caroline tramped back upstairs and sat at her desk. She heard shuffling in the hallway and knew Cameron was right outside her bedroom door pacing the carpet. If she were clever, she could knot bedsheets and climb down the balcony, but that seemed like a great deal of trouble to go to in order to win a few pence and drink some red wine. She opened a blank notebook and stared at the blank page. Her muse had definitely deserted her. What with the alleged threat on her life, the constant monitoring, and Edward's inconvenient, insidiously tempting presence, she could barely think straight. What she needed was a diversion or she thought she might start to throw things again.

Just in the knick of time, Cameron tapped on the door and

entered. "Lady Christie, Hazlett says you have a guest below. A Mrs. Bannister."

Caroline frowned. "I know no one with that name."

Instantly, Cameron produced the gun from its holster.

"Oh, good grief! Put that away at once. It's probably some poor soul collecting for charity."

Cameron shook his head. "Unlikely. A high flyer if I'm any judge. I caught a look at her from above before she went into the parlor. Hair black as night, big blue eyes, and a body that—well, never mind," Cameron mumbled. "Hazlett says she's come to ask you about her sister Charlie. What kind of a name is that for a woman?"

Caroline grinned in understanding. "Ah. It must be the Divine Deborah. It's all right, Cameron. I don't know why I didn't recognize the name. Mrs. Bannister is my friend Charlotte's sister. She lived next-door, although I never met her."

He snapped his fingers. "I knew it!"

Caroline couldn't help herself. Cameron might tower over her, but she shook a fist in the direction of his somewhat crooked nose, his only apparent flaw. "Yes, she may have lived here once, but she's a respectable married woman now. Don't be such a prig. You've no idea the suffering some of the residents of Jane Street have gone through. Young women have very little opportunity for employment and are always at the mercy of predatory men. Sometimes selling their bodies is the only available choice open to them. It would behoove you to leave your judgment to God."

Chastened by her tart lecture, Cameron stepped back into the hallway, his shoulders drooping in a satisfactory manner. Caroline appraised her own shoulders in the mirror. She was wearing one of her new dresses, perfectly proper, more wine-colored than scarlet—quite plain really. She fastened an amethyst brooch on the bodice and added amethyst earbobs. She had been too dispirited the past few days to affix her usual sparkle to her person, but the prospect of an interview with the notorious Divine Deborah was reason enough to shine. Deborah's sister Charlotte had disappeared from Jane

Street, not entirely without warning. Charlotte had told Caroline she planned to leave, but had gone without saying good-bye. The whole house was shuttered and silent, a mystery Caroline itched to solve.

"I'll accompany you downstairs," Cameron said, blocking her at the door. He had recovered his superior height and attitude.

"You may wait in the hallway. I have nothing to fear from Mrs. Bannister."

"You don't know that," Cameron said stubbornly. "She could be in league with the men who have plotted against you."

Caroline sighed. Her good gossip opportunity was not to be ruined by Cameron.

"Look," she said, trying to make her tone as reasonable as possible, "Mrs. Bannister is the new daughter-in-law of an earl. I doubt she would be foolish enough to risk her rise in society for some petty revenge upon me. I've never even met her before."

"Then maybe she's not who she says she is."

"You worry too much, but I suppose I should thank you. Please, Cameron. I'll leave the doors open and you may station yourself right outside. I will not let Mrs. Bannister get the better of me, but if she attempts anything untoward, I'll yell my bloody head off. Or maybe stab her with a letter opener. All right?"

Cameron blushed again at her curse, but nodded in agreement. What kind of soldier had he made if a little vulgar language was a problem?

She found the new Mrs. Bannister in the green downstairs parlor, her gloved hands holding a Sevres plate which she put down at once. Clearly the woman was examining its provenance. Just as clearly, she did not seem ashamed of her snooping. Instead she curtsied gracefully, raised her eyes, and put a lovely practiced smile on her face. Wearing a stunning gown of peacock blue, she was the sleekly polished image of her sister Charlotte—there was no doubt she was who she said she was.

"Lady Christie, so kind of you to see me. I am Mrs. Arthur Bannister."

The words sounded like magic coming from her lips. Caroline knew a little about Arthur, and he was not magical at all. She extended two fingers. "Do make yourself comfortable, Mrs. Bannister. May I ring for tea?"

"Thank you for the offer, but I won't inconvenience you. Or my husband, Arthur. He is waiting outside in our carriage. We've just come back from our honeymoon, you see."

Deborah was the picture of delight over her new station. Caroline could not remember ever being so pleased to be married, although she must have been at one time. Edward had saved her from her cousins, and for that alone, he should be enshrined in some heroic pantheon. "My felicitations on your marriage. I understand from your sister that it was rather sudden."

"Yes, a whirlwind courtship. But I couldn't say no to my Arthur. Charlotte was minding the house for me, but there is no one next door now, not even any staff. Would you happen to know what's become of her?"

"I do not. I was hoping you might be able to tell *me*."

"Oh, dear." Deborah fiddled with a loose coal-black curl. "I imagine she's gone back to her silly little cottage in the country then."

Caroline thought Charlotte was far more suited to a silly country cottage than a Jane Street residence. Charlotte Fallon was definitely not mistress material. Deborah, on the other hand, despite her recent marriage was still in full courtesan mode—every gesture, every smile set on a well-worn course to charm. It was no wonder men fell at her feet, but Caroline was impervious. She could see the vulnerable woman beneath the glittering surface and felt a bit sorry for her. It must be so very tiring always being pretty and pleasant.

"If you see Charlotte," Caroline said, "tell her I have

taken inspiration from her. My closet is positively exploding with red dresses and my husband is apoplectic." Actually, that was not true. Edward seemed rather sanguine every time she entered the room in one of her red dresses. They were not having the desired effect at all.

For the first time Deborah Bannister expressed a natural look—one of confusion—but nodded in agreement, her careful curls bouncing. "Of course. I shall write to her." There was the slightest pause. "You have not, perhaps, heard any news of Sir Michael Bayard?"

Caroline knew this was not an idle question. Deborah had left her sister in her place as Sir Michael's mistress when she ran off with Arthur Bannister. Poor Charlotte had not been able to hold out against Bayard's masculine conceit and had been hopelessly in love the last time Caroline had spoken to her.

"I'm afraid not. He's not been seen on the street in some time. As you said, the house is closed and the servants gone."

"Well, I'm sure they both landed on their feet," Deborah said, rising. "Thank you so much for your time, Lady Christie. I'm most sorry I didn't make your acquaintance earlier."

Caroline thought if anyone had landed on their feet, it was Deborah Bannister, nee Fallon. Once one of London's most sought-after mistresses, she had managed to hook a husband after a string of high-born lovers. Most Jane Street girls would never be so lucky, living out their old age rationing out the gifts of their youth. No wonder they were anxious to acquire one bauble after another to keep themselves warm in a future winter. Once their beauty faded, as it inevitably would, there was nothing left to fall back on but cold, hard cash.

Caroline shook off her dismal thoughts as she saw Deborah Bannister to the door. She knew she couldn't save every girl in the neighborhood—she could barely save herself. Although her writing had proved more lucrative than she had ever dreamed, she gave much of the compensation away. There was always some poor soul who needed it more than she did. After all, how many red dresses and Sevres dishes did she need? She had redecorated her house recently out of necessity. When Edward had placed her there, it looked very much like the wicked love nest it was supposed to be. The paintings alone were enough to make a whore blush. If Cameron had seen them, he'd probably have swooned. It had taken Caroline a few years, but room by room she had upgraded her surroundings. The only holdover from the previous tenant was the carved bed and the ceiling mirror, and it remained solely because the workmen feared the plaster would fall down upon their heads if they removed it.

Her interview over, Caroline climbed the stairs back to her neat desk. She hadn't written anything in days, since even before Edward had turned up on her doorstep. Garrett was not going to be pleased with her lack of progress. She dipped her pen in the silver inkpot and held it over the page. A splash of ink fell and spread merrily over the white surface.

"Hell and damnation!" Frustrated, Caroline tossed the pen down. What was she to do with herself? She couldn't write, couldn't visit, couldn't shop, couldn't even settle her mind long enough to read. Mrs. Hazlett had banned her from the kitchen as well after a long lecture on how unsuitable it was for a baroness to cook. She had absolutely nothing to do except wait until Edward came back from Parliament, when they would circle politely around each other at dinner, then fall into their respective beds in agonizing propriety. Her eye fell on the neatly made-up camp bed and she stifled an urge to take an axe to it.

Weeks ago, Edward had decided she would be his mistress, even if she was already his wife. They had burned up the sheets before that last, sad morning. Caroline couldn't even remember the details of it, except she had finally told him the truth. Whatever words she had used, they had been too effective. He had stayed away, and now, even though he was back, treated her as if she were a distant relative. He hadn't made the least effort to make her change her mind about her ill-conceived abstinence policy. How foolish she'd been to set such impossible ground rules before he moved in. Impossible for her, at any rate. Edward seemed to be having no difficulty keeping to himself.

He was divorcing her and probably welcomed the space between her bed and his, miles and miles across the flowered carpet. He was only there out of some misplaced chivalry because she was still technically his chattel.

That would change soon. Even if Edward said Andrew was no longer involved, he'd cook up something with that stuffed shirt Maclean. Caroline would be happy to help. Maybe she could haul the handsome-even-if-his-nose-was-slightly-off-center Cameron into her bed to speed the process along.

Her lips quirked. Now, *that* would be a scandal. And probably impractical. Cameron didn't seem to have one iota of sin in him, poor devil. The thought of seducing the man, despite the mighty challenge, really had no appeal. There was only one man Caroline wanted to seduce, but she had lost her touch.

Chapter 14

The broken shutter banged against the hinges in the maelstrom. The forces of nature were upon them, and nothing was safe from being swept away.

—*The Villa of Deceit*

Cameron was waiting with a candle when Edward finally came home. The session in Parliament had gone late, then he'd met Mulgrew in a dingy public house where he was not apt to be recognized. Mulgrew had shaken the guest list out of the Everdeens at some considerable expense to Edward and made the necessary inquiries. The most likely culprits— Pope and Douglass, who were present at the party—had been interviewed and intimidated by Mulgrew and several of his larger agents. As Mulgrew was plenty large himself, Edward was inclined to believe the threat to Caroline was now moot. To make sure, he would deliver his own threat in person tomorrow. If the so-called gentlemen worried for their social standing, a Christie had the power to ruin them with a few well-chosen words far more effectively than all the books Caroline could write put together.

He should feel vindication. He should be at peace. But there was no longer any reason to stay on Jane Street, and that made him rather cross.

Cameron helped him shrug out of his jacket in the shadowy hallway. "Good evening, Lord Christie. Lady Christie is already to bed."

"I should hope so. It's very late."

"May I get you anything before you turn in?"

"No, Cameron. I've already eaten, and drunk more than my fair share of ale." Mulgrew had insisted on toasting to their success and had stood a few rounds. Edward expected it would all be covered by the exorbitant bill that would arrive tomorrow morning. "How did Lady Christie pass her day?"

"She stayed in her bedroom in her flowery robe for the most part, muttering over one of her notebooks." Cameron caught Edward's cool look and hurried on. "I couldn't help but see what she wore, sir. She left the door wide open. This afternoon she had a visitor."

Edward's heart quickened. "Oh? Who?"

"A Mrs. Bannister. Don't you worry. I made sure she was who she said she was. It seems the lady used to be a neighbor. They spent a few minutes in the parlor, then she went away."

Edward watched as Cameron struggled mightily to suppress a yawn. His sleeping conditions were even worse than Edward's, sharing the box room with the pot boy up at the top of the house. It was a wonder they all didn't roast alive up there in the sweltering summer heat. "Thank you. I'm sure you'll be glad to know things will be back to normal tomorrow. I met with Mr. Mulgrew this evening. He's satisfied no harm will come to Lady Christie."

"Does that mean we'll be going home, my lord?"

Edward began to unwind his neckcloth. "I believe it does. Pack up my things tomorrow morning if you would and arrange to get them to Christie House. I have several appointments, but should be back in time for dinner."

Edward sat on a hall chair as Cameron jacked off his boots, as they had done every night Edward returned so late. There was no point in disturbing Caroline at the late hour. Stocking feet would be quieter. The longer he had stayed with her, the easier it was to absent himself in the evenings. It meant he missed Mrs. Hazlett's cooking. Missed seeing Caroline across the table. But when he left, he would not miss the rickety camp bed or the fact that Caroline was sleeping half a world away, forbidden to him.

He leaned back in the chair, a depressing weariness overtaking him. Tomorrow night he would undress in his own luxurious suite instead of a foyer, every amenity at his fingertips. He would not be sneaking upstairs like a thief clutching at his rumpled clothing. He'd have his soft feather bed and his spectacles and a good book, a snifter of brandy at his bedside. Somehow the thought did not cheer him as much as it should.

What if he temporarily forgot Caroline's edict and crawled into her bed tonight? One last fling before he formalized their deed of separation. A divorce was not possible—his integrity would not allow it—but a legal separation agreement was long past due. Will had hounded him about the too-casual way he had set up Caroline on Jane Street for five years. With his marriage a closed book, albeit one with a dog-eared page near the beginning, Edward might find a mistress and get on with the business of being a healthy, normal man.

Trouble was, he thought ruefully as he mounted the stairs behind Cameron's flickering candle, he didn't want just any mistress. He wanted Caroline. Still, after everything.

Cameron left him standing in the pitch darkness of the hallway. Edward disrobed before the door, folding the rest of his garments neatly for Cameron to deal with in the morning. He turned the handle. The room was no longer bathed in moonlight but dark as sin. Despite his caution, he banged a knee on the camp bed, which was slanted at an odd angle. One of Caroline's tricks to set him off balance, like those indecent nightgowns and red dresses and rich foods. She needn't bother. He was already tilted at a crazed angle, about to fall face-first onto his sword.

He crossed the carpet in silence, pulled by her Siren-like call to his blood like Odysseus. Reaching his hand out in the dark, his palm hit one carved bedpost. Not far then. Would she simply roll over in sleep or wake and argue? Would she welcome him in warm half consciousness? Stifling a curse, he stumbled on the covers that had migrated to the floor and almost fell on top of her. He sat down gingerly, then reached for her.

Nothing. His hand felt air. Pillows. No wife whatsoever.

"Caro?"

No response. Perhaps she was in the little dressing room taking care of her needs. Stretching his weary body on the bed, he willed himself to relax. When she returned, she'd either throw him out, ignore him, or melt. He was hoping for the latter.

He waited. The room was drenched in silence, no movement from next door. Edward sat up. "Caroline?" he said, his voice louder. Bumbling about in the dark, he wrenched open the door to the dressing room.

"Caroline!" A lingering scent of jasmine was all that remained. Feeling his heart kick up in panic, he managed to light an oil lamp on the bedside table. He saw at once the door to the little balcony was wide open, the curtains still in the breezeless summer night.

He vaulted across the room and skidded to a stop. There on the iron railing was a knotted, twisted sheet leading to the garden below, unmistakable evidence that someone had climbed in. *My God.* Had they taken her while he was politely drinking inferior ale with Mulgrew? Where the hell was Cameron during her abduction? How long had she been gone?

"Caroline!" His voice was hoarse, desperate. He would kill whoever took her with his bare hands, then kill him again.

The sounds below were faint, but they intruded into his murderous rage. "At last! Good evening, Edward."

"Caro! Where the devil are you?" It was too dark to see a bloody thing, but he thought he saw a wisp of white on the garden bench.

"I couldn't sleep," she said with a sigh, so quietly he almost fell off the balcony bending to hear her. "When I can't, I often come down into the garden. It's so peaceful. But I couldn't get past Cameron on the stairs. He hasn't let me outside in days."

"So you climbed down on a rope of sheets?" he asked, incredulous. "Are you mad? You could have broken your neck!"

"Nonsense. It's only two stories. I used to do it all the time at home. Of course, then I had Nicky's breeches on. Yours were way too long. I did try them on. But I couldn't get back in. The last sheet gave way when I was coming down. My knots are not what they once were." There was a hint of wistfulness in her voice.

Edward gritted his teeth. Of course Caroline Parker would be an expert in breeches and breaking the rules. How long had she been out there anyway? Anything might have happened to her, sitting beneath the faint stars. "And you couldn't come in by way of the back or kitchen doors?"

He imagined he saw her shoulders shrug. "They were locked. If I'd had a hairpin, I might have picked them. I used to be good at that, too. Everyone had gone to bed. Except Cameron. I could see him through the glass pacing up and down the hall, regular as clockwork. I didn't have the nerve to ask for his help, you see. He was quite explicit in his instructions. *Your* instructions. He would have felt an utter failure to find I'd escaped, and despite the fact he's been *most* annoying, I didn't want to upset him. You're very late, Edward."

To his everlasting regret. He felt as though he'd been robbed of ten years of his life in the past ten minutes. "Hang on. Don't move. Not one inch."

He tripped over the bedclothes again and went into the hallway, where he stepped into his pants in record time. He didn't bother with anything else. Racing down the stairs, he sprinted through the hallway to the back garden door. After struggling with a hellish combination of locks in the pitch black hallway, installed recently to keep Caroline safe and *completely* unpickable, he pulled open the door and ran smack into Caroline on the grass path.

They fell in a tangle of limbs and white nightgown. Edward raised himself to look down upon the shadowed face of his wife. It was not too dark to see her smile. He caught his breath. He had not hurt her. "You moved, didn't you? I told you to stay on the damned bench."

"I've been sitting there for hours. I didn't expect you to be quite so energetic leaving the house. You shot out like a ball from a cannon—there wasn't time to move away."

"I was worried, you little fool. When I couldn't find you—"

She shifted under him, the silk of her gown slicing his bare chest. The night was hot, but Edward felt goosebumps rise up the back of his neck. The angry words died in his throat.

"I was just fine. I got so bored, I tried to weed. I probably pulled up half my plants in the dark. Don't you think we'd better get up?"

Her breath tickled against his throat, her body soft beneath him. He could smell earth. The mélange of flowers. Caroline. Of course he should rise and help her into the house. Brush off the blades of grass and straighten the strap of her nightrail, which had slipped from her shoulder. A pale shoulder, vulnerable. Exposed. His lips covered a few inches of it, but they weren't enough.

Soon his hands joined the fray, long fingers skimming her alabaster perfection, freeing her breasts from the cloth that shred like a spider's web. Her nipples pearled in the starlight under his hungry touch. Edward kissed away her one obligatory protest because he sensed—*knew*—she was every bit as engaged as he in their mutual surrender. Her body didn't lie. She relaxed beneath him and her womanly moisture soon coated his fingers as he sought to pleasure her. Tomorrow—today—would arrive soon enough. Within the halls and walls of Jane Street, they would take leave of each other for a final time. In Caroline's pocket garden, there were no restraints. No barriers. She was as open to him as one of her lush scarlet and white-streaked roses, fragrant, complicated, exquisite. He turned long enough so she could release his member from its half-buttoned state. There was no time to remove his pants or tear away her nightrail completely—the abrasion of the textures on their skin only heightened their sensitivity to each other. She guided him home, seemingly as frantic as he to complete their coupling. His head flew backward in triumph as he seated himself inside her, the stars sliding above. He closed his eyes and permitted himself to feel . . . the incendiary velvet around his cock . . . the smooth skin and crumpled silk beneath him . . . the damp grass and tangle of russet hair between his fingers. They rocked together in almost agonizing slowness, savoring each thrust. For they each knew this was the end of it. The mutual torment had to stop. Caro was safe and he was—

He was a Christie.

He was an ass.

Those things were not compatible. Dealing with Caroline not only slid the stars from the sky but made him lose control. Caro couldn't change, nor could he. It was time—

She pulled him down to her mouth, sealing him firmly in her orbit, her kiss more than a rough brush of lips or clash of tongues. He tasted her tears and his own, bitter and sweet. How could he spill inside her, as he was going to do any second, then rise and leave? It was impossible.

But it was impossible to stay. Wasn't it? They were like chalk and cheese. He craved order and she blossomed in chaos. Their marriage had been the most miserable year of his life, worse than when Alice died. Caroline had lost her luster, too, becoming dimmer by the day until she had been tempted by Andrew Rossiter. He had asked too much of her—wanting her to be somehow *less*. Less Carolinian, more Christie. She seemed happy with her racy books and her racier friends. He'd kept her at bay for five years, save for the annual hellish birthday night. What on earth had possessed him to make her his mistress?

He had been angry. He had been high-handed. In his effort to put Caroline in her place he instead found his, gloved inside her and completely subject to the endless tremors surrounding him. It was no time to think, to be reasonable. With a howl he lost himself in temptation, no deliverance in sight.

When it was over, they lay side by side on the clipped grass. Caroline had pulled her nightgown down. Edward had pulled his pants up. The hazy stars winked down at them as they regulated their breathing and heartbeats.

"I met with Mulgrew tonight." Edward's words seemed foreign to him, as though the interlude with Caroline had robbed him of language.

"Oh?"

He heard the resignation. She expected her congé, and he would give it to her. Had to, for their own sanity. "He told me he had the matter of your safety at hand. He's spoken to Pope and Douglass. They denied everything, of course, as one would expect. But Mulgrew is satisfied there is no longer any danger."

"There's always danger. A meteor could fall and strike us both dead."

Edward blinked up at the stars. They seemed safely far away. "Or perhaps we could be devoured by wolves. Drowned in a trunk in the Thames. Flung down a cliff. Shot in a most uncomfortable place. Buried under the rubble in a disused mine. Have I forgotten anything else?"

He heard the smile in her voice. "Several. Never say you've been reading my books."

"Of course not. Beth lives to tease me about my fictional demise."

"I believe you were gored by a mad bull once."

"Ouch. Why can't you just slip poison in my port?"

"Done it. *The Dark Duke's Dilemma.* One of my earlier efforts. It didn't sell well. I've become progressively more bloodthirsty."

Edward sought her hand and brought it to his lips. "Perhaps you'll have a care from now on. While you may welcome my death, I should hate to have anything happen to you. Pope and Douglass may be warned off for now, but be careful."

"I assume you're leaving tomorrow?"

He dropped her hand gently back to earth. "Yes, Caro, it's for the best."

"I quite agree. Having you underfoot has been a trial." She sat up abruptly, shaking her long red hair free from grass clippings. Before he could stop her, she swayed up and marched off to the back door. It would be the camp bed for him again for sure.

"Hell and damnation!"

"What's wrong, Caro?"

"The blasted door is shut and I cannot get it open. Again. Did you not leave it unlocked?"

He hadn't a clue. It had been such a struggle to open the series of locks, his hands shaking all the while. He hadn't thought about anything more than fetching Caroline from the garden and giving her the lecture of her life. Instead he had fallen on her like a starved beast—a wolf—devouring *her*. But she was completely undead, a living flame of life who made his dull existence even more unbearable.

"Here, let me try." He stood, fastening his trousers, walking barefoot across the little lawn. The knob wouldn't budge.

"I'm sure we can rouse the servants."

Caroline tossed her head. "No we can't. Cameron's room is in the front. Both the Hazletts sleep like the dead and snore to prove it. I told Cameron to do as Ben and Lizzie do—stuff cotton in his ears at night, else he'd never get any sleep. What are we going to do?"

Edward thought a minute. "What about the garden doors?"

Caroline folded her arms across her chest in a vain attempt to press her torn nightgown together. "Cameron nailed them shut just this afternoon. I heard him before Deborah Bannister came. He doesn't trust me."

"As well he shouldn't. If you hadn't done this mad thing, we'd be inside, sound asleep in our beds ourselves. You'd be snoring to rival Hazlett."

"I don't snore!"

"I'm afraid you do. Like one of the piglets at Christie Park's home farm. I've had to listen to you all week."

"I never asked you to listen! I don't know why you had to sleep in my room anyway. You never did when we were married."

"Of course I didn't. A gentleman never sleeps in the same chamber as his wife. It isn't done."

Caroline shoved him into some shrubbery. "Isn't done? Is that a Christie tradition? I know many couples who share the same bedchamber."

So did Edward, but he was not about to agree with her. He liked his privacy. Needed it. Who wanted to tussle with Caroline all night long as she stole the covers and laughed in her sleep? Rubbed up against him like her damn cat, her cold feet on his calves? It was bad enough having to take breakfast with her in the morning, when she would prattle on about her plans for the day, never giving him a moment's peace as he sipped his coffee, peppering him with questions he had no intention of answering. Treating the staff like long-lost friends, and the children as equals. Caroline knew no barriers, had no filters, was like a child herself. A spoilt one. He brushed the pollen from his shoulder. "There's no need to manhandle me."

She smacked his chest again. "There is every need," she whispered furiously. "Thanks to you we'll be trapped out here all night."

"Wait just a minute! Whose bright idea was it to climb out a window?"

"I didn't plan for the sheet to come undone. I would have been back in bed by the time you came home and you never would have known the difference." She stomped away to sit back on the bench.

He followed. "You little fool. What if there had been intruders in the garden?"

"The garden doors are nailed shut. I just told you. I was perfectly safe."

"A determined man could scale the wall, Caroline." As soon as the words left his mouth, he knew he'd have cause to regret them.

Her smile was quite feral. "Fine. Prove to me how determined you are."

Edward straightened. "I have no need to prove anything to you. I've always kept my word. Done the right thing."

"Oh? Coming to my bed after all these years was *right*?

When you plan to get rid of me anyway? You are nothing but the basest villain, Edward. Being a wolfpack's dinner is too good for you!"

"So now you want me to plunge to my death over a Mayfair garden wall."

"I don't want you dead, Edward, although who could even tell you're alive? I just want you gone."

"Your wish is my command," he ground out. He'd show the little baggage. He headed for the spike-topped brick wall.

"Not that one. There's no one home, remember? Bayard has bunked it. Serena on the other side might still be awake. Her gentleman keeps very odd hours. She has extra keys to my front door."

"Even the new locks?" he thundered.

"She'd never hand them out to anyone but me or my staff. I trust her. We look out for each other on Jane Street."

Good Lord. He looked down at his bare chest and bare feet. Would the Janes look after *him*? If word got out, he'd be a laughingstock. It had only been because of his Christie-ness he was able to survive the scandalous denouement of his marriage. He had behaved with impeccable decorum, as if he'd not spent a year fighting like cats and dogs with his wife. No one save Will ever brought up the fact that he'd tucked Caroline away somewhere. Very few knew that the somewhere was Jane Street. How Neddie had figured it out was a mystery. If only his son had kept away, he'd not be standing there half naked.

"Very well." He tripped across a flower bed. Edward was tall, but the wall was taller. "I think if we can drag the bench over, I can boost myself up."

Caroline was not much help. Her end of the iron bench kept slanting down until she complained she'd bruised her toes and had to sit down for a while. The dark gray sky had brightened sufficiently for him to watch as she rubbed her plump white feet. She was barefoot, too. She seemed unaware that her right breast was completely unrestrained by the torn negligee.

"Maybe we should just wait until dawn. It won't be that much longer."

"Coward."

Edward bit back his retort. She was right. He was one. He couldn't cut Caroline out of his life, yet couldn't live with her. What was the expression? You can't have your cake and eat it, too. With a mere legal separation, he'd never be free of her, never be able to find a peaceful, normal woman to marry and help guide Allie to womanhood.

"Stand up. I'll get it the rest of the way by myself." With a grunt, he pushed the bench through some flowers, crushing the petals and causing their aroma to waft up in the night air. But nothing smelled as perfect as Caroline.

"You're ruining my garden."

"You're ruining my life!" Edward snapped.

"Good, because you've ruined mine, you odious, impossible, horrible"—she paused—"man!"

"Is that the best you can do? Why not blackguard or scoundrel? Rogue or miscreant?"

"It doesn't matter what you men call yourselves—you are fiends, every one of you."

Edward hopped up on the bench, running his fingers on the jagged iron spikes. He pictured one puncturing his lung, the life draining out of him as Caroline stood below, tapping a bruised foot impatiently. "I'm not going to do this, Caro. We're just going to have to wait for Mrs. Hazlett to light the stove in a few hours. She can let us in the kitchen door."

"I'll climb over then."

"You certainly will not. Even if I could toss you over, you'd probably land and break your neck. This place is like a fortress. It's a wonder there are not alligators in a moat."

"I told you I was safe! But, no—you had to exert your Christie control and make my life a living hell." She sunk down among the ruined flowers. "I rue the day my cousins ever took me to town. I would have been better off acting as an unpaid nursemaid for their brats than marrying you."

"My understanding was that your cousin James had other plans for you."

She looked up at him, her face stark. "Being his whore would have been preferable to being yours."

Edward felt something unravel within. "Take that back."

"Why should I? I'm nothing to you. Oh, you've strutted about all week acting Sir Galahad. It suits you to see yourself as a hero. But you're cold, Edward. So cold you make my blood freeze. I don't know how I could ever have thought I lov—" Her words stopped.

And his heart stopped, too, then started up with dizzying speed. He needed to get down off the bench before he fell but couldn't seem to move his feet. "What did you say?"

She pulled up her bodice. "Nothing of any consequence."

He stood rooted to the iron bench, its fancy curlicues cutting into his soles. Something swooped through the air—a bat, most likely. The silence in the garden made its own kind of noise, but he knew he'd have to interrupt soon—if he could find any words to say.

He clambered down from the bench and sat beside her. "If I'm so cold, why do you love me, Caroline?" he asked quietly.

"I don't know!" she cried. "It's terribly inconvenient. I shall stop at once."

He wanted to tell her he loved her too, but the words wouldn't come. They had never tumbled out with ease. He hadn't said them in years to anyone. But even unspoken, they were true, and she was right. It was terribly inconvenient, but he didn't think he could stop loving her. Ever.

So this was love. It was nothing like the ballads and sonnets and psalms, or the comforting closeness he'd shared with Alice. It was sharp, as sharp as the iron spikes on the wall, as ruining as the crushed flowers beneath his arse. Caroline made his blood boil and his mind turn to mush. It was more than inconvenient—it was inconceivable that Edward Allerton Christie could love Caroline Louise Parker.

But he supposed he did. How else could he explain the past weeks of insanity? It was more than the craving of her warm body atop and beneath him, more than his appreciation of her still-dazzling beauty. More than his desire for dominance.

"Holy God," he whispered.

"It's too late to pray, Edward. It's too late, period. You are right. We are completely incompatible. I want you to divorce me." She wrapped her arms around her knees and sniffed.

"I cannot, Caro. I decided that weeks ago. I don't even believe I can go through with a legal separation."

"Edward, what are you saying?"

"I don't know. I can't think. I never can when you're near."

"Well, someone has to! You can't keep reeling me in like a fish, then tossing me back. It's unconscionable."

"I'm sorry, Caro. I'm a cur."

She nodded. "Yes, you are. A dirty dog. With bloodthirsty fleas and other assorted vermin." She seemed satisfied with the analogy. He put his arm around her and she didn't resist, putting her head on his bare shoulder. The warmth of her russet hair pricked his skin and stirred his cock.

"What are we to do?" For once in his life, his Christie confidence had completely deserted him.

"I'm sure I don't know. Wait for Mrs. Hazlett to wake up."

"Not about *now*. About our future."

"We haven't got one, Edward. You of all people should know that."

"I thought I did, but I'm not so sure. What if we try again?" He must be mad to suggest such a thing, but the words had tumbled out without a moment of Christie forethought.

Caroline made a choking sound somewhere between a laugh and a sob. "I'm too old to change, Edward. And I don't want to. I'm not cut out to be a Christie, all proper and dull."

He put a hand to his heart. It *was* there, beating erratically, breaking just a little. "A direct hit."

"You know I'm right. You'd be ready to throttle me within twenty-four hours. Think of the children. Allie. It wouldn't do to upset her routine with me waltzing back into her life only to have it all fall apart again."

Edward brushed a tear from her cheek. "No. I suppose not."

"So it's settled then."

"If you say so." His throat constricted. Well, she had wanted him to *feel*, and now he did. It was appalling for a man his age to want to cry.

"It's for the best." She slipped out of his hold. "I've been thinking I'd like to make a fresh start. Go somewhere where no one knows me. A little cottage in the country, where I can write. Maybe I'll even stop penning such naughty books and try something edifying for a change."

"You'll stop killing me off?"

"There's no need to. I'm not angry anymore. With you *or* myself. We can't help being who we are, can we?"

For the first time in his life, Edward wished his last name was different. Wished *he* was different. Wished most of all that he didn't love Caroline when the discovering of it came too late.

"I'll look for a suitable property for you."

"Thank you, Edward. I have some money of my own, you know."

"Nonsense. You are still my wife, and I'm responsible for you." He would place her far out of reach, away from temptation, even if it killed him as thoroughly as Caroline's villains.

Unless . . .

He *was* a Christie. Christies might be proper and dull, but they did not give up. They knew their duty. They were dogged in the fulfilling of it.

He'd made his vows six years ago and meant them. He wanted Caro even more now, though it made no sense. They would probably wish each other to the devil within the first hour of mending their marriage.

But he had to try. How to convince her? Edward would approach the difficulties with his usual logic once he was alone and free of the confusion he always felt in Caro's presence. He needed to think, but first he needed to kiss her. She might think it was a good-bye kiss, but he knew better. Christies always did.

Chapter 15

A new life. It was everything she desired yet didn't dare
to dream of or deserve.

—Flowers for Flora

Despite the late hours the residents of Jane Street kept,
morning rose all around them. Windows opened, doors
shut, servants stepped into kitchens, and so did Mrs. Hazlett.
Caroline had been stationed on the steps to the kitchen door
for some time while Edward appeared to be lost in thought
on the hard bench, his eyes closed. They'd not said much to
each other once they discussed Caroline's real estate needs,
which were not particularly demanding. She would take
Lizzie with her if she'd go, but Caroline assumed Garrett
Marburn would have something to say about that. It had
surprised her when Edward said he'd sell the Jane Street
property. So there was to be no mistress in his future, as there
was to be no master in hers.

She rapped on the glass, causing Mrs. Hazlett to jump
quite spryly for a woman her age.

"Whatever are you doing out here, Lady Christie? Lord
Christie will have our hides!"

Caroline inclined her head toward the back of the garden,
then turned to the subject of Mrs. Hazlett's startled look. Edward wasn't thinking after all—he was asleep sitting up, his
long limbs loose and relaxed. "I had a bit of a misadventure
last night, but don't worry. All is well."

Mrs. Hazlett stared at the obvious disarray of Caroline's
nightgown. "I suppose your clothing tore itself."

"It had a little help." She would never make love to Edward again. The last time under the stars was a worthy memory, however. There would be empty years ahead to think on it. Too many, if Caroline lived as long as Mr. and Mrs. Hazlett. Edward had offered to send them from London with her, but a butler and a housekeeper would be superfluous for the kind of simple life she envisioned. Caroline could cook and clean for herself. But she would take Ben. Growing up in the country would be good for him, and her lessons with him would be good for them both, as long as Ben did not catch her out on her spelling.

"Come in, come in. Good thing it's so warm or you'd catch your death. The night air is dangerous."

Dangerous to Caroline's heart, at least.

She couldn't credit that Edward said he wanted to reconcile. If there had been a moon, she'd attribute the whole incident to moon madness. Thank goodness she had the presence of mind to remind him how it really was between them. It had been the hardest thing she'd ever done.

"I'm going upstairs, Mrs. Hazlett. Please tell Lizzie not to bother bringing breakfast. I'm exhausted. And Cameron should wake Lord Christie soon. I'm sure he has a full calendar." She paused on the stairs. "They will be leaving today. For good."

Mrs. Hazlett glanced up sharply. "Then you're safe?"

"Safe as a mouse in cheese."

"I thought—" Mrs. Hazlett tugged at her apron nervously. "I wondered if he might not take you back."

"Oh, no, Mrs. Hazlett. Whyever would he do that?"

"I see the way he looks at you, my lady. Like a hungry man and you're a meat pie."

Caroline laughed. "Well, I've been called many things, but never that."

"You know what I mean. I've not much way with words like you, an authoress. But it's my opinion, and Mr. Hazlett's too, that Lord Christie has warm feelings for you."

"We are to get a legal separation at long last, and I am

moving away from the city. Whatever he feels at the moment, he'll come to his senses. I don't want you to worry about your positions. Lord Christie will find you places, or you may retire with a generous pension. You've been more than kind to me."

Mrs. Hazlett pinked. "It's been easy doing for you, my lady. A true pleasure."

Caroline swallowed the lump in her throat. But she was going to put the past behind her, once and for all.

She fell asleep as soon as her head hit the pillow, oblivious to the tiptoeing removal of Edward's things from her room, unconscious of his absence in her life. If she felt the brush of his lips on hers as he bade her good-bye, it might have been a dream.

When she awoke in the early afternoon, it was to the sound of Cameron's soft cursing below, as he plied the long nails out of the garden doors. The balcony door stood open to the bright summer sun, and someone had untied the sheets from the railing. Caroline stretched and peered down as Cameron removed the final nail and put it in his pocket. As he turned toward the house, she gave a little wave. He inclined his head but kept walking. No doubt his pride was wounded after she outsmarted him, thinking he'd been so thorough. But soon there was to be no more visiting between the garden gates anyway. Caroline would have her cottage in the country. Her cat. Good heavens. She was taking a page from Charlotte Fallon's book.

Caroline was starving. And rather dirty. The soles of her feet were black from pacing in the garden, and her nightgown was a total loss. She wouldn't need anything so provocative again, not where she was going and who she would try to be. Before she had a chance to ring for a bath or breakfast—or would it be luncheon?—Lizzie knocked and popped into the room.

"Mr. Cameron said you were up. My heavens, you're a mess."

"Good morning to you, too."

"It's afternoon—nearly one o'clock, Lady Christie. Mrs. Hazlett said you had a hard night."

"It was not my finest hour." Save for tangling with Edward and tingling all over on the grass.

"Lord Christie was almost ready to sack Cameron this morning, but I told him no one can stop you when you really want to do something."

Caroline sat as Lizzie took a brush to her hair. "He's gone?"

"Yes. Quite early. Cameron boxed up everything and is on his way now, too. So we're back to normal," Lizzie said brightly, avoiding Caroline's eyes in the mirror. "Do you want to wash before lunch, or after?"

"A bath first, I think. Ouch."

"Sorry, but your hair's in knots. And there's grass enough caught in it to make a bird's nest."

One spring when she and Nicky were children, birds made a nest under the eaves of Parker Hall. She and her brother had watched through the grimy attic window as the couple settled in, hatched their babies, fed them. Then one morning, the nest was empty. Nicky had lectured her on the cycle of life, but Caroline had been inconsolable. She returned to the attic again and again until the snow fell, expecting to find the family snuggled together, back from their bird adventure.

She had missed country life whilst living in London. Exploring the bountiful grounds at Christie Park in Kent had been the one good thing about her marriage, besides the nights with Edward. Her Jane Street gilded cage was soon to be abandoned, but she could feel the loneliness already.

Caroline scooted over on the dressing table bench. "Lizzie, sit for a minute. I have a proposition for you, but I expect you to say no. I'm counting on it, for your sake."

Lizzie lifted a fair eyebrow but did as she was asked.

"Edward is going to buy me a house in the country. Something very small and out-of-the-way. I really will not require the services of a lady's maid, but I could do with a friend.

However, I believe my friend is about to become betrothed to another friend of mine. Am I correct?"

"He hasn't asked me yet. But I think he will." Lizzie twisted her fingers. "He hasn't seen my back, Caroline. I haven't let him do anything more than kiss me—and a few touches." She seemed embarrassed by the admission, showing a charming uncertainty for a young woman who had first sold her body at the age of fourteen. Lizzie walked to the window and stepped onto the little terrace. Caroline followed and laid a hand on her shoulder.

"Trust me. It will not matter to him. He will only love you more for your suffering."

"I don't want to be pitied!"

Caroline smiled. "I doubt what Garrett Marburn feels for you is pity, Lizzie. You're a beautiful woman. Smart."

"I was a whore," Lizzie whispered. Her eyes were bright with tears.

"And now you're not. We all make mistakes. It's important we don't let the mistakes make us." Caroline knew she should take her own advice. Her youthful folly with Andrew and her unhappy marriage did not need to chart her course for the rest of her life. "I'm going to start fresh, and you will, too. If you want, I'll speak to that slowtop. Why he hasn't offered for you yet is an absolute disgrace. Men are idiots."

"No, don't. I'll bring him 'round—when it's time. But what about you? Mrs. Hazlett says Lord Christie is going through with a legal separation."

"Yes. It's time now, don't you think? And I won't be on Jane Street at his mercy once a year. It's done. If I give him reason, perhaps eventually we will divorce."

Lizzie looked at her. "That means you'll have to have an affair. A real one this time."

"Would that be so impossible to imagine? I haven't lost all my looks, have I?" Caroline fluffed up her hair. Lizzie brushed it back down automatically.

"Of course you haven't. I just don't—never mind. It's not my place."

"Lizzie, you can be frank. We're more than just mistress and servant."

"I know, Caroline. I owe you everything."

"Let's not get carried away."

"I think you and Lord Christie belong together, whatever your differences."

Caroline shook her head. "I admit there's something between us, but not enough to build a marriage on. One must get out of bed eventually," she said wryly.

"What if you sat down with him and hashed everything out? Ask him what he wants of you?"

"One doesn't ask a Christie questions. One only gives the proper answers."

"I think it's worth a try."

"I appreciate your advice, Lizzie, but it's far too late. No, my plan is best. I'll leave here and start over. Stop writing. Be respectable. But don't tell Garrett yet. I expect he'll have a fit."

"He'll miss you."

"He'll miss the income I generate." Caroline laughed. "But the books haven't come easily to me lately. Better to stop while I'm ahead. I wouldn't want to repeat myself and kill off Edward the same way twice."

Caroline looked around the narrow hallway. It was far too crowded, but now that the hall table had been removed, there was room for the Hazletts, Lizzie and Marburn, and young Ben. Yesterday the removal men had packed up some of her things to carry into the wilds of Dorset. The rest she had bequeathed to the friends before her, the Janes, or the Jane Street house itself. The next courtesan would need a bed and a few sofas to recline on. A pity Caroline had wasted so much of her money on redecoration, but it was not the first mistake she had made.

She hadn't even seen the cottage she was to live in, hadn't even seen the man who had purchased it for her since the ill-fated night in her garden. It had taken a few weeks for Edward to make the arrangements. Her new life had been arranged solely by letter, which had suited her perfectly. She did not need to crick her neck gazing up at Edward's emerald eyes and listen to his dark velvet voice.

Gracious. She was thinking like a writer—jewel-toned eyes were *such* a cliché—which she was determined not to be ever again. She had penned her very last *Courtesan Court* book in a frenzy of packing. She hoped her public wouldn't be too disappointed. Her heroine, Cassandra, a notorious opera star, had decided to forego her lover Roderigo for a life in the country. She would sing in the local church choir only and give free music lessons to poor children. The ending was so abrupt Garrett had said she'd opened herself up for a sequel, but Caroline thought not.

She wasn't quite sure what *she* wanted to do next. She couldn't carry a tune herself. But Edward had written there was a large garden, so she could prune and plant and weed until she decided.

"Harold is safe in the carriage?"

"I put him in there myself. He wasn't happy to be stuck in that cage." Lizzie's chin quivered. "You'll come back for the wedding if we marry?"

"We'll marry, all right," Garrett growled. He had proposed, but Lizzie was yet to be fully convinced she was worthy of him. She was being particularly missish about becoming Mrs. Marburn. Caroline had already advised Garrett to kidnap her just like Lord Farringdon did to Felicia in *Lord Farringdon's Fickle Fiancée* and carry her off to Scotland, bound and gagged if necessary. Felicia had been very good with her fists, and not bright enough until the last chapter to realize that Lord Farrington was her one true love.

"Of course. You know Garrett's right. You won't get a better offer." Caroline suspected the next time she heard from them, the deed would be done and there would be no need for her to stand as matron of honor.

"Damn right."

"And *you*, Garrett Marburn, won't get a better wife. Be good to each other." She embraced them both.

"We shall miss you, Lady Christie." Mrs. Hazlett wiped a tear with the corner of her apron. Mr. Hazlett's eyes were suspiciously damp as well.

"I hope you both enjoy your retirement. I'll never forget how kind you were to me these last five years."

Ben shuffled behind the little crowd and stepped forward. "I thank you fer invitin' me, but Lunnon's me home. I don't hold with the country and cows."

Caroline chuckled. "I haven't any cows yet as far as I know, Ben, just my cat. But you behave for the Hazletts. They have need of a big, strong boy like you. And don't neglect your studies."

Ben rolled his eyes but said nothing else. Ben was perhaps not Caroline's most successful project, but he was the Hazletts' problem now.

Mrs. Hazlett handed her a hamper that had been at her feet. "Don't forget to eat your lunch and drink every drop of wine I packed for you. I know you don't hold much with spirits, but it will help to settle you bouncing around on the road. You don't want to be stopping at dirty posting houses for bad food. There's a flask of tea, too. Drink it all. It's just the way you like it—plenty of sugar."

It was the third or fourth time Caroline had been admonished to eat and drink the contents of the wicker basket. As she had no interest in sitting all by herself in some inferior inn, she had no objection. It was quite scandalous that she was traveling alone, but Edward's plans for a chaperone for her had fallen apart at the last minute. The maid he had hired became ill and there wasn't time to find anyone else. Caroline didn't mind. She had done for herself for years as Caroline Parker and expected she could do so as Caroline Christie.

It would take several days to deliver her to her new home. Just as she had requested, a hired coach was parked at her steps. Caroline didn't want to attract unwelcome attention with Edward's handsome crested carriage. It was past time to leave.

After another round of hugs and a bold kiss on her lips from Ben, Hazlett handed her into the carriage where Harold yowled a welcome. "Remember this, my lady. We have your best interests at heart. May you find all the happiness you deserve."

Touched, Caroline leaned down to give the old man a kiss on his cheek. She hoped the last two kisses of her life were not to be to a scruffy boy and an elderly butler. "Thank you, Hazlett. They don't make butlers like you anymore."

"I should say they don't. Now, you be careful. And keep in mind not everything is as it seems."

"Excellent advice. Good-bye! I'll write as soon as I am settled." She waved as gaily as she could manage, then settled back into the squabs of the coach.

"Hey there!"

Caroline looked out the window. All the current Janes, even the thieving Lucy Dellamar, had come out at the early hour, some wearing more clothes than others. They clustered around the sentry post at the iron Jane Street gate and tossed flower petals in her direction.

"Good luck! Be good, but not too good!" they cried in unison.

Caroline laughed. Then she cried a bit along with Harold as the carriage wound its way around the early morning traffic, missing her unlikely friends already. No doubt it was just nerves. She hadn't slept well and spent much of the night staring up at the big mirror over her bed. Without most of the furniture, the bedroom had seemed a bit spooky, so she'd let a lamp burn. Silly of her.

But she was leaving the bed behind, with its wicked naked caryatids. Too much had transpired in that bed to bring her any luck. Edward had written the cottage was partly furnished. She hoped so. She wasn't taking all that much with her.

Caroline loved to decorate. She was good at it. She'd transformed her family home on a shoestring once Nicky and Andrew had turned it into a hotel. But Edward hadn't let her change a thing at Christie Park or his house in town, one of the things that had stymied her so much during the year of her marriage. She was looking forward to assessing her new abode and improving it. There was plenty of money now. Edward's allowance was generous, and she still had her savings from the book sales.

Harold had stopped glaring at her and had curled up in a corner of his cage to sleep. Smart cat. But she wanted to keep her wits about her on the road. One never knew what might happen, although the coachman and postboy looked to be sturdy and dependable Yawning, she lifted the basket lid and took out the flask of tea. She unscrewed the top and drank directly from the container. With the rocking of the carriage, she didn't dare try to pour the liquid in the pretty china cup Mrs. Hazlett had packed. She wouldn't want to spill any on her new cherry-red travelling costume—which Edward would never see.

The tea tasted especially delicious, perhaps because she drank it straight from the flask. Caroline had always liked to break the rules. In fact, it was so good, she drank it all before they hit the London line.

Chapter 16

The fearsome footsteps came inexorably closer. Bound and blindfolded, Barbara knew her life was about to be altered forever.

—The Return of the Rogue

Who could imagine he had that rogue Garrett Marburn to thank for this brilliant plan? Edward had been beyond irritated when Marburn had the gall to come to Christie House to complain that Caroline had quit writing forever and was retiring to the country all because of him. The man went on and on how he'd miss Caroline, that she was his most successful author and an invaluable friend. She'd even given expert romantic advice! If her maid Lizzie didn't agree to marry Marburn soon, he was just to sweep her off her feet and drag her to Gretna like in some silly book she'd written. Caroline had assured Marburn all women liked the grand romantic gesture and a bit of mastery.

Edward had no need to carry Caroline off to Scotland. They were already married. But it was the ideal opportunity to get her out of town, to begin their marriage anew, with a set of clearly-defined rules. Alone. There would be no children to interfere—the boys were finally at university, and Beth had promised to keep a steadying hand, or perhaps two, on Little Alice.

It had taken Edward a few weeks to set the grand romantic gesture in motion, but once he set his Christie precision to it, things fell into place. First, he'd begged a copy of *Lord Farringdon's Fickle Fiancée* from his sister Beth. He locked himself in his study and read the thing straight through. Alternating between being appalled and fascinated, Edward took copious notes. Caroline was a much more worthy adversary than that nitwit Felicia, so he took it upon himself to alter the plot slightly.

Edward had no intention of sending Caroline to Dorset. Dorset was too far away from London, and he might be called back for some damned parliamentary emergency or other. No, Caroline was going to a perfectly charming borrowed manor house in Kent, not all that far from Christie Park in case the emergency was in the other direction. One never knew with Little Alice. He'd spent the last few weeks bribing, berating, and bullying the necessary people and was satisfied he'd be successful. Caroline had no idea what she was in for.

He smiled down at her on the seat cushion. His wife was blindfolded and gagged, curled up on her side. Her arms were tied up from wrist to elbow in front of her. And the best part? She didn't even know it. The empty flask of tea rolled on the carriage floor.

True, his approach was rather risky. But if he'd simply accosted Caroline on the road like some dashing masked highwayman as Farringdon did to Felicia, she would have recognized him immediately and talked his ear off once again on their unsuitability for each other. She would have been *reasonable*, when everyone knew it was up to a Christie to be the reasonable one.

She must have acquired a touch of reason by marriage. If he had to sit through one more lecture like the one that last night in her Jane Street garden, he'd commit himself to Bedlam. This time, she would listen to *him*. He had a whole week to convince her.

So here she was, quiet as a mouse. If she awoke, he'd give her the wine and that would keep her quiet until they got to his friend's property outside Ashford. The house sat on over one hundred walled acres. Caroline had appreciated the extensive gardens, Dutch arches, and Jacobean architecture on their previous visit. The Hazletts and Ben were already on their way to prepare her welcome. He would serve as lady's maid himself, and was relishing the task ahead.

But first they had to get there. If it had been up to the blasted cat Harold, he'd be streaked with blood and half dead. When Edward stepped into the carriage at the arranged spot, the cat had made an unruly commotion throwing himself against the bars of the cage, hissing and yowling, guarding his mistress with alarming fervor. Edward worried Caroline would wake up, but she was still his Sleeping Beauty. He had taken meticulous care in the arrangements, but he hadn't counted on the cat.

At least cats couldn't talk. It was imperative he not reveal that *he* was her kidnapper until he got her safely to Bradlaw House. He was wearing itchy new second-rate clothes from the skin out and had splashed a great deal of bay cologne all over his person to disguise the feel and scent of him. He'd practiced his villain voice for a week in case it was needed. He couldn't make himself shorter or less handsome, but as long as she didn't see him, she'd never know he had lost his mind and snatched his own wife. Once he installed her in their bedchamber, reasoned with her and then freed her, all would be well.

The thought of keeping her tied up was very appealing. He pictured Caroline spread open for him, her plump white limbs tied to the bedposts. If he were smart, he'd leave her gagged, for she was apt to make a fuss—

As she was beginning to do right this minute. He'd consulted his physician in a rather veiled interview to determine just how much of the drug should be added to the tea. Mrs. Hazlett had apparently erred on the side of caution.

Caroline gave a violent twitch and gurgled.

He swatted her backside. "Oy. See yer wakin' up. Do what yer told and no harm will come to ye." Edward thought he sounded quite ferocious. He hoped Caroline would, too.

Her scream was muted, but ear-splitting nonetheless. Harold joined right in.

" 'Ere now. Ye ain't got no cause for fussin' *yet*. You must be thirsty. Lie still and I'll get ye somethin' to drink."

Caroline's response was to flip on her back and kick him in the balls. How on earth did she know where to aim? Perhaps it was just luck. Not his. He bit his tongue and doubled over on the seat.

"Unh! Unh un uhn, oo unh!"

Her feet were flying at him. Clearly he should have tied them as well. It was not too late. Fighting nausea, he fought off her feet, too. When he had recovered sufficiently, he pulled a length of rope from the pocket of his coat, grabbed her ankles and wound them up tight.

"Unh! Unh unh unh unh!" She continued to tumble about like a furious red caterpillar.

"Shut up, ye little b-witch." It was imperative he get the wine into her as soon as possible. He felt as if he was wrestling with a bag of cats led by the redoubtable Harold. "I'll just take yer gag off, ye hear? If ye say one damned word, I'll slap it back on. Slap yer pretty arse too, see if I don't."

"Unh oo."

Edward was pretty sure she'd just asked him to do an anatomically impossible thing. Mindful of his fingers, he untied the fabric around her mouth. It was new, silk and clean, save for the drool.

"What is the meaning of this?" she asked, her voice unnaturally calm.

"Ain't got no meanin', missus. I got my orders. Now be a good girl and drink yer wine." He took the bottle and a glass out of the basket. If it weren't drugged, he'd be tempted to have some himself to kill the pain.

"I don't want any."

"Aye, ye do." He poured some into the tumbler and held it to Caroline's lips.

"It's poisoned, isn't it? Like the tea."

"Poisoned!" Edward scoffed. "If it was poisoned, ye'd not

be talkin' now, would ye? Ye'd be buried in a deep ditch I dug. Wormfood. C'mon, drink up."

Caroline took a sip, then spit it in his general direction. His reflexes were better this time around.

"Missed me, missus. Have it yer way." He fastened the silk back over her mouth in a trice.

"Unh unh unh, uh unh unh unh uh uh."

"Sorry. Can't unnerstand a bloody word." He picked up a sandwich and unwrapped it. "Umm-umm. This here's a good lunch. Don't suppose yer hungry either."

Caroline said nothing, her body deceptively still.

"Don't know where the next meal will come from, or when." He wasn't really hungry, but it was the only way he could think to pay her back for the vicious kick. He chewed loudly, smacking his lips, as he imagined one of the lower classes might do. Edward could only manage three bites before he quietly shoved the sandwich back in the picnic hamper, but not before risking his fingers to toss a slice of ham to Harold to shut him up.

"If I was in yer fix, I'd lie back. Have meself a nap."

Silence. Excellent. Perhaps she'd recognized the futility of trying to do him further harm. It was all for her own good. Once he'd convinced her to give their marriage another go, she'd thank him.

They'd been on the road all morning. Edward knew it was not much farther. He had hoped to carry a comatose Caroline into the house, but even if she was protesting in some form, no notice would be taken. The hired driver and his postboy had been paid well to turn a blind eye to any irregularities—a woman trussed up like a Christmas goose, for example. Edward had given a false name at the outset and they were to be left at a coaching inn in Ashford. His own coach had gathered up the Hazletts and Ben immediately after Caroline left Jane Street. They'd passed him a while back, where he transferred Caroline's small valise to them. There would be time to get the servants in place and for his coachman Munson to collect them.

He'd thought of everything except for the damned cat, who still glared at him malevolently despite the ham. Perhaps the creature would get lost in Bradlaw's deer park. Be gored by a wild boar. Carried off by an eagle.

Hm. There was something to be said for violent fantasies. No wonder Caroline had enjoyed her writing so. It must be powerful to make people behave in just the manner you wished. Lord knows, despite Edward's every effort, he'd not been entirely successful with his own family, and certainly not with Caroline. Well, that was about to change.

It was time to dress Caroline in the heavy black cloak. She was as unyielding as a block of wood, but he eventually covered her and pulled the hood down over her face. When the coach clattered into the yard, Edward climbed out, dragged her over the seat and threw her over his shoulder as though she were drunk. The innyard was empty save for Munson, who had scared off all comers and was idling in wait for him.

Edward dumped Caroline onto the leather seats, making sure her pert nose poked out between the blindfold and the gag. Deciding it would be safer to ride up top with his coachman, he left his wife and her cat and their seething fury securely locked below.

Pope and Douglass. Either one, the other, or both. They weren't foolish enough to accomplish the deed themselves— oh, no—they had hired the basest villain who stunk like a *Pimenta racemosa* tree to drug and kidnap her. The criminal smelled just like one of her brother's house party guests, a planter from the Caribbean islands. Caroline had never seen him, but his scent had lingered everywhere. It had taken a full three weeks to air out the room he stayed in.

Caroline lay flat on her back thinking, perspiring from the heavy cloak that had been bundled over her. Good-quality wool if she hadn't lost all sensation. The new vehicle was considerably better sprung than the first, not that it made any difference to her. Her kidnappers might be rich, but no matter how much money they had, they would be sorry.

The knots were fiendishly well tied. She hadn't a hope of escaping. She couldn't see or move or scream, but she could still hear. She'd concentrated on every word the bastard had said to her. She wasn't to be harmed if she behaved. *Hah.* That's what all her villains said, and they never meant it.

If she was being held for ransom, they'd contact Edward. If they simply wanted to torture her—or anything else, like kill her—she'd better start saying her prayers. There was a great dark spot upon her soul.

Edward would surely pay. He'd gone to a considerable amount of discomfort when he moved into her house after the first threat. Throwing money at a problem was much simpler than sleeping on the floor like some shaggy watchdog.

Edward. She might never see him again. Not that she'd planned to. Their break was absolute. She'd made that perfectly clear in her garden weeks ago.

Once she was taken to her destination, she would explain to Pope and/or Douglass that she'd already given up her writing, that she'd never harm a gentleman's reputation again by revealing any embarrassing or egregious truths. She was going to become a recluse in the country with her cat. Harold purred in solidarity across the way. At least her abductor had not left the cat behind. Thoughtful of him really. Harold had done nothing but growl and spit at her abductor, bless his brave little heart.

Caroline hoped her accommodations would not be too Spartan or spooky. One of her heroines had endured bats in a cave (*The Midnight Marchioness*), another, giant spiders in a dungeon (*The Baron's Bride*). She had nothing against bats or spiders, but didn't care to share her nights with them. She'd never get a wink of sleep, and she was so very tired. The drugged tea had yet to lose its power over her.

Her eyes welled up under the blasted blindfold in the reluctant realization that the Hazletts must be in cahoots with her kidnappers. No wonder her housekeeper had been so insistent she drink every last drop of tea. Perhaps Edward's pension had not seemed adequate to the old couple—they had put up with a great deal working for her. But she'd always thought they liked her, even when she had a temper tantrum or interfered in the kitchen.

She turned her cheek to the seat and sniffled. The texture and scent of leather was comforting. She took a deeper breath to calm herself and paused. There was something beyond the leather, something beyond the bay rum that lingered on the cloak after the kidnapper carried her like a sack of potatoes over his broad bony shoulder. *Lime.*

Caroline choked. Either her kidnapper had stolen the special formula that Floris mixed up exclusively for her husband, or she was being held captive by Baron Edward Allerton Christie. No wonder Harold had been so obstreperous. The cat was an excellent judge of character. It was she who was not.

The carriage was slowing to a halt. Caroline had been at war with herself the past few miles, wondering just how she would approach the man who kidnapped her. It was perfectly possible her nose was in error and she was not in Edward's comfortable crested coach. It made no sense for him to snatch her en route to the house he had bought for her, unless, of course, there was no house and his carefully neutral letters over the past few weeks were nothing but big, fat lies.

Picturing perfect Edward as a rough, ungrammatical villain was a stretch even for authoress Caroline, whose imagination often ran quite wild. Why would he affect such a persona? She might have taken such fright at being kidnapped she could have had an apoplexy and popped right off to her final reward. Fortunately she was made of sterner stuff, and at the first opportunity would beat the stuffing out of whoever had abducted her, be it Edward or some sorry stranger.

It was best, she decided, to play dumb, not voice her suspicions. At some point the silken blindfold would have to come off. What kind of kidnapper used silk anyway? All the evidence was pointing to her husband, who had quite obviously lost his mind.

The carriage door opened.

" 'Ere we are, missus. Come quiet-like. I'll carry ye upstairs, but yer not to make a fuss and make me drop ye. 'Twould be a shame to bruise that pretty arse."

Edward was inordinately fond of her bottom. She relaxed into her kidnapper's arms and sniffed. Nothing but bay rum. Her fingers made a limited sweep over stiff clothing. Her kidnapper had bought a new suit for the job. Oddly enough, the criminal dandy handled her just as Edward had the morning he had carried her from the garden and made her his mistress. Caroline was nine-tenths convinced the man who cradled her so lovingly was well-known to her, but a threat nonetheless. She debated writhing in protest, but saved her strength for what might come later.

They jostled up the endless stairs of a house that smelled of beeswax and roses. There was carpet underfoot, as their ascent was hushed. It was no cave or dank cellar. Wherever Caroline was to be kept—the attic? the roof?—it pleased her nose. As she was carried down a long hallway, she counted the steps away from the staircase. It would be helpful when she escaped to know just how far she had to run.

Her kidnapper turned suddenly and the scent of flowers grew stronger. The distant bleat of lambs caught her attention. A window must be open. An open window meant it was not nailed shut. Another escape route.

The man bent and deposited her on a lovely soft mattress. He took some care shoving a pillow beneath her head, but what she really wanted was a chamber pot shoved beneath her bottom. There was no way to request it, however, as her silken gag was still in place. Caroline heard the ominous click of the door and the turn of a key. She had been deserted without a word of intimidation or instruction.

Well. She was still covered by the hot cloak, so she rolled a bit to give herself some relief. She could probably roll right off the bed in search of a surface with which to cut her bonds, but decided against it. He really couldn't keep her like this forever.

Caroline used the time to tick off the known facts of her abduction. She thought back to the little farewell party in the hallway, remembering Mrs. Hazlett's agitation, once again realizing she had been drugged by her own housekeeper. Wherever Caroline was, it had not taken too long from London to get there—she'd felt the warm sun on her cheek when the villain dragged her out of the carriage so it was still afternoon. But the house didn't smell like Christie Park. Edward might have run mad, but he wouldn't take her to his family seat with his sister and daughter in residence, would he?

Then there was Harold. Harold hated Edward. The cat had made his displeasure known behind his bars, yet that might be a normal reaction to anyone who intended his mistress harm.

She could be all wrong about Edward's involvement. Then she remembered Hazlett's heartfelt words on Jane Street. *And keep in mind not everything is as it seems.* If that wasn't a weasely warning, her name wasn't Caroline.

It was all too vexing. Despite the deep feather mattress, Caroline was growing ever more uncomfortable between the tingling of her tied limbs and the urge to relieve herself. She should at least work on removing the blindfold and the gag so she could see where she was and scream properly. Flipping face down on the pillow, she butted her head back and forth, thrusting her tongue up, biting, groaning in frustration. She managed to free one eye and immediately turned to take in her surroundings.

The square room was handsome, opulent even. The walls were patterned an old gold, the furniture dark and massive. The bed she lay on could accommodate an entire family. An exquisite floral tapestry hung on one wall, and every flat surface was covered with vases of yellow roses, with a few daisies and greenery tucked in for contrast. *Glass* vases, which could be broken, the shards used as weapons of freedom.

Caroline inched over to the edge of the bed. The carpeted floor was far away. She lay on the sort of bed one needed to mount steps to get into, at least if one was as short as Caroline. Edward would have no difficulty at all, the bastard.

What was one more bruise or bounce? Caroline slid her legs over and hoped for the best. One ankle twisted hard as she landed. She wound up on her rump rather than on her feet, which was just as well, as hopping was not her forte. Hampered by the folds of the heavy cloak, she scooted along as best she could until she came to the penwork table near an armchair by the hearth. It was an attractive piece, its turned legs and curved column easily toppable by a determined woman with destruction in mind. Using a shoulder, she knocked into it as hard as she could. As the table tipped, the vase dumped out its water and flowers but remained unfortunately intact. It was heavy lead crystal, ideal for wielding in one's hand and cracking a skull or two, but in Caroline's current condition, useless to her.

She growled. Then she rolled, twisted, slunk. Chairs fell, andirons clanked, chamberpots emerged from their gloom— also useless and unbelievably tempting. Caroline was shrieking beneath her silk scarf as she caterpillared around the room, leaving a trail of frustration behind her.

"What the devil?"

Edward stood in a doorway, half undressed. He was stripped of his rough tweed coat and shirt, but still wore ill-fitting trousers and boots that had never seen the inside of Mr. Hoby's workroom. His hair was longer, his chest was bronzed, but he was definitely Edward, not a stranger who contracted kidnappings for a living. Caroline glared at him with her one eye and shrieked louder.

Edward surveyed the wreckage in the room. "Good God, Caro, stop. You'll hurt yourself."

"As if you care!" she shouted, but the words were naturally inaudible. He'd already dosed her with that vile tea and kidnapped her for heaven's sake, and now he was more concerned about a few bumps and bits of furniture. What on earth was he planning to do to her? She gave the chamberpot a vicious kick and her toes curled in pain.

"Hold still. I didn't plan on beginning quite this way, " he muttered. He got down on his knees and fumbled with her blindfold. She glared at him with both eyes. Caroline hoped she was sending the very clear message she hated him above all other men.

"I'm not fool enough to remove the gag or the bindings, so you'll just have to sit here and listen, all right?"

Caroline shook her head. No, it was *not* all right and never would be.

"I know you're angry. I'm sorry if I frightened you. You were meant to sleep through the trip, you see. I only pretended to be some thug in the event you woke up, because I needed to buy time to get you here. You would have tossed me out of the carriage if I came to you as Edward Christie, and given me one of your little lectures. All summer you kept pushing me away. But now we're together and we can talk like a normal couple, iron out our differences, start fresh."

Normal! Edward was as mad as the old king, but didn't seem to know it. He had a loopy smile on his face and appeared to think his scheme was a stroke of unsurpassed genius.

She might have to kill him to get her freedom. The thought had some appeal. It had taken her weeks to make peace with her decision, years really. No more trying to trick herself into thinking she could ever have a proper life. No more marriage. No more temptation.

No more Edward.

"I'm going to unfasten the gag. I warn you, the Hazletts and Ben will not come to your aid no matter how much of a fuss you make. I've engaged them for the week. They're getting settled in and will not be on duty until tomorrow. I'm to take care of all your needs myself, but if you bite me I daresay I will not be as effective as I might. Do we have an understanding?"

Again she shook her head. A week of enforced together-ness? The summer had nearly destroyed her. She'd lulled her-self into thinking love for her was almost possible, even though she knew better. What she and Andrew had done all those years ago was unforgiveable. If Edward discovered the truth—

Bad enough he thought he knew the worst. An affair with Andrew was nothing to what really happened between them.

No, she'd not make any of this easy for him or her wretched, betraying servants. Whatever they had planned, she was an expert in sabotage.

She chomped at his fingers for show, then uttered her first words in hours. "I must relieve myself. Untie me, or we both shall be sorry."

Edward raised a damnably elegant eyebrow. "Is this a ruse to escape?"

"Do you want to wait to find out? It won't be long." *That* was the mortifying truth. Caroline could not believe she was having a discussion about such a thing.

Edward reached into his ugly trousers and pulled out a lethal-looking knife. "You must promise not to run away."

"I made promises to you once. I shan't do so again."

Edward snorted as he sawed through the rope at her an-kles. "You had no intention of ever obeying me. Or honoring me or loving me. Our marriage was based on the flimsiest of foundations. It's time we set ourselves on a different path. We're older now, wiser."

"La la la," said Caroline. If her hands were free, she'd stick her fingers in her ears.

"You *will* listen to me. I'll make you."

"Do you intend to keep me a prisoner? For how long, Ed-ward? How did you wriggle out of your duties to the king's business anyway? I thought all peers had to be present in Par-liament for the Bill of Pain and Penalties." A Bill of Pain and Penalties indeed! If her hands were not still tied, Edward would feel the full weight of her wrath as lead crystal rained down on his head. She had exceptional aim from years of practice. "I'll show *you* pain, my lord, and you've not begun to pay the penalty for kidnapping me."

"See here, Caro. I haven't harmed a hair on your head, although it could do with a good brushing."

"I've been drugged! Blindfolded! Tied up, threatened, and scared out of my wits!"

Edward cleared his throat. It must have discomfited him to talk in such a villainous, ungrammatical way. "It was necessary. I know you too well." He avoided her feeble kick and moved up to her wrists.

"You don't know me! You know nothing! And I hope the king throws you in jail, if not for kidnapping me, then for leaving the trial."

"He won't. I told him I had a death in the family."

"Yours, I hope, because I am going to kill you!"

Edward put the knife back in his pocket. "Really, Caro, now who is threatening whom? If you want to be untied, you'll have to change your tune."

"This is unconscionable. You know I have to—oh, good Lord. Please hurry, Edward. I won't do anything." For now. But as she said, she'd make no more promises to him.

Chapter 17

"I am not afraid," Tatiana brazened. "Do your worst, my lord." His obsidian eyes glittered as brightly as the knife he held.

—*Lord Lancaster's Lady*

Despite her shrieking, the fiend had tied her right back up again. He left off the blindfold and gag, removing the dark cloak before he set her back on the bed. He dragged out a large copper tub from the adjoining room, then paraded back and forth shirtless with pitchers of steaming hot water. The sheen of perspiration on his muscled torso was quite gratifying, but she was not about to express any admiration. No matter what provoking thing she screamed at him from her perch, he ignored her, though his cheek muscle jumped at every word. He had taken a vow of silence, but at a cost. She had no such compunction, and would harangue him until her tongue fell off.

"Edward, I demand that you let me go on to Dorset. There *is* a cottage in Dorset for me, is there not? With a charming garden as you described? Hollyhocks? Hydrangeas?"

He poured the water into the tub. His ill-fitting pants slipped, and she caught a glimpse of his bare backside before he hiked them up again. He'd overlooked something critical in his grand plan—a pair of braces.

On his next return, she queried, "How did you persuade the Hazletts to be in league with you in this criminal enterprise? It must have cost you a fortune. A pity, for the money will not be of any use to them in jail." She said the last in her loudest voice, just in case they were hovering in the hallway. Her loudest voice, however, wasn't very loud—she'd hollered herself quite hoarse. Even from across the room, she could see the cotton batting in Edward's ears. Of course he wasn't responding, vile vermin that he was.

Why waste her breath when she could plan her escape? There were still three vases to throw, although the rest of the furniture looked impervious to breakage. Edward had tramped on and crushed the flowers on the carpet with his inferior boots, releasing their perfume. Under other circumstances, she would find the atmosphere impossibly sensual—a half-naked man toiling on her behalf, a well-appointed room in a remote country house (she was up high enough on the giant bed to see out the open window—nothing but rolling meadow and distant sheep), a bed large enough to contain any acrobatic activity she could dream up. But if Edward Allerton Christie the Elder had designs upon her battered and bound body, he was to be sorely disappointed.

Their talk that last night in the garden should have put an end to any hope of reconciliation. Despite the tender kisses, despite the scorching heat between them, they had agreed any further contact would be impossible. Caroline couldn't be his mistress, and certainly not his wife. Clearly Edward had forgotten and lost his sanity, but she was determined to remember and keep hers, for both their sakes.

At last he seemed satisfied by the volume of water. He sat down and wrestled off his boots, peeled off his stockings, stood up and dropped his horrid pants. Caroline shut her eyes, but not before noticing he was aroused beyond reason.

She waited in rigid resignation for him to carry her to the bath. Instead she heard a splash.

She cracked open one eye. He was scrubbing his armpit with his lime-scented soap, whistling. *Whistling!* She tried to shriek, but croaked instead.

"You know," he said conversationally, as if she were not tied up like a rabid dog, "I've become a terrible creature of habit. Some find the scent of bay rum pleasant, but give me my own lime cologne. My playacting the villain was as much torture for me as it was for you. I itch all over. I'm going to have Hazlett burn that suit." Water sluiced down his brown chest, beading on his nipples.

He lathered his bristled face and unkempt hair. This new, unimproved Edward confused her. He had never shared so intimate an act as bathing in front of her, except for the one time she'd barged into his dressing room and slipped into his tub uninvited. She'd made him like it in the end, but he was a man who thrived on a strict routine, and she was usually an unwelcome interruption. She had spent their year of married life weighted down by his continuous disapproval.

"Bastard." Caroline's old sense of humiliation fluttered to the surface. Perhaps he'd get soap in his eyes and go blind, she thought sourly.

He leaned back and poured water on his head, slicking back his long dark hair until every beautifully chiseled plane of his face was revealed. Then he pulled the wet cotton from his ears, tossing it among the flattened roses on the floor. "Did you say something?"

Caroline bit her tongue.

"This bath is so refreshing. I find travel arduous in the best of circumstances, don't you? You know, the water is still hot."

Caroline tasted blood.

"The tub is large enough for two. If you like, we can share it. Get the road dust off."

Caroline *would* like. She found herself furiously jealous of Edward's liquid display. "Will you untie me?"

"Unnecessary. I believe I'm perfectly capable of washing you. Everywhere." His smile was purely satanical.

"Absolutely not then."

"Don't be stubborn, Caro. I know how you like your baths. Do you remember the morning you surprised me in my bath at Christie Park?"

God, he remembered. Or could he read minds? "You were appalled at the disruption of your daily regimen. And your old valet—what was his name? The one before Cameron— couldn't look me in the eye for months."

"Well, as I said, it was a *surprise*. Poor Melrose didn't expect to find us in such a tangle when he came to barber me."

"I wish he'd cut off your—" She snapped her lips shut.

"Pardon? I must have water in my ears." He shook his head like a glossy spaniel.

"Nothing. Edward, while I appreciate your effort to get me in your clutches, I don't want to be clutched. I made that perfectly clear several weeks ago."

"I know what you said. I don't agree anymore. We may not be ideally suited to each other, but I'm sure we can find some common ground with a little work."

"The only time we'll find common ground is when we're both buried under it in the family plot. I assume there's still room for me at the churchyard?"

Edward looked a bit sheepish. They once had a discussion about her eventual placement. As an ever-organized Christie, he had dispassionately informed her of her future. Edward was to be the jam husband to his two wives' bread. The headstone was already in place, just waiting for the requisite dates. In Edward's case, Caroline hoped it would be *soon*.

"We have decades to go before we need worry about that, I trust." Edward rose from the tub, glistening like a pagan god. He bent, took the knife from his discarded pants and dripped across the carpet.

"You'll ruin the rug."

He glanced at the long water stain and the broken flowers. "I'd say it's already ruined. Bradlaw won't like it."

"We're at Bradlaw House?" Hope jumped in her heart. She'd been there before, but never upstairs. A small garden party had been held in their honor after she and Edward came to Christie Park to escape the gossip when they were first married. Lady Bradlaw had been all that was kind, conducting her through an exquisite parterre garden. Lord Bradlaw, a friendly, jolly sort, was a neighbor and one of Edward's oldest friends. Caroline never understood how such a warm, animated man could cope with the block of ice that was Edward.

He looked warm enough now, and a wave of her own heat suffused her cheeks. Edward loomed over her, deliciously wet and naked, the blade of the knife glinting in the sunlight. "Ah. You'd never manage a bluff in a game of cards—your expression betrays you utterly. Don't get any ideas. Tom and Susannah Bradlaw are still in town waiting on the king's pleasure. They can't help you run from me."

She made a gorgon-face at him. Let him understand *that*. She wouldn't need the Bradlaws' help. At least she knew where she was, and how to get back to London. She held her breath as the knife came perilously close to her heart.

"Go ahead. Stab me."

"Don't be ridiculous. Hold still."

Caroline waited for him to cut the ropes again.

Ping ping ping. The cherry-red buttons of her spencer bounced to the floor.

"What are you doing?" she rasped. The buttons had been fashioned to resemble little rosebuds and she had been very fond of them.

Edward frowned. "I'm not sure a knife will do. I'll be right back."

Hell and damnation. He was back with a large pair of shears before she could count to one hundred.

"I'll have you know this outfit cost a fortune!"

"I'll replace it." Mercilessly, he cut the sleeves of her jacket straight down her arms. He balled up the fabric and it joined the rest of the mess on the Bradlaws' carpet.

"You are a fiend," Caroline said behind clenched teeth. Much worse than her old neighbor Charlotte's lover Sir Michael Bayard.

"I've got to hurry. It wouldn't do for the water to get cold. You might catch a chill."

"I hope *you* catch lung fever!" She flinched when his hand snaked under her bodice as he cut the red kerseymere skirt down to the hem. She was left in nothing but rope and her chemise and stockings. Her half-boots had been removed long ago after the series of kicks.

Edward grinned. "No corset?"

Caroline would not dignify the question with an answer. As she had been travelling alone, it had seemed simpler to dispense with the contraption. Her destroyed carriage dress had been constructed with special boning at her direction.

Snip snip snip. Despite the warmth of the afternoon sunlight, her nipples contracted as her chemise gave way to air. Edward's hands trembled as he unfastened her garters. He had put the scissors down somewhere, but unless he untied her hands, he was safe.

For the time being.

She wondered how he'd get the stockings out from under the rope, but then he gripped her heels and cut the bonds. She lay still as death as he folded each stocking down with agonizing precision, his knuckles brushing her leg with each fold. Raising one limb, he massaged the pins and needles away with his warm, strong hands. Up and down, up and down, his fingers squeezed and released perfect pressure on the soles of her feet, her calves, the back of her knees. She forgot she was free to kick him as he swept up her inner thigh. His forefinger wandered just where she wanted it to. To her shame, she was wet and eager for his touch. Then he seemed to remember that the water temperature was no doubt cooling as her betraying body flared in heat.

"Can you walk or shall I carry you?"

"Carry," she whispered. She was too languid to step across the minefield of blossoms and cut clothing. He scooped her from the mattress and climbed into the tub, nestling her in his lap. His erection teased her cleft, but he made no move to insert himself in her aching hollow.

Her hands bound as if in prayer, she leaned against him as he covered her with his scent, the soap slick against her back and buttocks. Edward smoothed the bar over her hip, then swirled it around each breast until her nipples were stiff and rose-pink between the bubbles. She was his canvas as he painted every inch of her with froth, sliding back and forth over her sensitive skin. Her anger was slipping away as it always did when they were twined together. She closed her eyes and sought a fragment of sanity, but it eluded her as she fell deeper under his fluid spell.

His soap-filled hand stroked downward to her belly, then lower to her swollen clitoris. She opened her legs to him, desperate for more. He used a hard corner of the lime-scented cake in place of his fingers, rubbing with dedication until she drowned in sensation, his lips at her throat, his thumb at her breast. As she raised her hips in cresting orgasm, his cock sheathed itself in one deliberate thrust.

At last. He filled her as she shuddered around him, rising and falling, heedless of the water splashing over the rim, heedless of anything but his hard cock and hands on her hips lifting her from bliss and then back down. She was branded by his ownership everywhere as he embedded himself deep within her. His ragged breath tickled her neck, his teeth grazed her shoulder. The dark damp hairs of his chest curled against her back as his hand cupped her mound to keep her tight and taut against him as he emptied himself. She glided from wave to wave, helpless to find a shred of objection, to find a shred of *anything* that might pass for thought. She would be indignant later, make him sorry later, leave him later.

Later would come all too soon. For now she was content to be fitted to him in perfect harmony, her heart skipping as his cock pulsed inside her. The water had lost its warmth, but she was hot and heaving in his arms, reluctant to seek comfort anywhere else.

She stayed on his lap as he dipped a sponge into the pitcher, wiping cool water across her brow, down the bridge of her nose, circling the apples of her cheeks, soaking up the tears that fell. His lips rested in her hair as he smoothed a path to her throat. His touch was perfect in every way.

"I have waited for this for almost a month, Caro." His words were rough, reminding her of his villain-voice.

"D-don't get used to it. It won't happen again." But it would, if she stayed at Bradlaw House. She had to shake herself out of her sensual coma and do her own plotting.

"Ah. What will it take to make you change your mind?"

"There's nothing you can do."

"What if I free your hands?"

Caroline had practically forgotten she was still enslaved by rope. That was the least of her enslavement, but he must not know it. "It won't matter."

"Very well then." He lifted her up and slipped away. "I'll dry you off." He hoisted one long leg over the side of the tub.

"I can dry myself."

He reached for the stack of towels and draped one low on his hips. "It will be difficult if I don't cut the cords."

"You mean you won't?"

He shrugged. "You seemed to think it wouldn't matter."

"Well, it does matter! I meant there's nothing you can do to keep me here. To make me be your wife again." She couldn't hope or yearn or deceive herself that it would ever be different between them. Edward could never be less than a perfect gentleman, and she was as far from perfect as she could possibly be.

"We'll see." He pulled her up from the tub, then rubbed her vigorously with a linen towel. He fashioned it toga-style and Caroline was reminded of the debacle with the sheet so many weeks ago.

"Edward," she said, trying to blunt the edge of impatience in her tone, "this really is ridiculous. You are too old to be playing games with me."

"This isn't a game."

"What do you call it then? You are a grown man who disguised himself as a ruffian and took a woman by force!"

"Not by force. By cunning. And you are not just any woman. You are my wife. If you'll sit down, I'll brush your hair."

For the first time Caroline realized her own bottles and brushes lay on the vanity table. Mrs. Hazlett must have put them there. She imagined if she went into the dressing room, her clothes would be hanging neat as you please. Edward had persuaded her servants to conspire against her. Caroline knew just how convincing he could be, but she was not going to cooperate.

"Absolutely not."

"You've said that before. You really don't want your hair to dry like that. I'm having flashbacks to the illustrations of Medusa in my Greek textbook."

"I may have not had your classical education, but I believe if you looked into Medusa's face, you could see your own death," Caroline retorted, staring him down. "Well?"

"Sorry. Still very much alive. I'll have to take the scissors to the knots in your hair next." He had the gall to look rueful, as if the whole nightmare was not his fault.

"I'll brush it myself if you untie me!"

"I'm not certain I trust you yet."

"How many times must I fuck you before you trust me?"

Edward paled. "Don't reduce what we just did to simple fucking. It was more than that. Much more."

"Delude yourself then." She threw herself down on the bench. Her fit of pique was rather spoiled when the towel decided to come undone. Edward wrapped it around her shoulders like a shroud and she caught sight of herself in the mirror. Dead would probably be prettier. "Fine. Do whatever you want."

The brush tangled in the snarls despite Edward's best efforts. She longed for Lizzie—no, Lizzie was probably in on the trick, too. And Garrett! They had all of them deceived her.

She watched in horror as her eyes filled with tears again.

Edward noticed but misunderstood. "I'm sorry if I'm hurting you. Perhaps I should let you do it."

"Pl-please." She held up her shaking wrists.

Somehow she thought she'd feel more satisfaction when she threw the silver hairbrush and shattered the mirror. Even the first two vases did not quell the empty feeling she had in the pit of her stomach, but at least Edward dashed out the door in self-preservation. The third vase was too heavy to throw, or she was too tired, so she settled for carrying it to the open window and dropping it to the courtyard far, far below.

She discovered she was very high up in Bradlaw House, on the third or fourth story. The sheep were high on a faraway green hill. Sheep couldn't save her anyway. She was doomed, and down to her first and now last vase. It lay glittering and empty at her feet, a forlorn rose petal stuck to its lip. Caroline kicked it across the rug, succeeding only in hurting her toes again. She would save it for an emergency. There was bound to be one.

Chapter 18

Betrayed again. But how they would suffer for their perfidy. Her precious virginity but a vague memory, Jeannette ran through the mudflats with vengeance on her mind.

—*Ocean of Doom*

She assessed the damage. Without proper footwear, she'd slice her feet to ribbons. Her pretty red suede half-boots had disappeared, probably thrown out the carriage window by an injured and irate Edward. She tiptoed carefully to the dressing room, but was disappointed to find none of her imagined clothing. Whatever had happened to her luggage? And all her household objects she'd boxed up so carefully? She was left in that tower of hell with bath towels and bedding to clothe her body, which was now covered in gooseflesh.

And Edward's signature lime scent.

There was no point in sobbing—she'd lose what little voice she had left. Caroline climbed up the padded wooden steps to the bed and crawled in, pulling the brown velvet coverlet to her chin. What on earth was she going to do? She had weaponry aplenty, the sharp slivers of glass sprinkled like an ice storm on the carpet. Everything had shattered in a most satisfactory manner, although the pieces were more toothpick than lance sized. Her toes and twisted ankle hurt and she was hungry. *Famished.* Despite Mrs. Hazlett's urging, she'd eaten very little at breakfast. That meal seemed like days ago, when she was excited and nervous about starting her new life. Instead she was back under Edward's control, cold, naked and filled with frustration.

She flipped on the mattress, felt something hard and chilly

against her thigh. The scissors! Caroline sat up. She doubted she had the strength or the will to plunge them into Edward's heart if he ever came back into the room, but at least she could turn a pillowcase into a shift. She shook a thick down-filled bolster from its pretty embroidered rectangle. Yellow-centered daisies and a scroll of green leaves edged the fine linen, ridiculously cheerful under the circumstances. With a sharp scissor-point, she picked opened the seams wide enough to stick her head and arms through, then pulled it down to mid-thigh. She couldn't see the effect, as the mirror was crazed in a hundred pieces.

Caroline tugged the top sheet from its neat corners and set about cutting it into thick strips. When she was done, she had fabric to wind around and cushion her feet, tying the sandals with a jaunty knot at her ankles. There was plenty left over, in case she had to strangle Edward or make a bed linen ladder. The descent out the window was more than she wanted to consider, however.

It was time to tackle the room. In good conscience, she couldn't leave it for Mrs. Hazlett, even if the woman had betrayed her. Caroline wrapped a strip of linen around her hand and grabbed the coal scuttle. With each plink of glass to metal, she imagined dropping Edward off the roof, his brains dashing on the pavement below. There was still a great quantity of glass dust, but the little broom from the hearth swept it away. She gathered up the stems and flowers and heaped them into the coal scuttle too, but not before rubbing some ruined roses on her temples and throat to dilute the pervasive lime scent.

Satisfied that she'd made the room safer, she explored her prison cell. There were two chamber pots—intact—which she returned to the underside of the enormous bed. A massive tallboy was empty of everything, even dust. She doubted she was strong enough to tip it over to crush Edward, or slide it to bar the door. A pair of comfortable brown and yellow striped chairs sat before the empty fireplace. She righted the gold-leaf and black patterned table that she'd first knocked over, and returned the crystal vase to its center. Two polished brass candlesticks stood side by side on one end of the mantel. Moving one to the other end for balance, she checked its heft. It would make a considerable dent in Edward's head if he held still long enough for her to whack him. The brown toile-skirted dressing table held her comb, her rouge pot, an ivory tray of hairpins, and her new jewelry box. Caroline opened the lid to see her all her old glittery friends. She fastened a topaz and citrine brooch at her ragged neckline and clasped a topaz bracelet on her wrist. She found her hairbrush beneath the gold fringe of a curtain, sat down on the toile-cushioned window seat and counted one hundred snarling strokes.

The view below was lovely. Caroline was sorry the room did not face the elaborate formal gardens, but the brick-chevroned courtyard had a pleasing pattern. From there she could watch for any traffic, like a princess trapped in a tower. A long lime avenue led to the estate gates, which she would be exiting soon as she could figure out how. The hills beyond were still bright green, although a brief freak cold snap had turned some leaves, altering nature—just as Edward had altered her life those past three months. Even the last month, when she'd convinced herself she was done with him and everything that came before him.

Would she never get to start her life anew? She kept trying, only to encounter one stumbling block after another.

There was a slide of key to lock. Edward peered in through a two-inch gap. "Are you all right? It's awfully quiet in here."

"I ran out of things to throw." Not quite true, but he didn't need to know she held anything in reserve. "I'm hungry, Edward. Do you plan to starve me here?"

"That wouldn't suit my purposes at all." He entered with obvious caution, fully dressed in his own clothes. Caroline was not sorry to see a mottled bruise forming on his cheek where the second vase struck home. She was less thrilled with his bark of laughter at her own costume.

"How resourceful you are, Caro. I would never have

guessed. What's next? An evening gown made out of the curtains?"

She put the brush down before she threw it again. "If I must. The velvet is good quality. But I'd rather have my own things. Where are my clothes? My shoes? Where is my food?"

"All in due time. I confess I like how you look right now—rather like a woodland elf. All you're missing is a crown of daisies in your hair." He looked down at the carpet. "I see you've done some straightening up."

"Yes. Tell the Bradlaws to send me a bill. I'll be happy to replace the vases."

"I'll take care of that. I hope," he said, looking stern, "this will be the end of your childish tantrums. You must have been spoilt as a little girl."

Caroline felt a tantrum coming on. How little he knew of her. No one save Nicky had paid the least bit of attention to her—unless she made them. Her father had seemed to forget she even existed most of the time until she broke something he valued. Of course, most everything of value had been sold to cover his drinking and gambling and wenching.

"Yes," she replied, her tone glacial. "I was dreadfully spoiled. And there's my red hair, always a sure sign of temper, is it not? Yet, that was what you first noticed about me."

"Not quite. I admired the whole package as I recall. As did every man in the room."

"Yes. Entirely superficial admiration. No one bothered to get to know me, especially you."

"My greatest sin—which is why we're here."

"Edward, it's too late. You know me well enough. And I know *you*. We are both far too old to change our natures."

"I'm not asking you to change, Caro. Not really. But I am willing to listen to what you want in a husband."

"Not you! Never you! Never again!" Her hands fisted at her sides.

His eyes glittered for a moment, *just* like evil glass. So she had been wrong, after all. "I don't want to have to restrain you again, but I will."

Caroline's laugh was brittle. "Oh, my lord. How pathetic to realize that's the only way I'll endure your company."

"That's not true and we both know it."

Damn him. He was right as he always was. Part of her wanted to fling herself into his arms. But she hoped her other part would prevail.

"How long must I suffer here? Did you say a week?"

Edward nodded. "I hope you won't suffer, Caro. If you do, it will be by your own choice."

"You expect me to countenance kidnapping and torture? Curl up like a kitten in your lap?"

Edward walked over to the black marble fireplace and sat down in one of the chairs. "Please join me over here, Caro. I wouldn't want you to jump out the window."

"I have no intention of causing myself harm. Only you."

"I wish you'd reconsider." He gave her a most charming smile. Freshly shaven, his hair drawn back from his intelligent forehead, he was temptation itself. Caroline knew where that led. Then he extended a conciliatory hand.

His earnest effort was annoying, but she got up, crossed the room, and sat. She put her head back on the chair, closed her eyes and hummed.

"Give me five minutes, Caro, then I'll bring up a tray. It's a bit early for supper, but you missed lunch. I won't be joining you—I don't want a soup bowl thrown at my head."

Caroline's stomach rumbled. "I trust you won't drug the food."

"Of course not. And you needn't worry about what you ingested earlier. Dr. Wyatt told me it was perfectly harmless."

Yet another name to add to her list of enemies. At least her cat was faithful. "Where's Harold?"

"Prowling about. He and Ben are outside somewhere, exploring. I don't believe the boy has ever seen an open field in his life."

No, he hadn't. When Caroline found him, he'd been white as milk and stick-thin, begging on a seedy street corner. Over the objections of Garrett Marburn, who had accompanied her to a poor part of the city in the name of literary research, she had whisked Ben away in Garrett's carriage. It had taken several days to get him clean and calm and integrated into her household. It had been a tiny step toward the mother-hood she would never have.

"I hope they don't get lost."

"I gave him my compass. He's a bright lad."

"When he wants to be." She knew Ben was in awe of Ed-ward, the little traitor. "Are your five minutes up?"

"Almost. Tomorrow morning after breakfast I'd like to see you in Bradlaw's library."

"Do you want me naked or in this pillowcase?"

Edward winced. "Your trunk is outside in the hallway. I'm sorry I forgot about it." He stood. "I'll fetch it now."

He left the door ajar. For one mad moment Caroline con-templated pushing past him and running down the flights of stairs.

She wouldn't get far with sheets on her feet.

Edward carried the small trunk into the dressing room. Caroline had not packed much for her trip to Dorset, just a few changes for the several days' travel. But a flagon of jas-mine perfume was rolled up between her petticoats, and she would drown herself in it as soon as Edward left. "I'll leave you to unpack. Supper will be very simple. I hope you won't mind."

Caroline was hungry enough to eat the leather slippers she was thrilled to see at the bottom of her things. She waved Ed-ward away and hung up her dresses, just to get the wrinkles out. She was not moving in. Not staying, no matter what Ed-ward planned.

When Edward returned with the tray, she fell on the veg-etable soup with joy. Her bread was already buttered, the rare beef and cheese sliced—he'd taken the precaution of not including a knife. She bit directly into the juiciest peach of her life, its nectar dripping onto her pillowcase dress. She drank every ounce of the sweet red wine that filled her glass and wished there were more. She wanted to sleep tonight and wake up this morning all over again. Her day would be vastly different this time.

Morning found her in the same strange room, garbed in her own nightdress, a slant of bright sunshine slipping through a gap in the dark velvet. Caroline sprang up and rushed to the window. She looped back the drapes with their tasseled gold cords. There was no one about on the court-yard—no one with a tall ladder or a team of acrobats who could scale the walls and set her free. Her hair was not as long as Rapunzel's, and in any case, there was no prince to climb it. The point was to get *out*, not invite another vexing man into her boudoir.

Her hair was more tangled than ever. Good thing Edward had spotted the scissors and taken them away, or she'd be sorely tempted to cut the whole mess off. She sat at the dressing table, viewing two dozen little Carolines with two dozen hairbrushes in the cracked mirror. She needed to make herself ready for the morning's negotiation with Edward, her first and hopefully her last.

There was a rap at the door, then the turning of the key. Hazlett entered red-faced, whether from climbing the stairs, the weight of the breakfast tray or his mortification as her husband's accomplice.

"Good morning, my lady. I bring you Mrs. Hazlett's sincere and abject apology for her part in your abduction. We have nothing but your best interests at heart, you know." He set the tray down on the dressing table quickly, as if he were afraid to come too close, as well he should be.

"So you said, you old liar. How much did it cost Lord Christie to steal your souls?" Caroline asked in a forbidding voice.

"Why, nothing much above our usual weekly salary, my lady. Lord Christie was quite convincing in his ardor. Mrs. Hazlett and I thought you should give him another chance."

"Did you?" Caroline uncovered a dish of perfectly poached eggs on tiny toast squares. Their yolks would match the gold wallpaper, but she was not about to waste the meal on the walls. Who knew when she might find sustenance again? There was a dish of blackberries swimming in rich yellow cream, two enormous sticky buns, and a pot of chocolate. It looked like Mrs. Hazlett had made herself right at home in her new kitchen.

"Lord Christie instructed me to tell you to take your time enjoying breakfast. He will await you at your convenience in the library. Please ring when you're ready to come downstairs." He lifted the tapestry's corner to reveal a bellpull. Hazlett waited, looking hopeful. He could stand there rooted all day, and Caroline would not forgive him or his wife. She gave him the evilest of eyes.

"Is there anything else I can get you?"

She stabbed into an egg. "Oh, just my *freedom*. My life back! I don't suppose you'd hand over the key to this room so I won't have to ring any damn bells?"

Hazlett stiffened. "It *is* for your own good, Lady Christie. You are such a stubborn girl."

"I'm hardly a girl, Hazlett. I know my own mind, and it will not be changed. You're dismissed. In every sense of the word."

Hazlett drooped a bit as he left, but still turned the key in the lock.

Caroline drank her chocolate, ate her eggs and berries slowly, savoring every sip and bite. Edward could hang before she went downstairs. Although the buns tempted her, she wrapped them in a linen napkin. They would make a fine feast on the road when she caught the mailcoach in Ashford.

She had money in her reticule, but unsurprisingly Edward had not seen fit to bring it upstairs with her trunk. He must think her too besotted by her jewels to ever think of selling them, but sell them she would to buy a ticket home.

Where was home? Edward might have already arranged the sale of the Jane Street house to any one of the eager men lined up to install their mistresses there. But she hadn't signed her life interest away. While she still had breath in her body, the house was hers.

At some point while she slept, fresh water and towels had been delivered to the dressing room, although the bathtub was out on the carpet, still full. An oversight by Edward, but then he wasn't used to playing lady's maid. She blushed to think what she and her husband had done in it. Whatever else he was, he knew her body and how to bring it to pleasure.

Caroline washed and dressed with care, folding the black cloak over her arm. The bundle of buns was pinned to its lining with two enamel brooches. If he didn't agree to drive her to Ashford, she was in hopes Edward would let her outside to walk in Lady Bradlaw's garden. Alone. The pocket of her dark blue travelling dress was stuffed with jewelry. For good measure, she'd pinned the diamond spray on her shoulder. It was a minor Christie family heirloom, and would be the first to go to the pawnshop.

The soles of her leather slippers were thin, but Caroline knew she wouldn't abuse them for more than four or five miles. Six at the most. She wished she'd paid more attention to the mileposts when she'd lived at Christie Park. Walking over to the glowing tapestry, she yanked the bellpull hard.

Ben came up in place of Hazlett, who was probably lying down somewhere recovering from his earlier climb. The boy gave her a cheeky grin.

" 'ello, Lady C! Sorry if I gave you the flimflam. The country ain't near as bad as I thought. Lord C says he'll take me fishin' if he has time."

Fishing! She hoped they would drown. "Please see to it that the water in the tub is removed at once and return it to the dressing room. I am very disappointed in you, Ben."

"Aye, my lady. Knew you would be. But not all of us are cut out for schoolin'.'"

"I'm not talking about your lessons, you little heathen! I opened my home to you and you have repaid me by helping Lord Christie take me by force and keep me a prisoner against my will."

Ben looked around the comfortable room. "Don't look like no prison I've ever been in."

"You've been in prison?" This was something new.

"Not for more than a day or three. 'Twas a mix-up, Lady C. You can trust me now."

"Can I? When you'll do anything for the villain who promises to take you fishing?"

Ben chewed the inside of his cheek. "Lord C's most persuasive. Goes on and on about that Shakespeare play. Taming of the—Something. Some rodent, I reckon. Tell you what. If you ain't happy here—after a day or three—I'll help you escape. You been good ta me. No skin off my nose."

Caroline was momentarily speechless between Ben's mangling of Shakespeare and his offer to help her. So Edward fancied himself as Petrucchio? He had the wrong play entirely. *She* was Lady Macbeth.

"Thank you, Ben. I knew you would come through for me. I'll make it worth your while." She patted her pin for good effect.

"Don't need diamonds, Lady C. They'd only clap me in gaol again. Some blunt would be good, though."

"If you find my reticule wherever Lord Christie hid it, you're welcome to half."

"I'll keep an eye out. But you've got to give him a chance."

"What?" Caroline's vision of riding back in style to London dimmed.

"Lord C. He's gone to a lot of trouble. The Hazletts haven't slept a wink for weeks what with him badgerin' them. They're old and they need their rest. Give the man three days, my lady. If he don't come up to snuff, I'll filch the key again and set you free. Deal?" He extended a grubby hand.

"Two days, and not a minute more."

Ben gave a long suffering sigh. Who knew the little ruffian was such a romantic?

"Deal." They shook hands. Caroline laid the cloak down on the bed. It would be easier to have a proper plan in place than a chance flight from Bradlaw House. And Edward might get suspicious if she suddenly smelled of cinnamon buns rather than jasmine.

"You won't say a word of our arrangement to anyone, will you, Ben? I cannot trust the Hazletts any longer."

He straightened his spine, insulted. "I don't peach. Your secret's safe with me."

"Tell Hazlett you'll bring me my meals—that the stairs are too much for him."

"Shouldn't have no trouble convincin' him o' that. Poor blighter's took to his bed."

"Good. Serves him right."

"Lord C says he's movin' you to a different room. One o' the regular housemaids from the village is comin' to truck your things downstairs. Said his plan weren't watertight after all."

Caroline grinned. Edward must have been exhausted himself trudging up and down the stairs with her bath water. If she were closer to the ground, her climbing skills could be pressed into service once again if need be. It would be suicidal to try to escape from up that high.

She gave a squirming Ben an impulsive hug. "Excellent. I'll talk to you later in my new room. How do I get to the library?"

"Turn left at the bottom of the staircase. Three doors down. Cor, but there are a lot of books in there. Who would want to read them all?"

Caroline, if she were to amuse herself for the next two days. "Wait. We are counting today as the first of our days, are we not? After tomorrow you'll help me?"

Ben looked innocent. "Did you think I meant that? The day's half over now. It's nearly noon. Don't seem fair to count it as a *whole day*."

Hell and damnation. At least he knew his sums. "Fine. But after noon on Thursday, I will be leaving Bradlaw House with or without your assistance."

"That's fair. Do you think I can just throw this bathwater out the window?"

Caroline didn't stop to advise him. She had an appointment with Petrucchio.

Chapter 19

No one could force Magdelena to do the impossible.
Not her father. Not her poor dead nanny. Not her
brother Reynaldo. Certainly not the villain who had
kept her prisoner in chains to slake his sinful appetites.
—*Devil in Disguise*

Edward was seated behind a massive mahogany desk, a livid bruise matching it on his cheek. Caroline bit back a smile of satisfaction at its colorful progression and curtseyed. "Good morning, my lord."

"It's good afternoon, Caroline. I trust you slept well? You're looking lovely."

"Yes, even without any drugging, I slept like a baby. The bed was very comfortable. In fact, the entire room is absolute perfection. I just love it. For a prison cell it is first class. I've never considered the combination of old gold and chocolate brown before when I decorated, but I believe I'll have to give it a try in my new cottage."

Edward's dismay was comical to behold. "I hope you won't mind, Caro. I've arranged to move you to a more convenient location."

"More convenient for whom? I daresay it's good exercise for all of us to climb one hundred and twelve broad steps. I've never felt so fit."

"You've just walked *down*," Edward said. "Your new room is equally comfortable. And the mirror is intact."

"What color is it?"

"How the he—I'm afraid I can't remember. Some sort of blue, I think. Or gray."

"Any vases?" she asked sweetly.

"None. No Dresden shepherdesses, no bibelots of any kind."

"That's not very sporting of you."

Edward rubbed his cheek. "Be that as it may, I'm not here to talk decorating schemes, Caro." He leaned back in the padded leather chair and smiled as though he had a great treat in store for her. "Most ton marriages are business arrangements at heart—joining property or political ambitions. Lawyers spend hours on settlements and wills and codicils. If the couple comes to respect each other and hold each other in some affection after all that paperwork, it's considered miraculous."

"Are you dying, Edward? Is that your will there?"

He swept the papers under the blotter. "You sound awfully hopeful, Caro."

She shrugged. "You can't expect me to respect you and hold you in some affection after yesterday."

"I remember yesterday somewhat differently. The afternoon in particular."

The smug bastard. "I'm fixated on the morning. My abduction, you know."

"If I had thought there was any other way to get you here, I would not have resorted to subterfuge."

"Well, should the Christies ever lack funds, you can go about the country kidnapping heiresses." She leaned back in *her* chair. "I am waiting, Edward. What is your proposal for our future? You know mine. A cottage in Dorset. Are those papers you're hiding the deed? Where do I sign?"

"Um. Not a deed, precisely." Edward removed the papers from the blotter and shuffled them. He looked shifty. Nervous. Caroline went on alert.

"I've taken the liberty of making a little list for you. For us, really. I thought it best to put my expectations in writing."

"Your expectations? I have no interest in your expectations. But I *expect*," she said archly, "you know that."

"I'm hoping I can change your mind. What we have together, Caro, is rare. I admit I didn't know what to do about it while we lived together, but I think I've got myself organized now."

"How lovely for you. Organization is so helpful in general. In battle, for example, one must have the adequate number of weapons and provisions and so forth." She eyed a cloisonné ink pot on the desk. Edward snatched it away and dropped it in a desk drawer.

"Quite. I suggest you look upon this list as a kind of battle plan, a battle where we *both* win."

She twirled her wedding rings. She should have stopped wearing them long ago, but they were so very pretty. "You are not making any sense at all, Edward."

"Caroline, please hear me out. If I were your employer, there would be a set of rules. The time you were to report for work, for example. When you would be permitted to go to lunch. If you painted pottery, for example, how many plates you would finish in the course of a day."

"I don't paint. Nor do I play the pianoforte. I have none of the accomplishments one might expect for a gently reared woman. I wasn't gently reared."

"You are deliberately misunderstanding me. I don't want you to paint a bloo—blessed—thing. This is a list of suggestions—of my preferences—ways that might be pleasing to me if you chose to adapt them. I expect you to provide me with a similar list of how I might better please you."

"I don't want to be pleased by you. I want to leave—that would please me."

"Please, Caro. Humor me." He pushed a sheet of paper across the desk.

Caroline picked it up. Edward's handwriting was as precise and exacting as he was. She had no difficulty skimming his suggestions. "Only six?"

"I concentrated on the most important. The curbing of your temper is, of course, the most critical. I cannot have you destroying property and screaming like a banshee every time you do not get your way. As you can see, I've recommended some diversionary tactics you might take when life's vicissitudes irritate you."

The greatest vicissitude sat across from her. "I suppose that's reasonable," she conceded. Once the euphoria of destruction left her, she often felt a little foolish. She could count to ten or perhaps to twenty if the need arose. She read the second item on Edward's list. " 'There will be no unnecessary talk at breakfast.' " She looked up at Edward. "Would I be permitted to say 'pass the marmalade dear,' or is that taboo?"

"You know what I mean. When you wake you chatter like a magpie. A man can't think. I like to begin my day quietly with the paper and correspondence. In fact, it would be altogether better if you had breakfast in bed. We could meet later in the day."

"Don't count on it," she muttered. There was no point in reading the rest. She counted to ten, then tore the paper to bits.

"I was afraid you might do that. I made copies." He patted the sheets on the blotter. "My memory is not what it once was. I'd hate to leave a provision out. I advise you to do the same. The original might so easily get misplaced."

"How am I to make my list when you've taken the ink pot away?"

Edward hesitated. "You mean you'll write one right now? That makes me very happy, Caro."

"I might as well get it over with. I can tell you won't give me a minute's peace until I do."

"You—you promise you won't fling the ink pot?"

"That would be silly. The sooner I finish your blasted list, the sooner I can leave, yes?"

Edward pulled open the drawer and set the colorful enamel and metal ink pot on the desktop. "I thought we could discuss your terms. Perhaps in the garden. The weather is fine, and I remember how much you enjoyed your visit here."

"That was long ago. Six years. A lot has changed."

Edward stood. "Here. You take my place and write to your heart's content."

"Oh, I will." Caroline switched her seat and rummaged through the drawers for paper and pen. She sharpened a nib and discreetly dropped the tiny knife into her pocket. She hoped Edward wouldn't notice the bulge of jewelry.

What had happened to her Edward, the man who always knew his mind, the one who was a stickler for propriety? How could he think kidnapping and lists would transform their marriage? Had he fallen on his head or was he in the throes of early senility?

She supposed it didn't matter *why* he'd changed. He just hadn't changed soon enough. She would never forget the look on his face or his cruel words when it was clear he expected the worst of her.

But why should he expect anything else? If she was honest with herself, she'd given him no reason to think otherwise. In her heart, Caroline knew she did not deserve happiness and by marrying a man like Edward, had guaranteed it.

He turned on one polished boot heel and left her alone, inspecting the shelves. He found a book to his liking and settled into a burgundy leather chair across the room, gazing up now and then to check on her progress. She wrote as rapidly as she ever had when the muse had struck particularly hard. She bit her lip to keep from laughing. He wanted a list? She'd give him a list.

The clock struck one, a sonorous single boom. Edward crossed and uncrossed his long legs. She took another piece of vellum from the sheaf and began to copy the first page, her handwriting looping in crooked lines. She'd get no prize for neatness, but her creativity was unsurpassed. She tossed the pen down, black ink smudging her fingers. "Done!"

Edward put his book on a table and walked across the carpet, removing a pair of spectacles from his pocket. Caroline had never seen him wear them before. He'd made no concessions to his age when they were together, certainly not in the bedroom. He hadn't used the glasses to read his book. Perhaps he hadn't even been reading at all.

She handed him a paper. He took it to the mullioned window and held it to the light. "Your handwriting is so very difficult to read, my dear. Hm. Number One. Stab myself in the thigh with a—fuck?"

"Fork, you imbecile! Stab yourself in the thigh with a fork, hard enough to draw blood."

He looked down. "*Ten* times? Surely I would be successful at the bloodletting after the second or third round." He removed his glasses and calmly laid the list on the windowsill. "You are aware that puncture wounds frequently lead to infection. I might lose my leg."

Caroline shrugged. Legs, arms—there was too much of him already.

"I would still expect you to engage in conjugal relations despite my infirmity, you know. Once I'd healed, of course. In sickness and in health was a part of your vows."

"Just as I promised to honor and obey you, which I will not! Ever!"

"We'll see about that. Are the rest of your items equally reprehensible?"

"No," Caroline said sweetly. "Some of them are worse." Wait until he got to number eleven. Hitting one's balls with a cricket bat couldn't possibly be comfortable.

"Caroline," he said, his voice stern, "obviously you are not taking the purpose behind this list seriously."

"Oh, I'm serious! Just as serious and organized as you are, Edward. I even numbered my requests."

He picked up the paper again and turned it over, squinting. "Forty-seven?"

"I can think of more if you wish."

He crumpled up the vellum and tossed it out the window.

"I made a copy."

"And I'll throw it out, too. Stop playing games, Caroline. I want this marriage to work. I see nothing wrong with a sensible list of expectations from each other. Most marriages could benefit from a set of ground rules. Why, we didn't even know each other when we married. It's only natural that there were—problems."

"Problems? You hated me! Your children hated me!"

"Nonsense. You weren't what we were used to."

No, she certainly had not been staid and proper. Once she was Lady Christie, it was as if every impulsive imp she harbored within banded together to wreck everything she'd wanted: to be away from her cousins, to have a home of her own, a husband, a family, no matter how dreadful Little Alice was. The imps had fought over inconsequential things, thrown valuable objects.

Allowed themselves to get caught in the arms of another man.

There was something *wrong* with her. Caroline knew what it was, but Edward must never find out.

"Edward, I am not your employee. I don't want to be your wife. If you cannot see clear to divorce me, at least send me out of your reach. You promised me a cottage—with hollyhocks."

"I—I was unable to secure one in a timely fashion."

Caroline gasped. No wonder Christies always told the truth. They made very poor liars. "You never even tried!"

Edward scrambled around the corner of the desk and grabbed the ink pot again. "I did try. Then I thought better of it after Marburn came to me."

"Garrett told you to kidnap me?" That was much worse than Garrett knowing. To think she'd made the man a fortune.

"No, but he repeated your advice about running off with your maid Lizzie. I read that book, *The Farringdon Farrago* or some such—where the hero plays highwayman and kidnaps what's-her-name. I thought if I got you alone without any interruptions we might become reacquainted, so to speak."

He read her book? Caroline thought the world was coming to a screeching halt. She expected toads to drop from the sky and pigs to fly and the sulfur scent of brimstone to knock her right on her ample arse. Lucifer himself had taken possession of Edward Christie to torment her for her many mistakes. She counted to twenty-two. "Reacquainted? How many acquaintances do you drug and tie up? Even Lord Farringdon was not such a fiend. No, Edward, you've lost your chance with me. Five years ago I humbled myself. Begged you."

Edward turned away. "I was angry."

"Were you? You never really said. And you never gave me time to explain."

"What was there for me to say, Caroline? Did you want me to throw something? Let me correct you. As I recall you said a great deal—most of it nonsense. If I'd arrived half an hour later, what I believed would have been true anyway. Rossiter was in love with you and our marriage was hopeless. You were half naked . . . and well kissed," he added.

"He—he tried to blackmail me!"

"The poor fool was as desperate to have you as I am."

Rubbish. Andrew needed funds—he'd said as much. Even if she sold every jewel she possessed, she could not have come up with the astronomical amount he'd asked of her to keep their prior relationship a secret from Edward. His ready alternative had been to start an affair.

She had almost agreed. How that would have helped Andrew pay his bills she had no idea, but he probably would have bided his time until she sold the silver or a painting on the wall. But Edward had come home as a birthday surprise. The surprise had been on him.

She felt sick to her stomach reliving the worst period of her life. No, not the worst, a little imp whispered. Not even close.

"I want to go upstairs—to my new room."

"Caro, please—"

"No, I cannot talk to you anymore. Not right now."

Edward had remained composed and reasonable through-out most of their conversation, even when Caroline threat-ened him with bodily harm, although she thought he was beginning to sense his ultimate defeat. She would not, could not do what he wanted.

"Very well. I'll show you."

He led her up a double flight of stairs to a sunny corner bedroom overlooking the parterre garden. The walls were not blue or gray, but a soothing silvery green, the color of lambs' ear. The curtains and bedspread were floral chintz, lending the impression the garden had come indoors. It was much more feminine. Caroline wondered if Edward had ex-pected to share the other, more masculine room with her.

The surfaces were bare, except for a little dressing table. The maid had lined up her toiletry items. Her jewel box stood open.

Edward frowned. "What's this? Where are your trinkets?"

Caroline patted the comforting lump. "In my pocket. I wasn't sure about the staff."

"There's just the Hazletts and Ben, a few day girls from the village. Most of the servants accompanied the Bradlaws to town and much of the house is shut up. I'm sure you needn't worry about theft. The Bradlaws wouldn't hire people they couldn't trust."

"Why not? I did."

"Don't be too hard on them, Caro. They do care about you."

"So they keep saying. It's a mystery how everyone seems to think they know what's best for me."

"Maybe they do. Maybe you should listen."

"La la la."

Edward went to the door. "I'm off then." His lips twisted. "Perhaps to find a fork. I'll expect you downstairs for dinner at eight."

She heard the inevitable key turn. Locked in again. Caro-line hoped the sticky buns were still in her cloak. Dinner was a long way away. She looked around. There really was nothing satisfying to throw. So she screamed instead—for quite a long time—until her throat hurt and she became bored.

There were books in her trunk. Her own. Resigning herself to one more day of captivity, she curled up in a chintz-covered chair and began to read, even though she already knew the ending.

Chapter 20

> "Just once more, I beg you." The Marquess of Raven-
> wood kissed her fingertips. Lily could do nothing but
> comply.
>
> —*The Marquess and the Mistress*

At seven o'clock there was a tap at the door. Caroline
scrambled up from the bed and brushed the crumbs off
her blue dress. "Enter."

The key turned. She expected a maid, but it was Edward
the eternal water-bearer, carrying a pitcher. He was fully
clothed in handsome black and white attire. Some towels and
a suspiciously bright red evening gown were draped over an
arm. "I thought I'd help you get dressed for dinner."

She looked down at her ruined dress and spied a sticky bit
of cinnamon-coated pastry she'd missed. "I am dressed."

"But I've bought you a new gown."

Her mouth opened, then closed. She touched the oily fabric in revulsion, half expecting to see bloodstains on her fingers. "Were you blind? I can't wear that!"

Edward blinked. "But it's red. You love red."

"Not that red. It's hideous." In fact, she'd never seen a
more ghastly dress in her life, edged in stiff black lace that
looked sharp enough to cut into her skin. "The only way I'll
ever wear that is if I'm in my coffin. And even then, it's horrible enough for me to come back from the dead to claw it off
me."

"I shall never understand you."

"Exactly." She flounced over to the dressing table. Knew
she was flouncing, too. Every move she made was exagger-

ated impatience. Her hair had tumbled down during her nap and she sighed dramatically.

Edward set the pitcher and dreadful gown down. "Here. Let me help you with your hair."

She suffered through the brushing, the tender touches on her nape and temples. He seemed hypnotized as he stroked through her copper curls, no doubt hoping she was equally mesmerized. Well, she wasn't. She grabbed the brush away and twisted her hair up every which way with some pins, then splashed some water on her face. "There. I'm done."

Edward took in her wrinkled dress. "Are you certain you don't want to change? If not the dress I brought for you, perhaps one of your own?"

"Why? Are we entertaining the king? Oh, but no. I remember. He thinks you're in deep mourning. Who did you tell him died?"

Edward examined his spotless white cuff. "Your mother."

Caroline struggled with her twitching hands. How they wanted to snatch up the hairbrush and heave it against the wall. "My mother? You never even met my mother! For that matter, neither did I!"

"I'm sorry, Caro. It seemed like a good idea at the time."

"Edward, I'm beginning to think you have lost your mind completely. This is no way to go about winning me. Killing off my poor dead mother, buying me a dress fit for the cheapest of whores, locking me up for hours on end, not to mention the whole kidnapping scenario. What has happened to your good sense?" She put her hands on her hips, feeling very much like *his* mother.

He gave her a rueful smile. "You've driven it from me."

"I? I've done nothing."

"You don't have to. You just *are*."

She supposed that was a compliment. Edward was as inexplicably drawn to her as she was to him. To discover that their separation had pained him enough to go insane should have pleased her, but it didn't. She wanted the rational Edward back, who recognized her for the hoyden she was: the woman who talked too much at breakfast; who made love too loudly; who broke things and climbed out windows; who ran away.

"Let's walk in the garden before dinner. I'll get a wrap." Some fresh air would do her good. The sun had dropped low in the sky, but there was still plenty of daylight left to examine the intricate knot garden. Earlier from her window she had glimpsed late roses, rust-red and yellow chrysanthemums, cosmos, anemones and alstromeria.

But when she and Edward stepped onto the path, Caroline saw nothing but tenting rolls of burlap and heaps of straw covering the plants and shrubs. Bradlaw's gardeners had been busy while she napped, protecting the plants from the uncertain nighttime temperature. It had been unusually cold for September, the threat of a nighttime frost frightening gardeners throughout the Home Counties.

"Drat! I had so wanted to see the flowers."

"I invited you out here this afternoon. I understand the gardeners do this every evening and remove it all in the morning. How tedious for them when everything will die away soon. We'll come outside tomorrow."

Edward cut an odd figure in his formal evening clothes amidst the humble burlap and straw. The only thing odder would have been for her to be wearing the ghastly red dress. That was one article of clothing that would not be going back to London with her.

She supposed she'd have to leave all her belongings behind when she escaped. Wondering if Ben had made any progress finding her reticule, she sat on a bench beneath a canopy of bittersweet vines. After a moment, Edward removed a handkerchief from his pocket, dusted off the bench and joined her.

"You needn't dress up on my account, Edward. I don't care what you wear."

"I planned a candlelit dinner with lots of romantic trimmings." He sounded as dispirited as the brown garden surrounding them. Caroline wrapped her paisley shawl tighter, watching the sunlight fade on the windows of Bradlaw House.

As far as romantic places went, Bradlaw House and its famous garden had been an excellent choice. Too bad her heart had hardened.

"We're not far from Christie Park," she said, changing the subject. "Do you plan on visiting while you keep me prisoner?"

"No. I wanted this week to be for us. Only us. No distractions."

"That sounds awfully dull."

"It needn't be. Caro, I know you're angry." He touched his bruise, then covered up his action by rubbing his jaw. She saw he was freshly shaven, in anticipation of how he thought he'd spend his night.

Was she too angry with him to let him take her to bed? She thought not. In a few days she'd be shriveling up, not a spinster, no longer a wife. The prospect filled her with little satisfaction.

"I told you yesterday I wanted us to make a fresh start. After today's debacle, do you think we can forget it and make that fresh start tomorrow instead? I'm putty in your hands, Caro. I'll stand for anything you say. Or throw. Please tell me there's still a chance for us."

"This isn't one of my books, Edward." She picked a few orange berries from the vine and tossed them into a flower bed, where they pinged off the burlap and bounced back at her feet.

"Marburn tells me you're done."

"For the time being. I need a break. It's exhausting imperiling my heroines. It's exhausting being imperiled."

They sat in companionable silence for a while as the sun slipped behind the trees and the air chilled. Edward glanced at his timepiece. "Mrs. Hazlett must be nearly ready for us. Will you join me in a drink first?"

"No, I want to keep a clear head. You could take advantage of me."

His cloudy green eyes met hers. "I had hopes to."

Caroline stood up. Who knew? He might get lucky.

* * *

The candlelight flattered her, even in her plain wrinkled blue dress. Edward was secretly relieved she'd rejected the strumpet gown. That's what came of entrusting one's valet to go shopping for women's clothes. Cameron must keep company with very fast females on his off hours to have picked such unsuitable attire, or else he simply hadn't absorbed the lessons of Jane Street during the short time he was in residence. None of Caroline's neighbors would have worn something so shockingly vulgar and they were the epitome of strumpets. Edward had been too busy the past weeks tying up loose ends so he could dedicate a week to Caroline to visit a modiste himself. Seven days now seemed both too short and too long.

He was certain he could not keep her here, even if he locked her in. Judging from the jewelry stashed in her pocket earlier, she meant to escape at the first opportunity. Perhaps he'd let her.

He'd been a proper gentleman all his life, save for the few hours yesterday on the road. While he'd allowed himself to feel a frisson of power over a helpless female, he was over that. He couldn't hold his wife against her will. Whatever he'd hoped to accomplish, it was clear his mission was a failure.

Except he still got to watch Caro across the table. See her break a roll apart. Take a tiny sip of wine. Dab white linen against her luscious mouth. His appetite for food had deserted him, but his hunger for Caro had not. He was a fool. Once again.

She covered a yawn. He pushed back from the table. "I'll escort you upstairs. You must be tired."

"I am, but I don't know why. I slept the day away. Most of the morning, too." She folded the napkin into a neat square and stood up.

Edward offered an arm. "Being imperiled is exhausting, as you said. I didn't mean to cause you harm or worry, Caro."

"To the end of my days, I'll never understand what you were thinking."

"Let's call it a temporary lapse of Christie judgment. I've reverted to my old boring self."

Caroline looked as if she wanted to say something, then focused on the stairs. Thank heavens there weren't so many to climb. They were in front of her bedroom door before he knew it.

"Goodnight, Caro." He contemplated a kiss, but thought on the whole he should not subject himself to such torture. So he was surprised when she stood on tiptoe to kiss him.

Heaven. Honey. Every sweet lick drove him to despair. He had missed his chance to keep her, if not yesterday, five years ago when his pride had dictated a dismal future. His actions since had done nothing but cement Caro's determination to cut all contact. If it was her way of saying good-bye, he needed to remember each brush of her fingertips, each thrust of her tongue, each flutter of his heart.

She fell back against the door and Edward fell with her, her plush softness cushioning his lust. Trapped between the wood and his own rigid manhood, she made no effort to repel him; rather she held his shoulders firmly, drawing him down in her kiss. He opened his eyes to see hers closed, the fan of black lashes flickering on her cheeks. By rights they should be tipped with bronze, but Caro was nothing if not unique, even to her eyelashes. She appeared to be concentrating as hard as he was, her mouth a petal unfurling with such sweetness it broke him.

What started as the merest brush of lips changed to devouring possession. Who possessed whom Edward wasn't sure, for they took turns slanting their lips over the other, their tongues tasting and tangling, their hands busy exploring. The light from the sconces wavered. Anyone could come upon them in the hall to see Caro struggle blindly with his neckcloth, to see his hands covering her breasts under the blue cloth, to see her leg raise to wrap him closer. In minutes he could take her up against the door like a common harlot, but Caro was uncommon. She deserved better for their last night together.

He wondered if she'd take a lover. He knew he wouldn't.

He groaned, but Caro interpreted it as abandon and rubbed herself against him like a hungry kitten. He fisted her skirts, sliding under to her smooth, cool thigh. He couldn't see it except in his mind's eye—the dimpled white expanse of flesh above her stocking, so soft, so vulnerable. He would kiss her there later if he could, mark her as his, at least for tonight. She shivered as he swept up to quickly find her heat, two fingers impaling themselves inside her slick, tight passage. His thumb circled the apex of her womanhood, already stiff and swollen for him. Only for him, at least for tonight.

Tonight was all they had. Tomorrow he'd send her away as she wished. He pressed into her in desperation. She was the one groaning, drenching his hand with her desire, angling her hips to sink him deeper in her folds, to force him to rub harder, to kiss her as though his very existence depended upon it. He fought for breath and wits as her hand freed his cock, curled about him and stroked him upward. He needed much more than her hand, much more than tonight. With a savage mental curse he lifted her, fitting her onto him, her legs locking around his, and held her up against the door.

He was seconds away from spilling into her. In the hallway.

Edward dragged himself from her mouth. "Caro, hang on. I've got to get you inside."

"You are inside," she whispered. "And it feels so good. Please, please don't stop."

"I must." He clung to her fiercely with one arm as he fumbled with the doorknob. It would quite ruin the mood if he dropped her. Slamming the door behind them, he lurched toward the bed, Caro wrapped around him, nipping his lips and driving him wild. Wilder. His skin was on fire. Everywhere. Too many damn clothes on both of them, but there was no time to divest himself of anything but his seed.

He had barely edged them to the bed when she contracted

around him, her rippling muscles drawing him up to the tip of her womb. He tipped her backward, strumming her bud as she came apart on the counterpane, her spine curving closer to him, her breasts begging for their release. He tore at her bodice with his free hand, but the wretched dress was impervious to his assault. He settled for kisses to her collarbone, her throat, her swollen pink mouth. He released everything he was into her, riding her to mutual oblivion.

Just for tonight. The waves wouldn't stop, each thrust and shudder building upon the last until he collapsed mindlessly exhausted onto a heap of clothing and a gasping Caroline. His cock still jerked and her passage still trembled, an echo of the power between them. The thought of withdrawing from her caused him acute pain, but it would be more painful still to keep her skin from his. The bits of her body he could see were slick with sweat and scented with jasmine. He needed to see every inch of her again before she was forbidden to him. Each soft rose-tipped breast, each curve of her hip, each toe. Her plump thighs, the swell of her belly, her beautiful bare mound with its tiny heart-shaped freckle, as though Venus herself had branded her for love. Edward would keep his wife in this bed as long as he could, which would never be long enough.

He pushed a copper strand from her damp brow. "We are not done. Not yet."

"Speak for yourself, my lord. I cannot imagine being more done than I am now." Her voice was rusty from her cries.

"I'm confident I can convince you otherwise." His thumb traced her cheekbone, then swept across her well-kissed lips. If she opened them, she would taste her own honey.

She turned her face and pushed at him ineffectually. "Edward, do get up. I'm roasting. Burning up."

"My plan precisely. I think it's past time we removed our clothes, yes?"

She scrunched her red-gold brows. "I don't like the sound of 'we.'"

"All right. I shall remove *your* clothes." He eased out and lay on his side, examining the row of buttons on her bodice. Caroline's skirts were hiked up to her waist but despite her objection she made no effort to pull them down. Excellent. Seeing half of her was better than seeing none of her, but he wouldn't let those damn buttons get the best of him again.

He would start with her black slippers and her stockings and her garters. He sat up, the room swimming a bit. She had wrecked him—certainly wrecked him for any other woman. He looked down at his ruined clothing, thankful he'd given Cameron time off so he'd be spared the disapproval. Taking one of Caroline's feet in the palm of his hand, he pulled the grosgrain ribbon from its knot at her ankle and tossed the shoe aside. Her cotton stockings were beige and practical for travel, no pretty embroidered fleur-de-lis or tiny clocks, but her garters were a different story. The rosettes were studded with winking crystals and seed pearls, a pretty boon for a knight to carry into battle. He untied one and rolled the stocking from her calf.

Caroline lay still, her silver eyes closed.

"You won't kick me?"

She shook her head into the pillow as he began to knead her arch, rolling her heel in the cup of his hand as his long fingers traced a line to her toes. He felt her relax into his palm, her foot growing heavier, her other limb splayed in abandon to reveal her glistening cleft. She sighed as he tugged at each toe, working the knots out, rubbing her sole as earnestly as he did her swollen bud earlier. He lifted her calf and bent to kiss the little line behind her knee, allowing his hands to wander a bit farther north. She tapped her still-shod foot onto the coverlet.

"Ah. I'm getting carried away. I almost forgot." He made quick work of undressing her other foot. "I can see it's cross with me." He lightly kissed each toe, massaging all the while. Caroline let out a whimper which he took for an invitation, so he kissed his way up her leg, his hands smoothing and stroking in tandem.

He was hard again already. Molten. Her scent and his

filled his senses as he parted her and feasted, filling his mouth with her tender pink pearl. She convulsed beneath him, still greedy, still his. For tonight.

He gazed up though his lashes and saw Caroline struggling with her tiny buttons in frustration. She was half mad. Clumsy. His doing. He smiled and swiped his tongue deeper and felt each tremor against the tip. She abandoned the buttons and held him to her center, her words incoherent but her body stating plainly its need. Edward happily obliged in her drugging embrace, each kiss justified by her response. He could imagine doing this with no one other than Caroline, swallowing her bliss, tasting his own triumph.

She begged him to stop, yet he felt her fingers run ragged in his hair, each stroke a second late mimicking his tongue, as though they were dancing to the same tune from across a sensual divide. She crested again and again, sobbing his name. His common English name had never sounded sweeter or meant more.

And still they were dressed. Ridiculous. He gave her a final kiss, sat up, and tore off his jacket.

"Oh, no. No more," she whispered.

"We have tonight, Caro. Only tonight."

She nodded. "I can't—you can't—we must put an end to this. You know it as well as I."

He didn't agree, but was not going to ruin what was between them with an argument. But if he didn't shed his clothes, he'd burn up like a dry forest hit by lightning. Caroline was his lightning, his flame. He could taste the ash of her leaving already.

He fingered the little blue bone buttons. He saw they were shaped like little flowers, each petal sharp. Caroline always had an eye for detail. Why she couldn't see how much he loved her was a complete mystery to him. "What fiend sewed these on?"

She batted him away and began to unfasten them herself. "It's just because I'm hot. We are not going to—you know. Ever again."

"I know what?"

"You know," she said, glaring at him.

He slipped down next to her. "It doesn't seem fair, Caro. This last time was all for you. When do I get my turn?"

"You've had your turn. Too many turns. I can't keep tumbling into bed with you, Edward. Especially since I'm very, very angry with you."

He lifted her chin, but she wouldn't meet his eyes. "Yes, I could tell how angry you were. You were just chock full of—anger, was it?"

"Now you are mocking me. Of course I responded to you. I'm only human. But *you've* been the fiend, tying me up and carting me off to the country like this. I want to go away. To-morrow."

"All right."

She opened her mouth. "You don't mean that. Not really."

"Of course I mean it. A Christie's word is his bond."

"Then this is our last night together." She didn't sound as happy as she might have.

"If that's what you want."

"I do. It's exactly what I want." She pulled the blue dress over her head and dropped it to the floor. The finest French batiste shift still covered too much of her, but Edward saw the gratifying shadow of her nipples beneath the fabric. He continued to undress until he was shorn of everything but a massive erection.

Caroline closed her eyes. "Oh, no. I simply can't."

"There won't be anything simple about it, Caro, I guarantee that. For the *last* time should be special, should it not?"

The flush had left her cheeks and throat. Caro was alabaster in the lamplight, as beautiful as a marble statue. But her body was damp and warm against his, though not for long. He broke the spell deliberately. "You must promise me something."

She curled into his shoulder as though she had forgotten

they would not be lovers again. "No. No promises. I've said all I'm going to say. You said I could leave tomorrow."

"This is not about us. I've had word from Lord Douglass." Edward's sister Beth had sent a footman with the letter to Bradlaw House that afternoon. Edward should have sent *her* to buy a proper red dress. She was one of the few who knew of his reconciliation plan, and had encouraged him with unrestrained enthusiasm. Obviously, she'd read too many of Caro's books to recognize romantic drivel did not work in reality. *Lord Farringdon's Fickle Fiancée* had been a dismal failure if even after the passion of the past few hours, they could not put their marriage to rights.

He felt the immediate emptiness when Caro rolled away. "Now what? Don't tell me you mean to keep me by sleeping against the bedroom door like some bloody great mastiff for the rest of my life. I won't be threatened by these amorphous plots. Or by your misplaced sense of chivalry." She sat up, her hair a crimson thundercloud in the lamplight. "This is it, Edward. The last fling. Don't think you can scare me into staying. We are absolutely, completely, one hundred percent over."

Edward felt deflated. Gut punched. She meant what she said. It was the last time he would ever see her creamy skin or feel her wet velvet around his cock. He would send her home tomorrow. Buy her the promised cottage far, far away. In America if she'd go. There was no point in further discussion. Her very presence would break his heart. By having this conversation now, he was ensuring it was, in fact, the end. Any further arrangements they'd make would be free of feeling. He would summon Cold Christie and that would be that.

"You've made yourself quite plain I'm not wanted. We'll talk about the formal end to this marriage tomorrow when our heads are clear." He doubted his head would be clear anytime soon, but he'd not bore her with any more entreaties. His Christie pride forbade him lowering himself any lower. At least he'd have a shred of dignity left when he handed her up into his carriage tomorrow afternoon. "Please listen. He tells me Pope has not entirely gotten over your insult to him."

"But you spoke to him yourself weeks ago!"

Edward nodded. "I did. And he was most convincing in his assertion that he was not the man Rossiter overheard in the garden. I thought he might actually haul off and sock me, he was so full of righteous bluster. But Douglass warns me that Pope seems more desperate than ever. He's had some financial reverses and blames you."

"I? As though I have anything to do with the Exchange! This is ludicrous, Edward. Why are you telling me?"

"I just want you to be careful in the future, when you will no longer have my protection." The thought of Caroline rattling around by herself in the country pierced him. But he'd hire servants. Get her a real mastiff if necessary. Harold wouldn't like that one bit.

"I've already promised not to write any more books. I don't see what else I can do."

She was off the bed, reaching for the old red poppy robe on the chair. To his surprise, Edward realized he would miss the robe, and the lush white body beneath it even more. Their lives were about to change, his back to the well-worn groove of propriety. Speeches in Parliament. Stultifying dinner parties. Estate matters. Only his children would have the power to set him off-kilter. He nearly looked forward to Neddie's next mess.

Caroline's world would shrink even further. She'd be buried in the country. No naughty tea parties, no naughty books. A living death for a scarlet butterfly like Caro. But it was what she wanted.

He wondered how long she would last. "You won't miss writing?"

Caroline shrugged. "It hasn't been easy the past few months. I may have run out of ways to murder my characters."

Edward would have been sublimely happy to have died in her arms a few minutes ago. But he had responsibilities. Duties. Cutting Caro loose as requested was one of them.

She belted the robe and sat at her dressing table, untangling the thicket of curls. He didn't dare to get up and help her tonight. But he needed to get up. Put on his clothes and go. Turn the key in the lock for the last time. Lie awake down the hall knowing she was under his borrowed roof, breathing the same night air as he, perhaps feeling the same regret. She would be close, yet a world away.

Tomorrow they would conclude their business. He would be generous. He'd set his man of business out at once to buy her some damned country house with enough damned flowers to choke a herd of goats. Hire a staff. Double her allowance. Will would rail at him, but his money meant nothing. There would be plenty for Ned to run through, and more than adequate provisions had been make for Jack and Allie. Edward was not so distraught that he longed for death. The years ahead stretched empty before him, but he would manage. Christies always did.

Chapter 21

Esme looped the length of rope around the lone linden
tree. The valley was vast beneath her, but what choice
did she have?

—*Escaping the Earl*

She could not wait for Ben to help her. If she stayed another
day, it would mean another night in Edward's arms. No
matter what she said—and she had said it all, spelling out
how it was the *very last time* every time they had made love,
all three times—she didn't trust herself to keep her word. If
she succumbed to Edward again, she might as well lie down
in the road and wait for the London stage to run over her,
just like in *Beauty and the Baronet*, only at the last minute
the baronet pulled the beauty from certain death and into his
bed. Edward would do the same. She could *not* keep opening
to him—not her mouth, not her legs, not her heart. Nor did
she want to open her ears to listen to a new list tomorrow.

She looked at the little bedside clock. It would be later on
today. They had spent quite a long time in bed, Caroline ini-
tiating several moments she meant to remember. The last desperate, drowning kiss. The last graze of her nipple between
his teeth. The last twisting thrust of his hips. Even though she
tried consciously to cling to the concept of "last," another
day spent at Bradlaw House would make her lose her resolve. Edward would be immaculately civil, his gleaming
dark hair brushed back, his face impassive. He would grant
her everything he thought she wanted and more. Likely she
would be the best-set-up estranged wife in England. In Europe. In the world. And she would be bound to thank him in
the only way she knew how.

There was not a hope of her sleeping with Edward's scent on her bedding. On her. She opened the door to the dressing room. Very conveniently, the armoire had crisp white sheets stacked on the top shelf. But she would not be changing the linens. Just her clothes, because even the wrinkles of her blue dress had wrinkles after what Edward had put her through.

Caroline pulled the last fresh dress from its hanger—a simple slate gray travelling costume with a narrow skirt and tight-fitting matching jacket. She sponge-bathed with the cold water in the pitcher, dug clean undergarments from the drawer where the invisible maid had arranged her few possessions, and buttoned up the silver buttons herself as best she could. Her difficulty was a reminder that she had indulged herself far too much the past few months. If she weren't careful, one could tip her sideways and roll her down the street like an empty wine barrel. Declaring her hair a hopeless cause, she braided it and tucked it up under a black straw bonnet. Her jewels pinned safely into a pocket in her skirts, she began knotting the sheets together with all the expertise of one of Admiral Nelson's sailors.

Dawn was not so very far off, and the road from Bradlaw House led straight into Ashford, a busy market town. While she might have wished for her vanished half-boots, her black leather slippers would have to do. She laced them up her stockings, tying them as tightly as she did the sheets. Once she had dropped her line out the window, she discovered she'd underestimated. With a sigh, she pulled a fragrant rumpled sheet from the bed and added one last length. She dragged the chintz chair to the window for an anchor, hoping it wouldn't catapult over the window frame and come crashing down on her head. The furniture in the first room was much heavier, but Caroline had to escape from where she was. At least the drop to the ground was much more manageable. She could do it with her eyes closed.

And did, barring a disconcerting moment when a gust of wind twisted the makeshift rope and swung her into the bricks of Bradlaw House. She contained her yelp and slipped to freedom. The house was dark and quiet behind her. The only sound was the rattle of dry leaves that would fall soon and the thudding of her own heart.

She ran along the building to the front courtyard, down the tree-lined alley to the iron gates that stood at the end. They were, mercifully, wide open, an egregious oversight on Edward's part. If she turned right, she would wind up at Christie Park in less than an hour. Ashford was to the left, easy walking on a well-surfaced road, although the overwhelming inky blackness of the country night gave Caroline pause. By walking at a steady pace she should reach Ashford by daybreak. She shivered into her jacket, wishing she'd thought to bring the kidnapper's cape with her. It would be a memento of the odd adventure of the past two days, and useful besides. However, the sun would soon warm her on the way. No doubt she'd be so crammed into the coach to London with other travelers she'd be too hot for comfort.

She patted her pocket, confirming that the sharp lump of stones and gold and silver was still there. She hadn't taken all her treasures, but had every confidence Edward would eventually return her possessions to her, even Harold, who would have made an uneasy companion dangling from a window had she been able to find him. Edward would do what was right. He always did, although he'd made a detour of late, making her his unwilling mistress, holding her captive, and not only with ropes and keys.

She was finally free, the wind in her face, her steps lively. Walking to Ashford was not so very arduous. Caroline was not perfectly sure how she would barter a ticket with a trinket or two, but decided to worry about that when the time came. She had to concentrate on the dips and curves of the road and the insidious pebbles that seemed to roll under her every step.

Despite the chill, her armpits became damp and her thighs slapped together rather unpleasantly. She would be chafed and chapped, but who would ever see her red thighs? With each stride she became more aware of the soft life she'd led in

London. Her breath was ragged although she moved at a snail's pace. She was alternately cold and hot, which made no sense at all. What a pity it would be if Edward found her lifeless body in a ditch. He might mourn her, but it would solve the problem of him marrying again. She imagined the next Mrs. Christie, like the first, would be a paragon of virtue and good taste.

Caroline couldn't remember the last time she was truly virtuous. Even her desire to free Edward was more for her sake than his. She was a selfish creature, chock so full of foibles she didn't have a name for them all.

She laughed out loud, causing something in the grass to dart and scurry. She was so foolish. One couldn't die from walking and sweating and feeling sorry for oneself. It was rather ridiculous wearing a bonnet in the dark without a soul to see her, so she loosened the strings to let the air cool her scalp. The straw hat bumped on her back with every step and her braid slithered from its coil. She wiped a drip of perspiration from her left eye, not that she could see a bloody thing. She could hear, though—odd shifting and rustling, croaks and cries, all the usual sounds of a country night. Once, she had been used to them. She'd spent many a Cumberland night as a girl roaming the fields and woods with Nicky. She was no longer so intrepid. London streets might be unsafe, but she'd be delighted to have the company of a few merry inebriated gentlemen and hard pavement beneath her feet.

The air was redolent of leaf mold and damp. She sniffed. Rain was coming, she was sure. Perfect. She trudged on in the gloom, checking the sky every few steps for the black to give way to gray. A handful of stars winked down, most obscured by the scuddering clouds. Caroline sent a brief prayer upward that the rain might hold off until she was closer to Ashford and was rewarded by a wet plop on her nose.

Hell and damnation. She was already wet underneath her clothes. What difference would it make if she got rained on over them? Wet was wet. She shoved her hat back on her head and picked up the pace until a wicked stitch in her side was impossible to ignore. A low rock loomed ahead and she sat, catching her breath.

And was very glad she did, for she heard the jingling of a harness and the steady clopping of a horse in the distance. For one frightful moment she thought Edward had discovered her, but this particular horse was moving too slowly to be ridden by an angry husband. The creaking roll of a cart could be heard behind it. It must be market day in Ashford.

She stood up uncertainly, waiting to spy the conveyance and its driver. Folks were kindly hereabouts, or had been the brief time Caroline had been at Christie Park. Her walking days might be over. She kept well to the side of the road, not wishing to frighten the horse or its driver, and made her voice as sweet as warm honey. She waved a black-gloved hand in the air, not that anyone could see it.

"Hallo! Hallo! Hallo!"

The rumbling wagon came closer, its lantern swinging on a pole. Caroline saw the dark outline of its driver and a looming piebald workhorse.

"Whoa there, Ajax. And what have we got here?"

"Good morning, sir!" Caroline said brightly. "I'm on my way to Ashford. Could you possibly give me a lift? I'd be happy to pay you."

The man raised the lantern, casting Caroline in an unwelcome pool of light. "By all that's holy, you're Lady Christie, you are. Haven't seen you in these parts in years, but I'd never forget you or that red hair of yours. Does Lord Christie know you're out in the dark and rain?"

Of all the rotten luck.

Caroline widened her smile. "Do I know you, sir?"

"Wouldn't think so. Ham Mitchell. I'm a tenant of one of your neighbors, Lord Bradlaw. I can't take you back home to Christie Park, you know. It's market day. And I'm late already."

His name was unfamiliar. She'd made an effort with Edward's tenants, but had never felt sure of herself as lady of the manor. She was not Alice and never would be. Caroline had probably made a great many mistakes with them, just as she had with everyone else.

"Oh, that's quite all right. It's our home in London I'm going to."

"On foot? Without a maid?"

She could imagine his suspicious face even if she couldn't quite see it. "It's a very long story, Mr. Mitchell. I promise you I'll make it worth your while if you take me up in your cart." The horse whickered and Caroline rubbed his ugly nose. She trusted its owner was just a simple farmer, and not a murderer. It would be most inconvenient to have walked all this way to wind up dead. She sneezed.

She hoped it just was a reaction to the horse. Lung fever would be no picnic. Girls were always falling ill and delirious in her books so the heroes could nurse them through and discover the deep and abiding love that had hitherto been absent in their flinty hearts. Caroline had no wish to be nursed. Or dead. She just wanted to get to Ashford without incident.

"I don't know as I should. Lord Christie is no one I'd like to cross, and that's a fact."

Bother Edward and his reputation. "I won't take up too much room. You won't even know I'm in the cart. I don't want to delay you, Mr. Mitchell. It's raining, and you must be anxious to get your produce to market. What have you got back there under the tarp?"

"The best turnips you ever tasted. Courgettes and runner beans. Potatoes, leeks, and beetroot. Don't change the subject. Are you running away from your man?"

Caroline stuck her chin out. "Lord Christie and I are separated, Mr. Mitchell. Surely the gossips have told you that."

"Don't listen to gossip much since my wife passed. What are you doing on this road then?"

It might be difficult to bribe a widower with jewels, but maybe he had a daughter—and a purse with change in it she could swap for her semiprecious finery. "I'm so sorry about your wife, Mr. Mitchell. I'll tell you everything if you give me a ride." Cold rain dripped from the brim of her hat down her neck. "Please, Mr. Mitchell. *Please.*"

"I shouldn't. But I will." He hopped off the bench and gave a brief bow. Caroline quelled her desire to throw her arms around him and kiss him. "Can't stuff you under the canvas. You'll crush the vegetables. You'll have to ride up top with me."

"I shall be delighted, Mr. Mitchell."

After a mile or two, her delight and desire to kiss him had vanished. Caroline was convinced Mr. Mitchell had not bathed for quite some time and envied his wife her death. But as the rain pelted down, she told a much-abridged version of her story, grateful she had experience prevaricating and writing romances. Every sentence or two, she brought her gloved wrist to her nose, inhaling the wet leather so she would not have to inhale Mr. Mitchell. She made no mention of drugging and kidnapping, but painted Edward as the villain of the piece.

Mr. Mitchell seemed squarely in Edward's corner, however. "So, you're telling me he gave you one more chance, and you've run away."

"Perhaps I've not made myself clear. We had a marriage of convenience, but it wasn't convenient for anyone, least of all my husband. We never got along, not for one minute." Except in bed, but she was not going to shock the poor man. She'd already told too much. "It's much better we go our separate ways, as we've been doing these past five years. I've quite a terrible temper, you know. If you were married to me, you'd think I was a perfect shrew." She sniffed her gray sleeve, hoping for a trace of jasmine.

"A man likes a woman with some spirit," Mr. Mitchell countered. "I miss fighting with my Abby, and that's the truth."

"Have you thought of marrying again?"

He snorted. "Who would have me?"

"Your holding is prosperous, is it not? I imagine you're a very hard worker."

"Aye, that I am."

"Well," Caroline said, "you can provide financial security, which is very important."

"I don't want to be married for my money."

Caroline thought a very great deal of money would have to be involved to overcome his rank odor. "Tell me about your house. Is there a bathing chamber?"

"Abby used a copper tub in the kitchen."

She could hear the smile in his voice as he remembered, but she had to bring him back to the present. "Do *you* use it, sir?"

"If you're telling me I offend your nose, I know it," he said gruffly. "I've been too busy with the harvest to worry about washing. I was hoping this rain will take some of the dirt away."

She patted his arm. "You'll never catch another woman unless you take better care of yourself, Mr. Mitchell. Women are superficial creatures. A bit of soap and a good scrubbing, and they'll be putty in your hands. You'll see."

He was silent. Caroline hoped he wouldn't dump her on the side of the road for her unsolicited advice. It was one of the oddest conversations she'd ever had, and considering her unusual neighbors, that was saying a great deal. "I'm sorry if you think me too bold. I told you I was a shrew."

"I reckon you mean well. I'll think about what you said."

The rest of the journey was very quiet, save for the rain spattering the canvas and the horse plodding through puddles. Caroline imagined she looked as wretched as Mr. Mitchell smelled. As the sky lightened, the rain did not let up. Caroline was chilled to the bone. Soaked and miserable.

She cheered up when they passed a white-painted signpost. Not much farther. "Mr. Mitchell, I don't suppose you know of a jeweler or pawnshop that is open at this hour of the morning?"

His fuzzy gray eyebrows knit. "Don't tell me you don't have any money."

She smiled. "All right then, I won't."

"Lord have mercy. You're cork brained. Lord Christie is well rid of you, I'd say."

"That is what I've been telling you these past five miles."

"What are you planning to sell?"

"I have a few trinkets."

He pulled in the reins. "Whoa, Ajax. Let's see them."

Oh, dear. If he tried to rob her, she supposed she could bolt from the cart and make a mad dash into the woods. How lowering to think her confidence in him had been misplaced. Her face must have betrayed her alarm, for he growled at her.

"Don't look at me like that, Lady Christie. I'm not going to take advantage of your stupidity. If I'm to go a-wooing again, I'll need something to sweeten the pot. After I take my bath, of course." He patted the purse tied to his belt. "I can trade you your fare for a bauble or two."

"I do beg your pardon. The last few days have been very stressful."

"Aye," he said sarcastically. "Your husband sets you up in a fine home and wants to read you a list. Sounds brutal."

"You men all stick together." She took off her gloves, unpinned her pocket and pulled out the lumpy handkerchief.

Mr. Mitchell's eyes widened. "You really are a ninny-hammer. What if I weren't me but some rogue? I could steal you blind."

"I'm a good judge of character," Caroline lied.

"Hmpf." His thick fingers picked up Edward's pearl ring.

"Oh, no, not that one." She slipped it on her own finger. "Maybe this?"

He picked up a cameo ring and held it up to his eye. "Too plain."

"You really can't go wrong with an Italian cameo, Mr. Mitchell. Look, here's a matching pin. They're not plain at all. Just look at the detail!" In fact, they were not her favorites, and certainly worth the sacrifice if she could get to London.

"I don't know."

The man drove a hard and expensive bargain. Caroline

had to throw in a rose-gold bracelet and a silver chain before he forked over any money. She would have been far better off waiting until a jeweler opened.

"The next Mrs. Mitchell will be a very lucky woman," Caroline said graciously, if she had plenty of clothespins for her nose.

Ashford was bustling with energy, although the day was gray and gloomy. Mr. Mitchell was not offended when his offer of a turnip for the road was refused, and dropped her in the yard of the inn fifteen minutes before the first coach was to leave. Caroline purchased her ticket and a pasty, and earned the opprobrium of the other passengers as they took in her lack of luggage, sodden clothing, ruined shoes and the lingering aromatic aftermath of Mr. Mitchell.

It was not quite dawn. Caroline waited nervously, expecting Edward to clatter up on the cobblestones on a white steed, until she climbed into the coach and watched the rain drip down the window pane. At each posting house, she sank deeper into the squabs, hoping Edward had not discovered her perfidy.

The bells of London finally woke her from a doze. The rain had stopped and the world was bathed in sunshine, streets and rooftops sparkling with diamond drops. She was home. Almost. And happy, of course. How could she not be? She was dry and determined to put the past behind her.

Chapter 22

The castle's cold walls surrounded her, each shadow a wretched wraith of remembrance.
—The Prince's Promise

The hack left her at the corner. She was on Jane Street. Again. It was the logical choice. The only choice, really. There was no Dorset cottage to run off to. There *would* be if Caroline could persuade Edward to buy one for her. If he didn't throttle her first when he found her, which he would. Eventually. Possibly even later today. She hoped he'd be reasonable. She simply couldn't have stayed at Bradlaw House while he made another list stating the terms of their separation. If he did come, she would tell him to let Will Maclean earn his keep and do the honors, then close the door in his face. She really couldn't afford to see Edward ever again.

Serena still had spare keys and was surprised and delighted to see Caroline, even in her extreme dishevelment. Although her neighbor was getting dressed for an outing with her protector Lord Buckley, she offered Caroline a quick cup of tea. Caroline demurred, anxious to get as settled as she could next door.

Her footsteps echoed through the half-empty house. She'd only been gone three days, but realized she'd been saying good-bye to the house for weeks. Despite the brilliant September sunshine slanting through the parlor windows, Caroline had an overwhelming desire to go to sleep. She set her hat on the windowsill and eyed the emerald-green sofa. No. She'd be better off upstairs in bed, sleeping the rest of the day and night away. She was too tired to be hungry. Tomorrow she'd shop for provisions, although there was probably something to eat below. She could cook perfectly well for herself. Hell, she might even manage another courtesans' tea on her own if she borrowed some dishes. She'd have to ask Maclean where Edward had taken all the boxes meant for her nonexistent new home.

Trudging up the stairs, she took note of the empty squares on the wall where her paintings had hung. She wouldn't try to get anything back. She hoped she wouldn't be there long enough to mind the lack of decoration.

The bed was stripped, just as she'd left it the other morning in order to make things easier for Lizzie and Mrs. Hazlett, curse them both. Not bothering to find sheets or even undress, she stretched out and her problems disappeared nearly at once.

Suddenly, she was jerked up, a hood pulled down over her face. If she hadn't been dead asleep, she might have fought back sooner. Turning her hands to fists, she punched through the air. "Not again. Edward, you've got to see reason!"

"Shut up." He squeezed both her hands together and tied them tight.

"Fine. I suppose you think I'm *chattering like a magpie* again. I haven't begun to chatter."

"Shut up, I said!" So he could still hear her, despite the muffling of the fabric on her face. She could barely hear him, but Edward seemed very angry, an unusual show of choler from Cold Christie. She'd known he wouldn't like it when she ran away from Bradlaw House, but this rough handling was ridiculous. Did he think his absurd domination would make her change her mind? How many times did she have to tell him their marriage was over? Ended? Concluded? Finished? She couldn't think of any more words to describe it without her dictionary. Furious, she slipped from his grasp and rolled off the bed.

Silly man. He should have remembered from the last time to tie her feet up first. He grabbed her arm and she played possum long enough for him to draw her closer. Poor Edward. But he deserved it. He was *not* going to dragoon her twice and get away with it. She kneed him hard, reveling in his mumbled string of curses. He fell backward onto the floor with a thump. From the cracking sound before he landed, he might have hit his head on one of the naked nymphs on the bedpost.

Caroline tugged at the hood with her bound hands, finally shaking it off. She froze. The man on the floor wasn't tall or slender or elegant like Edward. The man on the floor wasn't Edward at all. He was a monster. Lord Randolph Pope. *Randy Poop.* A rather dead-looking Randy Poop.

Had she killed him? She was torn between horror and an odd sort of happiness. But then his chest rose, and horror won. She needed to get out of the house before he woke up and all of him rose to come after her. Whatever he planned was surely worse than anything Edward had done.

Of course Edward would not be so stupid to try to capture her heart again through control. It was she who was stupid, returning to an empty house. Edward had warned her about Pope but she hadn't paid any attention. Thanking Providence she'd slept in her clothes, she raced down the stairs. It took forever to unset the locks and turn the door knob with both hands tied.

Caroline cried in frustration as her damp hands slipped on the brass handle. There were no guards at the end of Jane Street to run to yet. They didn't come on duty until darkness fell. If she got out, she'd go to Serena's and lock herself in.

Success! The door pulled open and she tumbled down the steps—straight into Edward. A strange mud-spattered horse was tied beyond him to the tree in front of Number Seven. It looked tired, but its rider did not. Caroline had never seen a more wonderful sight than her husband, full of towering rage, lips set in a thin grim line, road dust and dirt covering him from head to toe.

"What are you doing here?"

"What are *you* doing here? You left me without a word! I had one last morning with you, or did you forget? Did you think I wouldn't follow?" He reached for her. Caroline darted away but not fast enough. He caught her face in his hands as though he was about to kiss her. And then he did.

The kiss was not friendly or polite. It was a kiss of possession, of anger, of white hot heat. Caroline sagged in his arms as he lanced her with his tongue, slicing through her defenses, making her witless. She could easily remain witless forever. Each fingertip along her jaw branded his intention to keep her at his mercy. Yes, this was exactly why she had fled. Why she had to stop his delicious assault, even beyond the danger upstairs in her house. She pushed feebly against Edward's chest.

"Unh."

Impossibly, the kiss deepened. He held her in a straitjacket embrace, crushing her into his travel-stained coat, as though he wanted to absorb her into him. His hands splayed wide across her back. His tongue warred with hers, and she was no match for him. He swept in, conquered, mastered. She could do nothing but shiver. Even the idea of Pope coming up behind her to bash her head in didn't seem so terrible. At least she would die in Edward's arms.

He broke the kiss. "You're not wearing a cloak."

Caroline looked up at him stupidly, her lips still tingling. Why was he talking about what she was wearing? Unless he planned on getting her out of her clothes again. *No.*

"Come, you'll get chilled. Let's go back inside and we can—talk."

"No!"

"Look, I know I made a mistake—with the abduction. And the list. But I swear to you, Caro—"

"No, it's not that!" She raised her wrists. "I may not be wearing a cloak, but I *am* wearing this rope bracelet. Lord Pope is upstairs in my bedroom. We have to get away before he wakes up. He might be armed."

It was Edward's turn to be slack jawed. "What?"

"He—he attacked me while I was sleeping."

Edward's lips went white. "Oh, Jesu, Caro. I'll kill him."

"No, no, it's not what you think. He didn't touch me that way. B-but he put a hood over my head and tied my hands." She couldn't help but smile. "Like you, he forgot about my feet. I kicked him, really, really hard, and he fell."

"He was still after you. I was right then."

"Yes," Caroline said in annoyance. "Aren't you always? But we can't stand on my front steps kissing and talking. I was going to Serena's next door when I bumped into you."

He shoved her aside and down a step. "A very good idea. I'll join you once I've taken care of Pope."

"No, Edward! What if he has a knife or a gun?" She grabbed his arm but he twisted away.

"Obey me just this once, Caro. I won't let him kill me, I promise."

Edward appeared unmovable above her, rather like a white knight come to the rescue. She had never loved him more than she did that moment.

She poked him in the chest with a shaky finger. "I won't ever forgive you if something happens to you. I will *not* be a merry widow."

"Go."

She wavered. "Should we send for a constable?"

He shook his dark head. "I don't think so. I'll talk some sense into him. I'll come as soon as I'm done."

Caroline bit her lip, playing for time. She couldn't let him go in there alone, could she? "Even after you spoke with him before, he didn't give up."

"He will this time. A kiss for good luck?" He was smiling at her as though he hadn't a care in the world.

"There isn't time for kissing."

He smiled down at her. "There's always time for kissing, Caro. A quick one." He bent and brushed her lips. It was an entirely different kind of kiss, and all the sweeter for his restraint. It was she who threw herself headlong into his embrace, losing control. She drank in his taste and his scent of lime and horse, drowning her senses with essence of Edward. He untangled her gently. "Go. I'll be fine."

Caroline watched him mount the steps. The door still hung open. He stepped inside, pausing on the threshold. "I absolutely forbid you to follow me," he said quietly. He shut the door, and she heard the resolute click of the new locks.

Damn! She couldn't sit around gossiping with Serena and do nothing. Serena had more keys to Number Seven even after giving her the front door keys. Caroline could go through the garden wall and enter by way of the kitchen or back door. But first she had to get the cords cut from her wrists. She hurried down the sidewalk, tripped up to Serena's door and lifted the lion's head knocker.

Serena had a butler, as did all the ladybirds lucky enough to find themselves safely off the stage or out of the alleys and onto Jane Street. Putney was no Hazlett, but proper just the same. He hadn't batted a rheumy brown eye when she turned up earlier looking like a drowned rat, locked out of her own house. He didn't react now, although he took in the rope with a quick flick of his ascertaining eyes. Caroline had no way of knowing how long she'd slept. The sun was still a vibrant orange ball in the sky, but surely her arrival twice on his doorstep in various states of distress in one day was unusual. Caroline confirmed it by her next words.

"Putney, lock every door and window. Fetch a knife to untie my hands. Do you have a gun as well?"

Putney took it upon himself to alter the order of the orders. He reached into his pocket, unsheathed a small knife and efficiently sawed through Caroline's bonds.

"Yes, Lady Christie. I believe there is a gun in the household."

"I need it."

"Do you plan on shooting someone, my lady, or would you like me to do it for you?"

Caroline swallowed her laughter. Putney was a gem. Rubbing her chafed wrists, she followed him and his jingling keys around the ground floor as he checked the locks.

"I'm not sure yet, but I don't think your involvement is necessary. My husband is next door."

Putney paused at a heavy red velvet drape, allowing himself the tiniest frown. "Lady Christie, if I may be so bold, I don't advise that you kill your husband. The murder of a peer is a very serious offense. I'm sure the legal separation will be adequate."

Everybody knew everything on Jane Street. "You misunderstand, Putney. I was attacked by Lord Randolph Pope. My husband plans to do something to him, I'm not sure what. I'd feel ever so much better if I helped him."

"Are you an expert with firearms, my lady?"

Caroline thought back to her unsupervised childhood. She and Nicky had shot their share of pickle jars and pots. "It will all come back to me, I'm sure. Really, I'm going quite mad with worry. Could you hurry?"

The butler drew himself up. "It is my responsibility to protect the lady of the house. As Miss Serena is off with her gentleman until tomorrow, it is my duty to protect you. I was once quite good with my fists, you know. I daresay it will all come back to *me*."

Caroline was skeptical. If Putney had ever fought, it was in the featherweight category about a thousand years ago. But his arms were folded across his narrow chest and he looked implacable. "Oh, very well. If Serena's not even here, we won't worry about locking up. Let's go."

"I am sure Lord Christie would not appreciate it if we interrupted him. I expect he told you to stay away and that he would come here when it was over."

"How did you—Wait, I just thought you said you'd help me. What was all that talk about being a fighter?"

"Indeed. If our security is breached, I shall ensure with my dying breath that you are safe. If you feel my fists are inadequate, I shall position myself at the front door with a truncheon. But you will not leave the premises, Lady Christie. Lord Christie would have my hide if I enabled you into danger."

"Oh, for heaven's sake! My husband could be lying in a

pool of blood right this minute and that revolting viscount heading for France!"

"Doubtful. Lord Christie seems eminently qualified to deal with the task at hand. Would you care for a cup of tea, Lady Christie?"

"I don't want any bloody tea! I've already been Pope's prisoner once today. I won't be yours." Caroline raced to the front door. It was, as she requested, locked.

Putney came up silently behind her. "Perhaps a sherry then. Something to calm your nerves."

Caroline felt her heart go black. "Give me the keys, Putney. If you don't, I'll find that truncheon."

"Now, my lady. You'll thank me in the end. And don't get any ideas about going upstairs and climbing out the balcony window. Miss Serena told me all about *that*."

She had been too good for too long—except for the interlude with Edward, when objects came so easily to hand and were tossed with smashing satisfaction at the walls. At him. Caroline picked up a particularly ugly vase. Serena would be grateful it was gone.

Putney looked at the fragments at his feet. "Tsk, tsk. Lord Buckley gave that to her, you know. There is plain white ironstone in the kitchen which has much less sentimental value. Shall we go belowstairs?"

Caroline admitted defeat. She was behaving like the spoiled child Edward accused her of being. But if she never heard him accuse her again, she'd simply die. She burst into tears.

Putney placed a gentle hand on her shoulder. "There, there. It will be all right. We'll give Lord Christie a quarter of an hour, how's that? If we've no news by then, I'll go round personally and find out what's what."

"I—I'll go with you," Caroline sniveled.

"We'll see." Putney went to the drinks cupboard and poured her some sherry. "Oloroso. Excellent, as I understand."

Caroline took a small sip. She had never been much for

drinking spirits—at least that was one fault she did not possess. Oh, a glass or two of champagne with Edward when she was nervous or love-flushed. A drop of brandy when she had a cold. But she'd seen firsthand what alcohol had done to those she loved, and would never follow them to their graves in that manner. She smoothed her wrinkled gray skirt, imagining she must look like she'd been run over by a dray cart. *Love Lane*, as she recalled. She'd once wished such a denouement for Edward, but now she prayed with every ragged breath that he would be safe.

So she could send him on his way again.

The brass clock on Serena's mantel ticked along. Putney puttered about the room, trying to appear is if he wasn't trapping her within. Just when she thought she'd go completely mad, the knocker sounded on the front door.

Caroline raced to it, leaving the elderly butler far behind.

"Don't open it yet!" he huffed. "Look out the sidelight to make sure it's Lord Christie."

Edward's tall form was visible through the wavery glass. Caroline threw open the door and screamed.

"Shh, Caro. It's not my blood. Everything is all right, I swear."

Caroline reached for Edward's ruined cravat, which was spattered with bright crimson droplets. His coat was torn, and he'd made an attempt to wipe more blood from his left cheek, streaking it from beneath one eye to his shadowed jaw. "D-did you kill him?"

"Just planted him a facer. Or several. I suppose I broke his nose, but he was no beauty to begin with anyway. Caro, come inside and sit down. I must talk to you."

She looked out to the empty street. A few leaves fluttered across the sidewalk. "Where is he?"

"You're safe. He's on his way home to pack, and then he's taking a little trip."

Caroline's panic reemerged. "You just let him go? What if he comes back?"

Edward took her by the elbow and drew her into the hall. "He won't. I promise. Let's go into the parlor."

Putney hovered, but one look from Edward sent him scurrying elsewhere.

Trembling, Caroline sat back on the ruby velvet sofa. "You've terrified Putney. He was very kind to me."

"I'll make it up to him later." Edward went to the drinks table, poured himself a brandy and downed it in one swallow. Caroline's sherry glass was still nearly full, but she had no desire for it. Her hands shook too much to hold it.

Edward had an odd smile on his face. "Pope and I had a little chat. It seems he blames you for his current predicament. Once you exposed him in that book of yours—what was its name?"

"*The Vicious Viscount.*"

"Very apt. He has been unable to bed any woman successfully since its publication. His wife left him, you know. High class courtesans will have nothing to do with him, and rightly so. They know his reputation after reading your book. *Everyone* in the ton does, it seems. No one wants to take a beating for Randolph Pope's pleasure no matter how large his purse. He was forced to resort to common streetwalkers, where he failed to perform despite repeated use of the rod on those poor souls. Not only that, he picked up a rather unpleasant affliction. You've made his life quite miserable, Caro."

"Good."

"Now who is the vicious one?"

She had no remorse. She had tended to Lizzie's back. "Wh-what was he planning to do to me?"

"Nothing half so sinister as we might have expected. He was going to hold you for ransom, a rather modest one when all is said and done. He wanted me to pay for his treatment at an Austrian spa for gentlemen he'd heard about. It seems he's spent what's left of his fortune on quack remedies for impotence. No doubt there are just as many quacks in Austria, but at least he'll be on the Continent and not in Mayfair. I've readily agreed to provide him with the blunt. With any luck, he'll fall off an alp and that will be the end of him."

"*The Count's Courtesan.*"

"I beg your pardon?"

"Nothing. What happens when he is cured and comes home?"

"Should the cure prove efficacious, I expect he'll be too busy being his old self to worry about us. But he's not a well man, Caro. The years of debauchery have taken their toll. You overpowered him rather easily, did you not?"

Caroline thought about it. She hadn't seen Pope fall backward, just heard the spectacular results. He had looked quite gray-faced and grim once she'd got her hood off. For a few seconds she'd thought he was dead. Maybe it *was* close to his appointment with the devil.

"You told me you spoke with him before, and yet he still tried to harm me."

"Yes, I spoke with him. When I confronted him this summer, he of course denied making any threats against you. Dressed me down for sending Mulgrew and his men to warn him off. Swore it must be Douglass who was to blame for anything Rossiter heard. But it was Douglass who wrote to me telling me Pope was becoming increasingly unhinged. I told you that at Bradlaw House last night. And still you ran away."

Caroline felt a twinge of shame. "I'm sorry, Edward. I wasn't thinking about Pope."

"When I discovered your room was empty late this morning I thought Pope had taken you. I've never known such despair. But then I found the bedsheets strung together. I realized you were up to your old tricks. And I was angry, so angry I had to talk myself out of giving you a spanking when I met you on the steps."

He had kissed her instead, quite memorably. "A spanking? Surely I'm too old for that."

"I wonder. Someone should have raised their hand to you long ago. You've run wild all your life."

He didn't know the half of it. And wouldn't.

"But," he continued, "I'm willing to overlook your impulsivity. I put a great deal of pressure on you at Bradlaw House. No wonder you wanted to teach me a lesson. This time we'll just sit down like two normal people and—"

"What do you mean 'this time'?"

"We keep starting off on the wrong foot. I'd like to pretend the past six years never happened, but I'm a realist. I was even ready to let you go after last night, Caro. I told you so. I heard all your 'lasts,' every one of them. There was no need for you to climb out windows and frighten farmers. Mr. Mitchell sends his regards, by the way."

Yes, she had been adamant about leaving. But it was she who was not ready to let him go, which was why she ran away.

"Yes, you'd convinced me. Utterly. I spent all night working on another list and was prepared to send you home in comfort. I even let you sleep in, figuring you were exhausted from our last night together. Every time I said the words 'last night' in my head, Caro, I felt as if I were stabbed—by a fork. But then, I finally went into your room, and you were gone. The window blew shut in the rainstorm, you see. I didn't see the sheets at first. I thought you'd been abducted, and I realized I could *not* let you go when I found you." He reached to cup her cheek. "If we can simply forgive each other for the past, we should be able to make our marriage work."

"I don't want to be forgiven, and I don't want this marriage to work, Edward! How many times must I belabor the point? We are not suited. You think I should be *spanked*, for heaven's sake! I'm much more than a spoiled child. I am a woman who knows her own mind, and I know that I don't want to be married. To you, or anyone else."

"Balderdash. You write romance novels. Of course you believe in marriage."

"They are made-up stories, Edward, written out of boredom and for coin. Not everyone deserves a happy ending."

His gaze was steady. "You think so little of me to deny me happiness?"

"It's not—oh, please, Edward, I've had a rotten day. I walked miles and got soaked and rode in a vegetable cart! I'm worn out from travel and attempted kidnapping. I-I *smell*. Just leave me alone and we can discuss my philosophy of life another day."

"No. I want to know why you don't think you deserve a happy ending."

"It was just a figure of speech. I meant not everyone *gets* a happy ending. Life is frequently unjust. Lovely people have dreadful things happen to them. You lost Alice too soon, for example. My brother died." Her throat constricted. She was so tired she didn't have the strength to battle back the tears.

"I want you to tell me, Caro. It's time."

She wiped her cheeks. "You won't understand."

"Try me," he said softly.

Chapter 23

Celestine had committed an unconscionable crime. No
one must ever know her secret. No one.
                              —*Secrets and Seduction*

She told him it was impossible for her to think with him so
close to her on the couch. She limped over to the window,
and he felt some guilt for continuing to press her. But the air
was suddenly charged between them, the truth floating just
beyond his fingertips. The red maple tree in front of Number
Six was a blaze of glory, almost as glorious as the river of
tangled red hair falling down her back. He'd not been able to
manage it at all playing lady's maid at Bradlaw House,
though it had been most enjoyable trying. He wanted to
gather her in his lap, brush her hair, soothe her, make love to
her. Instead he counted the clicks and whirs of the mantel
clock.

She was silent for the longest time. He had almost given up
waiting when she began, her voice raspy. "I will tell you
everything. And then you will see why this is pointless. You
will hate me."

"I will not."

She gave him a lopsided smile. "We shall see. I won't go
back to the very beginning. Needless to say, you are right.
My childhood was as naughty as you imagine. My father
didn't concern himself with me much, so I can't remember
ever getting spanked. I'll start with Andrew, shall I? That was
when my life got interesting."

Her tone was so bitter Edward nearly asked her to stop the
forced confession. But she rushed ahead. "Andrew came to

live with us when I was seventeen. He was so beautiful I could not help but be dazzled. He seduced me. No, that's not right. We seduced each other. He'd had—he'd had a truly terrible life. His guardian found him on the streets of Edinburgh and made him his catamite. Andrew was only seven years old."

Edward was appalled. No one, not even his rival Andrew Rossiter, deserved such a fate. "That's indefensible."

"Yes. Andrew thought that was all there was to life. It was all he was used to, all he expected. He took up with my brother when they were at school. They were—they were lovers."

"I went to public school. That's not as unusual as you might think."

"I know that now. Some men do not like women. My brother was one of them. He was *nothing* like Andrew's guardian. He would never have harmed a child."

"No. Most men of that persuasion would not. They are simply seeking affection like the rest of us, although they can be hung for it. That guardian was a predator of the worst kind."

"He was. I'm glad he's dead." She traced a circular pattern on the glass. "When I found out about Andrew and Nicky, I was devastated. I thought Andrew loved *me.*"

"He did. He told me so." *And I saw it with my own eyes. Twice. Once, five years ago in my wife's bedroom.*

It wasn't Caroline who had convinced him she was unfaithful. It was the look on Andrew Rossiter's face. Edward had seen a man deeply in love who was determined to have what he wanted. Needed. By any means necessary, such as blackmail. And then weeks ago, when Andrew came to warn him, there really had been no doubt he still had strong feelings for Caroline's welfare.

"Well, he loved Nicky too, in his way. He tried to explain it, but I wouldn't listen. I felt used. Disgusted. I confronted my brother. I said some horrible, hurtful things. I threw things at him. Hit him, too. Nicky never said a word. Not one. Then he went to his room and shot himself." Her voice cracked completely.

Edward bounded up from the distant couch to hold her. She made no protest as he tucked her hair behind her ears and smoothed the tears from her cheeks. "That's awful, Caro. But it wasn't your fault."

"Oh, wasn't it? He didn't die, Edward. He lived a week until Andrew and I killed him." She broke away.

"No. I don't believe you."

"The doctor said he'd never get better. The bullet could not be removed. He was—they call it a vegetative state, Edward. He couldn't see or hear or think. He lay in bed like he was in his coffin already, not moving. Andrew and I talked about it, then Andrew put him out of his misery."

That was also not as unusual as she might think. "That was a kindness, Caro. Surely you see that."

"Kindness!" she cried. "We killed him! Our selfishness destroyed him!"

"He destroyed himself, Caro. It was his choice to put a bullet in his brain. It was he who was selfish to hurt the two people he left behind."

She shook her head. "I knew you wouldn't understand." She turned her gaze back to the empty street.

Edward took her hand in his. "I understand this," he said. "It doesn't matter to me what you think you've done in the past, or what you'll do in the future. I can't change the fact you loved the wrong man first. But you love me now. I know you do."

Her gray eyes silvered with tears. "I destroy every man I love. I kill them off, even in my books. Look at Nicky. Andrew has been lost for years because of me. You deserve someone better. Like Alice, who'll be quiet and proper."

No wonder she had been so determined to be wild and provoking. She didn't *want* their marriage to work, not really. To her mind she had found the deadest bore of a man to marry—a Christie carrying on the conventional Christie traditions—someone who would never stir the confusing, guilty jumble of feelings she had for Andrew and her brother. And they might have had such a marriage, one of polite strangers, if sensual sparks had not ignited between them. Edward once resented her for her incendiary effect on him and had become colder. Perversely, his coldness had only made her hotter, ever more desperate to drive him away.

They were a pair of idiots. If only they had been truthful with each other from the start. But it was never too late to tell the truth.

A feeling of blessed relief nearly overwhelmed him as his words tumbled out. "I didn't have the same feelings toward Alice as I have for you. There. It feels good to say it. I mean no disrespect toward Alice—she will always be a part of me. She was my youth, as Andrew was yours. She gave me my children and was a wonderful wife and mother, but she wasn't Caroline Parker. I can't live without you, Caro. I don't want to. I've tried, and it hasn't worked."

She snatched her hand away. "You can't live with me either!"

Edward took it back and pressed it firmly between both palms. "Well, that's because you didn't read my list."

"I read it!"

"Was there anything on it so impossible?"

"N-no."

He felt her working her hand out of his grasp. "I'm not going to let you go, you know. Even if you haul off and kick me as you're wont to do. I must have you teach those tricks to Allie."

Her voice was barely above a whisper. "I'm not fit to raise a little girl."

"She's not so little. Tops you by at least half a foot, I think."

"Edward! You know what I mean. How can you even think of letting me near your children?"

He swept her up and down. "True. You are far too great a temptation to the boys. It wouldn't do to have them fall half in love with their stepmother. You'll have to wear one of those lacy caps to cover your hair and practice a stern expression. There's not a doubt in my mind they will do something to deserve your disapproval in short order. Cambridge seems a hotbed of depravity, very different from my day."

"Be serious. I've just told you terrible things. And I wrote all those horrible books and consorted with courtesans. You cannot possibly want me back in your life."

"Why can't I?"

"Because—because you're *Edward Christie*!"

"And who is he?" Edward asked quietly.

"He's—you're—oh, this is impossible. Go away."

"You just don't listen." He put his arm around her and brought her back to the red velvet couch. "But I have the rest of my life to convince you and I'm not going to give up. You've had a very hard day. I think you're too tired to run away again. So, here is your choice. You may stay here in Serena's house for the night, or come back with me to my town house. I'm not expected back so soon, and I daresay things will not be as comfortable as they might be. Most of the staff is on holiday."

"With pay."

"Why, yes. Of course."

"That's an Edward Christie thing to do. Not many men in your position are so kind to their servants. Even your offer is an Edward Christie thing—you gave me a choice to stay here where Mr. Putney and Serena's staff can take care of me, or I can go with you to an empty house. You didn't have to tell me that."

Edward was puzzled. "But it is the truth."

"Yes. In all the years I've known you, Edward, you've always been truthful. Too truthful sometimes. Except for the time you plotted and pretended to be a wicked kidnapper. I made you turn against your nature. You didn't do the right thing, the sensible thing."

"It seemed right and sensible at the time. Felt good, too, except when you unmanned me in the carriage. I got you into my clutches, didn't I?"

"You did. But why?"

"I told you at Bradlaw House. You were unreachable any other way."

"No, Edward. I know why you kidnapped me. Why do you *want* me? I've done nothing but make us both unhappy."

"You're right." Despair washed over her face at his words. "You just said I always tell the truth. It is a fact that when we lived together, you did everything possible to poke and pick at me. Being with you was unsettling, like snuggling with a rabid hedgehog." He was gratified to see her lips twist for a second. "You incited the children to riot—"

"I just wanted them to have some fun," Caroline interrupted.

"Well, yes, that's one way of looking at it. But Christies believe fun is overrated. Didn't you hear? Ah, I believe you *did* hear. You thought marriage to me would be most unexceptional, like sailing on a smooth, glassy sea, the wind barely moderate. Bland as blancmange. Dull as ditchwater. Absolutely no fun at all."

"You were the first man to propose," Caroline said tartly.

"Yes. It seemed the prudent, practical thing to do to ask a woman I'd known four days to marry me. That, my dear, was not at all Christie-like. In fact, that was the beginning of your corruption of me."

"I suppose I forced you to think with Little Edward."

"I hope you don't think of him as *little*. He would find that most offensive."

"Stop trying to charm me! It's not like you! You're supposed to be all stiff and grumpy."

"I can attest to the stiffness. A minute in your presence and I am granite. I can demonstrate if you wish."

"I do not wish! Edward, I realize that physically we are compatible—more than compatible. But sex is simply not enough to build a marriage on."

"I agree. That's why I made up the list."

Caroline groaned. But she didn't rise and flee upstairs, or ring for Putney, or look to throw any of Serena's rather hideous bric-a-brac. Edward felt hopeful for the first time in days. Their past was spread out before them like a torn and tattered blanket. They could mend it if they tried.

"Caroline, you asked me why I wanted you. I can tell you honestly that I don't know. You're not convenient. I can't control you, or myself when I'm around you. You cut up my peace. You make me ache. I have every expectation that all my hair will turn gray or even fall out if you come back to me."

Caroline bit her lip to prevent her smile. "Edward, I have given you the opportunity to make a pretty romantic speech. Is this your best effort? Pain and baldness?"

"I am not a romantic, Caro. I am a Christie, and as such I'm not used to declaring my affections. Perhaps I need lessons. But I have feelings for you, and you alone, as impossible and obstinate as you are. I would not kidnap any other woman."

"That's something, I suppose. It would be a chore to keep finding other women trussed up in your carriage or your bed."

"You will be the only one trussed up in my bed—if you wish it."

"I do." She sighed. "But I don't deserve you."

"Rubbish. Caroline, the past is the past. Every bit of it. Every mistake you've ever made—every mistake *I* have made— cannot be undone. But we would not be who we are without them. I expect we will make more mistakes in the future. It won't be so awful if we make them together."

She shook her head. "Christies don't make mistakes."

Ah! He had her now. "Then we are in agreement."

"I haven't agreed to anything!"

"Oh, but you have. Christies don't make mistakes. I am a Christie. I want you. Therefore, it is not a mistake to want you, because Christies don't make mistakes. You can't argue with that. It's logic."

"Love isn't logical."

"No, it isn't," Edward said soberly. "I love you, Caroline. I never knew what love was until the night in your garden when you said we were done. It's come late for me, but not too late for us, I hope."

With three little words, Edward discovered that kidnapping, jewels, and logic were completely superfluous to winning back his wife. Christies always told the truth, and if he said he loved her, it must be so. Inconvenient, impossible, but true. She melted into his arms and wept on his shoulder. His coat was ruined already. He fished a handkerchief out of his pocket.

Caroline blew her nose in a most unromantic fashion. "You love me?"

"I've just said so, haven't I? What do you think all this has been about?"

"Take me home, Edward. To Christie Park."

"Tomorrow, at first light. Tonight you'll rest right here." He cupped her upturned face and kissed her. "Do you suppose Serena has a mirror on her ceiling too?"

"We cannot make love in Serena's bed!" Caroline said, horrified.

"Christie House it is then. Putney!"

The butler materialized as though he'd been standing inches away from the door. "Yes, my lord."

"Thank you for assisting my wife earlier. I am deeply indebted to you."

"I was only doing my job, my lord."

Edward reached into his pocket and pulled out a fistful of bank notes. Putney looked as if he might swoon, but managed to accept them with alacrity.

"There is the matter of a vase, Edward," Caroline said contritely.

"Have Miss Serena send me a bill. I will take it out of your allowance, Caro. Your pin money will dwindle down to nothing if you do not rein in your temper."

Caroline lowered her eyes. "Yes, Edward."

"Do not think for a minute you are fooling me with this submissive act."

Caroline chewed a lip. "No, Edward."

Edward threw up his hands. "It is definitely time to remove you from Jane Street. You've gone mad, or I have."

Putney cleared his throat. "Perhaps you've gone mad together, my lord. May I send for your carriage?"

"I've a poor old horse tied up out there. If you can have somebody see him home to Christie House, I'd be obliged. My wife and I will walk home. If you're up to it, Caro."

"Yes, Edward."

He waited until they were on the sidewalk, then swept her up in his arms.

She yipped like a startled Pekingese. "Edward! What are you doing?"

"Carrying you home, my love."

"Put me down at once! You can't carry me through the streets of Mayfair in broad daylight! People will talk! And I'm too heavy!"

Edward kissed her forehead. "You are not," he lied. "And let them talk. I want the world to know that Baron Christie has found his baroness and will never, ever let her go again."

Caroline relaxed in his arms. "Yes, Edward."

Caroline's acquiescence was bound to be short-lived, but he had a pretty good idea what to do with it for the next few hours. All he had to do was not drop her on her beautiful white arse. He thought, on the whole, he was absolutely up to the tasks ahead.

Chapter 24

And they lived happily ever after.
—*The Baron's Bride*

Edward picked up the grubby letter from the tray, broke its seal and uttered an oath.

Caroline knew the rules. No talking at the breakfast table. She spread more marmalade on her toast, focusing on the pattern of the silver spoon. It was quite lovely, with tiny lilies of the valley entwined with some indefinable flower. She returned it to the jam pot and took a bite.

Edward looked as though he were choking on his own toast, which lay untouched on the plate before him. She wouldn't ask about the contents of the letter. It was enough just to sit with him in Edward's—*their*—lovely breakfast room at Christie Park. The room hadn't needed much in the way of redecoration, just some drapes, plants, and new pictures on the wall, so it was the first one she'd tackled. She'd be poring over wallpaper and fabric patterns for the rest of the house later with her sister-in-law Beth and was itching to get started. She took a large swallow of tea.

"Hell and damnation!"

Still, Caroline said nothing. The rules really were not so onerous. Edward was most particular about his morning routine, although he'd altered it recently to spend it—and the previous night—in her bed. *Their* bed. One of *her* rules. He still kept his old bedroom, of course, but seemed to wander into it only to keep Cameron busy.

Perhaps the letter was about the children. Alice was upstairs terrorizing her new governess, but the boys could have achieved most anything to set their father off. They were very busy sowing their wild oats at Cambridge. Entire fields were sprouting up, even if it was October. Caroline waited.

Beth didn't have her scruples. "Good Lord, Edward, what is it? Caro and I are dying of curiosity."

Edward looked up, straight into Caroline's eyes. "This is from Andrew Rossiter."

Caroline felt the pleasant air suck out of the room.

"He writes to tell me that he is *dead*, and wishes me to facilitate the transfer of his bank funds so I can purchase him a house on some Scottish island. Oh, and I'm to hire him an Italian-speaking governess."

"Andrew is d-dead?"

"Not in the strictest sense. It seems he got into a spot of trouble and needs to go underground. But for all intents and purposes, the man we knew as Andrew Rossiter has gone on to his reward, wherever that might be."

Caroline felt momentary relief. A tiny part of her heart would always belong to Andrew, but Edward had staked a larger, truer claim. "But why is he writing to *you*?"

"Because he saved your life."

"He did not! You did! Actually," Caroline said, reflecting, "I saved it myself."

"Well, he's taking credit and wants a favor in return. Apparently his other acquaintances are unreliable."

"You are certainly reliable," Beth said stoutly. "Christies always are."

"Yes, well, this is one task I'm going to parcel out to my man of business. I can't go traipsing about Scotland. I'm on my honeymoon, and will be for the foreseeable future." He gave Caroline a quick grin and put the letter in his pocket.

"I wonder what happened." Caroline peeked up through the tangle of her dark lashes, but Edward was already reading the newspaper.

"Better that you are not aware of the particulars." He put a finger on his place in the article and gave her a stern look

over his spectacles. "There seems to be some danger involved. As far as you know, your old friend is still in Italy. If
you hear of the accident, you will be as shocked as anyone."

"What accident?"

"That's enough, Caro. Let me finish my breakfast."

Silence resumed, broken only by the sound of cutlery and
the delicate mastications of two Christies-born and one
Christie-by-marriage.

If she wanted to, Caroline was sure she could get the
whole story out of Edward in bed. But she'd have to get him
back into it first.

She rose from the table unsteadily. "I-I'm not feeling quite
the thing. I need to go upstairs."

And suddenly it was true. She felt light-headed. Her stomach roiled with bits of bread and egg and tea. How dreadful
it would be if she lost her breakfast in the breakfast room.
Caroline was sure no Christies were ever so imprudent to be
sick in the potted palm.

Edward turned a page. "It won't work, Caro. You'll not
worm anything more out of me."

"Edward!" said Beth. "Look at her! She's green!"

"I am?" Suddenly she *felt* green. The color of boiled cab-
bage or one of those nasty garden slugs. The pattern on the
new curtains undulated like a stormy sea. Edward caught her
before she fell.

"Beth, send someone for Dr. Wyatt!"

Caroline closed her eyes to keep the room from spinning.
How ironic to finally be where she wanted to be—in Edward's arms—and she was too sick to enjoy it. She felt like
she was dying. Life was completely unfair.

Edward carried her upstairs as if she didn't weigh a thing,
when she knew her portly Parkerness was in full force. Ever
since Edward had come back into her life, more than her love
had grown. Her new clothes did not fit. She'd have to cut
back on the marmalade, which seemed an easy goal, as she
never planned to eat anything ever again.

Edward hovered solicitously, unlacing her, providing her

with a cool cloth and a basin, which to her shame, she used twice.

"I am disgusting."

"Nonsense. You are ill. The doctor is on his way. Hush now."

He closed the curtains against the morning light and sat like a sentinel in the dim room.

"I love you," Caroline croaked. "If I die, I want you to marry again. A proper girl next time."

"You've ruined me for proper, Caro. And you're not going to die. I won't allow it."

The doctor arrived and nearly departed just as quickly when Edward would not leave Caroline's side. After a resentful, blustery lecture, he examined Caro and stepped back.

"I can't believe I was forced to leave my breakfast table. This is hardly an emergency."

"Is it merely indigestion?" Caroline asked. There had been two slabs of rare roast beef on her plate last night, as well as Yorkshire pudding and nearly half a bowl of trifle at midnight. Edward had shared, but if she were honest, she ate most of it.

"You are increasing, Lady Christie. Congratulations, Lord Christie. I'd say your nursery will have a new arrival sometime late winter. February or March, I should think. I'll come back next week and you can pepper me with those questions you're longing to ask, but right now I'm going back home to my bacon and ale."

Caroline waited to speak until Dr. Wyatt left, mostly because her ears were ringing. She was not entirely sure of what she'd heard. The distractions of the past few months were enough to throw anyone off. In truth, when she gave any thought lately to her lack of courses, she thought she'd simply dried up.

"A baby? How can that be?"

Edward looked down at her, his face a study in love. "The usual way, Caro."

"But—but I'm barren."

He kissed her fingertips. "It seems not."

"I'm old."

"I'm older." And judging by his smug expression, proud he was still extremely capable in the bedchamber. The baby was proof of that.

"But you won't have to grow fat and bear it!" Caroline said, a bit cross. She would be as big as a house when it was done, doomed to wearing the new drapes. Or maybe a tent. No wonder she'd gotten so stout, but at least until today she had not felt a moment of sickness.

Edward frowned. "I would do it for you if I could. Aren't you happy about this, Caro?"

"Happy? I'm terrified. And so excited I'd jump about if I weren't sure I'd vomit again. A baby! *Our* baby. What if I'm a horrible mother?" she blurted.

"Impossible."

"But this baby will be a Christie. I don't know how to raise a Christie."

"You've made some headway with Allie."

"I have, haven't I?"

A series of thuds overhead belied the point, but the new parents resolutely ignored them.

Edward chuckled. "You were my mistress when we created this child, Caro. Perhaps we were too proper before."

"You can't tell her about our past! It's too shocking."

"Oh, I think *he* can handle knowing his father was a randy devil in thrall to the most beautiful redheaded witch in the kingdom. I hope he finds a redheaded witch of his own when he's old enough to appreciate her. With your warm heart, you'll make sure of that, Caro. He can't go wrong with you for a mother."

"*She* can't go wrong with you for a father. I hope she'll inherit your temper and not mine. We'll have to pad the nursery walls." Caroline sat up. Too quickly. The room tilted sideways. "Oh!"

"What is it?"

"Bother, I'm dizzy again. But get Beth to bring up the wallpaper and paint sample books. We can plan the nursery! A soft yellow I think, just in case it is a boy. He wouldn't like pink at all."

"I shouldn't think so. No Christie boy will ever be fond of pink. Except, of course, where it counts." His hand slipped under the covers.

Caroline felt the blush flutter to her toes. "Edward!"

"Pink. So sweet. Delicious. I'm much like Dr. Wyatt. I'm still hungry."

"But—"

"Not a word at breakfast, Caroline. You promised."

Caroline tried, but inevitably a few sounds squeaked out. Edward did not seem to mind at all.

Keep an eye out for SEVEN YEARS TO SIN
by Sylvia Day, available now!

Alistair Caulfield's back was to the door of his warehouse shipping office when it opened. A salt-tinged gust blew through the space, snatching the manifest he was about to file right out of his hand.

He caught it deftly, then looked over his shoulder. Startled recognition moved through him. "Michael."

The new Lord Tarley's eyes widened with equal surprise, then a weary half-smile curved his mouth. "Alistair, you scoundrel. You didn't tell me you were in Town."

"I've only just returned." He slid the parchment into the appropriate folder and pushed the drawer closed. "How are you, my lord?"

Michael removed his hat and ran a hand through his dark brown hair. The assumption of the Tarley title appeared to weigh heavily on his broad shoulders, grounding him in a way Alistair had never seen before. He was dressed somberly in shades of brown, and he flexed his left hand, which bore the Tarley signet ring, as if he could not accustom himself to having it there. "As well as can be expected under the circumstances."

"My condolences to you and your family. Did you receive my letter?"

"I did. Thank you. I meant to reply, but time is stretched so thin. The last year has raced by so quickly; I've yet to catch my breath."

"I understand."

Michael nodded. "I'm pleased to see you again, my friend. You have been gone far too long."

"The life of a merchant." He could have delegated more, but staying in England meant crossing paths with both his father and Jessica. His father complained about Alistair's success as a tradesman with as much virulence as he'd once complained about Alistair's lack of purpose. It was a great stressor for his mother, which he was only able to alleviate by being absent as much as possible.

As for Jessica, she'd been careful to avoid him whenever they were in proximity. He had learned to reciprocate when he saw how marriage to Tarley had changed her. While she remained as cool in deportment as ever, he'd seen the blossoming of her sensual nature in the languid way she moved and the knowledge in those big, gray eyes. Other men coveted the mystery of her, but Alistair had seen behind the veil, and *that* was the woman he lusted for. Forever beyond his reach in reality, but a fixture in his mind. She was burned into his memory by the raging hungers and the impressions of youth, and the years hadn't lessened the vivid recollection one whit.

"I find myself grateful for your enterprising sensibilities," Michael said. "Your captains are the only ones I would entrust with the safe passage of my sister-in-law to Jamaica."

Alistair kept his face impassive thanks to considerable practice, but the sudden awareness gripping him tensed his frame. "Lady Tarley intends to travel to Calypso?"

"Yes. This very morning, which is why I'm here. I intend to speak to the captain myself and see he looks after her until they arrive."

"Who travels with her?"

"Only her maid. I should like to accompany her, but I can't leave now."

"And she will not delay?"

"No." Michael's mouth curved wryly. "And I cannot dissuade her."

"You cannot say no to her," Alistair corrected, moving to the window through which he could view the West India docks. Ships entered the Northern Dock to unload their precious imports, then sailed around to the Southern Dock to reload with cargo for export. Around the perimeter, a high brick wall deterred the rampant theft plaguing the London wharves. The same wall increased his shipping company's appeal to West Indian landowners requiring secure transportation of goods.

"Neither can Hester—forgive me, *Lady Regmont.*"

The last was said with difficulty. Alistair had long suspected his friend nursed deeper feelings for Jessica's younger sister and had assumed Michael would pay his addresses. Instead, Hester had been presented at court, then immediately betrothed, breaking the hearts of many hopeful would-be swains. "Why is she so determined to go?"

"Benedict bequeathed the property to her. She claims she must see to its sale personally. I fear the loss of my brother has affected her deeply and she seeks a purpose. I've attempted to anchor her, but duty has me stretched to wit's end."

Alistair's reply was carefully neutral. "I can assist her in that endeavor. I can make the necessary introductions, as well as provide information that would take her months to discover."

"A generous offer." Michael's gaze was searching. "But you've just returned. I can't ask you to depart again so soon."

Turning, Alistair said, "My plantation borders Calypso, and I should like to expand. It's my hope to position myself as the best purchaser of the property. I will pay her handsomely, of course."

Relief swept over Michael's expressive features. "That would ease my mind considerably. I'll speak to her at once."

"Perhaps you should leave that to me. If, as you say, she needs a purpose, then she'll want to maintain control of the matter in all ways. She should be allowed to set the terms and pace of our association to suit her. I have all the time in the world, but you do not. See to your most pressing affairs, and entrust Lady Tarley to me."

"You've always been a good friend," Michael said. "I pray you return to England swiftly and settle for a time. I could use your ear and head for business. In the interim, please encourage Jessica to write often and keep me abreast of the situation. I should like to see her return before we retire to the country for the winter."

"I'll do my best."

Alistair waited several minutes after Michael departed, then moved to the desk. He began a list of new provisions for the journey, determined to create the best possible environment. He also made some quick but costly adjustments to the passenger list, moving two additional travelers to another of his ships.

He, Jessica, and her maid would be the only non-crewmen aboard the *Acheron*.

She would be within close quarters for weeks—it was an extraordinary opportunity Alistair was determined not to waste.

Turn the page for a peek at one of the stories in
SO I MARRIED A DEMON SLAYER,
featuring Kathy Love, Angie Fox, and Lexi George—Angie's
"What Slays in Vegas" . . .

Sunlight stung her eyeballs even though she hadn't opened them. Shiloh covered her eyes with her arm and groaned. She felt dizzy, weak. Her head throbbed with the worst hangover since that three-day wine binge through Sodom, Gomorrah and Zebiom.

And she hadn't even had any alcohol last night.

She stretched, sore from last night's activities with Damien. At least one thing had gone right. Damien had been exactly what she needed.

In fact, he was amazing.

So why'd she feel like hell?

She blinked against the bright morning, wishing she could lie in bed for the rest of eternity. Maybe she'd just close her light-blocking shades and go back to bed.

She didn't even remember making it home last night.

In fact, she didn't remember anything after that blinding orgasm. Strange. That had never happened to her before.

A flutter of a grin crossed her lips. If she was going to remember one thing, let it be her night in the Lust room.

She groaned into a sitting position and threw one leg onto the floor, stopping short when her toes came in contact with carpet. Her bedroom had hardwood floors. Shiloh's eyes flew open and she gasped as she saw a nicked wooden end table. A white ceramic lamp. Beige curtains. She was in a hotel room.

Out the window, she could see the roller coaster at the New York-New York hotel. Oh thank Hades. She flopped back against the pillow. She was in Vegas. Okay. She placed a hand on her chest. She was a few blocks from home. No need to panic.

Breathe.

Although something on her left hand didn't feel right. It was like a heavy weight on her finger. She glanced down to the hand on her chest and shrieked. There, on her left ring finger, was a gold band with a diamond on it the size of Switzerland.

She stared at it like she'd never seen one before. In all fairness, she hadn't. At least not on her hand.

From her right came a bellowing snore. She scrambled off the bed and stood staring down at Damien, tousled and wickedly naked.

What the hell happened last night?

She didn't remember a thing.

She rubbed her temples. *Think, think, think.*

Okay. She went to work, bribed the fairy, practically mauled Damien. That part had been a lot of fun. She'd felt her power flow out of her in an amazing orgasm and then . . . nothing.

Just a cheap hotel room, a hot man and a diamond ring.

She yanked at the gold band. It was big enough to slip off easily, but it refused to budge. The obnoxious diamond clung as if it were welded onto her.

It glinted in the morning sun, mocking her.

She couldn't be married. Succubi didn't get married. Ever.

Her eyes stung and she rubbed at them. Even if she wanted to get married, she couldn't marry a client from the Lust floor. It didn't matter that he was the best sex she'd had in a thousand years.

And how dare Damien sleep at a time like this?

"Get up!" She crawled across the bed and yanked him onto his back. Her heart stuttered when she saw that he wore a gold band on his left finger too. Oh Hades. She'd *been* afraid of that. "Wake up. This is an emergency!"

He threw his arms up over his eyes. "What's the . . . ?"

"Damien"—she yanked his arms down—"what did you do to me?"

He gazed at her with bleary eyes, confusion tumbling across his features. "What are you doing here?" he asked, his voice gravelly and a bit too indignant for her taste.

She smacked him with her pillow. "That's what I want to know."

He sat up faster than she expected. She could see he was still woozy. "Don't touch me," he warned.

"You sure didn't mind it last night," she shot back, pleased when a flush crept up his neck. Bull's eye. "Now fess up. What did you do to me?"

With the grace of a cat, he was out of bed. He strode toward a shiny silver suitcase on a luggage stand, displaying his frustratingly perfect butt.

He yanked the case open, his eyes on her the whole time. "I didn't do anything to you." He reached inside with one hand and grabbed hold of something she couldn't see.

Frankly, she didn't care. "You made me pass out. Want me to show you what happened next?" Maybe he had some memory of it. She shoved her obnoxiously ringed hand at him. "You married me."

He blinked twice and slowly removed his hand from whatever was in the case. "I couldn't."

She planted a hand on her hip. "Check your hand, sweetie."

He lifted it out of the case and went white as he stared at the gold ring on his finger. "I can't be married," he said to his hand.

She had to smile. Briefly.

Oh, who was she kidding? This was a mess.

Shiloh stalked toward the window, wanting to get as far away from him as she could. This was too much. It had to be a mistake. Getting married meant giving her power away. Seducing only one man for the rest of her life. She couldn't do that. She had a job. A career. Her boss was going to kill her.

She stumbled over an empty champagne bottle as she

scanned the room, trying to make sense of what had happened the night before. A gigantic pink teddy bear with an I Heart Vegas button sat next to a half-empty room service tray and what appeared to be her wadded up dress.

He slammed his suitcase closed. "What did you do to me last night?"

She turned to find him glaring at her, menace in his eyes.

"You were the one with the fancy shot, you jerk. You drugged me." Which proved he was a fool because drugs didn't work on her.

"You were the one who drank it," he said, yanking a pair of jeans from the closet.

Did she ever. She watched him pull on a pair of worn Levi's and remembered just how she'd drunk *the cocktail* off of him. She felt a delicious tightening between her legs. "Fess up. What was in it?"

He sighed and drew a hand through his hair. "I suppose it doesn't hurt to tell you now." He placed his hands on his hips, which only made his abs look better, damn him. "I gave you truth serum. It was *supposed* to make you cooperate." His jaw flexed. "Instead, you seduced me."

"That's my job!"

"You made me pass out," he accused.

"Me too. I don't remember anything after our screaming orgasm."

He looked like he could grind marbles with his teeth. "Don't say that word."

"*Orgasm?*" she asked, watching him flinch. "What are you? A prude?" She felt something slippery below her foot. "Oh," she gasped as she realized she was stepping on a photograph of her and Damien posing with a minister.

She snatched it off the floor.

There she was, radiant in her gold dress, smiling like it was her wedding day. She had both arms wrapped around Damien, who had a hand on her hip and a rose in his teeth. They stood under a trellis with a red and gold sign that read The Hitching Post Wedding Chapel.

"Yeek." She tossed it back on the floor.

He'd found photos too. Stomach tumbling, she hurried over to where he was sitting on the edge of the bed, flipping through a stack of pictures. She gasped at the proof of their post-wedding limo ride. Shiloh and Damien kissing underneath the Las Vegas sign. Shiloh and Damien pretending to be tigers outside the MGM Grand. Shiloh and Damien inside the limo, kissing like the ship was about to go down, while long-haired, painfully skinny members of a rock band cheered an toasted them with bottles of Captain Morgan. He squinted and studied the last picture closer. "Who are these people?"

And don't miss UNWRAPPED,
a sexy holiday anthology from Erin McCarthy,
Donna Kauffman, and Kate Angell,
coming next month!
Turn the page for a sample of Erin's story,
"Blue Christmas" . . .

"Santa can suck it." Blue Farrow kept an eye on the high-way and tried to hit the buttons on the radio to change the station. She was going to grind her teeth down to nubs if she had to listen to Christmas songs for another twelve hours. It was like an IV drip of sugar and spice and it was making her cranky.

Was she the only one who thought a fat dude hanging around on your roof was a bit creepy? And why were those elves so happy in that Harry Connick Jr. song? Rum in the eggnog, that's why. Not to mention since when did three ships ever go pulling straight up to Bethlehem? She wasn't aware it was a major port city.

Yep. She was feeling in total harmony with Scrooge. "Bah Humbug," she muttered when her only options on the radio seemed to be all Christmas all the time or pounding rap music.

Blue had never been a big fan of Christmas, never having experienced a normal one in her childhood since her flaky mother (yes, flaky considering she'd named her daughter after a color) had done Christmas experimental style every year, never the same way twice, disregarding any of her daughter's requests. The trend of feeling tacked on to her parents' Christmas had continued into Blue's adulthood, and this year she had been determined to have a great holiday all on her terms, booking herself on a cruise with her two equally single friends. She had turned down her mother's invitation to spend the holiday with an indigenous South American tribe and her father's request to join him with his barely-legal wife and their baby girl, and instead she was going to sip cocktails in a bikini.

Maybe.

The road in front of her was barely visible, the snow crashing down with pounding determination, the highway slick and ominous, the hours ticking by as Blue barely made progress in the treacherous conditions. Planning to drive to Miami from Ohio instead of flying had been a financial decision and would give Blue the chance to make a pit stop in Tennessee and visit her old friend from high school, but the only thing heading south at the moment was her vacation. It was Christmas Eve, her cruise ship departed in twenty hours, and she'd only made it a hundred miles in six hours, the blizzard swirling around her mocking the brilliance of her plan as she drove through the middle of nowhere Kentucky.

She was going to have to stop in Lexington and see if she could catch a flight to Miami, screw the cost. Not that planes would be taking off in this weather, but maybe by morning. If she flew out first thing, she could be in Florida in plenty of time for her four o'clock sail time. All she had to do was make it to Lexington without losing her sanity from being pummeled with schmaltzy Christmas carols or without losing control of her car in the snow.

When she leaned over and hit the radio again and found the Rolling Stones she nearly wept in gratitude. Classic rock she could handle.

But not her car. As the highway unexpectedly curved and dipped, she fishtailed in the thick snow.

Blue only managed a weak, "Oh, crap," before she gripped the hell out of the wheel and slid sideways down the pavement, wanting to scream, but unable to make a sound.

She was going to die.

If there hadn't been anyone else on the road, she might have managed to regain control. But there was no stopping the impact when she swung into the lane next to her, right in the path of an SUV. She wasn't the only idiot on the road and now they were going to die together.

Blue closed her eyes and hoped there were bikinis and margaritas in the afterlife.

Santa was the man. Christian Dawes sang along to the radio at the top of his lungs, the song reminding him of his childhood, when he had listened carefully on Christmas Eve for the telltale sound of reindeer hooves. Tossing the trail mix out for the reindeer to chomp on, putting the cookies on a plate for Santa, the magic and wonder and awe of waking up to a ton of presents, those were some of his best memories.

Someday when he had his own kids, he'd create all of those special moments for them, but right now Christian was content to play awesome uncle, arriving on Christmas Eve loaded down with presents for all his nieces and nephews. His trunk was stuffed with spoils, and he'd brought enough candy to earn glares from his two sisters and potentially make someone sick. But it wasn't Christmas until a kid stuffed his face with candy then hurled after a session on the sit and spin. That's what home videos and infamous family stories were made of.

Unfortunately the lousy weather was slowing him down on his drive from Cincinnati to Lexington. He'd left work later than he'd intended anyway, then by the time he'd hit Kentucky, he'd been forced down to thirty miles an hour because apparently the road crews had taken the holiday off and had decided not to plow. He hoped his family wasn't holding up dinner for him at his parents' house.

If he wasn't gripping the steering wheel so hard he would call someone and let them know he still had a couple of hours ahead of him, but he had no intention of reaching for his phone. A glance to the right showed a car next to him, but other than that, he could barely see the road in front of him. He needed Santa to dip down and give him a lift in his sleigh or it was going to be midnight before he arrived.

What he didn't need was a car accident.

In his peripheral vision, he saw the car next to him slide, spinning out so fast that Christian only had time to swear and tap his brakes before he hit the car with a crunch and they went careening toward the guardrail. When his SUV stopped moving a few seconds later, despite his efforts to turn the skid, he had the other car pinned against the railing.

"Shit!" Christian turned off his car and leaped out, almost taking a header in the thick snow, but terrified that he'd injured someone. "Are you okay?" he asked, yelling through the howling snow as he peered into the driver's side window.

The major impact of his SUV's front end had been in the backseat and trunk, so he hoped if there was an injury it wasn't serious. But with the snow smacking him in the face and the window plastered with wet flakes, he couldn't really see anything.

He knocked on the glass and when it started to slide down, he sighed in relief.

"Are you okay?" he said again now that the person in front of him could hear him.

"Are you okay?" she said simultaneously.

He nodded.

She nodded.

And Christian became aware that he was staring at the most strikingly beautiful woman he'd ever seen in his whole life.

GREAT BOOKS,
GREAT SAVINGS!

When You Visit Our Website:
www.kensingtonbooks.com
You Can Save Money Off The Retail Price
Of Any Book You Purchase!

- **All Your Favorite Kensington Authors**
- **New Releases & Timeless Classics**
- **Overnight Shipping Available**
- **eBooks Available For Many Titles**
- **All Major Credit Cards Accepted**

Visit Us Today To Start Saving!
www.kensingtonbooks.com

All Orders Are Subject To Availability.
Shipping and Handling Charges Apply.
Offers and Prices Subject To Change Without Notice.

3 1901 04909 4065